The Midnight Man

The Midnight Man

CHARLOTTE MEDE

KENSINGTON PUBLISHING CORP.
http://www.kensingtonbooks.com

BRAVA BOOKS are published by

Kensington Publishing Corp.
850 Third Avenue
New York, NY 10022

All Kensington titles, imprints and distributed lines are available at special quantity discounts for bulk purchases for sales promotion, premiums, fund-raising, educational or institutional use.

Special book excerpts or customized printings can also be created to fit specific needs. For details, write or phone the office of the Kensington Special Sales Manager: Kensington Publishing Corp., 850 Third Avenue, New York, NY 10022. Attn. Special Sales Department. Phone: 1-800-221-2647.

Brava and the B logo Reg. U.S. Pat. & TM Off.

ISBN-13: 978-0-7582-2367-8
ISBN-10: 0-7582-2367-6

First Kensington Trade Paperback Printing: August 2008
10 9 8 7 6 5 4 3 2 1

Printed in the United States of America

It is not the strongest of the species that survives, nor the most intelligent, but the one most responsive to change.
—Charles Darwin

Chapter 1

June 1860

O*blivion* is what she craved.

Strands of blue smoke snaked along the low ceiling. The room was hushed, its plush red upholstery absorbing sounds of both pleasure and pain. It was a place people came to forget, to slay their demons by slaking their desires.

Helena Hartford sank deeper into her chaise, unable to resist the images that bled before her eyes. It was always like this. Her work could make her forget anything, even the tightness in her lungs and the fear gnawing at her bones.

Her mind was already elsewhere and her fingers itched for her palette and brush, the crimson, blue, and flesh tones of the room fusing in a cacophony of color. That man in the corner. She watched as his high, starched cravat was loosened by the nimble fingers of the half-naked young woman kneeling by his side. His eyes were closed as he sucked hungrily on the opium pipe between his lips. It was an Hieronymus Bosch canvas come to life.

Nearly three hundred years ago, the Dutch painter had captured all too well the symbols and iconography of sin and human failings. She noted several men, lounging next to the broad stairway, eager to make their ascent to the private rooms on the second floor.

Helena's eyes narrowed at the assembly of *guests,* all of them scions of England's noblest and wealthiest families who in the dark pursued pastimes that wouldn't hold up to the bright light of day. The world could be an infinitely forgiving place—if you were male. And a friend of the noble Duke of Hartford who now lay deep in a cold grave.

Helena's smile was cynical as she focused on the small blue pipe delicately balanced on the side table so that its contents would not drop out. When she had first arrived a few minutes past midnight, there were several raised eyebrows, an unusual reaction in a venue renowned for its discretion. Helena Hartford, the widow of the old Duke of Hartford, was known for her flaunting of society's strictures. *But this . . .*

She took hold of the pipe with surprisingly steady hands. The warm smoke filled her lungs, its sweetness a new sensation. Another inhalation, then another. To forget, to obliterate the fear, to fall into the comfort of nothingness.

They would never dare to look for her here. She knew she was safe for the moment because for anyone to divulge her whereabouts would be to disclose secrets so ugly that even society could no longer look away.

She sank into the cushions of the alcove just as her limbs began to relax, the room coalescing into a swirl of patterns on a canvas. Time was suspended in a blanket of pure physical sensation.

The voices beyond receded like a bad dream. With vision simultaneously sharp and blurred, she examined the pipe with preternatural concentration. The contours were smooth beneath her fingers, etched with a stream winding into an endless horizon, a perfect, perspectiveless landscape. She placed it carefully on the side table before welcoming the soft red cushions that enfolded her in their embrace. She was alone in her private cocoon. Images, elusive as butterflies, danced behind her eyes, their scorching yellows and virulent blues carrying her away to a place where she was finally free. No father, no husband, no fears.

She blinked slowly, then focused.

The hand on her wrist was beautiful, large and strong, and male. A sinewed forearm, the shirt cuffs turned back, led to shoulders that blocked her view of the salon. Broad shoulders, but sculpted beneath the fine linen shirt, no cravat, and a waistcoat with the top two buttons undone. A torso she suddenly ached to draw.

She couldn't see his face against the dim light of the chandelier. He was sitting on the chaise, leaning over her, saying something. The deep voice was rough velvet.

"I've seen your work."

She pushed away the haze clouding her thoughts, unable or unwilling to concentrate as a ribbon of fear unfurled deep in her chest. "You have." It was more of a statement than a question. Her artist's eye traced his body, a sculpture that was large-boned, long-limbed, but elegantly made. Like nothing she had ever seen in real life. More like a hallucination or a bronze at the Victoria and Albert Museum.

"It's magnificent."

He was so close that she could detect his scent, the ocean, sun, and something else. Languorousness seeping into her bones, her words were slow to come. "I must have misunderstood." She heard herself laugh, the sound throaty and low. "Most of the critics, not to mention the friends of my late and beloved husband, aren't that generous in their praise."

"You're bitter."

The blue-gray smoke combined in the air between them. "How discerning of you, sir. Whoever you are." The metallic taste in her mouth stung as a flare of panic flickered in her chest.

She made to sit up and couldn't. Although he wasn't touching her, she instantly felt caged by his body limned in the shadows of the alcove. Closing her eyes, she tried to shut him out, following the shapes and patterns her imagination conjured. A stream distorted by sunlight. A face shattered into geometric planes. A rough-hewn mountain range. She was only vaguely conscious now of the low and constant sounds of strangers humming in the background.

Then the hand skated down her arm and a jolt of awareness pulled her back. And all she could do was focus on his touch, as compelling as the opium in her bloodstream, the calloused fingers moving slowly over the sensitive skin of her wrist before he pressed one finger into her bare palm. A shiver traveled from the top of her spine to the tip of her womb.

She opened her eyes. *What if he is one of them?* The thought crawled out the thick morass that was her reality. She wanted to move, to run, but she couldn't, held down by a force of nature invading her senses. The urge, out of nowhere, was contradictory and overwhelming: to reach up and loop her arms around his neck, then trace the hard muscles and warm skin of this man's body. First to feel and then to draw him.

"What's in that head of yours, Helena? In your mind's eye?" The low gravel voice mesmerized and she'd barely registered that he knew her name. His hard fingers traced a sensual pattern on her palm, the fine veins of her wrist.

From under heavy lids, she strained to discern his features. He was so close she could track the cadence of his breathing, the rise and fall of his chest. "What I see?" Her breath was shallow and the words cost her some effort. "Inspiration? You think this is where it comes from?" She gestured to the small blue pipe with her free hand. "Not from here, not from this."

"Then from where?" The dark voice led her on, as surely as if he'd leaned closer, his lips hot on the curve of her neck. Beneath the heaviness of her limbs, she felt an unfamiliar need, a tightening in her chest that was equal parts desire and dread.

"Most people believe I'm mad." It was more of a whisper than a statement.

"Why?"

She shook her head against the enveloping, smothering

cushions. "Because of what I do and how I do it." Explaining anything more would not help, even if she could.

"I saw your entries in the *Salon des Refuses* in Paris." He cupped her cheek, sketching her ear, the slope of her shoulder. Her insides turned liquid and her skin hot.

Desire coursed through her, foreign and frightening, desire for this stranger whose face she couldn't see. His voice and his body, the here and now that could blot out the terror that hovered in the air around her. From far away she watched herself as, with leaden arms, she reached up to pull him down toward her. His muscles were granite beneath her hands.

Her blood rushed and she breathed in his scent. "You're what I need," she murmured. "To escape, just for a little while . . ."

She was on the margins of awareness, her physical senses as keenly attuned as the finest instrument. The heaviness pooling in her abdomen and the swelling of her breasts were exotic terrain, her body suddenly alien to her experience.

She felt the heat of his breath with its tinge of warmed brandy and tobacco. "I can do that for you, Helena. I can do whatever you desire." His voice caused a muscle to spasm low in her belly. A strong arm slipped under her back, caressing her waist with infinite slowness, burning through the protective layers of skirt and undergarments. His fingers ran up the middle of her back and her shoulder blades tightened in response.

Helena's body inclined toward him with the inevitability of a magnet to the south pole. He was there, his warm breath inches from her mouth, and all she wanted to do was touch him and be touched by him.

"Good Lord, who's that you're rutting with, man?"

A voice intruded, like a rock hitting the stillness of a pond, heavy with alcohol. A shuffle of footsteps and then the slurred exclamation. "Not that I can see from this vantage point, but I'd swear by my dead mother-in-law, hellish harridan that she was, may she rot in hell, that you're about to rut with the widow Hartford. Not bad, not bad at all, I'd say. You've done well for yourself, old boy."

The words penetrated the thick fog of opiates and desire. Helena stiffened. Wide shoulders still blocked her view, but the man who held her was as fixed as a mountain range and didn't move a muscle. He didn't have to.

"You must have a death wish, Lord Beckwith." The threat, in that low gravel voice, was as casually delivered as the crack of a pistol shot at dawn.

Helena closed her eyes, willing reality to disappear.

Lord Beckwith's casual tone suddenly took on a distinct quaver. "Good God, I meant no disrespect. . . . Truly, I didn't quite realize . . . who you . . . er . . . were . . . are."

"I suggest you turn fast on your heels and exit this establishment if you'd like to see the next sunrise."

All signs of dissipation in Beckwith's manner miraculously cleared like rain on a summer's day. "Of course, of course." A restrained cough, the clasping of hands in supplication. "And you can count on my discretion. Certainly . . ."

"The alternative doesn't bear contemplation."

There was no response. Lord Beckwith had disappeared into the blue smoke of the salon, leaving behind a keen mortification and the unwelcome awareness of having been discovered virtually *flagrante delicto*, in a public space, albeit one of London's most luxurious and louche opium dens. Helena opened her eyes against the panic that seeped like cold water back into her veins, the rising curtain of reason beginning to reassert itself. She struggled to sit up, pushing back her hair.

"Thank you." She placed her hands at her temples to keep the room from spinning. "I'm not usually like this. . . ." She took a shaky breath. "I just couldn't deal with him . . . with anyone at present."

They were sitting side by side, and for the first time, in the shimmer of the chandelier's light, she saw his face clearly. As the momentary dizziness subsided, she was struck by an overwhelming masculinity, of sharp planes and angles, of unfamiliar ground. The men in her circle were and had always been refined, the cream of the aristocracy, their features softened by hours of leisure and undemanding days marked by nothing more important than a meeting with one's tailor or a card game at White's. Even the models she sketched were malleable clay, young and unformed, in comparison with this man.

This man was cut from a distinctly different cloth. The nose was strong, the forehead broad, the mobile mouth above the clean architecture of a stubborn jaw bracketed by lines. Lines of hard-won experience. Only a slight indentation in the chin alleviated some of the starkness. His eyes were light gray, disconcertingly opaque, revealing nothing.

"Are you all right?"

She felt like the fifth ring of hell on a bad night. A headache began its steady beat, deliberately mocking her. "I'm well, thank you," she lied, sitting up straighter, hoping to clear the vestiges of stupor that still numbed her brain. Again, she was struck by his size as he loomed beside her, taller, broader, stronger. Her imagination careened wildly. This man, she sensed in the pit of her stomach, would not be easily dispatched.

"What to say in a situation like this?" She licked her dry lips, the words as brittle as a social cliché. "It's a bit awkward, certainly." The useless sentiment drifted into the smoke-thickened air. "No need for introductions. Better that we just take our leave without much more fuss," she continued, fully aware that she was rambling. She couldn't quite recall the words they'd exchanged and didn't want to remember the strange feelings that had threatened to smother her with their strange intensity. With an evil eye, she looked at the pipe on the low table between them.

He caught her glance. "Opium is a powerful drug."

"As I'm quickly learning." Uncomfortable with the conversation, she smoothed the folds of her dress. Only then did she realize that her bodice was flecked with paint, lines of ochre and bright red, evidence of futile hours spent in her atelier earlier that evening.

A smile deepened the lines around his mouth. Strong white teeth flashed against darkened skin and she wondered if he had spent the past six months in an exotic clime. Whoever he was, unlike her, he seemed stone-cold sober.

She was never one for denying the truth. The headache urged her on, and on a shallow breath, she said, "You're clearly familiar with my name, sir, and you believe I'm here to indulge in certain proclivities, which I don't bother to deny. However, I would ask you not to consider these previous moments as representative of, well, of anything, of anything . . ." she faltered, looking down on her lap as though she would find the words there to continue. "It's probably best that we forget this encounter ever occurred."

His smile broadened and he threw an arm across the back of the chaise and crossed one booted leg over the other, the muscles straining against the superfine of his trousers. He was clearly not of the indolent class, and he clearly had no intention of making the situation easier for her.

"By that I mean you caught me at a bad moment, sir." Her headache was a tight band around her forehead and neck, clearly her punishment for having explored forbidden territory. But the fog was clearing and she wondered whether it was for the best because, at the moment, reality was not her friend. And then she recalled Lord Beckwith's hasty retreat.

She licked her dry lips. "Who are you?" She looked up at him, arching her neck in an attempt to loosen the knots that were in danger of cutting off her circulation.

He observed her closely before answering, and she didn't want to look away from eyes that seemed to absorb the darkness around them.

"I don't believe we've met," he said finally. She was relieved that he spared them the charade of rising and sketching a bow. "Nicholas Ramsay at your service, Lady Hartford."

Helena shook her head, dispensing with anything resembling tact or savoir faire. The name, without a title, meant absolutely nothing to her. Possibly a good thing if it indicated that he didn't run with her late husband's crowd. "I'm at a distinct disadvantage, sir." As always, her reputation had preceded her. "You know more about me, clearly, than I about you."

He caught her with his expressionless eyes. "I shouldn't think that would disturb you, Lady Hartford. From what I've gleaned, you're a woman who lives rather freely, doing exactly as she pleases, regardless of society's demands and strictures."

An arrogant, and a monumentally ill-considered, assumption. She felt unaccountably irritated because here was yet another man bestowing his estimation on her behavior. Her head pounded and her blood warmed to low simmer. "And that's what you think, is it, Mr. Ramsay?" Helena returned both hands to her lap and tried to keep the scorn from her voice. "And so what does please me? You seem overly well informed about my likes and dislikes."

"I'd be overly bold in answering that question."

Helena's eyes narrowed. "Your reticence is far from disarming, Mr. Ramsay, or even remotely convincing." As though this man were afraid of anything. His long legs, the muscles hard, were mere inches from her own. He was immaculately, expensively dressed, although his garments lacked the usual embellishments favored by fashionable men of society.

Her reaction to him made no sense and even the opium in her system didn't account for the fact that moments earlier, before this wave of irritation and anger, she'd been all but ready to take him to her bed in a headlong rush of desire.

Desire. Passion. They belonged to the exclusive terrain of her work and little else. Until now.

She was a fool if she didn't acknowledge this was a dangerous man. Lord Beckwith had.

She dared another glance at his strong profile, the radiance from the chandelier gleaming against his thick hair cut unfashionably short. The full force of his gaze was disquieting more so because she doubted that his eyes ever reflected the light.

Silly, fanciful thought.

"I don't believe this conversation is going much of anywhere fruitful, sir," she said, shifting away from him on the chaise in an attempt to bring the unfortunate encounter to a quick close. Something was wrong here and she didn't have the luxury of finding out what it was. "I believe I'm ready to depart for the evening. I shall have a hansom called."

As she moved to rise, she felt a hand, hard and strong, on her wrist.

"I didn't take you for a coward, Lady Hartford."

Still shaky on her feet, she sat back down on the chaise. She desperately hoped to make a quiet exit. "Whatever you believe about me is inconsequential, sir."

He leaned forward and his power struck her like a physical force. "Please let me go." But he didn't and she knew she couldn't afford to make a scene. Not here. Not anywhere. Not anymore.

"You're not a coward, so why not be honest with yourself? What did you feel moments ago? Fear?" His voice dropped to a lower register. "Or desire?"

The timbre in his voice had changed to something possessive, something dark. His eyes bored into hers. "Whatever you're running away from, I can help—better than opium," he said in silken tones. "I came here for you tonight."

A fresh drug slammed through her body, rushing her senses. Her face flushed with heat and he hadn't even touched her. Yet. Hidden in the folds of her skirt, his fingers slipped around her hand.

"Look, I can't, not here," she murmured, confused, the pressure of his hand indecent and arousing. He bent close and she shut her eyes.

"Yes, you can, Helena." He brought his mouth close to hers. "And you will." A heavy thrum pulsed between her legs. She felt his lips on her forehead, her cheeks, her eyelids. And then her mouth.

He pushed her gently back into the cushions. The luxurious press of his lips made her believe that the whole night stretched in front of them. The sweeping stroke of his tongue began a tantalizing rhythm—lazy, sensual thrusts and withdrawals that seduced with the subtlety of a master and the intent of an invading army. The taste of him made her breath come faster, the sweep of that clever tongue sending bright waves of shock straight to her breasts and between her thighs. Unwillingly, she lifted her hand to trace the sharp angle of his jaw before the other grasped the nape of his strong neck.

His arms pulled her close as he turned her face, slanting that devilish mouth down her throat where he took small bites along the sensitive curve of her neck, following with the touch of a warm tongue. Helena arched beneath him, only to have his lips return to her mouth to begin again. Shaking with reaction, she threaded her fingers through the short silk of his hair, a soft moan escaping from her mouth to his.

"I have to go," she murmured, disoriented and weak, half-heartedly curving away from him. "This isn't right. . . . I'm not feeling myself." Her body vibrated, in response to him or the remnants of the opium, she wasn't sure. Before she could catch her breath, he rose to his full height and pulled her from the chaise. Stumbling against him was like slamming into a wall of rock, and she barely reached his chin. Her lassitude instantly vanished and she tried to focus on the fine ivory buttons that marched up the front of his shirt.

"I have another place in mind if that helps." Ramsay had yet to release her, the iron band of his arm around her waist.

Helena lifted her face to his, aware of the gray eyes that were cold against the warmth of his embrace and the heat of his words. This was no ordinary man. *I came here for you tonight.*

And suddenly she was afraid.

"Who are you? Why are you even here?" The questions

spilled from her lips in no particular order. Looking frantically around the room, she pulled away and, miraculously, his hands dropped to his sides, hands that were large and all too capable with their hardened strength against her skin. "What is it you really want from me?" she whispered. They always wanted something.

He looked down at her with those empty eyes and it struck her that his face could have been minted on a Roman coin. Hard, cold, and resolute.

"I meant what I said earlier, Lady Hartford. I can give you what you want."

The room was closing in around her, the red walls like the chambers of a heart. "I have an ample choice of lovers." Her voice was pure bravado. She quickly glanced over her shoulder again in the hope they were not being observed. With some distance between them, her pulse slowed and her blood cooled. What remained was familiar—fear. Ramsay knew who she was, had known, when coming looking for her. In her earlier stupor, she had allowed herself to deny the obvious.

She began to shiver despite the hothouse air of the salon. Suddenly, the red velvet and dark shadows were all the more oppressive, smothering, the pall of smoke catching the back of her throat. She had to leave and only a broad chest and over six feet of solid muscle stood in her way.

"I'm sure you do." He kept his voice neutral. "But this has nothing to do with seduction, Lady Hartford, regardless of the unusual circumstances. If it makes things easier for you, think of this initial meeting as a detour, although a pleasurable one, I'll admit."

Her head snapped up. "A detour?" Her jaw clenched. "I'm leaving, right now."

"And I'm going with you." Before she could react he pushed her toward the front doors of the house. He moved casually, elegantly, despite his size and as though escorting women from one of London's most illustrious and debauched opium dens was a daily occurrence. The light from the wall sconces flickered, the scenes around the room a bacchanalian land-scape. No one noticed when he gestured to the majordomo to retrieve her cloak.

Head throbbing, Helena tried to reclaim her arm discreetly. "If you think that I won't scream . . ."

"As though anyone would notice in this milieu."

"My driver is waiting. He will be alarmed and alert the authorities."

"There is no driver. You mentioned earlier that you would call a hansom. And secondly, the last thing you need is to alert the authorities. As you well know."

Without releasing her, he drew her cloak around her body. His hands on her shoulders and at her neck were heavy with intent.

She looked up at him with a fury in her eyes. "Did Sissinghurst send you?"

"We'll talk more about this later," he murmured into her ear, "and here comes Madame Congais. I suggest we act like lovers. It will assure a smooth exit."

Before she could protest, Helena was hauled up against Ramsay's chest, his total physicality suddenly more frightening than any of Sissinghurst's threats. She lowered her eyelashes in self-defense just in time to see Madame Congais, in full sail, sweep over to them.

"Leaving so early, Monsieur Ramsay?" Her French accent was as artificial as the reddish glint in her hair. A shrewd businesswoman, she worked hard to ensure the ultimate in discretion and service for a clientele that ranged from the House of Lords to wealthy city merchants. She waved theatrically, gesturing to the wide staircase leading to the second floor of the house. "I could have your favorite suite prepared, of course. Was it not to your liking last time?"

Helena stiffened against Ramsay's chest, pretending not to hear the strength of his heartbeat or the fact that he was a regular at Madame Congais's establishment. He pulled her even closer for the woman's benefit.

"Everything was superb as always, Francine. We are simply ready to take our sport elsewhere this evening."

The words rumbled low in his chest, his body brushing against her breasts, forcing her to hold her breath. She jerked spasmodically, but Ramsay propelled her back toward the door and whispered against her lips, smiling as if he were telling a lover's secrets. "I'm your best chance, Lady Hartford. If you're as intelligent as I think you are, you'll take the opportunity just handed to you."

He lowered his head, his lips hot and possessive on the vulnerable side of her neck, and yet she sensed that he watched the room.

Her voice was acid sharp, pushing him away because her body couldn't. "You're a fool if you think that I'd leave here with you," she hissed, refusing to wrap her arms around him. In response, he pulled her hips more tightly toward his and she swallowed a gasp of outrage. "You're the one taking advantage of this opportunity!"

"Don't flatter yourself, Lady Hartford."

Over Ramsay's shoulder, Helena saw Madame Congais's majordomo open the door. Damp night air swept into the corridor.

Four men. Their eyes immediately fixed upon her.

The short one, on the top stoop, held a pair of manacles, dully glittering in the sputtering gaslight of Regent Street. Before she could struggle against the arms that imprisoned her, she heard the words—words that echoed from her nightmares.

"Lady Helena Hartford." Her breathing stopped, but she wasn't going to scream. She bit down on her lower lip, tasting blood, as she stared at the shackles and then up into the stony face of the constable.

"On the orders of the Bishop of London, you are hereby charged with immoral insanity."

Panic knocked the last of the air out of her lungs, and her legs nearly buckled beneath her. The constable's lips moved, the summons a dagger in her back. "To be immediately transported and committed to Bethlem Royal Hospital."

The room spun and she heard prison doors clanging shut, the shuddering sound of cold metal defining her fate as clearly as a knife at her throat. Ramsay's hard arms tightened around her along with the realization that he was the one wielding the knife that was going to end her life.

He was delivering her to the gates of hell, to a future of misery, degradation, and hopelessness.

To Bedlam.

Chapter 2

"**I**s it done?"

The Bishop of Sissinghurst placed a meaty hand on the head of the child kneeling in front of him. Smiling benignly, he helped the small boy to his feet before giving him his blessing and a sticky treacle. His love for children was as genuine as the ruby-encrusted crucifix dangling from his cassock. Each Sunday afternoon, select children from the local poorhouse in Shoreditch visited the Bishop of London's manse in the shadow of the great Cathedral of St. Paul.

The towheaded boy, his face gleaming from a washcloth scrubbing earlier that day, scampered from the room, clutching his sweet. A broad smile wreathed Sissinghurst's face, outlined in the sunshine pouring from the stained-glass window. He sat down heavily in an overstuffed wing chair. "Well, Deacon Mosley," he repeated, "once again—is it done?"

The younger man, with the delicate features of a cherub, nodded crisply, clasping and unclasping his hands in front of him with an eagerness that grated like a choir singing out of tune.

"My lord Bishop, I'm pleased to report that we have been successful."

The bishop arched his brows, deliberately misunderstanding. "*We* have been, have we? You know I dislike hubris in a man purporting to do the work of God."

Mosley's fine features tightened. "I shall take my punishment willingly, my lord Bishop."

Sissinghurst smiled thinly. "I'm sure you will, Mosley, I'm sure you will. Simply remember, I can always find more willing acolytes if the spirit—and flesh—is unwilling." The bishop gestured to the elaborate rosewood table. "A glass of port if you please, Deacon."

Relieved to be given a task he could dutifully perform, Mosley carefully measured the drink into a glass, aware that the bishop was abstemious in most of his habits, including his taking of wine and spirits. One serving a day was all he allowed himself, although meals, of course, were the exception. A large man, Sissinghurst satisfied himself at the table with a prodigious and frightening appetite.

"I'm waiting for an answer, Deacon Mosley." The tone was similar to the one that bounced off the cupola of the cathedral each Sunday morning.

Mosley carefully placed the glass on a side table next to the bishop before answering.

"I did have several gentlemen follow Lady Hartford to determine her whereabouts," he stated, keeping his voice suitably calm, although secretly his spirit rejoiced in hunting down culpable prey, particularly when performing the will of God.

"And?" The bishop took a careful draught of his port.

"I don't expect you to recognize the name of the establishment where we found her—Lady Congais's."

"What about it?"

Mosley cleared his throat. "An opium den, my lord Bishop. And worse."

Sissinghurst flushed red, the alcohol and triumph reaching his head simultaneously. He savored the information, like a mouthful of his favorite trifle, for a moment. "How absolutely wonderful, Deacon. An opium den. Another filthy abomination to add to a lengthening list of sins. And you alerted the authorities, of course."

"I did, Your Grace."

"Well done, well done, indeed."

The silence in the room was marred only by the ticking of the clock. A gift from his late uncle, the Duke of Hartford, the oak-veneered piece with its gilt bronze mounts dominated the room.

"She's on her way, then, I presume?"

"You presume correctly, my lord."

Sissinghurst rose heavily from his chair, pursing his lips, and began pacing. As a corpulent man, he moved heavily on his feet.

"Moral insanity, particularly among women, is not to be tolerated." He directed his homily to the rafters in a voice that could cause terror in the stoutest of men. What he didn't mention was that with Lady Hartford's incarceration came a monstrous fortune that was now his to oversee as her legal guardian.

"And, of course, a simple life away from temptation and self-indulgence will prove beneficial to Lady Hartford's mental condition, I have no doubt." He added significantly, "Mental hygiene is all important. Her licentiousness knows no bounds and can no longer be tolerated. As we well know, madness is a result of moral weakness, which my uncle's widow has in great abundance. This last incident is but more evidence." The bishop turned sharply on his heels, his color rising once again, disgust clear on his face. "The salaciousness of her so-called art work. Truly, Mosley, this will prove her undoing."

Mosley bowed his head in acquiescence, quelling the elation rising in his soul. He thought of the brutal ill-treatment meted out to the insane. Harsh, unhygienic, crowded conditions where cholera and fevers flared, Bedlam was God's punishment on earth. For a penny, eager spectators could peer into cells to view inmates and mock their antics. Once per month, visitors were invited to wield long sticks, poking, prodding, and enraging those who no longer had the freedom others took as commonplace. He thought of Lady Helena Hartford and a strange lust thickened his blood.

"It is God's will," he said.

Ignoring the Deacon and his zealous proclamation, the bishop continued, self-righteousness beetling his brow. He gazed at the clock and pursed his lips. "I don't know what my uncle was thinking when he took her to be his wife."

Mosley nodded vigorously while struggling with the rising temperature in his loins, hunger igniting his wayward thoughts. Lady Hartford was beautiful and flamboyant in a way that would appeal to any man and, in particular, to a man thirty years her senior seeking an elixir to prolong his vigor. He inhaled sharply, recalling the rumors of the duke's widow paying young men to pose nude for her. Then, of course, there was her huge personal fortune—which she was proceeding to give away to charities with wild and outrageous abandon.

The bishop gave up his pacing and sank back down in his chair, fingers drumming the ornately carved arms edgily. "I don't want her to receive any special treatment. Penance is good for the soul," he said sourly. "She has much to atone for, foremost of which consists of squandering my uncle's fortune on the homes of *wayward women and their offspring*, not to mention the schools." He shook his head with exasperation. "If I were not to intervene, there's no saying where she would turn her attentions next. Charity belongs in the hands of the Church," he concluded, selectively forgetting that the fortune he was referring to had come to Lady Hartford by way of her family. "She cannot be incarcerated soon enough. And if additional inducements are required to tame her spirits, well then, we shall be obliged to examine the alternatives available to us. As a matter of fact, I would like you to take up this point with the mad doctor himself."

"Very good, my lord Bishop."

Sissinghurst sighed and took another sip of his port. "Now

that Lady Hartford has been dispensed with and with my uncle's legacy in the proper hands, we can continue our good works, can't we, Mosley?"

"Indeed." The deacon watched as the bishop picked up the Common Book of Prayer carefully positioned at his elbow. Removing his spectacles from their case, he thumbed through the pages, impatiently looking for something he couldn't find. "And about that other matter, Deacon," he said absently, as though inquiring about nothing more important than the running of a local parish.

The words trailed off, but Mosley cleared his throat and said firmly, "I have made preliminary investigations."

"And?" The bishop peered over his spectacles. "You may sit if it makes you more comfortable."

Mosley lowered himself into a chair across from Sissinghurst, his mouth set in a thin line. Excitement shone from behind his pale skin and he began his recitation as though reading from the Holy Scripture, hands folded on his knees.

"The X Club meets once each month at the Athenaeum Club," he said, as always watching for Sissinghurst's most minute reaction. "It comprises nine men who support theories of natural selection and academic liberalism. What brings these men together is, in their words, *a devotion to science, pure and free, untrammeled by religious dogmas.*"

The bishop's eyes narrowed, transformed to raisins lost between his doughy cheeks and heavy brow. "Continue, sir."

Requiring no further encouragement, Mosley barely stopped to take a breath before continuing with the blasphemy. "The objective is to provide a forum that encourages freedom to express unorthodox opinions and the freedom from clerical interference in science."

Sissinghurst sneered. "Heretics, all of them, who are willing to overturn the heavens and worse, the earth," he muttered. "The fools. And it began with that godforsaken treatise."

"*The Origin of Species,*" Mosley supplied, his fingers flexing on his knees as though shaping something malleable that could later be crushed to nothing beneath his heels.

The bishop snorted in contempt and slammed his empty tumbler on the side table in agitation. "Nine men who work together to aid the cause of naturalism and natural history. And undermine God's work on earth. These benighted souls have far too much power in shaping the social landscape in England, Mosley. Just last week that fiend Huxley was in the factories again, spreading his lies about social progress to the sons of toil . . . ridiculous notions and potentially destabiliz- ing. He sets himself up as a type of Cromwellian, a revolu- tionary fighting for the advancement of science based on merit rather than on patronage and aristocratic privilege." The bishop seemed to run out of breath, an almost personal anger fueling his tirade. "If I could, I would condemn Charles Darwin to the burning fires of hell."

"We must overthrow this dangerous clique of allies," echoed Mosley, leaning forward in his chair to make his point, an angel stepping out of a fresco. "They are not only populariz- ing hostility to religion but galvanizing the working masses. I would sacrifice my life to see it done."

"And we will, we will see it done," Sissinghurt continued, but this time more slowly and deliberately, having calmed himself with the last dregs of his port. "With my uncle's legacy now under my control, we have resources to do God's work on earth, to ensure everyone has and keeps to his place. This infidel socialism is rampant on the factory floor and cannot be countenanced." His tone was implacable. "But you've yet to tell me, Deacon, who are these men of the X Club and where are they getting the funds to fuel such dissension?"

Mosley sucked in his cheeks, worry written large on his expression. "A question that requires an answer, my lord Bishop. As we well recognize, science should belong to the province of wealthy gentlemen with the resources and leisure to pursue their interests, or to those who can obtain the backing of rich patrons. Behind them stand archbishops and vicars of the Church of England, holding fast to the notion that all of nature is the working out of God's divine plan." He frowned before continuing. "Men like Lubbock, Huxley, and Busk, however, are middle-class professionals who lack the means to foment radicalism much less destabilize the Church of England. But there's one among their ranks, Tyndall, who in my early contacts with him could prove to be less certain in his views."

The bishop did not sound happy. "Inconceivable how a man like Huxley, the son of a schoolteacher and a cockney mother, could rise to such influence," he grumbled. "Use whom you must, but I want you to discover who is funding the work of the X Club. It's of utmost importance that we undermine the machinations of these heretics who would mount an assault on the divinely ordained social order."

Nodding vigorously and as eager as a medieval crusader, Deacon Mosley bolted from his chair. "Consider it done, my lord Bishop."

Sissinghurst fixed Mosley with a stare while picking up the glass at his side and taking the last lingering drop of port. "See that you do and keep me apprised. Money, of course, is no object now that I have secured the late Lord Hartford's legacy. But we have little time to lose."

He shifted in his chair, caressing the carved armrests thoughtfully. "And send in that little street urchin posthaste. I would like to see if he has committed his catechism to memory. In my experience, the impoverished, if left unattended, remain heathens. However, with the appropriate ministrations, they become the Church's staunchest—and most productive—allies."

To emphasize his point, Sissinghurst snapped shut the Book of Common Prayer and tossed it to the side. "And on that last matter, Mosley, ensure that Lady Hartford never sees light of day again. A weak vessel is our Lady Hartford." He sighed dramatically, his voice dropping ten degrees. "Bedlam is the only place for her to atone until, that is, our Lord sees fit to dispatch her to the hereafter where torment surely awaits."

Chapter 3

The light from the gas lamp swam before Helena's eyes.
No one moved. It was a frozen tableau, except for the
fine trickle of cold perspiration that inched down between
her shoulder blades. Ramsay's arms held her like a vise, his
strong profile turned to stone.

Then Madame Congais shifted, the rustle of her wide bombazine skirts breaking the spell. She pushed aside her majordomo with admirable vigor and addressed the constables on
her doorstep directly through thinned lips.

"I shan't have this, absolutely out of the question," she
said with the cool tones of a barrister mounting an argument
in court. "I don't care if the Archbishop of Canterbury himself sent you, but I shall not have a disturbance in my home.
I have guests," she added, too astute and too experienced to
blush or dissemble, "and I will not have them exposed to such
mayhem." Throwing the ruddy-faced constable a shrewd
glance, she continued unabated. "As a matter of fact, I believe
that there are several judges gracing my table this evening
who would, without doubt, look askance at such an inexcus-
able interruption."

Ramsay pushed Helena behind him, his broad back blocking the doorway. "Gentlemen . . ." he began.

A chill shot up the back of her neck, followed by a pure surge
of survival. Spinning around, she launched herself through the

hallway, bursting ahead. A quick left and then back through the main salon, and if there was anybody following, she didn't want to know. The inhabitants of the salon had dwindled to a few drunken sops, their eyes unfocused and their snores reverberating in the darkness. Holding her breath, she leapt over a man lying on the floor, directly in her path. The lamps were turned down low as she continued her way to what she thought was the back of the residence.

Tension tight in her chest, she reminded herself to breathe. She wouldn't, couldn't think of Ramsay now, or wait until she felt his hard, hot exhalations on the back of her neck, the cruel grip of his hands. She should have known that he was involved with Sissinghurst, and if it hadn't been for the fog shrouding her reason and her senses . . . She wiped the imprint of his strong features, those empty eyes, from her mind.

A light hand skimmed her shoulder and she jumped. "Lady Hartford," Madame Congais whispered, pulling her toward a dimly lit corridor to the right of the salon. "This way."

Her mind now blazingly clear, Helena made a quick decision to trust the woman, as though she had any other choice. Leaving behind the richly paneled décor of the main house, the passageway narrowed to emerge into the kitchen where kettles gleamed and the smell of baking wafted in the air in incongruous contrast with the decadent luxury and musky perfume of the main house.

Pulling her cloak more closely around her, Helena first looked for an exit and then into the eyes of her unexpected benefactor. Madame Congais was older than she first appeared, with delicate papery lines fanning out from her rouged lips and cheeks. A canny intelligence emanated from her like the bouquet from a finely aged wine.

"You needn't explain, Lady Hartford." Madame Congais kept her voice low, suddenly losing her French accent. "I should know better than most how unfair the world can be to women." She continued moving, pulling her toward the small exit leading to the courtyard behind the kitchen. "The authorities can be held off for a few moments longer, but you must make haste. Now, have you a place to go?"

Helena weighed her options—all appallingly dismal—deliberating how much to reveal. She glanced at the small window outlining the alleyway, anticipating that she was a few miles from Soho, but with her sturdy shoes she could arrive at her destination within the hour. *If* she wasn't being followed. She refused to entertain the prospect. Terrifying enough that she had brought the authorities to Madame Congais's door.

"I must apologize, madame," she said, realizing full well that trouble clung to her like a black cloud, as her father had always reminded her. "I've jeopardized your enterprise by bringing the law to your establishment. I would dearly like to make amends. If you need anything, ever . . ."

Impulsively, she lightly touched the older woman's arm. "And, yes, I think I have a place to go. Not here in Mayfair, but there's a friend . . ." She thought it better not to complete the sentence. "I'll go on foot, so as not to attract notice."

Madame Congais colored beneath her fine makeup before stepping away, her pride visible in the straight set of her spine. "No need, no need at all to make amends," she said briskly, pursing her lips. "I know about your generous donations to the Ladies' Association for the Care of Friendless Girls and the schools, of course. You do enough already and very openly, with no regard for your own reputation."

Helena shook her head, unable and unwilling to explain what compelled her to give away much of her fortune. "I have the means, after all. It is no great thing." Yet it was the least she could do with the obscenely large inheritance that seemed to attract far more misfortune than it ever did good.

Madame Congais ushered her closer to the door, the set of her jaw firm. "But go, go now, Lady Hartford. I don't know how long Ramsay can detain them."

At the mention of the name, Helena's ears strained for the sound of footsteps and suddenly she was cold, inside and out. "Detain them? I'm not so sure." Uncertainty simmered beneath the statement. "Nicholas Ramsay's appearance at your establishment here tonight to meet with me was surely no coincidence."

Madame Congais stopped with her hand on the door frame. "There's not much time for discussion, Lady Hartford." She frowned, the corners at her eyes fanning out in fine wrinkles. "Let me simply say that you're quite right in assuming that he's not the type of man that does anything without purpose."

"You know him well." The question was rhetorical. Of course, *Francine* knew him well. Helena wondered what she was doing, wasting time, and for what exactly? She needed to leave, *now.*

Madame Congais opened the kitchen door quietly but noted Helena's expression with seasoned expertise. "I won't lie to you, Lady Hartford. Ramsay is both dangerous and powerful." She paused significantly, as though sorting through memories she had long ago stored away. "I have, shall we say, a great depth of experience with those of the opposite sex, and I will warrant you this—Nicholas Ramsay defies definition of any kind."

The words were enigmatic, breeding ever more suspicions like noxious weeds in an overgrown garden. Helena kept her voice low, despite the fear gathering beneath the surface of her tenuously controlled calm. "The warning comes just soon enough and I'm now doubly in your debt." With a quick farewell, she slipped into the alleyway.

She sped down the narrow slope into the low fog and around the bend, past several stables and kitchen gardens. Her rapid footsteps echoed hollowly against the soot-stained walls of old buildings and along the uneven cobbled streets. Mindlessly, she raced past stone enclosures, green hedges, and hissing gas lamps, every shadow looming menacingly with renewed threat.

Pressing onward, muscles straining, she refused to give

into panic. Her thoughts careened along with the blur of buildings and vegetation scattered with the images of Ramsay, Sissinghurst, and the duke merging into a sickening montage. She was afraid to look over her shoulder, and instead ran as if pursued by hell's demons.

After a good fifteen minutes, she skirted around a curve to emerge on Leicester Square. The area was deserted and it was only an hour away from sunrise. She risked a look behind her and slowed to listen but heard no sound of pursuit, ignoring the scuttling noises coming from behind an untended shrub. Once the haunt of a few respectable families, the area was now filled with prostitutes, music halls, and small theaters. And artists. But even they were now abed.

Breathing hard, she resumed her hellbent run, her lungs absorbing the lingering aromas from the cheap eating houses that dotted the area and scented the gritty air. She rounded a puddle of slop and tore away from the square, scanning the horizon. Turning right, she made for another street that she knew would take her farther uphill and away from the shackles that awaited her at Madame Congais's.

Finally, she allowed herself to slow, attending to the rhythm of her feet and the more measured beat of her heart. Chest heaving, she spared one more glance over her shoulder before turning abruptly into a mews, all former carriage houses, lined up like chess pieces in the dark. Adjusting her eyes to the gloom after the relatively well-lit streets, she counted three entryways before knocking softly on the fourth.

Answer, please answer. Helena adjusted her cloak, shook out the folds, and smoothed her hair, desperately hoping that she didn't look like a wild thing. Then the door opened.

She flung herself into a bony chest and a pair of long arms, unable to hold herself back, her sense of relief spilling from every pore. "Thank God, you're in, Horace. Thank God, you're in," she breathed, looking up into the kind eyes of the older man.

Without asking questions, he pulled her inside, shutting

the door firmly behind them. Holding her quaking shoulders, he examined her face closely. "What is it, my dear? What's happened now?"

Helena forced herself to straighten away from him, gathering her remaining strength around her like tattered rags. "I'm so sorry to disturb you, Horace," she said, struggling to regain a semblance of composure. Despite her mad flight, she felt gripped by a strange chill that had taken over her body since her escape from Madame Congais's. She regarded the rumpled man in his late forties, his sparse brown hair hiding a balding pate, with something like hope. His eyes were a generous warm brown.

"I could think of nowhere else to turn," she said simply.

Horace Webb studied her quizzically, a frown marking his high brow, before gesturing her to take a seat by the hearth where a few embers still burned. The low-beamed room of what was formerly a stable was rustic, furnished in chintz and paisley for comfort rather than fashion, and ringed with canvases in various states of completion. For once Helena's gaze did not linger on the images that crowded the small parlor.

Horace was still fully dressed, his waistcoat hanging open, but there was no sign of his mistress. Sitting down before the fire, her cloak billowing around her, she felt her heart slowing. "I apologize for this rash intrusion, but I was counting on the fact that you often work late into the evenings," she rambled, reminding herself that this was her old friend who had supported her through many battles, despite his own often tumultuous personal life. "I'm sure Perdita has already retired for the night."

"You're in trouble," Horace said bluntly, already pouring her tea from an earthenware pot that stood on the low table between them. "And, yes, Perdita has already retired."

"When am I not?" Helena took the cup, relieved that her hands weren't shaking, and sipped the tepid liquid gratefully.

Webb ran his palms down the front of his waistcoat, his

features pinched and drawn. The silence between them was thick with memories, a shared past that had more shadows than either cared to acknowledge.

Webb would never forget the day he'd first met the rash young woman who was the daughter of a wealthy city merchant and who would proceed, in the coming years, to upend every last convention held dear to society. Six mornings a week, Burlington Gardens in London was invaded by a group of girls weighed down with portfolios, cases of drawing materials, and in one particular instance, overweening ambition. Already a member of the Royal Academy, he'd spied Helena setting up her easel on the dew-wet grass, a powerful landscape inexorably and inexplicably taking shape under her young hands. It was a portent of things to come and, sure enough, her talent had rapidly outstripped his own.

"You refuse to learn, don't you, Helena?" Memories and resignation laced his tone. He remained standing, one hand in the embroidered pocket of his waistcoat. "Your willfulness has never been productive."

Helena set down her tea, the porcelain clattering. She knew exactly to what he was referring, a continuing sore point between them. "Even if I hadn't enrolled in the Royal Academy, my father would still have married me off to Hartford." A well of sadness shone from her eyes even though her voice was emptied of emotion. "He wanted the title, and the old duke wanted my money."

"It was not the worse misalliance, surely. You might have compromised, taken private lessons, confined yourself to water colors and rubbed along well enough with the old duke."

Helena shook her head, feeling weary, silently and reluctantly acknowledging the Webb family connection with the duchy of Hartford. As with her late husband, Horace's background was far more illustrious than hers, but however much she depended on him for his personal friendship, she could not understand the duplicitous life he continued to live, seemingly without emotional repercussions or societal censure. Married to Isabelle, with whom he shared four children, he maintained a separate household with Perdita only two miles down the road but a world away.

"Men have an easier time of it, managing to be upstanding gentlemen and wayward bohemians simultaneously." She directed her words and irony to the smoking embers of the fireplace before returning to look at him directly, compelled to make her argument heard for at least the hundredth time. "And as you well know, I was one of the first female students who qualified when the Royal Academy Schools began accepting women. I couldn't turn my back on the opportunity, not just for what it represented for me, but for what it represented for my sex."

Horace sighed heavily. "I don't deny you that opportunity, my dear. You know how much I admire and have supported you in your artistic endeavors. It's simply that you continue to draw attention to yourself unnecessarily." He winced when he recalled the first study she presented to the judges of the academy. It was audacious, an affront, a deliberate assault on the classical standards set by the establishment. And this at a time when female students were confined to drawing from the antique, followed by a slow progression to still life and then onward to the draped female model. "I've only ever wanted to help you," he said with a stab of anguish.

Helena's expression softened. "I know, dear Horace, and you can't realize how much I've come to rely upon you to preserve my sanity in these past few years."

Webb grimaced at her unfortunate choice of words. To mask his growing anxiety, he walked over to an easel and adjusted a drop cloth to cover the image of a pleasant drawing room scene. Helena had raged inconsolably the day her father had terminated her studies at the academy and had locked her in her rooms for a fortnight. When she emerged, dry-eyed and resolute, he had promptly married her off to a man who was more than twice her age and whose expectations for wifely behavior were set in the Middle Ages.

"I thought your life might become more peaceable once the duke had passed away."

Helena hesitated for a moment, then rose to join him at the easel. "You know it didn't." They didn't talk about her outrageous behavior, her flagrant taking of lovers, her shocking, incomprehensible work, and the fortune she was intent on giving away. "And that's why I'm here. Just for a short time to collect myself before I return to my atelier."

Webb looked at her silently, and an understanding born of a shared obsession burned between them.

Helena lifted her chin. She never was good at keeping secrets from him because there had never been any need. "The constabulary appeared at Madame Congais's tonight. Looking for me," she said brusquely.

He froze. "So it's come to this. . . . What were you thinking, going to Congais's?"

"I wasn't thinking."

"You never do."

"I just wanted to escape." She gestured to the canvas on the easel. "I haven't been able to draw, to paint, to do anything worthwhile since that damned Sissinghurst began his campaign."

"And Madame Congais's was a solution?"

"Not all of us are as adept at compartmentalizing our lives, Horace. You would never give up your painting." The words were more resentful than she'd intended.

"Helena—you risk too much." Anger seeped into his usually mild tones. "You know he's the Bishop of London and he can make good on his threats."

"To have me committed, you mean? Yes, I know that the Bishop of London has the ability to do that and much more. But what can I do? If I can't work, I might as well stop breathing. And don't tell me you wouldn't do the same. You're as obsessive about your work as I am—if not more so."

Horace pulled the drop cloth back over the canvas, his impatient movements communicating anger and frustration. "If your work is so important to you, have you considered compromising with the bishop? Being more diplomatic, for a start, and selecting more appropriate subjects and approaches for your painting?"

Helena shook her head mutely, Horace's suggestions inconceivable.

He picked up a paintbrush by the easel and then almost immediately put it back down, his brow furrowed with concern. "Your very freedom is at stake. And there is nothing I can do to help you if you persist in this willful and headstrong path to self-destruction."

"It's already too late," she said, crossing her arms over her chest. "Sissinghurst has amassed evidence to support my incarceration, and the authorities are so close, I can feel their breaths on my neck." She shivered. "He sent one of his emissaries specifically to entrap me this evening, I'm sure of it." Her pulse began an erratic beat, her mouth suddenly dry. "Is the name Nicholas Ramsay familiar to you?"

Horace's kind eyes widened in disbelief as his hand once again closed around the paintbrush. "Ramsay, did you say?"

She nodded, watching carefully for his reaction.

The older man looked away for a moment before relinquishing the brush to take both her hands in his. "My dear girl," he said, worry lacing every word. "You don't want to know this man, trust me. If Sissinghurst has enlisted his aid, you are in grave danger indeed."

Helena pulled away, the chill returning to her bones. She remembered Madame Congais's warning along with Beckwith's hasty retreat. And her own galvanic response to the man, the shiver that had run from her head to her core at his touch. "So do your worst, Horace." She straightened her spine in defiance. "What and who could possibly be worse than Sissinghurst? Tell me?"

Horace gently released her hands and glanced briefly out

the room's one window. It was quiet, except for an early-morning robin beginning its song. "Nobody really knows," he said slowly, "and that's the dilemma."

"Knows what, exactly?"

"Who Ramsay is and where he comes from."

"Then why all the trepidation whenever his name is mentioned?"

"Ramsay is possibly the richest man in England. He could buy and sell the monarchy, the House of Lords, and Parliament several times over. Rumor has it that if he ever decides to call in his chits, the world would end as we know it. And I'm exaggerating only slightly."

Helena shrugged, unable to reconcile the Faustian powers of a wealthy potentate with the intensely physical man from Madame Congais. Nicholas Ramsay had exhibited none of the rarefied airs of the insanely rich. Quite the opposite, her instincts told her. He belonged to the open seas, to exotic terrain and savage mountain ranges. "Wealth alone does not make one dangerous. I'm still not clear why he instills such"— she paused awkwardly for a moment before concluding—"fear."

"It's what he does with his money, Helena, that's the sticking point. As well as the fact that it's unclear how and where he amassed such a stupendous fortune. There are rumors as I've mentioned, one more unsavory than the next."

Her throat was suddenly dry, her legs unable to support her. Looking for a place to sit, she collapsed onto an embroidered ottoman before the fire. "You'll need to explain because I still don't understand."

Horace looked relieved that she was finally paying heed to his warnings. "The little I know can't help you, I'm sad to say, my dear, and if anything, the less you know about Ramsay, the better."

The room fell into silence except for the light warble of the lone robin and traces of watery sun leaking into the room. Helena looked at her old friend, at the lines of worry etched in his forehead. A feeling of dread swept over her. "You aren't in his debt, are you, Horace?" she asked, bolting from the ottoman to his side. "I shouldn't ever want you to risk your reputation or your family or Perdita by associating with someone as dangerous as this man. If you need more money, you only have to ask and I'd be more than willing to help."

He looked at her hand on his arm, a strange expression on his face. "No, I'm not in his debt," he said stiffly, a strange formality infusing his words. "But I thank you, as always, for your concern. I'm fine at the moment."

Helena dropped her hand, feeling awkward. The specter of financial doom had always clung like a fine mist over Horace's dealings, a delicate issue for a family whose name had been associated with nobility and wealth for centuries. She hurriedly changed the subject.

"It probably doesn't matter, anyway, what you know or don't know about Ramsay. In a few short days I shall disappear into the continent for several months at least until Sissinghurst's campaign loses some of its luster for him," she added bitterly, hunching further into her cloak.

Horace frowned, their previous conversation seemingly forgotten. "But where will you go? What will you do for funds?"

Helena pulled the collar of her cloak up around her neck, preparing to leave. Morning had broken and she didn't dare make her way through the streets later in the day. "I've been funneling some money into an account in Paris for the past several months, so no need to worry, even if Sissinghurst does manage to seize my inheritance."

"And how will you manage to avoid him—and this Ramsay fellow? Europe is hardly beyond the reach of powerful men, my dear."

Helena's back was against the door. "I don't have much choice, Horace. I must take this risk to pursue my work elsewhere."

"Or?" he asked.

Her voice cracked with revulsion. "Or spend the rest of my days shackled in a filthy cell. Slowly and inexorably going mad."

After the early-morning sunshine, the narrow stairway to the attic was dark as a tomb, but Helena knew the winding steps to her atelier as though by heart. The rest of the building was empty, save for boxes and containers, detritus from a former tenant, the A.R. Burrows Shipping Company, that had long ago decamped to a more favorable location closer to the dockyards. Several years earlier, she had instructed her solicitor to buy the property for her under an assumed name, as a refuge from the official residence of the Duke of Hartford on Belgravia Square.

She was exhausted, perilously close to collapse. After leaving Horace's carriage house in Soho, she had made the trip to her atelier in short order. The early-morning streets had been empty, only workmen and domestic servants going about their business while their betters slept untroubled by the demands of the oncoming day.

The stairway came to an end and she carefully moved the old flowerpot on the grimy windowsill. The key waited for her, its familiar scrape against the lock a reassuring counterpoint to the chaos that had overtaken her life just a few hours earlier. The door opened on well-oiled hinges and she was struck by the welcoming aroma of turpentine and paint. And something else. Her eyes adjusted to the gloom to take in the floor-to-ceiling windows covered with drapes against the outside world.

She sensed, rather than seeing, that something was desperately wrong.

Panic shot to her brain. She slid low into the dimness, nausea rising in her throat. Her two easels, usually positioned in the middle of the room, were hacked into slivers, like children's wooden toys, now broken and useless. Paint pots, palette knives, drop cloths littered the floor. The cherry wood cabinet, which had held a few simple dishes, sketchbooks, and favorite novels, was smashed, fractured glass creating a crystalline sparkle on the frayed Persian rug.

Her canvases, her paintings. She stiffened as if she had just been struck. Her work had been slashed into ribbons with an unholy vengeance and flung against the wall.

She covered her mouth with her hands. Her back slid down against the wall until she was almost sitting on her knees, bent over. She was going to be sick. It was then she noticed something else, a detail that had caught her unawares earlier. The aroma, the sickly sweet aroma of a cheroot. Raising her head, she caught the small orange flame on the far side of the cavernous room. It glowed from the chair nestled in the corner where the wall met the ceilinged windows. A dark outline sat in the deep shadows, a curl of smoke mocking her.

Her throat went dry, her nausea dissipated by pure, undiluted rage.

"Who are you—you sick bastard!" Her hands shook as she quickly righted an overturned lamp, grasping clumsily for a match to light the wick.

She heard the faint sound of a pistol being cocked. But before she could respond, the man's voice said, "Allow me."

Frozen, she watched as he rose and pushed aside the heavy fabric from the window. Harsh sunlight escaped through the gap, glinting off his pistol still trained on her with iron resolve. She stopped breathing.

That low gravel voice. "Hello again, Lady Hartford. Surely you didn't think I wouldn't find you."

Chapter 4

She stood a pale ghost, eyes wide with fury. And for a moment, Nicholas Ramsay believed everything he'd heard about her.

That she was wild, reckless, mad.

He let the heavy fabric of the curtain fall back against the window.

"*You sick, sick bastard,*" she repeated as though in a trance. She moved slowly toward him amid the carnage of the room, oblivious to the gun that never wavered in his hand. A small part of his brain told him that she was more than he had expected, more beautiful, more willful. And more dangerous.

"Only a monster, a diabolical fiend, could wreak such destruction." She breathed fire, continuing her walk toward him. "Shoot me, I don't care, because if it's the last thing I do, I'm going to exact my revenge on your black soul." She glanced scornfully at the pistol; then he saw her eyes alight briefly on one of the palette knives balanced perilously on a small end table. Her right hand convulsed at her side as she clutched at the handle. The angle she would have to swing it toward him was wide as a canyon. But it didn't stop her.

In a seamless movement, he closed the gap between them, knocking the knife from her grip. He could feel her heart hammering against him as the muzzle of his pistol cut into her side. The dark gloss of her hair was silk against his chin, her slenderness hiding a tensile strength that was surprising. She was vibrating, from anger, exhaustion, and shock.

"Get it over with," she spat, her violet eyes clouded with pain. "I would rather die than tolerate this heinous destruction. Or rot in some asylum with vengeance eating away at my sanity. What are you waiting for?"

He was reluctant to release her, time decelerating to align with the ebb and flow of her breathing, the pulse point beneath the translucent skin of her throat, the plushness of her lips. She'd stopped struggling and he felt an immediate, gut-clenching need.

He hadn't liked it at Congais's last night, and he didn't like it now. Women had come and gone like common currency in the past two decades of his life, assuaging his desires from London and Paris to Buenos Aires and Jakarta. Making it doubly hard for him to account for his groin tightening like a fist. It didn't help him feel any kindlier toward her.

"I'm waiting for you to stop acting like an hysterical she-cat."

She jerked against him, brushing up against his hardness. His jaw clenched.

"What do you expect? Coming in here, laying waste to everything I value." She glared at the discarded palette knife lying at her feet. "I would kill you if I could."

"I'm not easy to dispatch and a few have tried. Although you're the first woman, as far as I can tell."

"Let me go."

"If I do, it looks like I'll have to kill you." Which would defeat the purpose of it all. He pulled her closer to make his point, the slender roundness of her buttocks against his hardness an agony more exquisite than the most evil torturer could devise.

Her shoulders slumped and some of the fight went out of her. He felt sorry for her. Almost. But then sentiment was not in his nature, and if it ever was, it had been driven out of him long ago.

As though she had pulled a switch, her body became sinuous, the lines and curves melting into his hands. "Let go of me and we can discuss this," she said softly, deceptively.

"You'll behave?" he asked into the silkiness of her hair.

Immediately, she stiffened. "*Behave?* Bloody hell—I'm not a child," she bit out through clenched teeth. "Women are not children and needn't be addressed as such."

"I fail to see the distinction," he murmured conversationally. In his experience, women, whether high born or low, were after much the same thing—to be taken care of, pure and simple. And class divisions made little difference.

"Sod you!"

"Watch your language," he mocked, but he loosened his hold, still keeping an arm around her waist. "Are you ready to have a civil discussion?"

Her silence was not convincing. He slid the pistol into his waistband and eyed the still-open door of the atelier. The room looked as though it had been on the receiving end of a monsoon, and he'd seen a few in his time in the farthest reaches of the globe. To his experienced eye, the chaos didn't look to be the handiwork of London's street runners. He took in the savaged canvases, the broken glass. More like someone nursing a malevolent, savage hatred.

Someone like him.

He began backing her toward the iron stairs leading to what he already knew was the rooftop, stopping when the motion of his body sent her ankle against the bottom step. He pushed her down until she was sitting. Oil from a broken flacon coated the step and seeped into the hem of her skirt.

"Don't even think of moving."

She glared up at him with molten disgust. "What is it you want? Other than to wantonly destroy something you can't even begin to understand."

With a hand on the banister, he leaned over her. "You believe I'm responsible for all this." He deliberately crushed a piece of glass under his booted foot.

The deep blue of her violet eyes darkened. "I don't know how you're involved with Sissinghurst, but trust me, I will make you pay." Despite her brave words, she had the appearance of a brilliant butterfly pinned under glass. Exactly the way he wanted her.

He knew that she still wore the same plain blouse and skirt, with its paint-flecked apron, beneath her serviceable cloak. The fact that she didn't look or act like the spoiled heiress she undoubtedly was made no difference to him.

"I take that to mean that you didn't believe me last night when I said that I can help you, Helena." He reached out to run a finger down the side of her face. He expected her to flinch, but she held still.

"So it's merely coincidence that you're here amid this outrage." Her voice escalated from shock to betrayal. "And at Madame Congais's earlier?"

"I didn't say that." His fingers followed the line of her jaw to the point of her chin. Her skin was petal soft in contrast to the glitter in her eyes. "As I recall, you didn't hear me out, given your rather hasty departure." The finger made a slow descent along her throat.

She licked her lips, in fear or desire, he couldn't say. She had a beautiful mouth, wide and full, and damned sensual. He watched objectively as his fingertip met the small inch of skin exposed by the opening of her cloak.

On a quick, indrawn breath, she said, "And I'm supposed to take you at your word?"

"It would make things so much easier for you."

"Ah, yes, the pistol."

"I was expecting the possibility of company." He dropped to one knee between her feet so his face was inches from hers. She pressed her body back against the stair to get away from him, an impossibility. The pupils of her fine eyes dilated, those same violet eyes, heavy with opium and longing, that had snared him at Madame Congais's.

She was warm. In the closed space of the atelier, her body gave off an elusive scent winding around him, a tourniquet cutting off his reason.

"I wish you'd stop touching me." She stiffened, her low voice close to pleading.

"Like this, you mean?" He sank his hands into her hair with enough force to loosen the pins. She started to shake her head, but he held fast, allowing a small measure of pent-up anger and burgeoning lust to rise to a surface he generally preferred to keep glacially smooth. One by one, the pins dropped to the floor.

He brought his other knee down until they were face-to-face. Her lips parted. "Did you mean what you said last evening?"

She was obvious in her desperation to assume a modicum of control. He smiled, quickly understanding what she was referring to. "About your work?"

She nodded.

"You're wondering if I lied, if I'm lying, when I said your work is magnificent."

It seemed as though she were holding her breath. Her hair beneath his hands was the heaviest silk. "What does it matter how I answer? You clearly believe I'm the mastermind behind this evening's events."

Helena met his hard stare. A fierce intensity, which he couldn't begin to identify, slashed through him. Her eyes were wary, her cheeks flushed, and he knew she had picked up on his monumental rage. *Good.* He threaded his fingers through the hair at the back of her nape, the lustrous strands loosening around them. The scent of lavender and musk drifted from the chestnut waves as they fell across her shoulder and breasts. His blood coursed and his erection pounded painfully.

"Please, I don't like this . . . this sort of thing." The words were unexpected. Coming from Lady Helena Hartford.

He decided to be deliberately crude. "This sort of thing? Sex?" he asked brutally. For a moment, he wondered what her relations with her husband and many lovers had been like. But then again, why should he care. "I find that difficult to believe. Because judging by your response last evening, I'd wager the Bank of England that you're a hot little piece." With the heels of his hands, he trapped the sides of her face, his fingers making tight circles on her temples. "Tell me." He brushed his mouth lightly across hers. "Tell me—do you like this?"

She expelled a small breath. He twisted his hand in her hair and pulled her lips to his, tasting the cushioned softness, deliberately playing her, his tongue a sensual invasion, slow and inexorable, his gentleness in inverse proportion to what he was feeling. His hands roamed, feeling the long line of her legs and the curve of her back. She swayed toward him, her eyes drifting closed. He knew that her skin would be hot to the touch and soft as satin against his hands. His mouth, when it opened hers, seared, hard and driving.

Pressing her against the sharp edges of the stairs, he cradled her head on his forearm. He tasted her, penetrated her, pushing his tongue deeper to draw on her breath. The smell, the feel made his blood pound as years of fury blended with the need to punish, to avenge.

Between gasps, she didn't pull away, but arched toward him, her mouth opening to the force of his tongue. Her hands, which had been clutching the railing moments before, now slid through his hair. A soft moan escaped from her mouth to his, her muscles relaxing beneath his body.

His mouth trailed to her neck where he tasted her tender skin and felt the rapid beat of her pulse against his tongue. With his free hand, he pushed her legs apart, bunching her skirts about her hips. Unresisting, the long legs fell open, encased in crisp, cotton petticoats. It always amazed him, the layers of fabric Western women devised to hide their sex. More erotic than the hundreds of naked tribeswomen he had seen over the years, Helena Hartford's legs in their virginal white tempted him with subtle eroticism. He stroked inside the fabric, from calf, under the sensitive knee, to aching thigh until he neared the opening of her pantalets.

He'd never been so hard, each brush of her against his body reminding him of the prison built by his past. The more he fed upon her, the more the hot pressure in his chest built. Her hands were touching him, slipping into the open neck of his shirt. He twisted her hair and pulled her lips close for a kiss, drawing deeply until they were both breathless and gasping.

But he wasn't about to let her get away so easily. She would have no choice, not with his large hand cupping her face, not with his impassive gaze giving her no place to hide. "You don't like sex," he repeated, his teeth tugging erotically on her lower lip. She suppressed a groan. "Then I wonder what it is that you do with your army of lovers."

Her hands stilled on his chest and her eyes flashed open, and he didn't like what he saw. Her expression was closed, as though her essence were hidden away, as far from his touch as she could get. "Lovers . . ." She expelled a small breath, yet tightened her hold on him. "Please." She bit her swollen lower lip. "I'm not sure about any of this."

He made sure his smile was predatory. "Then tell me to stop right now and I will." Sliding his hands underneath her cloak, he molded his palms to the shape of her. Her head turned away from him, but her breathing quickened to the rhythm of his hands.

"Open your legs for me." The command was deliberate.

Her voice shook. "I can't."

"But you already are." He kept his voice low, seductive. "You're spreading your legs for me." He watched as she squeezed her eyes shut, a flush beginning to stain the soft skin of her neck. Unerringly, he sensed she was close to climaxing, helpless against the demands of her body. He reached for the puddle of oil on the step next to them. He wanted to push her, drive her to the edge, expiate the rawness in his gut, cut it out like a growing cancer.

He dropped his mouth to hers, brushing her lips subtly, following with his tongue, just touching, tasting, and then deeper, harder as he began massaging the liquid into her thighs, stroking higher, the skin beneath his palms firm and slick. She threw back her head, exposing the long line of her neck. Her face was rigid with need, exactly the way he wanted her. Senseless, mindless, and trapped.

His hands continued their relentless journey, every movement accompanied by her sharp little breaths. He found himself riveted by the opening of her pantalets, the breach welcoming his fingers, the curls of her sex beckoning. He parted her flesh, exposing her.

He stopped breathing, a hot surge of blood pumping his erection. Sweat broke out on his brow. She was beautiful and he hated her for it. His fingers, coated with oil, slid between her already wet folds and she moaned, tightening around him. He slid in another and he felt a trickle of her moisture ease from her body. He pressed his thumb against the core that pulsed like a tiny heartbeat. Her hips began moving in a rhythm as old as time, and he continued to slide in and out of her, shaping her desire.

Her hips arched into his hand; then, trembling with need, she struggled to sit back on her elbows, her clothing bunched around her waist. Her hair was a wild tumble about her shoulders, her eyes glazed, lost to the world. Her mouth, with its full upper lip, tried to form the words. "Enough," she rasped, "I can't take anymore."

Ramsay's breathing shortened. "Is that so?" He stilled, waiting patiently for his reward. "But I think you can and you will, Helena. Sit up, bring your hands down, and hold yourself open for me."

The silence was thunderous. She shook her head, more at herself than him. "Why are you doing this to me?" Her fists were clenched in frustration.

Ramsay grit his teeth, her stare like heat from a fire. He would answer her question in time, but in his own time.

Right now, he was grateful for the lust drowning out the tortured thoughts he'd kept buried for the last two decades. He concentrated on that mouth, her long legs sprawled beneath him, and then just as he believed he was going to throw her up against the wall and shove into her, he heard the sound.

Coming from below, it was like the roll of a ship's masts on a windy day. Except it wasn't. Those were footsteps thundering up the narrow stairs to the top floor of A.R. Burrows Shipping.

He knew what was coming. And felt his blood run cold. In a few economical movements he'd pulled Helena's skirts and cloak back over her body. She looked up at him, her eyes clouding first with confusion and then fear as she quickly assessed the situation. Bundling her hair into a knot, she grabbed at a few pins scattered on the floor.

Seizing her by the arm, he hoisted her to her feet. "They're coming. For you, in case you haven't already guessed. There's no time for argument—you're going to have to trust me."

Chapter 5

Before she could reply, they'd crashed through the open door. Four of them, big brawny men swinging bats and brandishing pistols. She recognized none of them from Madame Congais's.

Ramsay pushed her under the stairwell. Fury washed over her, a hot pounding in her brain that she didn't stop to analyze. Head spinning and terror threatening to paralyze her, her vision contracted on Ramsay as gooseflesh chased up her arms and down her spine.

The numbers weren't good.

Ramsay didn't bother pulling the pistol from his waistband. Instead, he wound up and leaned forward, driving his weight into the momentum that lifted the first two men off their feet and sent them flying. He dove to the left, then staggered back, slamming his fist into the shoulder of the tall, wiry assailant barreling at him, his lips curled back in a snarl. He grabbed the bat from his hand, turned, and swung it at the last man standing. The wood splintered before it connected with flesh, making a sound Helena never wanted to hear again.

She watched as one of the men rose shakily from the floor, his face a rictus of pain. At the sound of his heavy tread, Ramsay turned, the move almost elegant, before throwing 200 pounds into an overturned easel with a thundering crash.

It was over before it started. The air hung with sweat, pungent and noisome, overpowering the lingering odor of paint and turpentine. Helena edged a step out of the stairwell, watching Ramsay's heaving back, her eyes tacking back and forth, containing her panic while measuring how quickly she could get through the open door. Away from these men, now broken and battered, littering the floor. But more important, away from Ramsay.

Amid the strangled silence she could hear the clicking of a clock, miraculously undamaged. Her moment was now. She wouldn't think about the heaviness between her thighs, the oil that still slicked her legs . . . *Don't think*. If she waited, if Ramsay turned around . . .

Not daring to move her head, she spied the palette knife out of the corner of her eye, discarded, where he'd tossed it after he'd twisted it from her grasp. She wondered if she would have the courage to use it. As though it would protect her from him. He had disposed of four men in the space of a heartbeat, moving with preternatural swiftness and a lightning rapidity that shocked her.

There was nothing left for her to think about; she could only act. Sensing her intentions, like an animal in the wild, Ramsay swung around. He stared at her until she felt him looking through her, not at her.

It was then that she lurched toward the door. There was a swift movement of air as she closed her eyes. She was not going to go easily, willingly, but his arm snaked out in one efficient motion, halting her escape.

This time she didn't struggle. He held her as though she were no more than a blade of grass, apparently relaxed, but his muscles were tight, ready to uncoil and attack. Towering over her, he was so close, she could smell the scent of blood, metallic and harsh, and the impact was of power and some deeply held fury that, she found herself praying, would remain beneath the surface forever.

He smiled in a way that didn't reach his eyes. "You know, Lady Hartford, we can't go on like this." At the same time, his right heel slammed the door violently shut, undercutting the irony in his tone.

"You're perfectly correct on that count." She wrenched her arm away from him and, surprisingly, he let go. Then he was gone, in two strides across the room back to the front windows, where he glanced, through the curtains, at the alleyway below.

Helena took in the closed door and the motionless bodies scattered like broken dolls on the painted wooden floor. A small river of blood, its source unclear, began to soak the edge of the worn Persian carpet. She looked away and into Ramsay's eyes, which were following her smoothly from across the room as his pistol had done earlier.

No chance of escape. Not now. Breathing deeply, she blocked it from her mind. Clearing her throat, she asked, "Are you hurt? There's so much blood."

He inclined his head before glancing back out the window. "Not to worry. Although a glass of water wouldn't be amiss."

She walked carefully, avoiding the debris, to the small pantry in the studio and opened a cabinet where a decanter of water waited, mercifully, undisturbed. With steady hands, she found two crystal tumblers and poured water into each.

Let him come and get it, she thought, a strange recklessness coursing through her, born of the knowledge she had little to lose.

Never taking his gaze from her, he took three steps and removed a glass from her hands. She moistened her dry lips and said nothing, but all she could think about was flight. There were four sets of stairs, narrow and twisting, and she knew instinctively that he'd overtake her in an instant.

She watched the corded muscles of his neck as he drank the water. His physicality, even in this simplest action, was overwhelming. The memory of his hands between her thighs, his mouth devouring hers, was like a hallucination. Her face burned and she hoped he couldn't read her mind. She took a quick gulp of water.

"Do you have any idea who these men are?"

Helena shook her head, cradling the tumbler between her two shaking hands. "They aren't familiar to me, but I have an idea as to who sent them." Her eyes darted around the room. At any other time and in any other world, the mayhem and carnage would have sent her into a spiral of panic, but just thinking of Sissinghurst hardened her horror into pitiless determination. "Can we be sure they will stay unconscious for the moment?" Her cool tone, she noticed, almost matched his.

Ramsay shrugged carelessly. "They won't cause any more trouble for a while." She thought about what had happened, and about how quickly and ruthlessly he had managed the attack. It didn't make sense that one of the wealthiest men in the empire handled himself like a felon in an alleyway ambush.

"I'd suspected they might come back looking for you," he said, his voice clipped, revealing no more emotion or information than a complete stranger would. Gone was the pent-up fury, the monumental rage that had burned through her skin when he touched her. It was as though nothing between them, *nothing intimate,* had ever happened. He set down his water glass and halfheartedly smoothed the front of his shirt, now splattered with blood. "I'd found the atelier destroyed when I first arrived. Believe me or not. But do believe me when I say that somebody hates you with a passion."

Her chin jerked up, unwilling to absorb his statement or his transformation. "You knew they were coming, and yet you allowed yourself to . . ." The words tumbled from her lips. "To engage in what we did, when you knew someone might . . ." She trailed off, her grip tightening on the glass to the breaking point.

The faint mockery in his voice was disquieting. "We can't

control everything in life, much as we might try. Besides which, I enjoy a certain amount of risk," he said. "And I think you're much the same, Lady Hartford."

The formal use of her name peeled back another layer from her frayed nerves. She stared at a precise spot on Ramsay's once immaculate white shirt, where the ivory button had popped off. For once in her life she couldn't explain herself, couldn't account for the collision of emotions crowding out every thought. Each moment she'd endured so far with Nicholas Ramsay was an outrage she could never hope to understand.

She looked into his eyes and saw cool calculation, an awareness that he knew exactly what he was doing and why.

Irritation and hopelessness fueled her impatience. "None of this makes any sense, at least to me, Mr. Ramsay," she said, infusing the words with iron. "Speak your business and let's have done with it."

Without taking his eyes from her, he sauntered across the room, broken glass crunching under his booted feet. He leaned against the windowpane, this time not bothering to lift the curtain to glance outside. "You still don't understand," he said finally. "Maybe you don't want to understand."

Helena set down her glass with a thud on top of the cabinet. "You're speaking in riddles, but I'm giving you one minute to explain yourself." She let out a short breath, feeling suddenly calm and certain. "Why should I believe that you have nothing to do with this wanton destruction? You've asked me repeatedly to trust you, to go along with you when all I can think of is *this*." She gestured helplessly around the room, trying to avoid looking at the four bodies slumped on the floor.

"You are asking the impossible!" For emphasis, she scooped up a piece of torn canvas, the corner a livid, vibrant green, before tossing it back to the frayed carpet. "I meant what I said earlier when I entered this room—if you have had anything to do with this abomination, you will pay."

"You're not in any position to be exacting retribution."

"Just watch me."

"That's your problem, Helena. You act on emotion. Try counting to ten from time to time."

"Damnit—I'm leaving." She kicked at an overturned chair with a jerk of frustration, making her way to the door.

He didn't bother to come after her, his supreme confidence unnerving. "Do you see what I mean? If you just stopped feeling for a moment and listened, it might do you some good."

"You bastard."

He cocked a brow. "A fine and accurate assumption on your part. But never mind that, are you ready to listen?"

A step away from the door, she whirled to face him. "Enough about what I'm supposed to feel or not feel, sir. I've had a lifetime of being dictated to by men, and I'm not about to have you of all people move me around like a piece on a chessboard."

He crossed his arms. "Then what do you propose to do to extricate yourself from this particular situation? It looks like you have half of London eager to ensure you rot away the rest of your life in Bedlam. Not a great prospect—unless you have a solution at the ready."

Helena hated the condescending tone and she evaded his gaze. "Not that it's any of your concern."

"That's where you're wrong. Again. I've said it a few times in the last twenty-four hours—I can help you." He glanced briefly out the window and then had her back in his sights like the marksman he probably was.

"Then you have a peculiar way of showing your regard."

"You've yet to give me the opportunity," he lied smoothly, no doubt the result of years of practice.

"It's been difficult—what with your unwelcome attentions." She regretted the words the minute she'd said them and could have bitten her tongue. She looked away from those hard eyes.

But his faint smile revealed nothing. "If you haven't noticed already, I'm not a gentleman, and in any case"—he held up both hands in mock defeat—"I refuse to give in to the charade that my attentions were in any way unwelcome. I recognize a woman's response, and frankly, I'm surprised at your hypocrisy."

Helena flushed. "Even your referencing this, this . . ." She was at a loss for words.

Ramsay shrugged carelessly, raising a dark brow. "Where is the free-spirited bohemian, the artistic soul, the woman who cares not a shred about society's strictures, the renegade who takes and discards lovers as though they were kid gloves?"

"You know nothing about me, sir." She glowered.

"I know you're supremely talented and about one minute away from being locked up in Bedlam for the rest of your life. What else is there to know?"

The man had a point. "You have a proposal, a solution?" She shot him an incredulous look. "And how do you intend to gain from it? I don't think the knight in shining armor is particularly your strong suit."

Her sense of foreboding didn't evaporate. It was heightened, particularly when she thought about the way he made her feel. This was what lust was, it occurred to her suddenly, a heady, reckless emotion emerging from a lethal combination of fear and attraction. She put her hand to her forehead and was horrified to find it trembling.

He scrutinized her closely, dissecting her with his eyes. "Yes, as a matter of fact, I do have a solution to your problems. And by the way, you're shaking."

The man didn't miss much. His stillness was unnerving, his opaque gray eyes giving nothing away, save that they could read her mind. Dear God, she hoped that he would never see into the dark of her soul that she trusted to no one, the part so well hidden, it kept her safe and whole.

"I haven't had much sleep," she muttered, forcing her hands to her side.

With a last glance out the window, he stalked toward her.

"If you don't leave with me now, you'll have the rest of your life to sleep away in your cell at Bedlam. And if, once again, you don't believe me, just take a look outside this window." He grabbed her arm. "You're about to receive a visit from half of London's constabulary."

Helena smothered a curse, trying to ignore the hand burning through the fabric of her dress. Her head snapped toward the door, but she knew it no longer offered an option.

She moistened her lips. "You could be lying. Those men could be yours."

"You know that is entirely illogical." He paused for a second. "Although something tells me there's more going on here. You seem to have quite a few enemies, Helena."

Before she could respond, he swung her toward the stairs. *Dear God, the stairs where they had nearly . . . just minutes ago . . .* She wouldn't think of that now.

"The stairs lead to the rooftop, which I'm sure you know, and into a back alley." The man was thorough, having checked out all the entrances and exits in advance. "Once again, you've got no choice but to trust me." He added coolly, "Twice in one day, how unfortunate for you."

She felt panic once again close her throat as Ramsay squeezed her hand, his movements calm and assured. And like an obedient child, she followed him through the atelier, up the stairs and onto the rooftop into the stinging light of day.

Chapter 6

It was like herding cats.

"Order, I say. Let us bring the meeting to order." George Busk cleared his throat and surveyed the men hovering around the heavy Queen Anne table, reluctantly taking their seats. A surgeon by training and instinct, he liked getting things done.

He scratched his heavy white beard impatiently. "We have many important matters to discuss this evening, gentlemen. Beginning with the debate last week up at Oxford."

An instant hush fell over the room. Seven heads swiveled in Busk's direction.

Joseph Dalton, on his left, puffed himself up like a balloon. "I do believe Huxley did an outstanding job! Outrageously good!" He punched the air for emphasis before scraping back his chair and sitting down decisively. The other men followed suit.

"Is he still up at Oxford?" asked John Tyndall, who had given up his work as an artisan to become a physical scientist, and had joined the X Club only two months ago through his association with Huxley.

"Indeed, Thomas will not be returning to London for another fortnight," confirmed Busk, donning spectacles to peer at the agenda before him. He shook his head imperceptibly at the long list of items before removing his spectacles with a snap. "I know, gentlemen, what is surely percolating in your fine scientific minds. It would be your wish that we move the Oxford debate to the top of our agenda."

"Hear, hear." The voices raised in unison.

Busk leaned back in his chair, waiting for the rumbling to calm down before continuing. "And since our host has been delayed"—he paused with the slightest unease—"I would suggest that we proceed with Dr. Dalton, who was present at the scientific conference where Bishop Samuel Wilberforce chose to speak against Mr. Darwin's views. I will cede the floor to you, sir."

Dalton bowed his head in acknowledgment. "Thank you, Mr. Chairman." He tipped his chair back and hooked his thumbs in the lapels of his melton jacket. "Having witnessed the debate firsthand, I can wholeheartedly endorse Huxley's new moniker, *Darwin's bulldog.*"

The room erupted in laughter with several of the men lifting their water glasses in a toast.

Raising his voice over the clamor, Dalton continued, "As we are all aware, the publication of Mr. Darwin's book last year proposing a mechanism for evolution, that is, natural selection, caused outrage both in the Church and in society."

Across from him, Edward Frankland nodded. "Implying, of course, that humans were not created by God but had evolved from other animals. And perceived as an assault on the divinely ordained aristocratic social order. This does not sit well in many circles here in England. And I must say, most unfortunate, that Darwin himself was too frail to attend the debate."

A chorus of agreement met the statement before Dalton interrupted. "Unfortunate, yes, gentlemen, but hardly fatal, as you'll discover if you would allow me to continue my account. First to set the scene." The men leaned forward in anticipation, waiting as Dalton cleared his throat before carrying on.

"The room was crowded to suffocation long before the

protagonists appeared in the hall, 700 persons or more managing to find places. The very windows by which the room was lighted down the length of its west side was packed with ladies, whose white handkerchiefs, waving and fluttering in the air at the end of the bishop's speech, were an unforgettable factor in the acclamation of the crowd."

Tyndall shook his head. "A behavior one would expect from the fairer sex."

Dalton ignored the interruption. "Wilberforce took the podium first, attempting to undermine Darwin's supporters with a provocative question: *Was Thomas Huxley descended from an ape on his grandfather's or grandmother's side of the family?* As you can imagine, a shocked silence blanketed the room.

"Huxley, just as formidable a public speaker as Wilberforce, responded sharply. And if I may quote: 'If then said I, the question is put to me, would I rather have a miserable ape for a grandfather or a man highly endowed by nature and possessed of great means of influence and yet who employs these faculties and that influence for the mere purpose of introducing ridicule into a grave scientific discussion—I unhesitatingly affirm my preference for the ape.' "

Dalton barely paused before the room broke out in cheers of approbation, several of the men pounding the table with enough vigor to have it shake on its legs.

"Well done, well done," Frankland applauded. "I'm sure Huxley's suggestion that he would rather have an ape for an ancestor than a bishop caused an uproar."

"As a matter of fact, yes. One lady actually fainted and had to be carried from the hall while Robert Fitzroy, Darwin's captain on his voyage aboard the *Beagle,* if you can imagine, brandished a Bible and implored the audience to have faith in God."

"Damn sorry I missed it," Busk muttered into his beard. "And a damn fine show, by all reports, although I must ask the question, Where does this debate leave us?" Like the bearer of bad news, his query cast a negative pall on the proceedings. "As we know, anyone who publicly supports scientific views at odds with accepted religious dogma risks ostracization and worse."

"There is much at stake," concurred John Lubbock from the end of the table. A short man with rounded glasses to match his girth, he had lost his position as head surgeon at King's College Hospital for his unorthodox views. "I have already heard it said that Wilberforce, the High Church, and evangelicals will organize petitions and a mass backlash. They propose to bring forward a declaration at the upcoming Anglican convocation reaffirming their faith in the harmony of God's word and try to make this a compulsory Fortieth Article of faith."

"And we have also learned that they will take their campaign to the British Association for the Advancement of Science," added Frankland soberly. "We find ourselves, indeed, as members of the X Club, involved in the struggle for freedom from clerical interference in science."

Busk stroked his beard contemplatively. "Clearly, this is simply the beginning. Huxley is not endearing himself to society by lecturing to workers who, apparently, arrive in droves to hear him speak. And vicars, in turn, are encouraging factory owners to dismiss freethinkers."

"It is rumored that while only half the nation frequents Sunday services, next to none attend from the slums," added Frankland.

Busk nodded. "I digress only slightly when I ask all of you to remember the night of our first meeting when Huxley proposed, in jest, that our club be named *Thorough Club,* referring, of course, to the concept of freedom to express unorthodox opinions."

"Although it was your wife Mrs. Busk, as I recall, who proposed our current name because it committed us to exactly nothing," reminded Tyndall, tapping his pen pointedly on the sheaf of papers in front of him.

It had also been decided that meetings would be scheduled on the first Thursday of each month with dinners taking place at St. George's Hotel on Albemarle Street, Almond's Hotel on Clifford Street, and then, finally, at the Athenaeum Club. Meetings always started at six in the evening so that the repast would be over in time for the Royal Society session at eight o'clock.

Save for this evening, an exception of which they were readily aware to the last man. Suddenly, they were all thinking the same thing.

"Has he arrived yet?" asked Lubbock from his end of the table. The imposing ancestral portraits of the fourth Marquess of Conway loomed over the assembly, as though each august personage were considering the question.

"He's somewhat delayed, I'd heard earlier from his butler," supplied Busk, somewhat reluctantly. He sifted through the papers before him, trying to ignore the fact that they were ensconced in one of the country's most ornate homes, invited by a usurper whose motives were about as transparent as the muddy Thames.

Conway House was overflowing with treasures that the late marquess had purchased in the decades before his untimely death late last year. Everyone knew that his life had been devoted largely to dissipation and foreign travel, making him a considerable connoisseur. He had snared Titian's *Perseus and Andromeda* and seventeenth-century gems such as Rembrandt's *Good Samaritan,* along with a trove of French furniture, gilt bronzes, and Sevres porcelain. Attracted to the luxury and refinement of eighteenth-century French art, the marquess, along with other English collectors, profited from the dissolution of many Continental collections during the French Revolution and Napoleonic wars.

And now, as everyone around the table recognized with painful clarity, 500 years of a family's wealth and riches were lost to a clever and monstrously powerful upstart.

"Survival of the fittest, all right," muttered Lubbock, not

unaware of the terrible irony in the situation. He looked pointedly at the heavy gold candelabra at the center of the table. "Very good of our host to fund our work and to invite us to have our meeting at his new home whilst he's in London."

Busk concurred, alert to the tension filling the room. "Very gracious, very gracious, indeed. He is abroad much of the time, I deduce, running his shipping and banking kingdom from all corners of the empire. Clearly a busy man. I'm certain his butler will announce his arrival, so in the interim, I suggest we continue with our agenda items, gentlemen, if you are in agreement."

Before the members could respond, Tyndall cleared his throat noisily, rising to stand behind his chair, gripping the high back. He surveyed each man with a piercing gaze from under shaggy gray brows, his muttonchop sideburns trembling. "Perhaps we *should* take this time and opportunity, gentlemen, to discuss more thoroughly the motivations and background of our host and benefactor. Shipping, banking— is that all we know? And is that enough?" Like a malodorous scent, the words hung in the air. "Because when we accept someone's resources, are we not as a matter of principle—"

"What exactly are you getting at, sir?" interjected Lubbock, throwing down his pen.

Tyndall's color rose along with his condemnation. "It isn't simply rumor that the late marquess was hastened to his grave by the unceasing demands of one monstrously, unconscionably wealthy individual, Mr. Lubbock."

Lubbock snorted. "Our host and benefactor simply rescued an old man from his own debauchery, not to mention the spendthrift and wasteful ways that would have landed even a peer in the poorhouse."

Tyndall squared his rounded shoulders. "And what of the source of that wealth? This man materializes out of nowhere, with fleets of ships and international banks at his command? Who is his family? Where did he come from?"

"You expect him to be listed in Debrett's, for God's sake, Tyndall?" Busk asked, his own doubts and unease warring with the exigencies of the situation. "Where are these suspicions coming from? You must have your own font of information, so do tell, sir. Because if all of this is about the source of our host's fortune, well then, that's an old story we should probably dispense with right now."

Tyndall gripped the back of his chair more tightly, his knuckles whitening. "As I have been unexpectedly called away earlier this evening, I shan't have time over our repast to elaborate—"

"So you won't be joining us for dinner," interrupted Busk impatiently.

"Precisely, all the more reason I should like to address the members currently present with some of my reservations, culled from the most impeccable sources, I will vouchsafe."

"*A capital idea, Mr. Tyndall.*"

The voice was a low growl, disarming and dangerous at the same time. And it came from the back of the salon where the richly paneled French doors had, at some point, silently eased open.

A tall man strode into the room, a grim smile spreading across his face.

The X Club's generous host—Nicholas Ramsay.

At first, she didn't know who she was. Where she was.

Panicked, she grappled for her name, clutching a pillow to her chest. In a hoarse voice she vaguely recognized as her own, she found it in the dark and began reciting it to herself like a creed or a well-worn article of faith, willing the curtain to lift.

The bed was wide with heavy satin sheets weighing her down. Only then did she remember.

Her work, the attack, Ramsay.

Helena bolted from the covers with a groan.

Her bare feet sunk into three inches of carpet before she

noticed the bed crown draped in blue-watered silk, the size of a small stage. The room was sumptuous beyond description, even for the standards of the Duke of Hartford and Belgravia Square. Rich wall paneling was interrupted by drawings of classical figures—she peered at a trio of nymphs frolicking around a fountain—quite possibly from Renaissance Florence. A pair of Louis IV Bergeres flanked the fireplace next to a small French desk made of exotic materials and set with a black and gold cup and saucer.

A gilded prison instead of Bedlam.

A quick exploration of the dressing room revealed her cloak, dress, drawers, corset, and chemise neatly pressed and waiting for her inspection. Bronze candleholders decorated an oversize English tall chest with eight drawers, next to a three-door French armoire, which, she discovered quickly, was empty. A water closet, equipped with the most modern fittings available, included a porcelain bathtub.

Back in the bedroom, a small mantel clock in ormolu and statuary white marble told her it was six in the evening and that she had slept nine hours since first stepping into Nicholas Ramsay's London home.

He didn't belong here. That much was clear.

It was impossible to reconcile the startlingly masculine and physically imposing man with the overly refined and studied décor of Conway House. Unless he had a wife, which somehow she doubted. He was too dangerous, too unmanageable. Her pulse jumped, the image of the bodies littering the atelier imprinted on her mind's eyes. She swallowed hard, the shambles of the previous night rolling over her.

Who was Nicholas Ramsay and what did he want from her?

She quickly unbuttoned the demure nightgown she was wearing, her fingers stiff with nervousness. Convent-made lace, virginal and pure, encircled the neckline like a noose, and she was reminded of the ridiculous confection she'd been forced to wear on her wedding night. And the look in her husband's eyes, cold and hungry at the same time.

With a sharp tug, the nightgown sailed over her head and onto the floor. Tossing it onto the bed, she recalled instead the tense silence that had accompanied her hurried arrival at the house north of Oxford Street midmorning. Fleeing from London's constabulary with Nicholas Ramsay to this house was madness, part of the cloud of unreality that refused to dissipate. She was determined Conway House would be a temporary prison, despite its splendid five bays on its south front and a large Venetian window at its center topped with three stories like a wedding cake.

Temporary. Because at this moment, Ramsay was all she had and she would make the most of him. Freedom would be hers at any price.

Her heart ricocheted in her chest. She hated running, but she would not wait like a lamb to the slaughter for Sissinghurst's men to make another appearance. If Ramsay was somehow part of the bishop's plot against her, she would manage that too. She closed her eyes against the image of his hands and mouth on her body, burning like a desert sun.

Her eyes flashed open. She wasn't pliant and she was never the docile doll her father or her husband had wanted her to be. Her moods, her outbursts, her unpredictability meant survival, an amalgam of determination and passion that neither her father nor her late husband had been able to strip away from her. Why then had she not been able to shut Ramsay out, to pretend?

Ten minutes later, she had completed her ablutions and impatiently drew her dress over her drawers, chemise, and corset. She was not a vain woman and her working garb had never included crinolines or hoops, fashion representing simply another stricture that had been forced upon her.

She hurried over to the exquisite French escritoire and penned a quick note on a page of smooth vellum to Horace

Webb. She didn't want to involve him any further in the disaster that was her life, save to spare him worry and apprise him that she was staying at Conway House until further notice.

A discreet pull on the servant's bell produced a maid who took away her missive but not before presenting her with a note on a heavy silver plate, the bold black strokes dark against the white paper, giving away the author.

Helena glanced quickly at the message. Her presence in the dining room was requested for eight o'clock.

Her pulse jumped. That gave her thirty minutes to discover exactly how to use Nicholas Ramsay before he could use her.

Chapter 7

Horace Webb put down his paintbrush and leaned back to observe his handiwork.

Early-evening light played with the muted blues and grays of the still life. The yellow of a pear did not glow and the sprays of white lilies looked like they formed part of a funeral cortege. He sucked in a deep breath, a miasma of disappointment and frustration spreading like disease through his body and mind.

He threw a drop cloth over the canvas, not bothering to wait until the paint was dry. It was useless. He was useless. His dream of achieving artistic greatness had never been farther from his desperate grasp.

The carriage house here in the mews should have helped, as should have Perdita, his charming and completely empty-headed mistress, so different from his stolid wife and their dull children. He turned toward the fireplace with its cold ashes and the teacup, half empty, abandoned by Helena earlier that morning.

Perhaps his father had been right. He should have simply pursued the life of a minor peer, rusticating in the country, hunting and fishing, while making occasional and desultory appearances in the House of Lords.

His gaze returned to the tea cup and Helena. Her father, Robert Peacock Whitely, one of the canniest merchants in

London, had more than once financed Lord Webb's fiascoes. In exchange, of course, for the right introductions to the aristocratic circles he so craved. Cruel man, but one who got the job done.

And all the more tragic for his beautiful and supremely talented daughter.

Webb's head turned at the sound of Perdita's light footsteps.

"Darling," she said in that breathless way of hers that he had first thought so charming in a muse. Her glossy blond ringlets bounced girlishly against her low-cut afternoon gown. "I have something for you."

She clutched two envelopes in her small hands. "But I won't give it over quite yet, my dear," she trilled coquettishly. "First, let me see what has been occupying your time and taking you away from me today."

Without asking permission, she swept over to the canvas and pulled aside the sheet.

A fist knotted in Webb's chest. There it was in all its dullness. He couldn't bare it a moment longer and looked away.

"Oooh, my darling, absolutely lovely. Look at all that fruit and those divine flowers!"

"Never mind, Perdita," he said tersely, snapping the sheet from her fingers and covering the offending painting. "What is it? If that's a message, please give it over immediately."

Her large brown eyes filled instantly with tears. "You're always so short with me lately, Horace. And those dresses you had me return to the dressmakers, and the leather gloves . . . when you said that I'd had enough pairs to outfit an entire livery."

It was the last thing he wanted to hear at the moment from Perdita, this litany of tiny injustices that she lay down at the feet of her impecunious protector. He ran a hand over the nonexistent hair on his pate. Importuning his solicitor for more funds was out of the question and would only serve to alarm him further over the hash his finances had become.

Good God, that any of the Webbs should even have to reflect upon, much less worry about, their finances had been previously unthinkable.

There was so much that Helena Hartford took for granted.

"Horace, my dear." Perdita's lower lip began to quiver, an indication of her sorry plight. She pulled a lace-trimmed handkerchief from her sleeve before giving him the missive, now dampened with her tears. "There are two here for you," she mumbled tremulously.

Turning away from the feminine snuffling, Horace tore open first one and then the second envelope, quickly reading the messages. When he looked up moments later, he felt a strange lightness suffuse his spirit.

Sharper than she appeared, Perdita managed to look concerned. "What is it, my love?" she asked.

"Fetch me my hat and coat."

She looked up, startled at his sudden change of mood. He spun around without a backward glance, leaving her swaying like a puppet on a string, confused, in the middle of the small parlor. A surge of energy swept through him. It was one of those moments, he convinced himself, that turned a life around, a moment that he, Horace Webb, would remember on his deathbed.

Time for him to take the lead, to reach out and seize what was, and had always been, his to take. It was like the tumblers in a lock had suddenly clicked into place.

With his hand on the door, he decided he could spare a moment's generosity for his mistress.

"I won't be dining in tonight, Perdita. And not to worry, I'll get my own hat and coat. And, my dearest, don't wait up for me as I expect to be very late."

He gave her a kind smile that was genuine to its core.

Helena threw back her shoulders and hitched up her skirts, the stairs disappearing beneath her feet. The house was silent, the curved banister beneath her palm slick with beeswax. On the ground floor a dining room appeared on her left with a long table set opulently and elegantly for eight. The ivory linen shone and the crystal gleamed with military precision, the only discordant note the three or four canvases piled carelessly, facedown, against the east wall. Distractedly, she remembered the vague rumors about Conway House and the late marquess, tales about his stupendous art collection, spendthrift ways, and catastrophic ruin.

As though she had time for useless speculation. She was running on instinct and not much else. She hurried past to the end of a hallway toward an open door that revealed the corner of a desk and shelves filled with books, their spines covered in gilt lettering.

With a quick glance over her shoulder, she slid into the library, her eyes darting around the room before coming quickly to a decision. Edging behind the desk, her hands made quick work of the heavy drawers, rifling through papers that looked to be routine correspondence. Pushing away a vague feeling of guilt, she quickly slid open three ivory boxes, all of them empty. She didn't know precisely what she was looking for.

As long as it was something, anything to use against Nicholas Ramsay.

But bloody hell, the library, like much else she'd seen in this blasted house so far, might as well have been a stage set at Covent Garden. No hint of the real man, no evidence of his past or his present.

Not that she had to remind herself that he was flesh and blood.

She looked up from the frantic search of the desk and surveyed the room like a thief with only moments to spare. Shelves upon shelves of books, a shuttered window and a leather settee, bracketed by two heavy lamps, facing the fireplace. Going through all the books would be madness, and she didn't have anywhere near the time. She gritted her teeth and appraised the room again, but this time stopping at the fireplace mantel carved from travertine marble. Why hadn't she noticed it before?

A crudely constructed model ship, amid the intricately wrought appointments of the room, caught and held her attention. Awkward and out of place somehow. Her knowledge of seafaring was scant, but there was something distinctly repulsive about the replica, its three masts with its square aft sails squat and ugly.

Sliding from behind the desk, she approached the fireplace, making out the script on the barque's bow. *Scindian.* She played with the name on her tongue, the lingering taste exotic and foul all at once.

And somehow she knew it belonged to Ramsay.

Chilled, she stepped back, imagining the carved wood in his strong, elegant hands. It was all she really had, that peculiar image and little else. A fanciful notion, perhaps, but she sensed she wouldn't discover much else. He was a cipher and intended to keep it that way.

She didn't need the striking of a clock somewhere in the house to remind her that time was running out. Easing her way to the open door, she heard a rumble of male voices spilling into the hallway and spied half a dozen older men filing toward the dining room. And for whatever reason, she suddenly thought of the duke.

She saw herself as a new bride sitting across from her husband, his nephew, the Bishop of London, and, never far from Sissinghurst's side, Deacon Mosley. Mercifully, an acre of polished wood and shining crystal separated her from the three men. Hartford was dressed impeccably as always, his high and elaborate cravat emphasizing that commanding look he directed at her.

"Not hungry, my dear?"

She didn't remember her specific reply, but she knew that she had pretended to eat, moving the food around her plate, anything to delay the humiliation to come.

"You're becoming much too thin," his nephew concurred, pinning her with his raisin eyes and puffing up his pigeon's chest. "I should think, uncle, that someone of Helena's, shall we say, rustic background, would have a more robust appetite. Perhaps she's simply putting on aristocratic airs for my sake. Totally unnecessary and ultimately unconvincing, I might add."

Mosley said nothing, he simply continued to stare at her, a strange fire burning behind the fine, pale features that could just as well have belonged to a choirboy.

"She is proving quite contrary," murmured Hartford, allowing himself a malicious smile behind a bracket of candles that burned at the head of the table. "But there are many ways to remedy that situation, to bring her to heel, as it were, nephew."

Sissinghurst chuckled, displaying large white teeth, amused at his uncle's cavalier tone. He continued as though Helena were not even in the room. "I'm sure you have it well in hand, sir, along with her quite magnificent fortune." He shoveled another forkful of meat into his mouth.

A door slammed somewhere in the depths of Conway House—the abrupt noise dissolving Sissinghurst's plummy intonation. Helena rubbed her arms against an imaginary chill and forced down the bitter memory. She took several deep breaths, her eyes arrowing back to the ship's model on the mantel.

No man—not Sissinghurst and not Ramsay—would ever bring her to heel again.

Suddenly, the house's silence pulsed with threat. She ripped her gaze away from the *Scindian*, her hands clenching and unclenching by her side. Perhaps it was the disturbing ship replica, the men in the dining room, those canvases piled carelessly against the wall. Her throat tightened and she frowned, her thoughts repeating like an echo in a cavern.

Those canvases.

With a surge of anger, she suddenly understood with a

clarity that cut like a knife. Bitterly, she complimented herself for missing the obvious. Wiping her sleeve across her face furiously, she became even angrier to find it come away damp with tears. Hopeless tears. She bolted from the library.

A blaze of gaslight illuminated the dining room, throwing into sharp relief a decorative symphony of formal wainscoting and frieze work, along with seven men rising in unison from a long table with expressions ranging from startled to wary at her entrance.

"I'll dispense with the pleasantries, gentlemen." Silhouetted by the open doors, she was suddenly fearless, anger replacing bitterness, running like molten lava through her veins. Her look should have scorched them. The men stared. She banished emotion from her face, knowing her tears had left no traces, and scrutinized each man, one at a time. "Do sit down as what I have to say may take more than a few minutes of your time."

"Lady Hartford, good of you to join us."

Behind her, the low voice raised hackles along her already stiffened spine.

Ramsay.

And if he so much as touched her now, placed a hand on her arm, she would fly into a million shards. She felt his heat as he passed her, so close, she could inhale his scent, already so damnably distinct that she would recognize it with closed eyes anywhere.

An admission that made her blood simmer all the hotter.

She turned around to face him. "You *bastard*. You *liar*."

There was a collective indrawn breath. Shocked by such language coming from a woman, not one man in the room spared a word.

Dressed in a simple black cutaway coat, Ramsay returned the look of steel in her eyes with his own. Stiffening as if she'd been struck, she refused to turn away and instead stared at the furrows that curved down from his nose to his mouth and led to the cleft that marked the center of his chin.

To remind her he was only human and as vulnerable as anyone else.

He smiled in a way that was entirely unconvincing. "I think we already established those facts early in our acquaintance, Lady Hartford." He gestured to the table. "Before you continue your tirade, I'd like to save you further embarrassment by introducing you to your dinner companions this evening."

She didn't spare the group—which was mesmerized by the scene playing out before them—a glance. "Don't try to placate me. Etiquette and introductions be damned!"

"You'll get all the clarification you want when you sit down and join us." He pulled out a chair. She didn't move. All she could focus on were those soulless eyes that were so intense the two of them might as well have been alone in the room together.

Helena crossed her arms against her chest. "You take me for a fool."

He raised a brow. "Then don't behave like one."

Her gaze shot lightning bolts. "Believe me, I won't. Because I'm going to ask you to explain those paintings in the corner. They belong to me, don't they? And they certainly begin to explain what you were doing in my atelier yesterday, despite your lies and obfuscations."

She turned to the assembled group, directing equal scorn at the spectators, still numbed into silence like a captive audience caught in a particularly awkward drama. "Yes, gentlemen, I will declare here and now that Nicholas Ramsay is, at best, a thief and worse, having entered my private premises without permission, with the intention of destroying and stealing my work."

"Lady Hartford, perhaps you should allow Mr. Ramsay a moment to explain," interrupted an older man at the head of the table. His gray beard gave him the appearance of an *éminence grise*.

"Explain what exactly, sir? That these canvases"—she gestured behind her—"don't belong to me?"

"Perhaps if you'd take a chair and allow us to start at the beginning, Lady Hartford, you might see reason."

"Ah, yes, sit down, be quiet, listen, and obey. I've heard it too often and I don't care to ever hear it again!"

She turned back to Ramsay. "The truth will out. Here and now." She brushed by him and grabbed the first canvas, hoisting it in the air, waiting a moment before turning it around.

Ramsay had made no move to stop her, but from the corner of her eyes, she watched him pin his gaze on her. The gaslight flickered and, abruptly, the room felt small, claustrophobic. Somebody cleared his throat. Another perched glasses on his nose in anticipation.

Quickly, she turned over the canvas. The blues and ochres of the portrait burned with familiarity, her scrawled initials in the bottom right-hand corner. Although the painting weighed little, her arm trembled.

Ramsay stood motionless, a faint smile on his face indicating that her accusations were no more than the ravings of a lunatic.

The older man who had addressed her earlier spoke first, peering at her over his spectacles like she was of a particularly annoying species of insect. "My dear Lady Hartford, as a man of science, I must protest that this little drama of yours proves exactly nothing."

Helena's smile was both bitter and triumphant. "Then perhaps we should allow Mr. Ramsay to explain how these canvases came to be in his possession. Mr. Ramsay?"

He leaned a shoulder onto the wall, a bored man waiting for the histrionics to stop and dinner to be served. "You're so eager to supply your own fiction that I don't see how any of my explanations could possibly compete," he said in a disinterested tone. "If I were you, I would be more curious to know why I would be interested in presenting you and your work to this august group of learned gentlemen this evening. But then in our brief acquaintance I've noticed that sober, second thought has never been a priority of yours, Lady Hartford."

Helena ordered her nerves to quiet. "Is that all you have in your arsenal, Mr. Ramsay—these banal observations? Which cannot take away from the facts. First things first—you were at my atelier yesterday and stole these canvases."

"Are you certain?"

"Most assuredly, I know these are mine. Examine the signature in the corner." She pulled the others away from the wall, each bearing her mark. She placed the first portrait prominently on the table. None of the men looked surprised.

"Yes, but are you certain I stole them." Ramsay's voice was hushed, yet the words were enunciated so clearly, the threat in each so palpable, that a shudder shot through her. He turned the full force of his gaze upon her and it sucked the air from her lungs. She looked away and at the canvas on the table, aware that the men were scrutinizing her like a specimen under glass.

"I don't know what you're talking about," she said coldly.

I saw your entries in the Salon des Refusés in Paris.

"Don't you?"

Her heart hammered. The heavy, sensual atmosphere of Madame Congais's. *Your work. It's magnificent.*

Ramsay straightened away from the wall and took a menacing step toward her. "Paris—where I purchased your work. These"—he gestured to the canvases—"to be precise."

Helena stared, speechless. The evening at Madame Congais's came flooding back in its earth-shattering entirety. Ramsay knew, these men knew . . . what exactly? Her thoughts tumbled like dice onto a table, assaulting her from different directions as she forced herself to digest the words and their implications.

He continued, his voice low and mocking, "What? No indignation, no righteous fury?"

Her nerves and her voice snapped. "You're playing with me, all of you!" She whipped around to face the men still frozen like figures in a group portrait around the dining table. "But I'm not easily led, gentlemen. Whether these paintings were stolen or purchased makes little difference in the end. Because I'm not easily coerced into doing something I don't want to do." She was responding with pure instinct now, undiluted intuition leading the way. Taking a ragged breath, she swept the room with her gaze.

And sensed that he had come up behind her. "Sit down."

Her head jerked around and, desperate to avoid his touch, she pulled out an empty chair and sat down. Folding her shaking hands on the table, she watched as the older men finally took their seats, Ramsay next to hers.

She tasted desperation and forced herself to focus on the Sevres turquoise and gold hand-painted plates set for the evening's repast, needing to cool her anger, collect her thoughts, and to distance herself from him. Ignoring the fact that if she so much as swayed six inches to her left she would be on his lap, it took all her discipline to trace with her downcast eyes the scrollwork around the edge of the plate with its scene of a man and a woman safely cavorting among brightly colored flowers.

Damn his black soul. The curse pulsed in her brain.

"Lady Hartford." Helena looked up to acknowledge the man with the beard who had spoken earlier. He was playing with his spectacles thoughtfully. "It may be advantageous to let tempers cool for the moment," he said with a smile both neutral and avuncular. "Perhaps we should begin again and offer introductions. By way of presentation, madam, we are members of the X Club, and Nicholas Ramsay is our host and benefactor."

She preferred to say nothing as he proceeded to introduce

his colleagues one by one. Doctors, naturalists, and scientists to the last man. When he finished, he added for her benefit, "You see, Mr. Ramsay has kindly offered to help us in our cause."

"Indeed." Her voice sounded strangled to her own ears. She ignored the fact that Ramsay's physical nearness all but immobilized her with the risk of brushing up against a hard arm or muscled leg. The threat was paralyzing.

Directly across from her the man who had been introduced as Lubbock, responding, no doubt, to her frozen expression, tried to add some much needed context. "You are aware, Lady Hartford, of the recent publication of Charles Darwin's *The Origin of Species*?"

"Of course," she responded stiffly. She had devoured the treatise only the year before, a few months after the duke's death. It had been liberating to be able to read what she'd wanted without having to resort to subterfuge. Her late husband, under the guidance of his nephew, believed books to be too stimulating for the female mind.

"Good," he said approvingly. "And I'm sure you are aware of the upheaval that ensued. Worse still, there are those who would like to see the work of reason and science silenced, a movement that galvanized the formation of our group and our mandate—to support scientific progress free from theological influence."

Helena's head jerked up impatiently. "A worthy cause, surely," she interrupted, "but I fail to see . . ."

Busk held up a hand. "Be patient, be patient, madam. All in good time. Please allow Mr. Lubbock to continue."

As though she had any choice in the matter.

"Thank you, Doctor. Lady Hartford, allow me to demonstrate." Lubbock rose from his chair and produced a roll of paper from a satchel at his side. Pushing away the fine porcelain and crystal in his eagerness, he unfurled the cylinder.

She was aware that Ramsay had scraped back his chair to better observe her reactions, as though he already owned them and her. She swallowed her irritation and focused on the chart displayed on the table.

With his index finger, Lubbock pointed to the set of diagrams. "You see, these figures illustrate the set of hominin species known to science in a given year. Each species is plotted as a box showing the range of cranial capacities for specimens of that species, and the range of dates at which specimens theoretically appear in the fossil record."

Helena nodded, irritation turning quickly to impatience.

"The sequence of diagrams shows how an apparent missing link or gap between species in the fossil record may become filled as more fossil discoveries are made."

"Of course," interrupted the man introduced earlier as Tyndall. "This diagram is based on highly speculative reasoning." He peered at Helena closely, careful to gauge her level of comprehension. "Is this all too difficult for you to follow, madam?" His muttonchops quivered.

She clenched her jaw. "I'm a woman, Mr. Tyndall," she responded dryly, "without doubt the more *highly evolved* gender."

Beside her, a smothered laugh. She resisted the urge to look over her shoulder, convinced she would only encounter Ramsay and his usual impenetrable mask.

Tyndall harrumphed his disapproval as Busk and Lubbock drew her attention back to the diagrams. "Indeed, indeed," said Busk, sitting his glasses on his nose. "Be careful what you wish for, Tyndall," he murmured diplomatically, trying to defuse an already tense situation. "And are you not expected elsewhere as you mentioned earlier?"

Tyndall frowned at the overt dismissal, groping for his pocket watch to peer self-importantly at the time. "Of course, of course. I mustn't delay. Many thanks for the reminder, Dr. Busk. I shall take my leave immediately. My apologies, gentlemen, Lady Hartford."

Busk continued as though the interruption had never happened, fixing Helena with a stern look.

"Now what we're talking about here, madam, is a transitional fossil or transitional form, the fossilized remains of a life-form that illustrates an evolutionary trajectory. Darwin has stressed in his work that this lack, this transitional form or missing link, is the most challenging obstacle to his theory."

"Which is where our host, Mr. Ramsay, enters the scene," continued Lubbock smoothly. "He has volunteered his time and resources to help us find proof of these intermediate forms. Indeed, in some places of the world there are many species alive today that can be considered to be transitional between two or more groups."

Ramsay sat silently, and it occurred to Helena that he was one of the stillest men she'd ever known. Like stone when it served his purposes, as it clearly did now.

"That's very generous of him." Her voice dripped suspicion. It helped to imagine that Ramsay wasn't even in the room, and she directed her response at the men around the table. "But what does he gain from his involvement in your cause? Is he simply a wealthy dilettante intent on finding the next esoteric amusement?"

Her bullet hit a mark. Suddenly, the room was restive, the air heavy.

Tyndall, still hovering on the edge of the room, was first to speak. "My thoughts exactly, Lady Hartford." She wasn't sure why his approval made her distinctly uncomfortable.

Busk shot Tyndall a dismissive glance, but his smile reserved for her was pleasant. "At this point I shouldn't concern myself with Mr. Ramsay's motives, madam, but rather with what your involvement might be in this cause. Was that not your initial concern?"

Helena was close to reaching her limit, all too aware that she was being strung along to a destination that was clear to everyone but her. She swore silently, telling herself that at the moment it was better to listen than to lash out.

Busk signaled to Lubbock to remove the diagrams from the table. "You see, Lady Hartford, we require evidence, hard physical evidence, to support our cause." The papers were hastily reassembled and disappeared into the tube.

She decided to play their game, for the moment. "Evidence of these transitional forms, you mean?"

"Exactly. And that requires a journey. And if the intermediate forms cannot be transported back to England, we require someone to capture their likenesses."

Understanding dawned. "An artist."

Busk's smile broadened. "Precisely."

Her eyes widened and then narrowed. "When you could choose from among the hundreds of artists in London alone? Why me?"

"We should allow Mr. Ramsay to answer that question," Busk supplied, peering at her over his spectacles. His tone was disingenuous, as though the matter were already resolved. "But then you'll have plenty of time to discuss the matter en route, I believe."

Helena stiffened. "En route? En route to where?" Slowly, reluctantly, she turned in her chair to face the man at her side.

Ramsay's smile was arctic, his appraisal sharp. With predatory elegance, he rose from the table. His eyes were shadowed and yet she knew in her soul that he relished her dread.

"To the other side of the world." He bit off each word. In the gaslight of the dining room, his offhand statement shocked her into speech.

"With you?" Her voice was a hoarse whisper. "You're mad!"

She released a long stream of air, her hand at her throat. Everything was going according to plan.

His plan.

Chapter 8

Helena bolted from the room.

She wanted to get as far away from that table, those men, and above all, Nicholas Ramsay. All she could hear was the thudding of her pulse, drowning out everything but the knowledge that he was right behind her, swift and silent as a jungle cat.

The thought came and went, between one footstep and the next, as she was lifted off her feet. Shocked beyond belief, she dangled in the air like a leaf from a tree. The man was strong, damn him, carrying her like she weighed no more than a piece of down, along the hallway toward the library.

With her arms pinned to her side, all she could do was kick at empty space and her own pride. "I won't be manhandled like this," she spat. "Who do you think you are? Hauling me in front of those men, that ridiculous X Club, as though I'm here to do your bidding."

"You're the one who ran from the room in high dungeon," he growled. "And I didn't haul you in front of anyone. I invited you to what I thought would be a civilized dinner, as you'll recall."

In response, she jerked in his arms ineffectually, renewed shock thrumming through her body in pulsating waves.

"Until I can calm you down," he added grimly, holding her away from his body like she was carrying a form of contagion, "we can't discuss this reasonably." In two strides he was in the library, slamming the door shut with his shoulder.

He dropped her onto the leather settee without ceremony, almost knocking over a heavy bronzed lamp.

Rubbing her throbbing arms, she gave him a look that could cut glass. "As though there is anything to discuss, sir. And as though I would even think of traveling with you to God knows where, on some harebrained scheme that doesn't even begin to make sense."

He threw himself down in the wing chair opposite her, watchful as an eagle with its prey in its sights. The light from the lamp cast dangerous shadows and she was startled again by the clean harshness of his features, the aquiline nose, pale gray eyes, and strong jaw. The only disconcerting element was the cleft in his chin, like a mark made by a sculptor. Even now, ridiculous woman that she was, it was a face she hungered to draw.

She gave herself a mental shake. *Plan, strategize, think.*

Don't think about what it was like to feel that hard chest beneath her hands, her body. Or his mouth, that clever mouth, on her hair, her neck, her legs. Her sense of foreboding grew along with the realization that she didn't understand what was happening to her. She, who had never felt so much as a whisper of desire, and yet this man, so still, so impenetrable, chafed her blood and her senses.

He was waiting for her to say something, lounging with his long legs crossed at his booted ankles. She looked at the ceiling, the swirls of plaster, and then to the fireplace where the disturbing ship's replica waited. Tension mounted, like the heavy atmosphere before a storm. Helplessly, she allowed her eyes to trace his lean calves and muscled thighs, the large and elegant hands, relaxed on the arms of the chair. Her artist's gaze was greedy for more.

Bloody hell, she was lying to herself now.

And the only truth she could trust was the tightness in her chest telling her to get away from Nicholas Ramsay. Far away.

"What are you thinking?" he asked. She jumped at the words.

"Why should it matter?"

His gaze was speculative, but his observation as accurate as a sculpture's chisel. "You're trying to determine your options for getting away, I'd surmise."

"As though you could blame me," she responded tartly.

He watched her like a lion on a savannah, sleek and still, waiting for the exact moment to attack despite all the benign words. "All I'm asking is that you listen carefully to what I have to say and to offer. I meant what I said at Francine's yesterday evening—that I want to help you."

She tilted her head, chin up. "As though I should give you a hearing when not a speck of this makes any sense from my perspective. You appear out of nowhere at Madame Congais's, only moments before Sissinghurst's men appear at her doorstep. Then I find you waiting for me at my atelier, which had been destroyed, as you claim, prior to your uninvited arrival. We flee the scene and now you would have me believe that you—a complete stranger—have a legitimate interest in my fate." She paused, trying to sit up straighter, the leather settee beneath her slippery. "That you care to get me away from Sissinghurst? Do you even know the man and what he is capable of? And that of all the artists in the world, you would choose me to help you with your cause?"

He shrugged and she was struck again, totally and irrationally, by the indecent breadth of his shoulders.

"No, I don't know the bishop personally, but suffice it to say that I've faced more formidable challenges in my lifetime than an overly ambitious cleric." His tone was dismissive. "And what's so difficult to believe? I see and admire your work in Paris. Make inquiries about you here in London, learn of your plight, and track you down at Francine's."

"My plight? Please save your condescension for other women of your acquaintance because I'm far from helpless, sir. As for Francine," the name slipping out before she could hold back, "it would seem that you know her well."

He crooked a small smile. "Why should it matter?"

"Rest assured, it doesn't."

"And that was your first encounter with opium?"

She didn't smile, wondering about this line of attack. "Why should it matter?"

"Only that something that good can be dangerous."

"I've read my de Quincey, Coleridge, and Shelley, not to worry," she said. "But you sound as though you speak from experience."

"We're getting away from the subject at hand." He changed the direction of the discussion smoothly, refusing to relinquish any ground. She wondered if those wintry eyes ever burned with passion or lit up with something other than careful watchfulness.

"Are we?" A simmering anger urged her on. She wanted to probe, excavate beneath the surface of that calm, stony exterior. It wasn't fair that he could remain so unmoved, so unshakable while she, her life and her freedom slipping from her fingers, should be cast into a whirlpool of conflicting emotion. "What if I proposed asking you several questions? Would you answer? It would only be equitable."

He slung one leg closer toward her, the physical proximity a form of intimidation. "Why wouldn't I?" he asked disingenuously.

As though the man had any intention of telling the truth, but at this point, she would grasp at anything to whittle away at his seemingly unshakable foundation. "Why have you aligned yourself with this X Club? You don't look like a man of science," she said bluntly. The light from one of the lamps shone directly over her face, leaving her vulnerable and exposed. She slid to the opposite end of the settee, more comfortable in the shadows.

He shrugged carelessly, but she was conscious that he

tracked her every movement. "I have accomplished most of what I want in my life. I consider this diversion a welcome distraction, and I have the resources to ensure that the objective, which we identified earlier this evening before your abrupt departure from the dining room, is met."

She didn't believe him for a moment and she hoped he knew it. Her eyes darted momentarily to the ship's replica. *Scindian.* And then returned to Ramsay. His expression didn't waver, but there was something—

"You're a man of the sea," was all she said, feeling her way in the dark.

"A reasonable assumption on your part." His voice was lower than usual. "It's not an unusual way for a man to make his way in the world. And it makes perfect sense for the X Club to make use of my experience and resources in this area."

She raised a brow. "I wouldn't know, but I suppose I have no choice but to take your word for it."

"Of course, with your illustrious background, you wouldn't know how many pennies to a pound, I'd warrant. You've never had to." Ramsay's smile was deliberate, his hands still relaxed on the arms of the chair. But she detected a crack, however slight, in the veneer.

"I perceive a hint of sarcasm in your tone, Mr. Ramsay." She slid to the edge of the settee, closer to him. "Suddenly we're discussing money. And your assumption about my birthright—well, that's perhaps unwise. But then I'm assuming all these unwarranted conclusions come from a self-made man who carries with him all manner of prejudices."

He leaned forward in his chair, so their knees were almost touching. Although it cost her some effort, she didn't shrink back. "Believe whatever makes you more comfortable, madam," he answered smoothly. "Wherever I or my resources come from should mean nothing to you. After all, did you ever concern yourself as to the origins of your father's or husband's fortunes? They were simply a means to an end—a way of providing you with an estimable life where your every whim and concern was no doubt catered to."

"Of course, Mr. Ramsay. My every whim and concern. You can't begin to imagine." Her voice was brittle. "But you would never understand that I did *earn my keep*." The last three words were as harsh as she'd intended.

He shook his head, barely acknowledging her words, and reached out to enclose her wrist. "What I don't understand is why you're reluctant to accept my offer." The hand was hard and unyielding, yet she didn't pull away. "You're looking for an escape. And I'm offering it to you in addition to my protection. You can't get away from Sissinghurst on your own. He's a powerful man."

His arrogance was appalling. He sat there with the lamplight bronzing the short silk of his hair, glancing off the austere plane of a cheekbone, resolute and overly confident. As though no one had ever for even one moment stood in his way.

Resentment, sharp as bile, closed her throat. "I'm an independent woman of means. I don't require a man's *help* and never will again."

Ramsay pushed harder. "You needed help several times these past twenty-four hours."

"Try being a woman in our world, Mr. Ramsay," she said with some venom and a pointed glance at his hard fingers trapping her wrist. "Experience what it's like having your intelligence and talent suppressed, the very core of your being smothered. And if that isn't enough, try being threatened with Bedlam and worse."

He paused several beats, but his eyes were unnerving, pushing her into a corner more easily than even his lean, muscled body could. "So you won't accept my help."

She rallied. "What you mean to say is that I won't do your bidding."

"I never said I would take away your freedom."

Images of the two of them on the stairs wavered before her

mind's eye. He'd been the conductor in that charade while she . . . She couldn't finish the thought.

She tried to loosen her wrist, pulling away. He didn't let go; instead, his fingers began a rhythmic massage on the inside of her arm.

She froze. He watched her reaction from hooded eyes. "I told you that I admired your talent, Helena." The voice mesmerized far more powerfully than opium ever could. "And there's every reason to believe you can put that talent to good use. While escaping from Sissinghurst. And think of it," he continued, his tone as persuasive as the tempo of his touch on her sensitized skin, "the Bishop of London, he will be none too pleased when we return with evidence that could very well undermine everything he's worked for."

They were so close now that his breath fanned her face. He was right and he was lying. She was sure of it. Her chest felt tight, a simmer of panic mingling with a pain so sharp it was like a knife twisting where her heart should be.

It was too much. She struggled for breath, her skin scalding hot beneath his fingertips, a warning that she had to get away from him, from this danger that she knew to be far more treacherous than what even Sissinghurst and Bedlam held in store.

"Again, why me?" she tried, keeping her voice calm. "You know as well as I that there are artists who devote themselves solely to the subjects of botany and wildlife, and would be far better suited to this venture than I."

"You are the best," he said simply.

Clever man, appealing to the unassailable pride she had in her work. She refused to let it go to her head. Or her heart. "But what or who exactly led you to me, Mr. Ramsay? That's the question I can't let go of." Despite her struggle for control, her voice had a desperate edge.

The oil in the lamp at her side was almost out, the light flickering menacingly at things to come. "You're still suspicious of my motives." His was a statement of fact that she had no need to answer. "Come with me," he said, abruptly pulling her from the settee. "I want you to see something that I know you will appreciate."

It was a form of reprieve at least and probably short-lived. Against her better judgment, Helena tugged her hand from his but followed him back into the hallway and up the staircase to Conway House's third story.

He took two steps at a time, transforming the hallway into a blur, and within minutes she found herself standing at the end of a magnificent corridor, with every conceivable space laden with paintings, sculpture, and porcelain, one example more splendid than the next.

She was speechless.

Frans Hals's *The Laughing Cavalier* stared back at her. She took another step, to take in a big, stylish Gainsborough portrait, *Mrs. Robinson,* alongside smaller portraits of the same sitter by Reynolds and Romney.

As if that weren't enough to fill her eyes and her soul, a few feet away waited William Hilton's oversized landscape *Venus in Search of Cupid,* whose centerpiece featured several winsome girls bathing.

"Quite something, isn't it?" asked Ramsay at her elbow.

She nodded, unwilling to break the spell. The corridor glowed with images that set her mind reeling. This is where she belonged, amid the paint, turpentine, and stretched canvas with a brush or palette knife in her hand. She expelled a deep breath. To draw, to paint, far away from the suffocating machinations and demands of the men who wanted dominion over her life and her freedom—that was her greatest wish, *her only wish.*

Her eyes devoured the vital greens and blues of the landscape as though her very existence depended on it.

She felt Ramsay's hand at her waist guiding her toward the end of the corridor. For once, she barely registered his touch, gliding past *Queen Victoria* by Thomas Scully and Thomas Lawrence's famous *Countess of Blessington,* who leaned out of the canvas with engaging forwardness.

A right turn and they left the grand hallway behind to enter a jewel box of a room. Small and windowless, acres of pink, dimpled flesh adorned the walls—paintings by Boucher, Fragonard, and Watteau.

It was dizzying. "This is almost too much," she breathed, collapsing on the eighteenth-century chaise longue drenched in crimson. Around her, shepherds courted curvaceous shepherdesses while Greek gods and goddesses frolicked with sensual abandon.

Her eyes fed on the feast and when, finally, she tore herself away, she noticed he still stood in the center of the room. She should be accustomed to it by now, but he was calibrating her every movements, as though her reaction were more than he expected.

"You're pleased—I thought you would be, but perhaps I didn't realize quite how much." His height and breadth seemed exaggerated in the pink and whiteness of the room. "Conway's collection is something to be marveled at."

"Conway's collection or yours?" she couldn't help asking, absently caressing the luxuriant silk of the chaise, absorbing the rich color through her skin.

His shrug was noncommittal, shoulders moving easily underneath the perfect cut of his jacket. "Yes, it's nominally mine. I own this house and its contents, but the vision behind the works of art it holds belong to the late marquess, something no one can take away from him."

"You're very generous."

He didn't respond directly but approached the small sculpture on a pedestal next to her on the chaise. Helena could tell it was heavy and bronze, the small brass plate bearing the title *A Circassian Slave in the Market Place at Constantinople.*

"Beautiful, isn't it?" she supplied, and then almost immediately, regretting her words, "if slavery in any way can be termed beautiful."

He lowered his head, and she had the momentary impression that he was shielding his expression from her.

"Exactly right, beautiful and ugly at the same time, Helena." The way he said her name sent a shiver up her spine. "Have you seen the Hogarths?" he asked abruptly, walking away from her to the opposite side of the room. He moved with none of the affectations of the men in her set. No wasted motion, no pretentious poses, just an athletic stealth that reminded her uncomfortably of an animal in the wild.

She rose to join him, unexpectedly riveted by the black and white engravings on the wall, wondering how she could have missed the eight etchings, so distinct from the rest of the art in the room with its eighteenth-century worldly sensuousness. She'd seen reproductions published in several pamphlets, the series depicting the decline and fall of Tom Rakewell, the spendthrift son and heir of a rich merchant who wastes all his money on luxurious living, whoring, and gambling, with the consequence of imprisonment in Bedlam.

For a long, heavy moment she stared at the last engraving. Her skin crawled. In the forefront, Tom Rakewell, maddened by his debauched life, was represented in a half-naked recumbent position, holding his head in agony. His shoes had been removed and he was being manacled by a keeper while the bewigged physician in attendance attempted to intervene. A plaster beneath his right breast suggested that he had been bled. Around him was a mad scientist plotting longitudes on the hospital wall and a mad tailor obsessed with measurement brandished a tape in his hand. A king, naked and urinating in his cell, was being visited by two ladies of questionable reputation. They concealed cruel laughter behind their fans.

It was a scene straight from Dante's fifth ring of hell, every desperate depravity known to humankind detailed in Hogarth's nightmare.

She clenched her teeth, her expression bleak. The connection couldn't have been clearer.

And she hated Nicholas Ramsay for making it.

She'd been bewitched by the collection, as he knew she would be. But he also ensured reality would intrude, irrevocably and irrefutably, when the time was auspicious. Her voice taut with emotion, she said, "What a coincidence and how convenient, yet again. Did you make special arrangements for me to see this too?"

Nicholas turned to look at her and she was sure her face had gone white. He crossed his arms over his chest thoughtfully. "It does rather clarify the argument." The statement was as cruel and arrogant as his stance. Helena swallowed hard and wrenched her gaze from his.

She couldn't get away from him fast enough, this powerful and ruthless man who appeared from nowhere to take what he wanted without remorse. This time when she fled there would be no turning back.

Forcing herself to stroll to the chaise with studied leisure, she sat down. Her artist's eye could not help but admire the way he moved, like the outsider he was, with a powerful, loose-limbed athleticism that had no place in parlors or sitting rooms. He made his way to her side, but he didn't sit, and she loathed the fact that she had to look up at him.

It didn't help that her nerves were already ragged, worn thinner still by her primal awareness of him, mixed with anger and a good measure of fear and desperation. And not for the first time she wondered why her entire life had been a struggle, a never-ending prison house of subjugation and submission, the accepted code of conduct reserved for the weaker sex.

A remorseless tide of memories swept over her.

"Of course you knew, dear uncle, that at one time chains had been used to restrain lunatics—before the *camisole de force."* Even in his younger years the Bishop of London had used any occasion to express his interest in moral weakness and its correctives.

And next to him, the choir boy, Deacon Mosley, sat hanging on to his every word like manna from heaven. Even more than her own husband and his nephew, he filled her with revulsion, the way his pale blue eyes with their blond eyelashes would settle on her person, staring for minutes on end.

She remembered rising to leave the table.

"Quite the humane advance over chains, I would imagine." The duke always enjoyed his postprandial conversations with his nephew, who was flying up the ranks of the Church of England. "What do you think, wife? You who always seem to have opinions about everything?"

"And you who never seem to care for them," she replied, realizing immediately that she would pay for the impertinence. Later.

Sissinghurst's glance was dismissive, always jealous when his uncle's attentions wandered away from him. "It was invented in 1790 by an upholsterer for an asylum for the chronically mentally ill near Paris," he continued pompously, relishing every detail like the finest morsels of chocolate.

Mosley hastened to add an original element to the discussion. "In its first incarnation, it was a vest of strong cloth with long sleeves that could be attached to each other and behind the back of the madman to prevent them from causing harm."

"Madman or madwoman?" The duke's laugh came out as a sibilant hiss.

Mosley responded with a sly grin.

Encouraged, her husband continued, "My dear nephew, you're a man of the cloth. All the more reason to suspect you already know about certain *other* proclivities that serve as restraints."

The comment was meant for her.

* * *

And now in this room with its rococo adornments, she felt the familiar deadness invade her soul and its welcome antidote that helped keep her intact and unreachable.

And in control.

Her life had always been a metaphoric *camisole de force.* Bedlam would simply be its physical equivalent, she thought wearily. Only if she retreated far enough inside herself could she break the chains that bound her because, as she knew better than anyone, what appeared as submission on the surface could hide a pitiless will.

She'd learned her lessons well. At best men were credulous creatures led by their baser natures. And this one—she glanced at Ramsay from beneath her lashes—would prove to be no exception.

The silence stretched wide and she focused for a moment on Watteau's iridescent *Voulez-vous triompher des Belles.* Indeed, how ironic, this decadent and relaxed sweep of a painting with its men whispering seductive words into the ears of their lady loves. Her limbs relaxed, and as though propelled by some otherworldly force, her body edged closer to Ramsay.

Finally, she said, "Yes, you're quite right." Her voice was low and calm, surprising even her. "This does rather clarify your argument. I don't have much of a choice, do I?"

She glanced up at him. His gray eyes were opaque, his smile empty, etched in the austere planes of his face. The hair on the nape of her neck rose. No man had ever looked at her with such dispassion, and just for a moment, she thought that doing what she must would prove impossible.

"Please do sit," she invited, patting the luxurious silk of the chaise. "So we can, as you've suggested, discuss this situation more fully."

He took a step closer and narrowed his gaze. "You are ready to see reason all of a sudden. I can't help but be intrigued." The upholstery dipped as he closed in beside her. Her stomach clenched. He was so near that she could see the creases that fanned out from his eyes, eyes that had probably squinted into the sun on the other side of the world. What had he seen, she wondered, what was hidden beneath that mask?

She felt hot, her skin strangely sensitized, but powerful nonetheless. A different kind of authority than when she held a brush or palette knife, but power all the same. No matter who he was or what he threatened, he was *only* a man.

She leaned toward him, and with her free hand she ran her open palm lightly up his chest, warm granite beneath the linen of his shirt.

He stopped breathing. Just as she'd intended. And stilled her hand with his own.

The lines bracketing his mouth deepened. "What are you doing?" A suspicious man by nature, he hadn't missed the fluid shift from unwilling quarry to eager seductress.

"You want me," she said, holding his gaze with her own. "I can tell. From the other night . . . at the atelier." Still nothing from him except a barely perceptible increase in the tempo of his breathing. So he wasn't made of stone. She could feel the steady beat of his heart against her hand.

Very carefully, demurely even, she tipped toward him to undo the top two buttons of his shirt, exposing browned skin beneath. Nothing more.

And then she waited for him to come to her.

She relaxed back into the chaise, watching him for a change from empty eyes. She felt nothing except rising anticipation, a director leading from the wings, shaping a piece of theater. She thought he hesitated for a moment, but then his body loomed over hers. The same heady scent of sun and wind, vaguely reminiscent, except this time, she reminded herself, she wasn't suffering from the effects of opium-inspired desire.

She felt a subtle tension in his muscles. Good. "What game are you playing, Helena?" His lips brushed her ear. She shivered, not in yearning but in triumph.

He shifted his weight so that just the surface of their upper bodies touched. With a callused fingertip, he grazed the side of her face. "You have an agile mind," he murmured. "But whatever you're planning isn't going to work," he said, beginning an agonizingly slow trail of hot kisses along her throat. He pressed intimately into the cradle of her thighs.

Precisely where she wanted him.

She arched her hips in response where she could feel the heat pooling in his groin. Running her hands over his shoulders and arms, she pushed ineffectually against his weight. "Let me," she said with an open-mouthed kiss at the base of his throat.

He straightened away from her, allowing her to slide her body like a blanket over his. He skimmed his hand under her hair and curled his fingers around her nape. For a moment, deep violet eyes locked with arctic gray. He took his time, looking his fill.

Her lungs locked. She didn't want him to know what she was thinking, feeling. She couldn't afford to. But it was that low, timbred voice that was nearly her undoing.

"Your machinations, Helena—don't think I don't realize you're planning something." The words vibrated from deep in his chest against her breasts. "Even I'm not arrogant enough to think that you're suddenly overcome with passion for me."

Then, at odds with his words and the erection that burned through her skirts, he took her mouth in a slow, soft kiss. It wasn't what she expected or wanted, that decadent press of his lips, a torturous tongue, slick and in motion, a not-so-subtle gauntlet thrown into the field of battle.

His hands, hard and strong, moved down her shoulders, brushing the sides of her breasts as they strayed down her arms. A tremor rippled down her spine and her world narrowed to what he was doing with his knowledgeable tongue, sliding it over hers, over her lips, her cheek, and then down her throat until he found the delicate spot behind her ear.

Her heart stopped, but her hips, against her will, arced against his.

She couldn't permit this. Couldn't let it go on, go further and risk repeating the hallucinatory moments that transpired at the atelier. The last thing she wanted. Feverishly, determinedly, she brought her arms up to pull her torso away from his body. She couldn't risk having his mouth playing on hers again, against her skin, heating her blood, confusing her.

"No, please, let me," she murmured repeatedly, steeling herself against the caress of a large hand on her backside. A liquid warmth pooled in her center, and her breath hitched in dread and alarm at the searing hardness of his huge erection.

She curved away from him like a bow and stilled, shocked. His cold eyes radiated a hostility and awareness that shook her to her soul.

"You're certain you know what you're doing?" he asked with soft menace.

And with those words she did know for certain that, despite the heat radiating from the lean muscled body beneath her, Nicholas Ramsay was a man who never let down his guard. A man who couldn't be seduced, distracted, or manipulated—unless he wanted to be.

And the knowledge frightened her more than anything else had in a long time, because she knew that with this man, the stakes were set high against her.

She brushed a finger across his lower lip, resisting her fascination with the cleft in his chin. Lowering her eyelashes, she began the slow work of undoing the next three buttons of his shirt. Against her will, she reveled in the feel of the beautifully delineated muscles beneath her palms, the crisp hair that scratched her cheek as she kissed her way down his chest, her mouth wet and open.

She made her voice thick with desire. "By now, as you can probably tell, I know what I'm doing, Ramsay." She sat up slowly to straddle his narrow hips with her knees.

He gave her a stony look. "Let's just say I'm not entirely convinced." But his hands continued to stroke her buttocks almost as though he couldn't help himself. His eyes tracked her movements like a machine, and yet she noticed his breathing slowed whenever she skimmed against the hot hardness pulsing at her core.

He shifted his hips beneath hers—and she wondered about the state of his willpower now.

"Allow me," she said, leaning down sinuously, ensuring her breasts brushed the lean contours of his chest while the juncture of her thighs continued its rhythm. "Let me do the work." Unbelievably, his erection gained another few inches.

Deliberately, she ran her open palms from her waist and over her breasts, her lips curved in a slow smile, for his benefit—and hers. With one hand she began releasing the intricate fastenings of her bodice, one at a time. His eyes were hooded, and a muscle in his lean jaw clenched. She smiled to herself as she felt his shoulders tense and, just like clockwork, his hands came up to cup her breasts.

His pupils contracted to pinpoints and he looked as though he were fixing a target in his crosshairs. The heat of his hands burned along the upper swells of her pale breasts, the fingers skimming, claiming ownership of every curve.

"You're making this much too easy," he growled.

"Indulge me," she said, pretending to lower her lashes. Across the room, she caught sight of one of Boucher's pink cupids, arrow poised to hit its mark. And close to the chaise longue and next to Nicholas Ramsay's head, the heavy bronze Circassian slave sat waiting to do her bidding.

Pulling the pins from her hair, she inched her way up Ramsay's hard body, deliberately lowering her half-exposed breasts closer to his face. Her loosened hair brushed his chin as she dragged a palm along the sharp line of his jaw before tracing the outline of his lips and flirting with the indentation in his chin.

"You're too beautiful," were Nicholas Ramsay's last words, his breath hot against her palm.

With her free hand, she grasped the bronze sculpture and, with determined momentum, swinging wide, heaved the heavy base at his temple.

The sound was less dramatic than she'd anticipated.

His eyes flashed open for a split second, fixing her with a pitiless stare, before shuttering closed. Beneath her, she could feel that he was still breathing, despite the wound at his temple quickly turning an ugly purple.

Terror welled at the back of her throat, trapping her breath in her chest.

She leapt off his body as though it were covered in hot coals, the pink of the room a panicked blur. Sliding more than running, she hurled herself down two flights of stairs until the sputtering of gas lamps was the only noise that greeted her in the deserted front hall.

She would not stop to think, forcing herself only to move, pushing open the heavy door and hurtling down the flight of stairs, staying close to the wall to avoid the beam of an outdoor light. For a moment, she thought to snuff it out, but that would only call the attention of the servants.

A warm June rain began to fall, the drops beginning to soak her dress. Walking away from Manchester Square with a calmness she didn't feel, she headed in the opposite direction of her atelier, avoiding the crowds close to Oxford Street.

His image burned behind her eyes.

Don't think of him now.

If possible, he'd looked even more dangerous where she'd left him. Lying there, immobilized and unaware.

Her pace quickened. A speedy escape to the Continent, and she need never see Nicholas Ramsay again.

A block from Conway House an emaciated dog appeared out of an alleyway to her right, loping along the cobblestones. Startled by something that told her to stop, she crouched low in a doorway of a small pub, its light illuminating the street. Voices warmed by alcohol barely penetrated her concentration as, in front of her, four elongated shadows grew out of the dark and blocked her path.

The rain began in earnest now, pelting off the cobbled road. She studied the advancing silhouettes caped in greatcoats. A smaller figure led the way, familiar somehow, slight of build, perhaps her height, a hood obscuring his features.

The wind picked up as he walked toward her through the rain.

She knew him, and impossibly weary of the games and the threats, she refused to cower. Instead, she stepped from the doorway where raindrops fell on her face like tears but did nothing to wash away the fury that rose from the depths of her despair.

Seething with outrage, she whispered through clenched teeth. "I've had enough of this, of you and Sissinghurst. What do you want, Mosley?"

Under the halo-like hood, his pale features glowed alabaster in the evening's gloom. "Now here you are, Lady Hartford. At long last," Mosley said in his reedy voice. Three large men circled around him protectively, but she recognized none of them from either Madame Congais's or her atelier. "You're leading us on a merry chase."

"What do you want?" The question was ludicrous because she knew the answer already. A trickle of sweat or rain, she didn't know which, slid down her spine. She was certain no one had followed her, which meant that Mosley and his men had been lying in wait. But how had they known she would be at Conway House?

Unless Ramsay had alerted them.

"You have the answer to that question, madam," he continued agreeably. "Come with me willingly and I'll ensure that the warden at Bedlam prepares an extra special welcome for you."

"You can go to bloody hell."

His rosebud mouth thinned and he clasped his hands, encased in light leather gloves, in mock alarm. "Now *that's* a threat coming from you, madam," he said silkily. "You would know the way to hell far better than I."

The moon threw a few rain clouds into sharp relief. She started to move away, but he gripped her arm, his thin fingers like talons. She glared down at his gloved hand and then up at him.

"I won't go quietly."

"Please don't. Just what you need, more evidence of your supremely unstable nature. All that bohemian nonsense, the unseemly reaction to your work in Paris. Now opium. And then running off with your latest lover, Nicholas Ramsay. So what are a few extra histrionics in public?" He shook his head disapprovingly. "The good bishop has always remarked on the fragility of your moral character, my dear, and today you must finally pay the consequences."

Helena's lips curled in disdain. "Don't insult me further by pretending to be interested in my moral character, Mosley, when all you and my uncle are interested in is my considerable fortune."

He squeezed her wrist sharply, but she didn't wince. "Your late husband's fortune, you mean."

"The money was my father's, entailed directly to me," she bit out and, with an exhalation of pleasure, aimed a well-placed heel directly over his instep.

With a howl of outrage, Mosley dropped her wrist and leapt back. As he stumbled, she spun around and bolted through the shadows. For better or for worse, the street was deserted. She hauled air into her lungs, ignoring the pounding footsteps behind her. The lone mongrel slinked out of the alleyway and barked in unison with the grunts from Mosley's men. If she could just gain several more yards . . . but her body was jerked backward and an arm snaked around her neck and waist.

They dragged her into the darkened alleyway redolent

with smells that assaulted with the stench of refuse and worse. Eyes stinging in pain, her neck stretched at a perilous angle, she watched as Mosley appeared out of the mist to stand a few feet in front of her.

He sighed dramatically, his usually wide blue eyes turning to slits. "That was most unwise, my dear, as I truly don't have the patience for this, *Helena*. You don't mind if I call you by your first name, do you?"

Mosley gave the signal for his man to tighten his grip around her throat. Pain jagged through her windpipe. Helena stared up at the starless sky, her hopes for escape dwindling along with her false courage.

"We shouldn't have to stand on ceremony, although that was always the case when I would take dinner with you and your husband."

"You always were a weasel." She choked out the words, the mountain behind her refusing to budge. In response, Mosley's two remaining alternates crowded in around her as though she needed reminding of the perilous circumstances. "Always trying to curry favor with the duke, with Sissinghurst," she added in a hoarse whisper.

Mosley cocked his head, considering, the raindrops shimmering diamonds on his hood. "You know what you need, Lady Hartford, if I might suggest?"

It began to pour in earnest, the rain slanting down through the narrow buildings, water sluicing off the greatcoat of the man who held her prisoner, plastering her dress to her shivering body. But the cold was the least of her troubles.

Mosley stepped in closer toward her until they were almost touching. She could feel his eyes crawling over her neck, her breasts, and down the length of her legs. Had she been able, she would have spat at his feet.

"What you need, *Lady Hartford*, as they say in the vernacular, is a *good fuck,* something your venerable late husband was too old and debauched to provide. Would have tamed you considerably, taken your mind and energies away from those lascivious paintings you were so fond of creating. Expiated all those unwholesome, un-Christian emotions."

The stillness of the night roared in her ears.

"None of your many lovers has been able to do a credible job either, by the looks of it."

Helena's eyes blanked from a thunderstorm of rage.

"Not even our mysterious Mr. Ramsay."

Mosley clasped his gloved hands together, walking around her as though examining the goods. "Well, we have plenty of time to see to those matters, never fear. Perhaps we'll arrange for a private room, initially at least, at Bethlem Royal Hospital. And then once we've seen that you're settled, you'll be able to share your newly acquired generosity with some of the other patients. There are many possibilities we can explore to help you manage your indecent proclivities, I'm sure."

Mosley continued almost dreamily, "I've already had most instructive discussions with the mad-doctor, a very nice gentleman named Munro, who informs me there are a myriad of cures we may avail ourselves of. Care to hear more?"

Helena refused to respond, turning her eyes upward to the darkening sky bare of stars and sodden with rain.

"Well, I shall continue in any case, simply to ensure that you understand exactly where it is you're going and what exactly you will experience there, my haughty, wanton Lady Hartford. Did I mention that Dr. Munro believes that forcing a patient to stand erect for an extended period of time while bloodletting has salubrious outcomes? No? Apparently, losing twenty to forty ounces of blood at one time is a wonderful therapeutic for calming mad people. I do believe that requires effectively removing forty-six percent of a patient's total blood volume. What—no response from Lady Hartford—and you who always seemed to have something to say at your husband's dinner table, as I recall."

Impossibly, Mosley's words receded, absorbed into the rain-slicked night. The sky above her was beginning to darken from dark gray to black, bright darts of light dancing before her eyes. She fought it as she fought Mosley's hideous words, but there was no escaping the heavy rag, damp with noxious fumes, pressed over her mouth and nose.

Her last thought was of Ramsay. She choked on his name—as a curse or a benediction, she would never know.

Chapter 9

It was a little-known fact that the Temple Church, just a stone's throw from St. Paul's Cathedral and an integral component of the Inns of Court, was built in 1185 by the Knights Templar and intended as their home in Britain.

The Bishop of London savored the knowledge, breathing in the musty air kept cool by beautiful, cream-colored Caen stone.

The oblong nave, cradling the wooden altar designed by Sir Christopher Wren, could do little to obscure the temple's circular design, there to remind the Templars of the Church of the Holy Sepulchre at Jerusalem, a round, domed building raised over the site of the tomb where Christ was buried.

Turning his back to the altar, Sissinghurst made note of the clusters of parishioners kneeling in the pews, heads bent, penitent and in need of guidance. He suppressed a grimace. Ministering to the great unwashed was not his life's work. Instead, he liked to dwell on the ten knightly effigies that lay in the crypt below his feet, reposing in eternal splendor, their lives given over to the pursuit of riches and power.

Clasping his hands behind his back, he made his way down the side aisle toward the confessionals. Above him mocked a circle of grotesque portrait heads, grimacing gargoyles with tails and talons designed to keep evil at bay.

Well, not today. He did make a point of enjoying the irony.

Of course, he would have preferred to keep his appointment with the poorhouse at Shoreditch. All those pitiable, potentially profitable children. The bishop heaved a sigh, cursing Mosley under his breath. He genuinely loved the little ones with their grimy, importuning faces, all the more for raising his profile with the Archbishop of Canterbury and the queen while presenting prodigious opportunity. To be seen as modest and humble, his interests turned away from worldly concerns toward Christian duty, and the higher good required an elevated moral tone that orphaned children happened to provide. Among other things.

The huge Norman door opened, revealing a man wearing greatcoat and top hat, damp from rain, which he didn't remove. The bishop kept his eye trained on the figure who looked to the left and right before setting his sights on a confessional in a dimly lit alcove a few feet away.

Let him wait.

For the moment, he wanted to indulge himself, immerse himself in the past, dwell on the power of the Templars whose grasp had spanned the known world. It was all, and had always been, about men and power, those who had it and those who didn't. Those who were let in and those who were shut out.

He traced the outlines of the ruby-encrusted crucifix around his neck reflexively. The details of initiation at the time were a closely guarded secret, later causing untold trouble as gossip and rumors spread about possible Templar blasphemy, and threats to the Crown. Even today, the Temple Church was a royal peculiarity—under the jurisdiction of the Crown, not of the Bishop of London.

How slowly things changed. Feeling doubly irritated, Sissinghurst adjusted his Canterbury cap, the soft, square-shaped covering on his head. He leaned his girth against a pew, and drew his thoughts back to the present and to Mosley, hoping the deacon would report back to him later that evening with good news, once and for all, about that chit, Helena Hartford.

He'd always hated her.

Despised her pride, arrogance, and adamant refusal to *behave*. And always competing with him for his uncle's attention, with her feminine deceit and unwholesome wiles.

Served the old codger right. Dying in his prime, port glass in hand and feet warmed by the grate, his death hastened, no doubt, by the attentions of a woman young enough to be his daughter. No wonder the flesh had given way—along with his reason.

Looking up at the vaulted spine running down the oval of the church, Sissinghurst cursed his uncle to the heavens. By some fluke of fate or a crafty solicitor's sleight of hand, the bulk of the duke's estate, the coffers of which had been handsomely filled by dint of Helena Hartford's marriage dowry, had reverted *to her* upon his death.

Dear Lord in heaven. The Hartfords hadn't seen any kind of real money since the seventeenth century, all the more reason for the duke, habitually drenched in drink and cards, twice widowed and without an heir, to marry the daughter of a mere city merchant.

The bishop pushed away from the pew, feeling his face reddening with anger. He lumbered toward the confessional, hoping that Mosley would finally get the job done so he wouldn't have to involve himself in these demeaning encounters, bothered by details that, at this point in his life, should fall under the purview of lesser mortals. Skullduggery had been a feature of the first phase of his illustrious career, but he couldn't afford to have errant debris clinging to his ecclesiastical robes.

He opened the confessional door and lowered his bulk into the compartment. Barely glancing at the plain wooden cross hanging over the grille, he pictured the man stooped on the prie-dieu kneeler on the other side of the sliding screen.

With a plump hand, he slipped the grille open.

"May God have mercy on my soul."

Sissinghurst let out an impatient breath. Damn Mosley's inefficiency. "Never mind the posturing, let's get on with the business at hand." He could barely make the outlines of a face beyond the lattice pattern of the grille.

A gentle sigh. "I'm disappointed, Your Grace. I was expecting a benediction, if not outright forgiveness. I remember my Sunday school lessons well and wonder when I might hear the words, from your illustrious lips, *Almighty God who forgives all who truly repent, have mercy on you, pardon and forgive you from all your sins, confirm and strengthen you in all goodness, and keep you in life eternal.*"

Sissinghurst could feel the man's sarcasm through the gilt scrollwork dividing them. The ill will was as palpable as a fist to the face. This so-called penitent despised someone—that much was clear—perhaps even himself, for giving in, succumbing to his baser nature. It was a circumstance, a deficit of the human spirit, that Sissinghurst in his long career had encountered often enough.

"We have no time for cant today, alas," he said dryly, the air in the confessional close with past and present confidences. "You were to have met with Mosley—what happened precisely?"

"Our rendezvous was cut short."

"Clearly, as otherwise you would be speaking with Mosley and not with me this evening. So for what reason was your assignation cut short?"

"I detect a tone of disapproval, which is quite unfair given the circumstances."

"You will allow me to determine what is fair or not."

"That is your business, ostensibly." The shadow moved

with ghostly stealth behind the grille work. "Church as the scales of justice, after all."

The bishop grimaced, deciding it best not to let his impatience show. "What went on with Mosley and, once again, why was your meeting cut short?"

A small laugh. "Because he had more pressing matters to attend to."

"And what could possibly be more important than doing the will of God."

"You may tell me."

The man was arrogant beyond belief, but Sissinghurst had parried with far better in his time and his lips thinned. "What exactly did you do for us, sir. I can tell that you're all too eager to tell me."

The voice moved in closer, becoming knife sharp and far more disturbing than it should have been. "I had always assumed you were an astute man." Sissinghurst imagined that he crossed his legs, shifting to get more comfortable before relinquishing a confidence like a gold nugget. "What I did for you, Your Grace, is to tell Mosley where to find Helena Hartford, which he couldn't seem to do himself."

Sissinghurst felt the flush of heat color his face, the walls of the confessional suddenly too small to contain his bulk or his ambitions. So the chit had managed to elude them once again.

But years of dissembling had schooled him in the fine art of keeping his tone even and smooth. "And so where did the good deacon finally manage to catch up with Lady Hartford?"

"What? No gratitude, Your Grace?"

He'd had quite about enough. "Unless you would like to feel the wrath of God, I would suggest you disclose the information you're holding so close to your vest."

Another chuckle and a soft breath against the grille. "Shouldn't I fear your wrath more than God's? At the very least, that's what I've heard." He lowered his voice mockingly, conspiratorially. "She's with Nicholas Ramsay, by the way."

The name was a shot fired in the dark, conjuring a triumvirate of money, influence, and power. The confined space was becoming warmer and Sissinghurst wished he'd picked up a hymnal earlier to fan the air.

God damn him to hell. Nicholas Ramsay. What did the man want with a woman like Hartford? He almost spoke the thought aloud before he was interrupted.

"Some say he sold his soul to the devil."

Others said that he *was* the very devil. The man moved above the law, both judicial and ecclesiastical. Sissinghurst tried to impart an illusion of calm, although they both knew otherwise. He glanced briefly at the unadorned crucifix hanging over the grille.

"Never mind the histrionics concerning Ramsay. The question remains—did Mosley manage not only to find my aunt but also to take her into his protection?"

"With my help and mine alone, Your Grace."

Sissinghurst allowed himself an inaudible sigh.

"Although, I find myself wondering about your ultimate intentions, Your Grace, if I might."

The man's impudence was staggering, although Sissinghurst also knew enough about human nature to worry about what lay behind the stunning presumption. "And why do you bother about my ultimate intentions, sir, when I thought your concerns lay in another direction entirely?"

"You find it hard to believe that I would care about the fate of Lady Hartford?" The question was posed with all the innocence of a saint. "Then you may be surprised to discover that I should like to be apprised of her whereabouts and her well-being."

He was giving orders now. Sissinghurst answered more sharply than he'd intended. "You may rest assured of her well-being." He didn't like the direction the discussion was taking and cursed Mosley once more for not relieving him of these tedious and irritating negotiations.

"How might I put this delicately?" the voice on the other side of the confessional probed smoothly. "Perhaps you're more concerned about the lady's well-being than I am."

A heavy, sinister silence.

Somewhere deep in the caverns of the church, someone coughed, a harsh, hacking intrusion. And, in that instant, the bishop knew that the man on the other side of the grille would like to see Helena Hartford *dead*. Sissinghurst almost expected the peel of church bells to accompany the realization, but then again, he'd seen, heard, and done too much in his lifetime to be even close to being shocked. He leaned forward, choosing his next words deliberately.

"Well, well. My errant and wayward aunt does seem to engender a myriad of sentiments." The man in the confessional would be shocked to discover that Helena Hartford was worth more to him alive than dead. Quite literally. But he could empathize with his perspective because, given the chance, he too would have preferred to lay the bitch in the ground and dance on her grave.

Instead, it would have to be Bedlam. A living death.

"She does, indeed. And the way Deacon Mosley was *handling* her earlier this evening, well, let's simply say that *even I* was alarmed, Your Grace. Such unbridled lust in a man of the church is positively unseemly." The sarcasm was thick. "Had it not been for the intervention of Ramsay, who knows what may have befallen the poor woman?" There was a sigh and a shuffle, as though the man were preparing to leave, giving the bishop the disagreeable sensation of being dismissed. The door opposite creaked open an inch, light from the nave diluting the dimness.

"My preference, Your Grace, would be to see the matter resolved with more *permanence*, sooner rather than later.

And take particular heed of Nicholas Ramsay, as dare I say, you may find yourself out of your league."

The statement was delivered with the arrogance of a royal decree. The balance of power had tipped. But not for long.

"Indeed." The lone word was frosty. Tasting irritation on his tongue, Sissinghurst made a note to have Mosley take care of this interloper as soon as feasibly possible. Intimidation never worked with him because he knew the frailties of humanity better than anyone. Everyone had a weakness.

Even the son of the devil himself. Nicholas Ramsay.

"And one last matter, Your Grace."

Sissinghurst didn't deign to respond as a lifetime of discipline had taught him when to hold his counsel.

"Deacon Mosley, if you're interested, which I'm quite sure you are, will meet with you shortly. In the crypt. He's had quite the evening, the details of which I'm sure he will be eager to disclose."

The bishop swore with an inventive fluency. The invective was bitter, and before he could swallow the last mouthful, he heard the confessional door closing softly.

Gripping the crucifix around his neck, he seethed. Preserving his dignity and minding his girth precluded rushing out in pursuit of the man. And yet—he mopped the sheen of sweat from his brow—despite his monumental disrespect, he could still prove useful.

After a decent interval, he exited the confessional sparing a look around the now-deserted church. The great Norman doors would surely be locked, the last parishioners back on the streets, their consciences now neat and orderly. He found himself breathing hard, not so much from exertion as from a suffocating anger that choked his blood.

Damn Mosley to hell for not looking after details with greater precision. How difficult could it be to dispense with a madwoman? It gave him pause, truly, as to whether he could leave the fate of the X Club in his delicate, white hands.

He shuffled to the back of the church, behind the nave and down the stairs into the chill air of the crypt. The smell of melting wax from the wall sconces accompanied his descent, reminding him of the liturgy of his youth, full and redolent of forbidden incense and papal indulgence.

The ten sarcophagi were waiting, glowing dully in the candlelight as though for him alone in all their regimented glory, ready to swear their allegiance to his will.

It was time to teach Mosley a lesson.

Leaving the door open behind him, he heard light steps scraping against stone, signaling the younger man's timely arrival. Sissinghurst didn't acknowledge his presence and began walking with deliberate ceremony amongst the tombs, stopping briefly by each one to admire carved hands crossed beneficently across a chest or to caress the hilt of a sword, at the ready for all eternity.

The silence stretched. Mosley remained motionless. The hood of his cloak was thrown back and his hair, burnished platinum, shone in the medieval candlelight. Sissinghurst knew how to draw out the tension, how to transform anxiety and fear to an exquisite level of torment.

At long last, he said, "You may speak." And turned to face the younger man who, in exaggerated respect, refused to meet his eyes.

"Your Grace," he began in that peculiarly soft voice. He took a step back before continuing, as though to ward off a coming blow. "We've encountered somewhat of a challenge, but I assure you, it can be resolved promptly and in a way that satisfies . . ."

Sissinghurst, one hand still hovering over the serene stone face of a Templar effigy, swept Mosley with a look that stopped the flow of words. More of a signal wasn't required. Mosley took two steps forward and fell to his knees, bending his head in supplication.

"Forgive me, Your Grace, for I have failed."

"So I've already been apprised." He looked down at the young man kneeling at his feet with a combination of distaste and power. "I learned that our quarry would have eluded your grasp had it not been for the aid of a confederate. I am not, as you well know, predisposed to easy forgiveness, because in the act of mercy lies only weakness. So do tell me, at the very least, Deacon, that we now have Helena Hartford under our protection." It was a test.

The head bowed lower in silence.

"As I thought." Sissinghurst crossed his arms over his chest, the ruby crucifix around his neck digging into his flesh with a welcome twinge of pain. "I would like you to explain the situation you found yourself in this night, fully and comprehensively, and without acknowledgment of the consequences to your own person. And it's best if you don't make me wait."

Mosley's thin shoulders shuddered, but he refused to lift his head, directing his confession to the floor.

"I found her. Initially."

"Tell me something I don't already know."

"And then I lost her."

"To whom?"

A pause no longer than an angel's breath. "To Nicholas Ramsay."

Sissinghurst closed his eyes in disbelief once more. To lose Helena Hartford to a man more powerful than any monarch, any Eastern potentate, a titan who could summon the prime minister, the Archbishop of Canterbury, and the queen to breakfast—

"You fool!" The words merged with the sputtering hiss of the candles. "Do you have any idea what you've done, allowing her to slip into the hands of a man whose earthly powers virtually know no bounds?" Strength leached from his body and for support he leaned into the cold stone at his back.

Mosley raised his head, his fine features paler than usual.

"I do realize . . . only too well. Your aunt has proved trouble-some from the outset." Behind the penitent mask, a flicker of hatred sprang to life. "We had her subdued when Ramsay appeared on the scene . . ." He flushed with anger at the memory.

Sissinghurst didn't want to hear it. He gripped the crucifix around his neck, the rubies biting his hand. "I don't require the details as I can clearly deduce the outcome of the situation."

Mosley remained kneeling. "Lady Hartford will reap her just rewards, I swear it, if I must crawl over broken glass to see it done." Venom lent a delicate rose to his cheeks. "And if I may, Your Grace, all is not lost as there is one important detail that I would like to recount." He lifted his chin fractionally with something like hope. "That may help us in our dealings with the X Club."

Sissinghurst scowled. "I trust that this important detail doesn't compound an already horrendous situation."

To his credit, Mosley didn't sweeten his next revelation. "Ramsay is the main support behind the efforts of the X Club," he said with a starkness that matched the gloom of the crypt.

Sissinghurst felt himself shrink, grow calcified, as hard as the tomb at his back. For a moment he was speechless, an avalanche of implications spinning around in his head. Light-headed, he said in a hoarse whisper, "You had better be certain of this, Deacon, because we *cannot* afford another disaster."

Mosley straightened his upper body, an avenging angel, and for the first time that evening held the bishop's gaze. "Unfortunately, I'm certain of it."

The bishop inhaled sharply and made himself move, pacing in front of the kneeling Mosley, his thoughts racing. "Lady Hartford and Nicholas Ramsay—I find the pairing too coincidental for comfort. There must be a reason, and not a good one, behind Ramsay's dogged pursuit of my aunt."

"I will find out, I swear to you, Your Grace." Mosley made no move to rise, becoming almost one with the cold stone beneath his feet.

"It can't be for her fortune," Sissinghurst muttered, discarding one rationale after the other, his sharp mind working quickly, "or for her parentage, which is common to begin with. And as for her beauty, it is surely tainted, what with her reputation." He stopped in his tracks. "All of these assumptions are worthless given we haven't much time. Where are they now?"

Mosley raised his finely lashed eyes to the bishop. He looked like a child awaiting punishment for a serious misdeed. "On Ramsay's ship, setting sail for South America."

Sissinghurst thought a blood vessel burst in his head. When his vision finally cleared, he focused on hauling breath into his constricted lungs. "And what are you"—he ground out each word—"planning on doing about it?"

The candles flickered and the light in the crypt seemed to dim. Finally, Mosley moved, clasping his hands in front of him as though in prayer or supplication. "I plan to get her back from Ramsay. More exactly, to have Ramsay return her to us."

Sissinghurst thought the young man, always mentally precarious, had finally lost his mind. Ramsay's ship, probably as well guarded as the crown jewels, was already floating beyond their reach on its way to the other side of the world— and he actually believed that he could force the vessel to turn around?

"What you say is making absolutely no sense, Deacon, and need I remind you that Lady Hartford's fortune is no good to us *if she's dead*." His voice grew flinty. "What is she to Ramsay—do we know?"

At the question, Mosley gave an almost imperceptible jerk. Then he stilled and his face assumed the mask of contrition, his eyes downcast and shadowed. "I'm not certain, Your Grace, but there is a shared history, I suspect, the details of which I will determine. However, in the interim, it is in our best interests to have your aunt returned to us."

"You're repeating yourself, Deacon, and I've yet to learn how you intend to accomplish this feat save calling out the British Navy."

A sly look passed over the younger man's beatific features as he straightened his spine. "Arsenic."

Sissinghurst resumed pacing. "What of it?"

"I had their supplies laced," he said simply. "The symptoms of intoxication usually occur within thirty minutes of exposure. Ramsay will have no choice but to turn back to England if he hopes to save his lover." The way he savored the last two words was not lost on the bishop.

Sissinghurst glowered. "You'd better get this right, Mosley, because if my aunt dies, our plans turn to ashes and dust." His options regarding Helena Hartford were a narrowing channel and he didn't like it. "And like most men who come within sniffing distance of my aunt, you display a decidedly unhealthy interest in her. Not that I would deny you your choice of reward, Mosley," he continued shrewdly, "but only if your assignment is flawlessly executed."

Wisely, the younger man did not respond except for a glow in the pale blue of his eyes.

Indeed, everyone has a weakness. And if he didn't, the Bishop of London would create one.

Which brought his thoughts back to Nicholas Ramsay, too powerful a figure to leave in the hands of the deacon.

Everyone, from the Exchequer and the Courts to bankers across the empire, was entirely too fearful of the wealthy upstart. Perhaps because they had too much to hide of their own.

He turned toward the stairs, his way lit by two brackets of flickering candles. Ruthlessly, he reached out and snuffed out the first branch before turning to the second. "You will remain here for the night, on your knees, to atone for your sins,

Mosley," he said absently, in the manner he might use to discipline a dog.

He approached the last cluster of candles and wrenched them from the bracket. His steps up the stairs were heavy. Plunged into darkness, he imagined Deacon Mosley swaying on his knees in the crypt, alone except for ten Templar effigies and his own fevered, misdirected prayers.

Chapter 10

R amsay watched her sleep.

Still in port, the *Flying Cloud* rocked gently as a cradle, barely disturbing the slender figure lying under the covers in his bed. He willed her to wake up, so he could see those lying violet eyes widening as she realized that she would never get away from him again.

The sheets outlined her sinuous body and his blood drove hard with anger, revenge, and God damn it, arousal. The pulsing at his temple where she'd landed her blow wasn't the only thing reminding him of his weakness for this woman.

What he really should do was kill her now, before she awakened, and in one easy motion erase the past and the burden he'd carried with him for two decades.

She moaned something in her sleep, a deep, throaty sound, and he turned away from where she lay sleeping, lost in the large bed, her hair a cloud spread on the pillow. He noted again, as he had that first night at Francine's, that physically she appeared nothing like her late father, nothing at all.

He looked out the porthole with its expansive horizon, just an hour from daybreak and still spangled with stars, but all he saw was her face, eyes lit with panic as she struggled against the men who'd seized her, the chloroform-soaked cloth held tightly against her mouth and nose.

In the rain and in the dark, his reaction had been involuntary, based on some primal instinct to get what belonged to him, because make no mistake, Helena Hartford was *his,* the one he wanted, even if for all the wrong reasons. And by God, he'd have her.

He couldn't even recall exactly what happened. It didn't matter. The man who held her dropped like a stone. Blood mingled with the rain. Grunts dissolved along with fractured bones and, in the end, he was standing alone with Helena Hartford in his arms in a downpour in an alleyway in London.

This wasn't going to be simple, but nothing in his life ever was.

He sat on the edge of the desk in the captain's cabin that extended almost the full width of his ship. The space had natural illumination, from portholes on the port side and through gratings in the quarter deck above. Once all the supplies had been loaded, they would shove off, possibly before the break of dawn.

Then Helena Hartford would be his to do with as he wished. And what he wished wasn't even remotely pleasant. For years he'd planned for this day, examined his options, one more horrific than the next, with the calmness of an accountant at his books. His first instinct was to simply end her life. Easily enough accomplished, a body washed overboard, his men on the ship sworn to secrecy and loyal to him to the death.

But then again, easy wasn't enough. Nothing would ever be *enough*.

The rustle of bed clothes caught his attention. She tossed her head, and with her white skin and wild dark hair, she looked like a goddess out of a Greek myth, although asleep, she seemed softer, more vulnerable. He had stripped her of her soaking clothing before bundling her under the sheets, actions that had tested every ounce of his willpower.

Christ, he'd been hard since the first moment they'd met,

his balls in her viselike grip. The small scar on his left temple was proof enough.

More than anything, it grated that he could still feel the imprint of her body against his, so supple and yielding, taste that full warmth so sensuous and so full of lies. He moved from the desk and took a few steps toward the bed. The sheet covering her was superfluous because her naked body was seared in his mind's eyes. The firm, high breasts, the hardness of her peaked nipples, the lush length of her legs tangling with his. Desire pounded his senses, the taste of her still on his lips.

Shoving his hands in the pockets of his breeches, he swore under his breath.

The ship shuddered, the muted commands of his men indicating that they would soon be under sail. He'd chosen the *Flying Cloud* from among his fleet for its great length, sharpness of ends, and proportionate breadth and depth, all conducive to speed. She'd recently sailed from London to Melbourne in under eighty-five days. The clipper was fast and slender, with a narrow hull that was deeper at the back than at the front, with acres of sails on her tall masts.

The floor rolled under his feet, but he felt strangely at home, his deeply ambivalent relationship with the sea scarring him in ways that he didn't care to consider. It was a bond that went deep to sinew and bone, born from memories of shackled bodies, the endless scream of seagulls and harsh terrain that seared to cinders both the present and the past.

Introspection was perhaps the one and only thing in this world that he couldn't afford.

The bitterness in his mouth was as sharp and pungent as the cold black coffee sitting abandoned on his desk. He played with the idea of lighting a cheroot, knocking the ash onto the Turkish carpet beneath his feet, and then deliberately grinding the embers under his heel. But he decided against it because needing and wanting—even so much as a cigarette—was a weakness. And he didn't like weakness.

Which was exactly the reason why he attached no sentiment to his life—or the life of Helena Hartford, heiress, artist,
and very probably harlot. A woman earning her keep on the
street was a prostitute, while one trading on her family name
and fortune to buy a husband was to be admired. In the new
world of affluent commoners, morality, or at least what traded
as morality, was magnified, and as an obscenely wealthy
man, he recognized that fact better than most.

A pit opened beneath his feet, but he didn't look away.
There in the depths lay his life. And the spectre of Helena
Hartford, the one way to obliterate his past. The only problem, and it was minor, was the unwelcome lust he hadn't
been able to shake for the past forty-eight hours.

He scrubbed a hand down his face, dark with stubble.

Let us be brutally honest.

He was a good lover but harbored no illusions that her response to him was anything more than a charade of passion,
learned at the knee of her elderly husband and subsequent
army of lovers. It was a convenient place to hide for Helena
Hartford, offering her a façade of control, and it was something useful he'd learned about her. Seduction had never been
his strategy. Either the woman was interested or she wasn't; it
would be an encounter free of pretense and doubt, and the
only way to fuck in his worldview.

The impression of her half-naked breasts still burned his
skin. And her eyes, wide and bewildered as she lay splayed,
those impossibly long legs, on the stairs of her atelier, his
voice urging her on. There was something there, a brittleness
that went beyond bourgeois reticence, and like the wolf he
was, he recognized the scent of anguish. That she was being
hunted down like prey by the Bishop of London and his pack
of hypocrites was one thing, but there was more. Much more.

Something he could leverage, something that he could use
to heighten her suffering. She was hiding, and he'd find out
from what. To break through that barrier would be the first

step on the way to building something resembling trust. Forty days together, confined to the sea, was all he would need. And then, he smiled bitterly, to have that trust stripped away, to be left moored, both literally and figuratively—well, that was the worst pain of all. Nothing could cut so deeply or permanently, no dank ship's hold, no deprivation and no chains.

He should know.

She stirred, and he turned around, his senses tuned to the smallest change in the atmosphere. Twenty years of watching your back did that to you. Although her eyes were still closed, he knew by the tightening in his gut that Helena Hartford was awake.

"You're going to have to look at me eventually." Crossing his arms across his chest, he remained standing a few feet from the bed watching her eyes slowly open, an ocean of violet. The sight of him was so sudden, so unexpected that she was confused, pushing the hair back from her face, half asleep, half awake. Then the dream shifted to reality and he could see a thousand images running through her mind.

"You must be hungry. Would you like something to eat?" The banality of the words was a good defense, heading off dangerous thoughts. Without moving, she stared at him, memorizing every detail of his appearance as though for later use. A few more awkward seconds, then she shook her head mutely, sitting up tentatively. She held the sheet to her chest, her hair heavy around the fragile bones of her naked shoulders.

Her gaze took in the cabin, the floor covered with a painted canvas drugget, the paintings on the bulkheads, and the coalfired stove that provided heat in cooler climes. Two chairs and a settee covered in green damask and framed by a large, round mirror filled the port side of the cabin, opposite a dining area with a table to seat a captain and nine guests.

"I think I remember." A frown knit her smooth brow. "The X Club, leaving Conway House, then Mosley . . ."

Her voice hit him straight in the chest, pure silk with the promise of a rich carnality. To head off the throbbing blood in his groin, he turned his attention to the stew and the pot of tea on his desk. "Mosley was the smaller one, I'm assuming," he said. "You may still be feeling nauseous from the effects of the chloroform. Have something to eat before we talk." He picked up the tray and set it by the bed.

The typhoon didn't erupt, at least not yet. Instead, she glanced at him warily as he poured her a mug of tea and then carefully reached for it, making sure their fingers didn't touch.

Ramsay watched the vulnerable line of her throat as she sipped the hot liquid. Maybe she didn't want to talk or maybe she was truly hungry, but for the next few minutes, Helena silently applied herself to the food he'd offered as though shoring up her strength for an upcoming storm.

"Do you remember exactly what happened?" he asked, keeping his tone deliberately neutral.

Maybe she was bargaining for more time, but she put down her spoon and carefully wiped her lips with a linen napkin before raising her eyes to his. "You can probably explain far better than I. All I know," she added, gesturing to the surroundings, "is that I'm on your ship. Exactly as you and the X Club had planned. And it doesn't look, at least right now, as though I have much choice in the matter."

He followed her line of sight to the doors and porthole and back again. While she appeared comparatively relaxed, the muscles in her shoulders were taut. The pulse point at her pale throat gave her away, as well as the almost imperceptible tightening at the corners of her eyes. She was looking for a means of escape.

"I don't awaken in strange men's beds every day of the week," she said, reading his mind. "And I don't typically assault men with heavy pieces of sculpture."

"So you do remember." They locked gazes, and the heat inside him turned up a few degrees. He tamped down the blaze ruthlessly. "Good thing that I recover rapidly."

"I'm sorry," she said halfheartedly.

"And I'll pretend that I believe you and accept your apology."

She shot him a hot glare. "I'd like to get up, please." Strength had returned to her voice, her shoulders above the white sheet straightening. She placed the tray carefully on the bedside.

"I'm sure you would—so you can find something else to hit me with?"

"I learn quickly. Clearly, it didn't work the first time."

"And a good thing or you would have awakened in a cell at Bedlam, courtesy of your nephew, the bishop."

"I don't quite know what's worse, an asylum or your ship speeding off to lord knows where on some mission whose connection to me is tangential at best." Her eyes transmitted a sharp acuity as she made to rise, first carefully wrapping the sheet under her arms like a shroud and then sitting at the edge of the bed. She looked as innocent as a woodland nymph, though God only knew he wouldn't recognize one if he'd shot it between the eyes.

He moved to her side and she froze, her hands clutching the sheet. "I can do this myself."

Bloody hell, he wanted to touch her. "Just in case you keel over. Particularly since you haven't your sea legs yet." She stiffened, but the skin of her naked arm felt like warm cream under his hard palm. "The water closet is to your left. Where you'll find some of your clothing as well."

"Haven't you simply thought of everything." Her tone dripped sarcasm.

She deftly detached herself from his grasp and disappeared through the small door. He tried not to follow the sway of her hips but stood waiting with his back to the door until she emerged a few minutes later, dressed in the brown smock of the day before and stocking feet revealing fine-boned ankles. She'd washed her face and strands of damp hair clung to the sides of her cheeks.

Glancing briefly out the porthole where the rising sun was pinkening the sky, she sat on the settee. Her knees set demurely together and with her shoeless feet, she looked like a young schoolgirl.

But the voice was low, direct, and damned adult. "Where are we exactly?"

So this was how it was going to be. He grabbed the end of a chair and straddled it, facing her. "We've just left England and we're aiming for Madeira and then farther south toward the port of Santa Cruz at Tenerife Island. We'll make a stop at the Cape Verde Islands to pick up fresh supplies."

Her jaw clenched at the starkness of his statement. "We're replicating Darwin's voyage on the *Beagle*, aren't we?"

And what exactly was she intending to do about it? Unpredictability was something he was beginning to expect in his dealings with Helena Hartford. Even though they were already miles out at sea, surrounded by saltwater, he wouldn't underestimate her desperation. She valued her freedom above all else, and though it cost him, he had to admit it was something they had in common.

"I believe the good doctors and scientists of the X Club explained in comprehensive detail what they require of us."

Her smile was cynical. "Us? Don't expect me to believe you aren't doing this for a very selfish reason."

He shrugged carelessly, resting his arms across the back of the chair. "I won't try to deny your claim, although I shouldn't let it worry you. You, on the other hand, have much to be grateful for—escape from Sissinghurst and his crew whose reach, I would suspect, doesn't extend all the way to Tierra del Fuego." Or to Nicholas Ramsay, for that matter. "You've escaped—which means you can stop trying to escape from me."

She crossed her legs demurely at the ankle. "And what do you expect in return?"

Images of her lying across his chest, flagrantly sensual and available, flashed through his mind. Every curve and every hollow in that beautiful body was primed for manipulation and deceit, all she'd probably ever known. Pleasure had never come into the equation.

"Just to do what comes so naturally to you," he said innocently. "You've been asked to draw and paint what we find to provide as evidence for the X Club's purposes."

"This missing link conundrum, you mean."

"Exactly."

"And you know where to look? Last time I explored an atlas, the Americas were quite a large continent." He almost smiled at the edge in her voice. Challenging him and the world was clearly in her nature, although the tendency hadn't done her much good to this point.

"When you're fully recovered, we can discuss the details. We have plenty of time before we get to Argentina. In the interim enjoy your reprieve."

Her toes curled into the rug beneath her feet. "Reprieve?" She raised an eyebrow. "More like I've just exchanged one prison sentence for another. My only hope is whatever we find in Tierra del Fuego can be used directly against Sissinghurst, because I don't expect much will have changed upon my return unless I have several new quivers in my bow."

For a second, Ramsay felt a stab of guilt, but it was gone in the space of a gunshot. His instincts were back on full alert because she was doing it again, exposing an astounding vulnerability that was as dangerous to him as a freshly loaded weapon. "Of course, and to use against Sissinghurst," he agreed smoothly.

Narrow eyed, he watched her with an intensity bordering on obsession. He could tell that she could no longer sit still, fully awake now and plagued by an awareness that she was effectively a prisoner—his prisoner—saddled with him for the duration of the voyage.

Good thing she didn't know the truth.

"And *your* motives in all of this are to remain obscured, I take it." She rose from the settee. "And I have no choice but to simply acquiesce." Shaking out the folds of her smock, she let her eyes drift to the door of the cabin, her desperation rising to the surface like a torrent from an underground stream.

He stood, shoving aside the chair. "Never mind about my motives. I'm concerned about yours because, unless you're courting a premature death, I wouldn't think about throwing yourself overboard. Or, for that matter, throwing yourself at me as you did at Conway House. Neither will help your cause."

He'd just raised the temperature in the cabin. Deliberately. Her hands curled into fists at her sides. "I don't recall hearing any complaints either at my atelier or at Conway House." She stared pointedly at his left temple. "Women can inflict damage, leave scars, as easily as men."

"That's a very old story," he growled. "You're not telling me anything I don't already know."

The tilt of her head, the narrowed eyes, the mocking tone— she would court disaster to the end. "The male of the species, as Mr. Darwin could probably attest to, is an extraordinarily simple creature, as your behavior last evening demonstrates," she said.

The depth of his annoyance came as a surprise to him, almost as much as the harshness of his response. He looked at her for a long, hard moment, then nodded. "I could generalize that although women are first, last, and always actresses, the theater is in your case obviously not your métier," he responded silkily. "I can see why you chose art instead."

The crude remark shocked her into action. She swung up her right hand to slap him, but he grabbed her wrist and blocked her knee to his groin. Like a wriggling fish on a line, he held her away from him.

"The truth rankles, doesn't it?" he bit out, tightening his

hold on her wrist. "Your performance, despite having the patina of carnality, has hardly been convincing so far."

She matched him glare for glare. "Perhaps it's because I didn't have much to work with, other than a coarse, brutish arriviste who can't even begin to even *attempt* masquerading as a gentleman."

He jerked her toward him, unwillingly breathing in her scent like the animal she was accusing him of being. "How little you know of me, Lady Hartford. You've just paid me a compliment."

She refused to look away but shifted slightly as though she were ready to leap for the porthole behind her. He tightened his grip, but with a quick wrench she broke free and dashed straight toward the door.

"It's locked from the outside, so don't bother," he drawled, stopping her in her tracks. "And only I have the key."

With her back to him, she stood ramrod straight. His hard fingers gripped her upper arm and hauled her back toward him. They were close enough that he could see the unvarnished fury in her eyes.

"You have made this impossible from the start."

"You're the one who keeps fighting a losing battle, Helena. Accept your situation and accept who you are."

"You mean the fact that I'm a woman who's supposed to leap into bed with you? As part of this Faustian bargain that's to keep me from Bedlam and Sissinghurst?"

"You're afraid of something and it's not me, Helena. That's why you keep doing this to yourself." The shackle of his fingers slid down her arm to her waist. "Accept it, take it for what it is, and free yourself, for once, from the subterfuge you've no doubt had to hide behind most of your life."

She looked at the ceiling and he swore she was fighting back tears. Clearly, his mistake, because her voice was hard when she said, "You can't know anything about it and don't even try."

He tightened his fingers around her waist, felt her stiffen and then, an instant later, relax into his hands. It was a reprise of the performance at Conway House, as though she'd suddenly assumed a mantle, a role, transforming herself from rebellious virago into seductive wanton. Experimentally, he slid his hands from her waist, up her arms, over her fragile shoulders and to her throat. She felt as supple as a purring cat.

But he could see the restrained triumph, in place of tears, behind the lowered lashes. Her tongue came out briefly to wet her full bottom lip, and he knew that mouth to contain the same duplicitous tongue that he'd felt against his own in that decadently pink room the night before.

The attempt at logic mocked him. He was rock hard and fated to stay that way whenever he was near her. His anger got the better of him.

"I'm not in the market for cheap whores," he said brutally. But his body reached out for her as if it had a mind of its own, his lips testing the softness of the skin under her ear. Stubble from his beard scraped against her throat as he pressed his thumbs into the rapidly beating pulse at the base of her neck. "This time we do it my way or no way at all."

The fine bones of her shoulder blades stiffened, veneer cracking, as the actress faded away. She stepped back from him and he let her, staring at him with her surprise—and disillusionment—starkly etched on her face. She knew that he knew—had seen right through her like a pane of shattered glass.

"I don't understand," she said, her breath unsteady. "What do you want of me then?"

Through the haze of lust, he recognized the torment and, in the anguish, the wide-open opportunity. It was a talent that had made him a very wealthy man.

"Why are you afraid to accept pleasure?" he asked, letting himself into the breach. "Passion at its best is an act of independence, a rebellion against forms and strictures. It's what you do with your painting, you let yourself go and you refuse to accept limits."

He'd struck a chord. She lifted her chin, her features outlined in the harsh light of the morning sun slicing through the porthole window and reflected against the mirror over the settee. "I'm surprised. I truly am that you realize what I strive to accomplish with my work." Her voice was a whisper and he knew the admission cost her some effort.

"And all the rest, the husband, the lovers, they left you cold, didn't they?" he continued relentlessly, recognizing opportunity when he saw it. "Trapping you in a pantomime of what desire should be. You were traded by your father for your youth and your fortune for a husband who demanded nothing more from you than that you be his plaything and his pocketbook. As for the lovers"—he deliberately backed away from her—"they couldn't break you out of the prison you keep yourself in, could they?"

Her face was stricken, her lips white, but he pressed on. "Now's your chance to find out the truth, Helena, about yourself, about who you are, and what you hold deep inside you, the passion, that you can then give over to your art."

His eyes never left her face, watching the play of emotions with the detachment of a general taking a body count after a battle. Already, she was melting, letting down her guard, her defenses easily breached, and out of nowhere, he felt a blast of unwanted pity for her.

He probably never hated himself more than at this moment, but then he despised Helena Hartford and everything she represented a million times more.

His voice low, he said, "Come to me when you're ready, and only then."

Her addiction to pleasure would be the beginning of the end.

Because in that final moment, when the *Flying Cloud* became a speck on Helena Hartford's horizon, leaving her behind in an alien land, emotionally devastated and physically cut off from everything she had ever known, they would come full circle.

And he would finally have what he'd worked toward all these years.

Revenge.

Chapter 11

It was like drawing the hot smoke of an opium pipe into her lungs and releasing it in a long, slow breath. A sudden wave of dizziness swept over her at the realization of what he was offering.

A drug that would help her forget—and make her stronger. A strength she could pour into her work. All it would take is a gesture, a step closer to that tall, uncompromising man who allowed her to catch a glimmer of desire she'd never felt would be possible for her. He was intimidating, yes, but right now he stood waiting for her to do what she wanted. Of her own free will.

When had that ever been a possibility?

Her body stiffened automatically at the thought of her late husband, what she'd been forced to do, to become. And then the lovers she'd tried to take in a feeble attempt at declaring her independence and freedom. She'd ended dismissing them all, her own deficits insurmountable, too difficult to overcome.

And now trapped on this ship with this man . . . Something lured her toward him, perhaps her fascination with his physical form, so pleasing to her artistic eye. The austerity of his jaw with its incongruous cleft, the aquiline nose, the deep-set eyes and—a shiver skidded up her spine—the tall, powerful body.

Ramsay stared at her a long moment with strange detachment; then, slowly, he began to remove his shirt. When he had unbuttoned it, he pulled the fabric from his shoulders and threw it carelessly over the chair.

His muscular elegance robbed her of her breath. He could be a sculpture, she told herself as she stepped toward him, the bright light revealing every plane and angle to her suddenly hungry gaze. Drawn by nothing more than her own curiosity and pleasure, she dared to trace the turn of hard muscles in his arms. Running a hand over his broad shoulders, she absorbed the heat of his skin, skimming her palm up to his nape where his pulse beat strongly.

He held himself rigidly under her hands. Lost in the sensation of seeing and feeling, she almost forgot he was in the room, his voice startling her. "What are you feeling now?"

She tried to hold the question in her thoughts, but she couldn't focus, overwhelmed by Nicholas Ramsay's devastating physicality. She'd seen, she had drawn from, and she had certainly touched, male flesh before in her life, but somehow this was different. Removed and intensely personal at the same time. "I don't exactly know, except what should be familiar is suddenly very unfamiliar to me," she said finally, telling the truth.

His eyes never left her face as he removed the next article of clothing. She was transfixed, for once not planning, not hiding but simply giving in to the moment. He made no move to touch her.

Daylight streamed into the cabin, but he was unconcerned. He opened his trousers without haste and then pulled them down over his hips. Taut flesh stretched over his ribs and down to a flat belly. The streamlined bulge of his thighs framed his erection, thick, strong, and straining toward her.

Helena's body hummed with a low charge of electricity.

Riveted, she leaned toward him, balancing on her toes. His lips were warm and firm, offering a silky sting that was magnified with each breath and subtle pressure of his mouth on hers. Emboldened by his seeming passivity, this jungle cat who allowed her to play with him, her tongue snaked out to caress his bottom lip.

He pulled her arms from around his neck, holding her hands away from his body. He stared down at her and she marveled again at his features, too harsh for conventional handsomeness. His was the face of a man who had weathered storm and tempest, endured isolation and drought, until every superfluous bit of flesh had been chiseled away to reveal the bare-bone structure beneath.

"What is it—what's the matter?" she asked softly. She had to hold herself back, fighting the unaccustomed urge to mold her body to a man's.

He shook his head, and other than his rock-hard erection, he remained seemingly unmoved, made of marble or bronze, which should be cool to her touch. But wasn't.

"It's not a matter of what I want, Helena," he said, his voice, which was slightly unsteady, the only indication that he was flesh and blood. "It's about what matters to you right now, what you want, and need."

Confusion bloomed on her face. She could feel it, a flush of heat rising to the surface of her sensitized skin. In response, he went to stand behind her, a hand on each shoulder. Slowly, he dragged his open palms down her waist and then carefully threaded them between her arms and sides until her own palm lay against her abdomen. She tensed, then sighed, as he moved slowly to stroke the base of her mound.

His hand burned through the fabric of her skirts. "You have to know your own pleasure before you can give it," Ramsay murmured very close to her ear.

She looked up to see their reflection in the oval mirror, her head thrown back against his bare chest, their hands locked. The image swayed in time with the gentle rocking of the ship. She felt and watched a gradual downward tug upon her smock, the buttons at her back miraculously freed from their moorings. She held her breath as first her dress and then her chemise loosened and slipped from her shoulders.

All she heard was her own rapid breath. Behind her she felt the size and strength of him, hard and heavy against her backside. His hips flexed against her.

"You're beautiful, but you know that. Take a good look." He slid his hands around her narrow rib cage to pull down the last bit of chemise that obscured her breasts. She forced herself to look into the mirror, at the rounded flesh, engorged and eager. She watched as he molded his palms to the shape of her, pressing his fingers into her sensitive skin, coming closer but still not touching her nipples. His gaze moved over her body as his hands roamed, squeezing, kneading. "Touch yourself, Helena, give yourself what you want."

She lifted shaking hands to cover his and then allowed them to skate over her distended nipples. Arching against him, she rolled them between her fingers, observing his glittering eyes in the mirror opposite them.

"Now, lift your skirts."

She met his hard stare and stopped breathing as her right hand, on its own accord, dropped to begin gathering her skirts, lifting them. Her white stockings, with their simple garters, framed the opening of her pantalets. "I don't see . . . what it is . . . you want me to do," she stuttered softly.

His mouth lifted with a predator's smile. Rock hard and unmoving, the granite of his penis burned the back of her thighs. "See if you're wet and warm," he said into the softness of her neck as he ran his hands on the underside of her breasts. "Let me help you." He fisted her skirts, which she had clenched between her fingers, into his hand.

She wanted to close her eyes against the sight of her exposed mound, the dark curls. But somehow she didn't, watching as though the two images in the mirror were pieces of art come to life. Ramsay's eyes never wavered as her hands left her thighs to part her own flesh.

She relaxed against him, opening herself, flingers sliding between wet folds. She gasped and her eyes fluttered against the trickle of moisture seeping onto her thighs. Instinctively, her fingers pressed against the fulcrum that pulsed and throbbed.

His words were harsh against her ear. "Bring your other hand down and open yourself wider, Helena, hold yourself open."

For a slight second she faltered, but she couldn't bring herself to keep her arms at her sides. She widened her stance, throwing back her head against his hard chest. She throbbed with every stroke, an almost painful craving that tortured her now with its burning need for release. Stiff and rigid with unreleased tension, her fingers moved with their own rhythm over the swollen nub of flesh, in tight, firm circles creating a hot, stabbing pleasure so fierce that her whole body convulsed against the press of her fingers.

His arms tightened around her ribs, his hands finally on her aching nipples, plying and pulling them. Her voice shook, the words incoherent to her own ears.

His fingers kept working her nipples. "There," he groaned, "keep going, keep feeling and let it wash over you."

Her thighs flexed and her knees weakened, the slick skin of her clitoris a universe unto its own. Intense sensation centered on the torturous pleasure of her own making, winding its way into one open, throbbing nerve.

She exploded, stiffening in his arms, her skin burning against his. She writhed under the waves of pleasure, her body rigid against the climax that pulsed hard and fast and uncontrolled. A low moan escaped her lips as she finally collapsed against him.

Picking her up from behind her knees, he carried her to the bed. She lay limp and mindless, her breath coming deeply, satisfyingly, filling her lungs as though she'd been deprived of air for years. He sat beside her in the linen sheets, his unreadable gaze holding hers.

She relaxed fully into the embrace of the mattress, her

thoughts a disordered jumble, aware, for the first time in an hour, of the gentle sway of the ship and her racing heart.

"I don't know what to say," she whispered, and her breasts were flushed, her voice full of unwelcome emotion she couldn't control. She rose on an elbow and looked at him, the muscles trembling slightly, a weakness she refused to acknowledge.

His jaw was tight as he braced his hands on either side of her, but his voice was curiously gentle. He shook his head.

"This had nothing to do with me and everything to do with you." Then he lowered his head as if to kiss her. Helena's pulse hammered and her lips parted, but he slowly pulled away from the bed. Not saying a word, she turned on her side to watch him move across the room, supremely unself-conscious of his magnificent nudity.

He pulled on his shirt and breeches.

"Get some rest while you can," he said. "Because where we're going, the weather is guaranteed to be rough."

And before she could respond, he was gone.

Chapter 12

For once he wasn't lying.

The next week brought a series of storms that had Helena confined to her bed, clinging to the mattress when she wasn't facedown in the bucket that someone had kindly left by the bedside.

They missed Madeira, their first port of call, because a westerly squall prevented the ship from making port.

And in all that time, she hadn't caught a glimpse of Nicholas Ramsay. Not that it mattered—his image, his touch, and his scent were burned into her body like brands. Exactly what had happened to her in this room, in front of *that* mirror, in his arms a few days ago?

Sitting at the captain's dining table, nibbling some dry biscuits, her first food in days, she forced herself to take stock and examine the possibilities with an unflinching discipline and an excruciating honesty that stripped her bare.

For the first time in her life, her body had not betrayed her—a fact that made just about everything that came before a lie, every sentiment a falsehood, and every calculation a blinding error. Whether she liked it or not, *and she didn't,* all her frailties were now exposed like a raw nerve—the dependence, the fear, and the denial.

As for the old duke, her mind cringed away from the memories. It was enough that she had lived with him and had been forced to share his bed for five endless years. She had fought and she had struggled, and now lived and worked with the scars to prove it. Horace Webb had once told her that she directed her rage and frustration into her art, transforming her work into a battleground of emotion and pent-up desires, a canvas for whom and what she really wanted to become. Dear Horace had been right.

The doors of her prison were slowly being pried open, offering her a glimpse of a freedom that she'd craved but never believed possible.

Passion at its best is an act of rebellion. . . .

Her breathing quickened at the thought. She wanted what Nicholas Ramsay could give her. To touch him, use him, like an opiate that opened up a world of horizons that had remained stubbornly closed to her. Not that she trusted the man. She tossed an uneaten biscuit back on her plate, biting her lower lip, the pain reminding her of an unpalatable reality. She considered the possibilities—that he was too closed, unreachable, made of stone, for God's sake, someone who would sacrifice his own pleasure, someone who didn't need her body . . .

He'd been aroused—make no mistake—dangerously, gloriously aroused. She could still feel the heft of his erection and the heat of his hands on her breasts, spanned against the whiteness of her skin. Such control. Such discipline. There was always a reason for everything and she knew better than anyone else that illusions were dangerous. Female bodies served as currency and, her instincts told her, like every other man, Ramsay would expect a handsome return.

A discreet knock interrupted her tortured thoughts. At her response, the cabin door opened revealing the steward, Mackenzie, whose face had become all too familiar to her over the past several days of dramatic weather.

"Anything I can do for you, madam," he asked with his pronounced Australian accent, and once in the cabin, moving efficiently to clear the table of her tea and biscuits. Small and lean, he might have been in his fifties, but he moved with the ease of a much younger man. "I trust that you're feeling better."

"Nothing at all. And, yes, thank you for your concern, I feel much better." She smiled for what must have been the first time in days. "You've been very kind, looking in on me, sir." She wondered distractedly if Ramsay had ever inquired about her well-being. Ridiculous, useless notion.

"You're most welcome, madam. And I would like to point out that as the weather has cleared somewhat, the captain has indicated it's permissible for you to move up on deck."

Either she had truly become accustomed to the rhythms of the ship or the climate had actually improved because she noticed that the floor under her feet moved with a smoother cadence. She left the table to look out of one of the cabin's portholes, hungry for a glimpse of the outdoors. An expanse of solid blue sky filled the glass. "Excuse me, Mackenzie," she asked, "but how far have we come since leaving London?"

A man of few, carefully chosen words, Mackenzie finished refilling a pitcher with fresh water before replying. "About two hundred nautical miles off Cape Verde Islands, madam."

"Will we be stopping to supply the ship?"

"I believe that's what the captain intends, to anchor at Porto Praya, on the island of Santiago."

Helena turned abruptly from the porthole to examine Mackenzie more closely. Clearly a valued retainer and perhaps more, he was, she sensed, loyal to Ramsay with an allegiance founded most probably on a long-term association forged decades earlier. Her thoughts returned to Conway House and the replica of that other ship, the *Scindian,* its squat and ugly outlines refusing to let her go.

"I haven't seen Mr. Ramsay in days," she said, looking for what exactly she didn't know. Her eyes swept the cabin absently, over the green brocade settee, built-in book shelves, and the gleam of a polished table.

"The captain's been very busy what with the squalls. He's spent most of his time with the men."

"I feel guilty having taken his cabin, and his table." And his bed, she thought wretchedly.

"He prefers taking his meals with the men as well, madam, so I wouldn't be worrying about it. And he takes his rest in the aft cabin."

She wondered how many men of Ramsay's means would allow themselves to consort with those consigned to the lower orders. "When did you first begin working for Mr. Ramsay, Mackenzie, if I might ask?"

He didn't look up from his task, replacing used water glasses with fresh ones from the walnut commode bolted to the portside of the cabin. "Many years ago, madam, many years ago." The answer was as vague as she'd anticipated.

"Please forgive me, but I placed your accent as Australian, so perhaps you and Mr. Ramsay met in your home country," she probed lightly.

His hands stilled and he looked up at her sharply, his chin jutting out with resolute obstinacy. "And what if we did, madam? The captain has lived many lives and my role in any of them has been minor."

She pulled her shawl from the settee and put it around her shoulders, the action a bid for more time. "I get that distinct impression—a man of many lives," she mused aloud for the steward's benefit. She sensed a defensiveness, or was it protectiveness, on his part. "But what of his family, his origins? To have amassed the wealth he is rumored to have—surely earlier in his life he must have enjoyed some advantages, beneficial connections and the like?"

"Perhaps you would ask the captain, madam." Mackenzie collected his tray, keeping his head down, and began making his way to the cabin door.

Helena stroked the fringes on her scarf. "And as though he would answer," she replied lightly.

Mackenzie feigned deafness at her remark. "Madam," he continued, edging out the door, "if there is nothing else?"

"Actually, there is," she said, gesturing to the glass-encased bookshelf. "May I help myself?"

"Absolutely, madam. The captain has emphasized that you have full access to anything in the cabin. And, as a matter of fact, I believe you will also find your drawing materials in the dressing room, where I also took the liberty of unpacking some of your things while you were indisposed."

Ramsay's reach was not only formidable but thorough. He'd managed in the space of twenty-four hours to ensnare her at Madame Congais's, enmesh her in the X Club's machinations, and get her aboard his ship—complete with her supplies and suitable wardrobe, culled, no doubt, from the duke's residence on Belgrave Square.

But about him, she still knew next to nothing. Other than that he released in her a potential for carnal pleasure that had ripped her wide open.

She glanced at the mirror that now seemed to dominate the cabin and looked away. Shivering, she drew the warmth of the shawl closer over her shoulders while Mackenzie left the cabin as discreetly as he'd entered.

Thirty minutes later, armed with sketchbook and charcoal, a book tucked under her arm, she leaned over the rail of the *Flying Cloud*, breathing in salt-tinged air. The cool wind and cresting waves blew at the lingering cobwebs crowding her thoughts.

No land in sight, only an endless color field of blues and grays. She played with the idea of returning to the cabin for paints and canvas, but the wind was coming up, making the prospect of drawing next to impossible. The rail of the ship came to her waist, and every few seconds the vessel heeled on a precarious angle, swells rolling into the hull, slicking the deck with water. She craned her neck and spied several men wrestling with the sails, their shouts to each other barely audible over the crashing waves.

But no sign of Ramsay.

She wondered who he was, this man who commanded fleets of ships and legions of banks flung far and wide in all corners of the globe. This man who would give up civilization to sail to the bottom of the earth to chase after what might as well be a unicorn.

Helena tucked herself under an overhang, momentarily away from the spray and the wind. Perching on a wooden bench, she opened *The Origin of Species*, which she had taken from the cabin's bookshelf. She scanned the pages quickly, looking for mention of the Cape Verde Islands.

The more she learned about the X Club undertaking, the better positioned she would be not only with regard to Ramsay but also when she returned to London to battle Sissinghurst. When the duke had died, she thought she'd at long last gained her freedom. How mistaken she'd been. Always ambitious, always striving, her late husband's nephew had assumed the role of her master with indecorous relish, relying on his fine command of subterfuge and the ways of power, hungry for gain at every turn and ensuring that he rose in social and ecclesiastical ranks with relentless appetite.

And, of course, as Horace had pointed out to her so many times in the past, with her inheritance at his disposal, almost nothing would be out of his grasp.

The prevailing winds were picking up, scattering pages of the book held on her lap. She looked up momentarily, scanning the deck, feeling ill at ease, as though someone had invaded her privacy. Once convinced no one was watching her, she dragged toward her a small barrel holding the remnants of rainwater. Propping up her feet to get more comfortable and stay out of the gusts, she continued reading, flattening the pages.

Absolutely, she thought a few moments later, glancing uneasily over her shoulder searching for what wasn't there,

Darwin's hypotheses could be disturbing to those in positions of ecclesiastical and political power. Including, and perhaps foremost, the Bishop of Sissinghurst. To allow that the universe, with its planets and stars, its animals and its creatures, was governed by immutable, scientific laws that bore no relation to a special, godly act was radical and even revolutionary in its implications.

And this revolution had begun with the most minute, seemingly irrelevant observations. Darwin had made detailed observations of a type of cuttlefish that populated the tide pools around Santiago, fascinated by their seemingly miraculous ability to change colors. He'd written with much excitement to Reverend Henslow about his discovery of a strange animal that could change colors at will.

She raised her eyes from the book, for a moment scanning the limitless horizon that swayed rhythmically before her. Nature was ruthless, she'd always suspected, a dispassionate, coldly rational mistress who made no promises and brooked no claims.

Water from beneath her feet had frothed the hem of her cloak, the sea closing in even on the proud *Flying Cloud*. From the corner of her eye, she saw a young sailor, brass buttons gleaming, balancing perilously on the gunnels of the ship, intent on what, precisely, she didn't know.

She rose, leaning against the ship's rail that divided wood from the churning water below.

The boy—and he couldn't have been much more than fifteen or sixteen—reached for several tangled ropes over the side, the set of his small chin unyielding. The large coils of hemp disappeared up into the billowing sails of the clipper.

Her shoes were now thoroughly soaked, slippery on the planked deck sluiced with saltwater. Again she sensed a pair of eyes drilling her back, but when she glanced over her shoulder, there was nothing to see but tangled rigging, ship, and sky.

The boy stretched, the rope a hairsbreadth away from reddened fingers. The ship tilted, a downwind sleigh ride, with rollers heaving up the stern and shooting her forward until the horizon momentarily disappeared.

The railing punched hard against her ribs. Before she could take a breath, the next swell heaved the boy into view once more, before dipping her back into the dark blue trough.

Her last rational thought was, *How many fathoms deep?* The ship rocked again, but this time as the horizon locked into view, the boy was gone.

A scream caught in her throat, choking her. Her cries ripped from somewhere deep in her belly warred with the wind and waves, and the monotonous creaking of the ship's timbers. She looked desperately for something to throw into the sea, *something, anything*, for the boy to hang on to. Slipping and sliding, she grabbed the small barrel behind her and hefted it onto the rail. Twenty feet below the froth of the sea, like liquid lace, danced mockingly beyond her reach.

With fingernails digging into the wet wood, she pushed, throwing the entirety of her weight behind the effort. Ribs aching, she climbed midway up the rail, skirts flapping damply in the wind, to give the final thrust.

The horizon tilted on its side and, for a nauseating moment, all she knew was a heavy pressure on the small of her back and the cold embrace of the ocean flying toward her. Her balance taken from under her, she sailed helplessly through the air. A drumming in her ears, the weight excruciating, and then the cut of the water, like hundreds of shards of glass, breaking her body.

She couldn't see, couldn't breathe, her arms flailing as the grip of the ocean claimed her, lost in a roar of silence. For a moment, she struggled to loosen its hold, to rise to the light above the enveloping darkness around her before her lungs burst. Brine burned her throat, and her heavy skirts clung to her legs like a funereal winding sheet.

Then a body beside hers grabbed her arms, shaking to get

her attention away from the terrifying void of bottomless water. Frozen with panic, she blinked several times, surprised that she could see anything at all. Dark green swirled around her and all she could make out were intense gray eyes, for once expressive, talking to her in blurred fragments of time.

Nicholas Ramsay slid arms around her waist, reading her expression, looking for signs that her terror was under control. They began to float, swim, Helena stiff as a board clutching the shoulder at her side. Emerald kelp swayed beneath them as though buffeted by a gentle ocean breeze and, if she looked up, she pretended to herself that she could see daylight break the top surface of the gloom.

Where was the boy? Her lungs seized.

Ramsay kicked powerfully and they ascended a few feet as a dark shadow appeared in the water above them. He slipped under her and pushed her toward the surface and the outlines of a small boat, his body as solid and unshakable as a dam.

Helena twisted wildly, churning the water, a heavy blanket of disorientation beginning to take over, a profound cold seeping into her limbs. The ocean floor beckoned, while hands grabbed her arms, pushing her through the liquid ceiling above her.

She took a huge, shuddering breath, hauling sweet, cold air into her blazing lungs. Blue sky replaced the gloom of the ocean, but with her hair plastered to her face and over her eyes she could barely make out hands grasping toward her.

Then she felt it, a hold around her ankles pulling her back into the water. Well beyond shock, she jerked frantically, grabbing and kicking like a frightened child. A sudden exhalation of breath and bubbles danced over her head, startling her. Lashing out at the hands grasping at her legs, her eyes stung and strained to see through the saltwater murk.

Then she saw them, Ramsay and another man, struggling. The stranger held a gleaming object like lost treasure in the gloom. Ignoring the compounding pressure in her lungs, she tried to swim toward them despite the anchor of her heavy skirts. They thrashed in the water like eels, Ramsay the taller of the two, as they drifted down together in a slow, macabre dance, into the kelp.

Helena kicked the water, lungs on fire, frantically mimicking the moves she'd watched Ramsay make moments before, going against her instincts toward the two grappling men. Ramsay slashed his elbow into his assailant's shoulder and punched a fist at his throat.

Her consciousness was beginning to flicker and she wondered whether she was finally running out of air. Her mind skittered—how long could Ramsay last? She thrust down toward the blurred images, and toward the taller, leaner man.

Too little, too late. He was weakening, his head sinking to his chest, losing awareness. His assailant was feeling confident, peering into the taller man's face, ready to leave him for dead.

In horror, she watched Ramsay's body go slack, the head bob, the precious bubbles of air subside.

Then the assailant turned toward her, an underwater creature prepared to devour her next. The drumming in her head was deafening, the pressure threatening to puncture her ears. She watched the attacker's head break the surface of the water momentarily as he rearmed himself for the encounter to come.

A quick jerk of his limbs and he was at her side. She reared back her numb legs and kicked hard against him, against the water, against her sodden skirts. Ramming her right elbow back, she thought he grunted in pain. She had connected with his chest, muscular and resistant, but the damage was slight. She was no match for either his experience or his strength but could only grab hold of his neck, digging her nails into the spiny bones of his throat. From someplace deep inside, waves of anger replaced terror, fueling an intense pleasure as his windpipe gave way like rotting flesh beneath her hand.

She saw the air bubbles behind his head before she saw anything else.

Ramsay rose behind the assailant like an apparition, spinning him around, then embedding the knife in his back with a definitive twist. Dark spots obscured her vision and she thought she saw the assailant reach for the knife at his belt. Without thinking, she grabbed the weapon from behind and twisted it from his grasp.

Blood poured from the gaping slash between his shoulder blades, discoloring the dark water in curls of wine-colored clouds.

It didn't take long.

The attacker convulsed like a windup tin soldier, his arms windmilling uselessly, then finally slackening and spinning in a gruesome ballet before descending into swaying strands of kelp.

Chapter 13

"**B**y Jesus, when are we going to get a decent wager around here?"

Not that heavy gaming was unusual at White's Club on St. James's Street. Sitting in the famous Bow Window where Beau Brummel had held audiences decades earlier, Horace Webb, uncharacteristically into his cups, endeavored to hold court.

Word was that the last thing Webb could afford was to lose a healthy bet. Membership in the club was limited to 300 members, each with sufficient financial padding to pen his entries into the Betting Book—one of the most recent and outrageous of which hazarded whether a man could survive a thousand hours underwater.

John Tyndall eyed Webb derisively. "You're looking rather worse for wear, old man, probably not the time to go searching for opportunities to increase the stakes, would be my guess."

The men had been schoolmates at Eton, and both knew that it was considered the height of bad taste to make mention of financial contretemps. Many a gentleman had kept up appearances without keeping up his payments to his tailor or his mistress's jeweler. Unlike the city's merchants who were becoming as wealthy as Eastern potentates, the landed gentry was facing particular challenges keeping pace and keeping face.

Tyndall dropped into a chair opposite Webb. "Is it the beauteous Perdita giving you reason to drink, not that a gentleman requires one. And if she is"—Tyndall drew himself up in his seat—"I would be more than pleased to offer my services."

Webb took another deep draught of his port. How he had labored over Perdita last night and this morning. To no avail, his manhood as limp as his pocketbook and as futile as his artistic ambitions. He couldn't paint, he couldn't ease his balls, and worse yet, his lawyers had contacted him yet again about his overdrawn accounts all over London.

His brown eyes clouded over. "Don't count me out yet, Tyndall," he said, marshalling a semblance of bravado. He straightened his waistcoat. "Positively detest dashing your hopes, but my affairs are perfectly in order, and Perdita has not given me my *congé*. And I doubt she ever will."

Tyndall bowed his head in mock acknowledgment. "Pleased to hear it, Webb, and of course, your artistic pursuits are proceeding swimmingly. How nice that you are able to find time and temperament to *dabble* in the fine arts."

Bollocks, the man was referring to his recent exhibition at Sass's Academy on Charlotte Street. The domestic subject matter, and its painterly execution, had been received with all the enthusiasm of a group of nuns at a bordello.

He shifted uncomfortably in the oversized chair. At the very least, his ambition had been to seek recognition as a fine academician, or at best, to inherit the mantle of Sir David Wilkie and his royal and aristocratic commissions.

Well, Tyndall had his own disappointments to savor. Although his former schoolmate had been born into a family whose lineage could be traced back to Hastings, his own dabbling in the sciences had been rewarded with sneers and guffaws from his own set.

"Heard about your recent publication—what was it concerning again?" Webb asked with an air of distraction. "The petrified sea urchin?"

Tyndall, choosing not to acknowledge the sarcasm, nodded importantly. "You see, Webb, I am attempting to reinforce the Linnaean Scala Naturae, the ladder of nature, whose great keystone is essential to the divinity of life, which posits that a new species cannot enter the world." Hence, Tyndall's and his fellow naturalists' obsession with the Aristotelian bent for classifying and naming.

Some of the alcohol was burning off in Webb's brain. "That would be nice, wouldn't it, Tyndall, our lofty positions in this world permanently fixed. However, isn't that counter to what Mr. Darwin has hypothesized, that it is futile to stabilize and fix what is, in reality, an unremitting flux?"

"Pure speculation. Not provable."

"Is that so? I shouldn't have thought," Webb said slyly. "I have heard it *speculated,* as a matter of fact, that right at this moment, a ship is speeding toward the Horn with the express objective of proving some of Mr. Darwin's *speculations* correct."

Tyndall replied with a stiffening spine of his own. "So you do look up from your paint box occasionally, Webb."

Indeed, he did, now more than ever, because much depended on the fortunes of the *Flying Cloud* and her passengers. "Any word on the project's progress?"

"No, and I for one don't expect any progress, even if they do return with the hold filled with fossils and the like."

"Return?" Webb looked doubtful, setting aside his port. "We're speaking of the Antarctic Peninsula, one of the roughest and most fearsome of the ocean's depths. Cyclonic lows of near-hurricane strength travel through the passage roughly every three weeks. Then there's the icebergs and pack ice. Ships are often blown north onto the Cape Horn reefs, destroying their sails and masts." He paused. "Not to mention mutinous shipmen."

Tyndall eyed him thoughtfully. "You seem incredibly well informed. And not hopeful at all," he paused significantly, "almost as though you have a personal stake in the matter."

Webb sniffed, running a hand through his thinning hair. "Not at all. Only that I'd heard there's a wager brewing as to whether the great and mysterious Nicholas Ramsay can pull it off. That's the wager I was alluding to when you interrupted my reveries, Tyndall."

"Just because a man can import opium through the Strait of Hormuz, doesn't mean he can navigate the Drake Passage, my man."

"Opium. Is that what you heard?" He played with a button on his vest. "I heard human cargo."

Tyndall shrugged with the insouciance of a man whose mind was anchored on higher ground. "Earning money is always a dirty business, no matter what the source, so I don't care to make distinctions, as I've explained to the X Club just over a fortnight ago."

And he could afford to, the bastard, thought Webb. With not much left to lose and his life depending on the course of the *Flying Cloud*, he decided to play the man and not his hand. He was betting *against* Nicholas Ramsay who had just two months earlier been seen leaving the Royal Exchequer's office amid reports that he'd left Gladstone's right-hand man virtually in tears.

Webb had little remaining to lose, his coffers empty, his artistic endeavors languishing. Not for him the boring but reliable life of the country squire, boxed in by convention and a miserly pension.

He would risk all. Even Helena Hartford.

He motioned the nearest steward to fetch the Betting Book.

"Care to make it somewhat more interesting, Tyndall?" he asked.

Delicately, the Bishop of London held a handkerchief to his face. The factory odor was particularly noisome today, almost, but not quite, overwhelming the cacophony of clanking machinery.

A little girl of about seven, a few feet away, frantically collected flying fragments of cotton from the floor while hissing machinery passed over her. Her head, body, and outstretched limbs carefully hewed to the floor, only a slight trembling and wide, darting eyes revealing her terror that she could be swept into its gaping maw.

Samuel Greg, the owner of the Quarry Bank Mill, followed the bishop's gaze. "I must disagree with the latest findings of the Factory Commissioners"—he said, bending forward and speaking loudly over the din, a bespectacled man of middle age in a finely tailored, double-breasted coat with fashionably wide lapels—"who have reported the scavengers to be constantly in a state of grief, always in terror, and every moment they have to live stretched upon the floor in a state of perspiration."

Sissinghurst nodded approvingly as the two men continued their measured walk toward the offices at the back of the building. "Idle hands—we know what these children need," the bishop said briskly. "As a matter of fact, in the short time I've spent here this morning, I've observed scavengers idle for four minutes at a time, and certainly I can't say they display any of the symptoms of the condition described in the Report of the Factory Committee."

Neither man offered to bring up the subject of the five-year-old boy whose flaxen locks had been rudely torn from his head earlier in the day.

The shortage of labor was distressing, and one of the solutions that the bishop himself had proposed to the poorhouses was to have factory owners purchase children from orphanages and workhouses. The children became known as pauper apprentices, signing contracts that virtually made them the property of the factory owner and a cog in the wheel of continuous production.

"I have eight children coming from Islington on Tuesday next and eight or ten more on Thursday," continued Greg, smoothly changing places with the bishop to ensure he was on the inside of the corridor and a safer distance away from the gigantic looms. "I had my choice from upward of fifty boys of different ages, all from very well conducted workhouses." He would be paid five pounds for each child taken and receive another five after the child's first year, thereby binding the children to the mill until the age of twenty-one.

"I'm sure it only takes the children a while to become accustomed to the whirling motion and noise of the machinery."

"Quite right, quite right, Your Grace."

"And so much kinder, after all, than sending them abroad to Van Diemen's Land, as was the custom in the recent past." And so much more profitable, the bishop knew as well.

Greg respectfully placed a hand on Sissinghurst's elbow, ushering him into his offices. "Indeed, yes, the colonies will have to wait when Britain herself is suffering from such labor shortages, although I must conclude that the convict ships still do a mighty trade, due to the low morals of the lower classes."

"The Church does its best, all the more reason for my presence today," intoned Sissinghurst, lowering his bulk into a chair across from a desk. "When Deacon Mosley comes to collect me, please show him in, would you, Greg?"

"Of course, of course, Your Grace."

"And by the way, those papers I asked you to draw up."

A shadow darkened Greg's brow. "I do have the way bills . . . however," he hesitated, "not that I'm questioning your reasons for doing this, sir, not at all, but there is enormous risk involving this particular man, as I'm sure you recognize. How prudent is it—"

The bishop arched a brow, his smile displaying his large teeth. "And why should any of this be of concern to you?"

Greg placed a hand where his heart would be under the fine fabric of his expensive waistcoat. "No concern for myself, at all. Not at all." He seemed shocked by the suggestion. "I am merely concerned for *your* well-being, Your Grace."

"I can and shall manage whatever comes my way, God willing," he responded, supremely irritated, dismissing Greg with finality. "Have the documentation delivered to my offices as soon as possible." The mere specter of Nicholas Ramsay transformed everyone into a trembling mass of unease, as though he were the prince of darkness himself.

Before Greg could back out the office door, Sissinghurst spied Mosley, his cherubic countenance flushed, in the corridor, the black fabric of his cassock swaying in time with his hurried movements.

"My apologies for my tardiness." He nodded to Greg, watching the factory owner take his leave before turning to the bishop. "I was delayed, but your conveyance waits outside, Your Grace."

"Shut the door, Deacon, we can talk here as Lord only knows no one can hear us over that ghastly din."

Mosley looked momentarily perplexed but turned to shut the door immediately, remaining standing. "I had thought you needed to return to the Church for services, Your Grace—"

The bishop cut him off sharply. "I can be late. This is much more important. I want to know why the *Flying Cloud* has not returned to Portsmouth, Deacon."

The younger man stiffened, pleating the fine cashmere of his cassock between nervous fingers. "I don't know what could have gone amiss exactly, as they should have had to turn around by now."

Sissinghurst waved a hand dismissively, silencing him. "It was your plan, this arsenic business." His voice brimmed with disgust. "All you had to do, after you *twice* lost my aunt, was to ensure that Ramsay and his *Flying Cloud* never left English waters."

Mosley was holding his cassock in a death grip. The only thing he had left was the truth, but it was a truth he didn't want to give up. "I believed that the arsenic lacing their supplies . . ." he started ineffectually.

The bishop blinked several times as if unable to understand. "I don't want more details, I want results," he said slowly. "And up until this point you have disappointed me immeasurably. Your time reflecting in the Temple Church crypt has done you not a whit of good. Now what am I to do with you?"

A queasy feeling slid through the younger man. "It may not be too late," he said.

"It's been too long already," the bishop said, brooking no argument. Thankfully, he had taken this Nicholas Ramsay business into his own hands. "All we can do now is hope that Ramsay keeps her alive and returns her to London. At which point"—he paused, raising his voice only slightly but it might as well have been a canon's roar—"we have two objectives. Firstly, to incarcerate Helena Hartford in Bedlam immediately, and secondly, to confiscate any evidence that the X Club could possibly use against us. Have I made myself clear?"

Mosley's face was pale with a thin sheen of sweat. He fumbled in his cassock for a handkerchief, mopping his brow. He had the look of a condemned man, a fact that didn't impress the bishop. "There's something else you're not telling me, obviously." He bit off each word like a piece of his tongue.

The younger man folded the handkerchief neatly, as though his life depended on it, before replying. "You see, Your Grace, I've come across some information about Nicholas Ramsay and his relationship with Lady Hartford." He shifted his slight weight from one foot to the other. "Something that probably doesn't bode well for our cause."

The bishop stood slowly, preparing himself for the coming blow. His small eyes beetled, lost somewhere between his jowls and forehead.

"If I understand things correctly," Mosley continued, his voice impressively stoic, "if I understand the history between the two of them, then Nicholas Ramsay wants . . ."

"Wants what?" Fury oozed from the bishop's pores and he took a lumbering step closer to the deacon.

"He wants revenge." Mosley articulated each syllable distinctly. He stared hard at the handkerchief in his hand. "And he most probably wants her dead."

Chapter 14

"Did they find the boy? Is he recovered?"

Helena stalked the cabin, dry clothes and a cup of tea laced with brandy gradually chasing away a bone-deep chill. Remnants of brine still soured the back of her throat.

"He's fine." The voice was low. She struggled to bring the room and Ramsay into focus.

He'd saved her life.

And killed a man in the process.

His short hair, still wet from the unexpected encounter with the ocean, was combed straight back from his face. He leaned against the captain's table, laden with steaming dishes, but despite the relaxed pose, she could see the cold tundra in his eyes.

She remembered the bodies—his handiwork—at her atelier. The glint of the knife in the ocean, the curls of dark, red blood. What kind of man was he? Since that night at Madame Congais's she'd never been more in danger, and with Nicholas Ramsay always close behind. It never paid to believe in coincidence, in happenstance, in fate, and she wasn't about to begin now. The fact that she exploded like a flare in the dark when he touched her, that she wanted him . . .

Good Lord, she swept a hand through her still-drying mass of hair. She couldn't even articulate what she wanted from him, although her body all but screamed for release when he was near. Her pulse accelerated, mocking her with its erratic rhythm. This was simply another complication she didn't need.

She threw him a look of undisguised hostility before continuing her pacing. "A boy like that is far too young to be working on a ship."

He crossed his arms over his chest, his tall, powerful body clothed in wool-twill trousers and an open-necked white shirt. "Boys far younger than he are employed both in the merchant marines and the navy in England. Besides, it is no business of yours how I run my ships."

"Of course not," she continued, concentrating on righteous annoyance rather than on the elephant in the room. "The great Nicholas Ramsay does whatever he wishes." She stopped in her tracks and glowered only to be met by silence. The steam from the soup tureen on the dining room table scented the air, doing absolutely nothing to allay the faint outlines of alarm gripping her. After what seemed like several minutes, Ramsay's mouth curved into an empty smile, which had the peculiar effect of sending shivers up her spine.

"What I would concern myself with, Helena, is how an assailant came to be aboard one of my ships," he said with soft menace. "And for the record, the young boy was on the *Flying Cloud* as an exception and a favor to an old friend of mine. As a rule, I don't employ children."

"Really?" She raised her eyebrows. "And how else does one become wealthy seemingly overnight than on the backs of the disenfranchised?"

He shot her an unfathomable look. "I find it curious that you're so eager to discover my *pedigree* while I'd wager a guess you have no idea how your own family came into its own fortunes. Or even care."

The image of her father flashed into her mind.

Brandishing the key to her room. Locking her away for weeks, vanquishing her paintbrushes and canvas, along with her freedom.

His face smug, marching her down the aisle, toward her soon-to-be husband with the lofty title. And berating her, at one of his few visits to Belgrave Square, for not yet producing an heir.

Saying good-bye to him on his deathbed had scarcely been difficult. And now, right here in the middle of the Atlantic, she couldn't conjure his exact features if she tried. And he was the last man, next to her late husband, that she wanted to talk about.

When she didn't answer, Ramsay pulled out a chair from the table. "Judging by the silence, I sense I've hit yet another nerve. Although I'm hardly surprised that you don't know how you came to live such a cossetted, indulged existence. Yes, don't look so alarmed at the mention of filthy lucre, horrifying though that might seem to someone of your rarefied sensibilities, shielded and protected from life's harsher realities." He gestured to the chair. "Now come and eat."

Something caught her attention—and it wasn't the offer of food. He returned her inquiring gaze with a look of such complete dispassion that she wondered if she'd misheard his words. It was the second time in their brief association that he had mentioned her father and her family. Curious. And possibly ominous because Nicholas Ramsay didn't do anything by chance. There was definitely something beneath that cool neutrality, that concentrated detachment, that strategic manipulation of her repressed desires.

Helena stopped pacing.

He hated her.

The thought struck her with the force of a rogue wave, followed by an undertow of confusion worse than what she'd experienced nearly drowning in the ocean just a few hours ago. She watched his lean, deft hands lift the lid from the soup tureen to begin ladling the broth into the broad white bowls. Crisp white napkins and heavy crystal goblets shimmered before her eyes.

"I'm not hungry," she said, meaning it, her mind working

quickly. He hadn't simply tracked her down at Madame Congais's after seeing her work in Paris, not that she'd ever allowed herself to believe that claim. Instead, he'd come looking for her with the single-minded determination born of something sinister, beyond anything the X Club had envisaged.

She watched him watch her carefully. With those empty eyes, he was like a predator waiting for any sign of weakness. There was a dangerous stillness about him, a power he controlled with ruthless discipline, allowing him to dispense lethal violence or cool dispassion, even in the throes of sexual mayhem. Almost as though the moments she'd spent in his arms, exploding with pleasure, had never happened except in her feverish imaginings.

Of course it had happened—for a purpose. His purpose. Which was what exactly? Lingering deep in her mind like an iceberg was the prospect that he was still somehow connected with Sissinghurst. She couldn't rule out an association. An elemental awareness of him heightened her anger and now fused with a large dose of fear.

"I need to move, to walk right now. Eating is the last thing on my mind," she said, abruptly stopping in front of the bookshelf for something to occupy her hands, quickly surveying the titles with their gold-embossed spines. She felt exposed, stripped of her usual protective layers that had kept her safe but imprisoned at the same time. Her hand hovered over a copy of Ovid's *Amores*.

From over her shoulder, she saw him advancing toward her with his casual, loose-limbed grace. "You're angry," he said, the non sequitur startling.

Not sparing him a glance, she took the book from the shelf and pretended to examine it closely. "I have every reason to be."

"Does it have to do with your nearly being killed earlier today or something else?"

They both knew to what he was referring, and it didn't concern drowning at the hands of an unknown assailant. She squeezed her eyes shut, clutching the book in her hands.

You have to know your own pleasure before you can give it.

Her skin flushed at the memory. She forced her eyes open to see him standing so close behind her that if she swayed so much as an inch—thank God, the seas had calmed—they would be touching. Which was the last thing her chaotic thoughts needed. "This is all very confusing," she said in what she hoped was a definitive voice, placing the book back on the shelf and forcing herself to turn around.

She looked up at him while her pulse thudded. They were so close their breaths mingled intimately and she could read absolutely nothing from his expression, not at all unusual, *damn him*. He looked down at her for a long, hard moment, supremely unmoved, yet intently, wholly, focused on her.

"Don't let it confuse you," he said simply, sounding not in the least like a lover but more like a man who was withholding something from her, something deep and dangerous, a rancor, or perhaps bitterness, that bordered close to hatred.

The words slipped from her mouth. "You don't like me, do you?"

For a moment, she thought she might get a reaction. A darkening of his eyes, his jaws clenching, the lips thinning in response. But no. He merely shrugged. "Sex for its own sake, at least in my experience, has little to do with *liking*. It is a skill like anything else, something to be honed and finessed. I trust that's what you've learned from our carnal encounters, Helena, and I meant what I said before—take what you can from it, you've nothing to lose."

If only she could sound as totally void of emotion and ruthlessly ignore the velvet sweep of sensation traveling up and down her body at the memory of those hands on her breasts, that mouth on the sensitive flesh of her neck. She could only imagine what it would feel like to have him touch her more intimately, to have all that controlled power inside her.

The inclination was totally foreign to her experience. Her husband and her lovers had professed technique, finesse, skill—only to leave her feeling humiliated, wretched, and alone. But when it came to Nicholas Ramsay, her body fervently begged to differ.

"Lose? Of course I have nothing to lose," she said, breath as unsteady as her legs, "as long as I keep my focus on ridding myself of Sissinghurst." She shifted under his close scrutiny, her mind working even faster. "So don't expect me to get all missish about all this. You've offered your services and, quite obviously, I've accepted." She swallowed hard. "Although I want to make clear that I still find your motives in all of this far from transparent. In short—I don't trust you. And I still don't think you like me."

"I'm not surprised." He took another move toward her with that silent tread of his. She licked her dry lips as he first placed one arm and then another against the bookcase, effectively caging her. "You're an intelligent woman," he continued, his wide chest blocking her view of the cabin, "who knows that there are a lot of people out there after her. But just remember one thing"—he leaned in closer, his thick, short lashes hooding his eyes—"that I'm not one of them."

It was no use. She couldn't control the effect that his physical proximity had on her body. Her pulse fluttered, her skin radiated an unaccustomed heat, and she felt like overripened fruit ready for his delectation. And he hadn't so much as laid a hand upon her. He didn't have to. "I don't believe you," she croaked. "Too much has happened since I met you, so much of which makes no sense."

He trapped her gaze, but his eyes were still cold and gray. "You know all you need, Helena. I'm here to help you. We're here to help each other."

His voice was mesmerizing, as momentarily persuasive as the gentle rock of the ship, and yet some part of her conscious thought broke through, warning her again that his detachment masked something far different, something dangerous. And *still* all she wanted to do was stroke that clean sweep of jaw, feel the lines of bone and muscle beneath her palms and fingertips. Desire unfurled deep in her stomach.

"I think I should eat something now," she improvised, backing away from him until the bookcase ground into her shoulder blades. He smiled congenially, lifting the corners of his mouth as though by rote, and she wasn't convinced in the least. Like a wolf playing with his prey, he pretended to let her go, dropping his arms harmlessly to his sides. She slid away from him toward the table.

The bowls filled with soup were still steaming, yet all she felt was a faint nausea at the thought of food. Her appetite hadn't been right since she'd started the voyage, perhaps a combination of bad weather and the strain of knowing that not the choicest of fates awaited her. Bending over to pull a napkin on her lap, she felt Ramsay's hand on her shoulder. The second he touched her, her body remembered the flex and play of his muscles beneath her touch, the painful craving he ignited, and the tidal wave of pleasure he unleashed.

She made a monumental effort to glance up at him. "You're not intending to join me?"

He remained standing, so close she could detect the faint starch of his clothes and that unidentifiable scent that was his alone. "I ate something earlier in the mess, but please go ahead."

Mercifully, he chose a chair opposite hers, and she thanked the gods under her breath for the physical space separating them. "I'm not really hungry," she said, playing with a spoon.

"Try," he responded, "and I'll make things easier for you by changing the subject to something that requires our more immediate attention." He leaned forward, his eyes intent. "While you're eating, you can tell me more about what happened out there and whether you recognized your assailant."

The spoon wasn't even at her mouth and she nearly choked on her soup. "My assailant? He's on your ship so shouldn't *you* know who he is . . . was?"

He poured her a glass of wine and pushed it toward her to drink. It wasn't a request, it was a demand. "Never saw him before in my life. And believe me, I caught a good look at the man up close. All I can presume at this point is that, some-how, he managed to stow away below."

Up close? He'd only stabbed him in the chest and back, which was certainly enough time to examine and memorize his features. As well as watch him die. Her hands shook as she reached for the wine. Taking a sip, she noted it was as bitter as the soup. Not unlike her life, actually, she thought grimly. Even on the *Flying Cloud,* thousands of miles away from England, her world was closing in on her.

"You should have known when you enlisted my aid—un-willingly need I remind you—that I would bring with me enough ballast to sink this ship," she said bluntly. She took several more mouthfuls of the soup. "Which puts me in your debt," she continued reluctantly, taking a few more mouth-fuls and watching the gold filagree at the bottom of the porcelain bowl appear.

He inclined his head slightly toward her, the late-afternoon light threading through the thickness of his hair. "For what?"

"Coming to my rescue, yet again." Her words were as dry as the desert. That was the problem, Nicholas Ramsay was hardly her salvation, and somehow she suspected that they both knew it. Every step she took with him was bracketed by danger that was becoming harder to define. At one point, the threat had simply consisted of her work and Sissinghurst, yet now she wasn't so sure.

He folded his hands carefully on the table, large, elegant, and a dark contrast to the white linen. "Someone would ob-viously like to see you dead," he said smoothly, as though an-nouncing nothing more important than the next course.

She put down her spoon, her stomach rebelling. "That's

what I don't understand. I sensed someone watching me while I was reading on deck. That man who came after me, came after us," she amended quickly, "he was intent on killing."

His voice was grim. "Killing you."

She reached for the wine, her fingers nearly snapping the stem of her glass. "Which is something I don't understand."

"Sissinghurst is obviously not an admirer of yours. Nothing we don't already know."

Suddenly, she felt dizzy, a metallic taste drying her mouth. There was a carafe of water farther down the table, but an unexpected stabbing pain in her stomach prevented her from moving.

"It's more than that," she said through dry lips, unable to bear the sight of the soup or wine any longer. She leaned back in her chair and placed the napkin against her mouth. "Sissinghurst would lose everything if I were to die. His only hope to secure my inheritance is to see me committed to an asylum wherein as my legal guardian he can dispose of funds however he chooses." A vise around her chest tightened, the jabs in her stomach traveling north. Out of nowhere, a sheen of cold perspiration coated her spine.

Placing the napkin carefully on the table and taking a deep breath, she rose from her chair, eager to breathe in some fresh air. The cabin tilted more than she'd anticipated and she stumbled over to the porthole. The sky was darkening, leaving only a pink streak where the sun had been. She tried to focus on the horizon, to stop the twisting and turning in her stomach, to right the cabin, which was tipping precariously on its side.

She noticed somewhere outside herself that the groaning of the ship's timbers matched the groans coming from her lips.

Ramsay's hands were on her waist, holding her upright. Unwillingly, she sagged against him. "Tell me what's wrong, Helena." The voice held an urgency that she was unaccustomed to, but his image was blurring and ominous in the fading light of the window. His face came closer to hers, blotting out the cabin behind him.

Black clouds dotted her vision, a staccato of unrelenting pain matching the harsh sound of her erratic breath.

"I don't know," she slurred, doubling over in his arms.

Ramsay caught Helena just before she slumped to the floor. *What the hell had just happened?* Only moments before she'd been pacing the cabin, a virago of energy, every sense on the alert, challenging him at every turn. And now this.

Lifting her in his arms, he carried her to the bed. Her eyes were closed as he tilted her face up and felt for a pulse beneath her ear. The rhythm was inconsistent and her eyelids fluttered. She twitched, her legs jerking spasmodically, and then curled into a fetal position as if to protect herself from powerful blows to her midsection.

He stroked her cheek to check for fever, a strange hollow in the center of his chest. "Helena? Wake up, tell me what's wrong."

Responding to his touch, she opened her eyes, clouded and bewildered. Blinking slowly, she struggled to swallow several times. "What—" She licked her parched lips and stared up at him, confusion and pain turning her eyes a darker violet. "What did you do to me? . . . Why are you trying to kill me?"

It was then he saw the trickle of blood at the corner of her mouth. Before he could reply, she recoiled as though bitten, curling into a tighter ball, away from his touch.

He crouched by the bed helplessly, watching the terror grow in her eyes as she doubled over in pain. Her dark hair was already dampening with sweat and curling around her stark white face.

Jesus. He grabbed a clean linen napkin from the table before returning to her side. She jerked away as he attempted to blot the blood seeping from her mouth. "Tell me what hurts," he asked again, doing a quick survey of her body. She didn't answer but her throat convulsed, and just in time he quickly moved his hand to support her forehead and then rolled her over.

It seemed to take forever and all he could do was hold her as her stomach heaved and her shoulders shook until, finally, the spasms subsided. Rolling her gently back onto the bed, he fixed his gaze on her colorless face, her blue-tinged lips. Her breathing was ragged and her eyes closed. The hollow in his chest deepened, and another part of him, at a great distance, wondered at the sensation.

It had been many years since his life had been out of his control, and yet now his hands shook as he attempted to clean up the mess at the bedside, sparing only a short bark for Mackenzie, who came running into the cabin moments later.

"Help me with this, would you, Mac?" he snapped. He turned back to Helena and attempted to place her beneath the bed's covers. Her body trembled, not from the cold but something else, shudders that she couldn't control.

"Fuck." He ran his hands down the length of her, looking for a sign and symptom he could possibly interpret. Damn, he should have insisted on having a ship's surgeon on board, but time had not permitted engaging someone for the journey. "This couldn't be aftershock," he said distractedly to Mac, brushing the hair from her face with a hand that suddenly seemed huge and clumsy. "She seemed fully recovered from what happened earlier in the day."

The steward was efficiently mopping up, throwing a heap of clean linens on the floor by the bed. His eyes were worried when he said abruptly, "Looks like poisoning to me. There's blood amongst the contents of her stomach."

Poisoning? It was as though someone had just landed a punch to his gut. She looked vulnerable, defenseless, lying there. Her confused state, the clamminess of her skin, the violence of the spasms wracking her body. *Poison.*

Which meant they didn't have a lot of time to determine the cause or the origins. His heart rate began to escalate. "All

right, let's get on with it," he said, rising from the bedside
and meeting Mackenzie's doubtful gaze. The steward's expression held nothing but skepticism. "There's not much we
can do, Captain, save keep her comfortable and see if she can
weather this."

"Bloody hell, Mac, since when do I weather anything?"
He scraped a hand through his hair trying to ignore another
blast of dread coursing through him. "Get me pitchers of
warm sea water and charcoal, and I want it now."

For the next hour, Ramsay worked steadily to remove the
contents of Helena's stomach. Years ago, he remembered, a
ship's surgeon had administered gastric lavage to a group of
sailors who had inadvertently consumed a poisonous herb
they'd sampled on shore leave in Tasmania. Over half had succumbed to the treatment or the herb, they'd never know, but
a lucky few had survived.

It was her only chance.

He never asked himself once why he should care that she
could die, so conveniently and in so much distress. She was
feverish as he pulled off the blankets, stripping her pale and
bare, before covering her again with a clean sheet. Mackenzie
stood at a discreet distance, taking away the used buckets
and returning with pitchers of warm water.

"How can you tell it's working, Captain?" he asked once.

"We can't," was his terse reply. "We can only hope the
charcoal absorbs whatever it is she's ingested."

He reached over and took her limp hand, so translucent he
could see the blue veins in her wrists. Such a talented, competent hand, the fingers long and elegant, now curled life-
lessly in his own larger one. If there was one truth he had
shared with her, it was his admiration for her work. When
he'd stood alone in the gallery in Paris, before he'd even met
her, he'd been struck by the impact of her work. It was a
small canvas, he remembered, depicting two figures rendered
in unapologetically bold and powerful strokes. He learned

right then and there that the daughter of Robert Peacock Whitely, Lady Helena Hartford, was not only a reckless woman but also a brilliant artist.

Her moans ripped him from his thoughts. He gripped her hand harder, noticing that the convulsions had receded along with her consciousness. After her last bout with the bucket, she seemed to sink into a deep sleep, her eyes sunken and shadowed, her white lips parted to accommodate her shallow breaths. She appeared as though her life were seeping out of her along with the deadly toxin.

There was not much more that he could do. His jaw clenched as he released her hand and eased her toward the center of the bed, turning her head gently to ensure she could breathe freely.

He looked at the clock; it was past midnight and he was a tightly coiled spring. Glancing at the table, with its half-empty glass of wine and the soup tureen with its cold contents, he began to think coldly and calculatedly again.

"I want all of our supplies dumped overboard, Mac. Tell the first captain," he said abruptly. "And check to see if any of the men are experiencing similar symptoms." He stroked the sharp stubble covering his jaw before adding, "It's curious that you and I have been eating with the men and we've been spared. Which leads me to think that the seamen's rations are untainted."

"Will see to it, Captain, right away."

"And leave the table as it is." It was evidence, the last thing Helena had consumed before falling ill. As the door closed behind the steward, he examined the table and its contents more closely. Helena's symptoms had appeared within thirty minutes of exposure to the toxin, which told him the dose was anything but small. He lifted the soup bowl scraped clean to his nose and detected a faint metallic odor.

Good thing that they would be landing in Santiago within thirty-six hours, if they had the winds in their sails. They could find a doctor and totally reprovision the ship, this time under his eagle-eyed command.

Like a magnet, his gaze went back to the figure on the bed. Her breathing was more regular now, but she lay still, too still. He ground his teeth till they hurt, unaccountably angry, in a way he didn't care to examine at the moment. Rationalizing was what he did best, but in the heat of this particular battle, it was all too hellishly complicated.

Yes, he wanted her to suffer, the way he had suffered.

Yes, he wanted her to trust him, so he could betray her the way he'd been betrayed.

And, yes, he still intended to leave her behind the way he'd been left behind with nothing but his wits and his youth to rely upon.

Which was why she couldn't bloody well die. Not now.

He clenched his fists, aware that he was turning into a blithering idiot, the plans he'd nurtured for two decades going out the porthole window because of his illogical reactions to a beautiful woman who was not allowing herself to be the docile pawn he'd intended her to be.

His gaze riveted to the mirror over the settee. Her reflection gleamed in its depth, her breasts in his palms, the nipples taut with need, her hands at the juncture of her thighs. And her face at the moment of orgasm, head thrown back, her eyes heavy with pleasure . . .

He shoved his hands deep into his pockets. Right now he just wanted her, damn it, *needed* her, to survive, and in the meantime, he just hoped he knew what he was doing. The trap could snap closed just as quickly on him if he wasn't careful. Because a different kind of toxin was invading his body, slowly and insidiously, and he needed a cold, clear antidote . . . now.

He strode to the bookcase and quickly surveyed the volumes, his hand falling on Decker's *Toxicology.* He quickly thumbed through the pages until he found what he was looking for.

Arsenic.

Of course, the king of poisons. A way of settling old scores and an instrument for advancement courtesy of its lack of color, odor, or taste when mixed in food or drink. And how effective as a single large dose, which could provoke violent abdominal cramping, diarrhea, and vomiting, often followed by death from shock.

> *Initially the patient experiences a metallic taste in the mouth . . . along with dry mouth. This is abruptly followed by severe nausea, vomiting, colicky abdominal pain. If the dose of arsenic ingested is large, cold clammy extremities and convulsions are followed by shock.*

It was all he needed to know and he snapped the book closed.

For the first time in hours he became aware again of the movement of the ship, the customary sounds of the sea that were as familiar to him as his own breathing. And with it came a preternatural sense of calm, colder and more lethal than any rage could possibly be.

Damn, it felt right and it felt good to be back in his own skin.

Someone, something, had invaded his territory.

An assassin and now poison—*on one of his ships.*

Whoever was behind this, they would pay. And if Helena Hartford died . . .

He refused to finish the thought.

Chapter 15

For the next twenty-four hours, Helena hovered somewhere between purgatory and hell. She was back under
the ocean where everything undulated in a nauseating motion, sending waves of convulsions through her body. Images
of corpses swayed in the murky depths, the gloom unrelieved
except for the glitter of knives and the surging form of
Nicholas Ramsay.

Violent tremors wracked her flesh, and hands clutched at
her head and shoulders. She pulled away from the face of the
old duke, wearing his cruel smile pockmarked with small,
yellowed teeth. Then Sissinghurst, his beetled brow and thick-
set form, threatening, smothering.

Don't, she wanted to say, but nothing came out except
deep shudders that disappeared into the jagged edges of pain.
Pokers singed her skin, wielded by Mosley, who tried to strip
her of her clothing despite her whimpered protests. Then he
faded along with Sissinghurst and the duke, while she spi-
raled into a huge void, falling into nothingness.

Opening her eyes hurt. She wanted to cough but she couldn't
because a heavy stone sat on her chest. Hands ran over her
body, familiar hands, their strength and gentleness breaking
through her awareness.

"Helena, take a breath. Just one more. Now another." The

voice was calm and reassuring and as far away as the next continent. With heavy limbs, she reached out to touch the voice above her. She traced the sharpness of cheekbones, the high ridge of a nose, the subtle indentation of a strong jaw. And slowly the heavy stone on her chest eased, ounce by ounce, until she felt her lungs shudder and heave into life.

When she finally awoke, she thought she was alone.

Both her mind and her mouth felt as though they were filled with cotton, and she was so weak it hurt even to blink. But when she blinked again, it was to see Ramsay sitting in a chair by the bed as though he'd been planted there weeks earlier. At least two days worth of stubble shaded his face along with even darker shadows under his eyes and the sides of his mouth.

"You're finally awake." The words convinced her that he wasn't an apparition from the underworld. "How do you feel?" He leaned forward in the chair, wrinkles in his shirt and breeches prominent.

Worse than she'd ever had in her life.

She squeezed her eyes closed to shut him out, disturbing thoughts tumbling to her mind's surface. The last thing she could recall was eating soup, drinking wine, and then the stabs of pain piercing her abdomen and Nicholas Ramsay breaking her fall.

She opened her eyes. He was watching her carefully, like some kind of experiment that might interest the scientists of the X Club. "I think I need to have something to drink," she murmured, her voice no more than a whisper against the burning of her throat.

He poured water from a pitcher and sat on the edge of the bed. "Sip slowly," he said, holding the glass to her mouth.

She managed to wet her lips and felt a trickle of moisture dribble into her mouth. Overwhelmingly fatigued, she let her head fall against his chest. His body felt warm and hard against her trembling form, a bulwark against danger and the unknown. She knew she was lying to herself, but just this once she couldn't be strong and wanted simply to melt against him. "Tell me what happened," she said. "How long have you been here?"

He placed the glass by the side of the bed. "You were poisoned. Arsenic, I believe. And Mackenzie and I have spent the last day and night doing what we could." The words were matter-of-fact.

Doing what they could to prevent her from *dying*? She lifted her head weakly as memories of their earlier discussion swept over her. "More attempts at killing . . . Why? There's no logic here." A bolt of horror shot through her and she dropped her head into her hands. "Dear God, was anybody else hurt? That poor boy. The crew?"

Before he could answer, she raised her eyes to his, anxiety clear in her voice. "Are you all right? More precisely, *why* are you all right?"

She remembered he hadn't eaten, not with her at least. Confusion, dread, and suspicion must be written all over her face. Yet she couldn't suspect him, could she? He'd saved her from an assassin and, by all appearances, saved her from poisoning. She shoved a tangle of hair from her face, tired and confused and weak.

Ramsay gave her a hard look, eyes narrowed beneath the black slash of his brows. "I see you're still reluctant to give up your suspicions about me." He rose from the side of the bed, leaving her bereft in a tumble of sheets. "Even though the facts speak for themselves."

They should, but they didn't, at least not to her. And yet, she glanced up at him, this previously contained, controlled man looked as though he hadn't slept in a week out of concern for her well-being. Yet his words held a strange warning tone she couldn't ignore. "If this is your way of extracting gratitude . . ." she countered.

His voice was tight. "It's not your gratitude that I want, Helena." He peered at her sharply. "It's your trust."

Unease swept through her, followed by indignation and a gradual strength returning to her limbs. "How can you expect me to trust you, after all that's happened? And why is it so important to you?"

"Because we're not going to get through the next several weeks together if you continue to believe that I'm the one trying to kill you."

The words were stark and unequivocal. She sank back into the pillows, her eyes holding his. There was no logic, none to be found, in the events that had followed her like a ball and chain since her first meeting with Ramsay at Madame Congais's. And what lay ahead could only bring more of the same.

"I don't know what to think," she replied grimly. Here she was barely alive and locked away on a ship gobbling up the miles on its way to South America and with a man whose aims were as elusive as writing in the sand.

In a gesture that spoke volumes, he crossed his arms over his chest. "If I have to, I can outline the threats you'll be encountering over the next few weeks, ranging from severe weather conditions, harrowing seas, unfriendly natives to intractable terrain and an elusive quest. And need I even touch upon the unknown dangers that your friends the bishop and his acolytes may still have in store for you?" He paused significantly. "Seems that trusting me is your only option."

Her fingers clutched the linen sheet more tightly. She was tired, so very tired of having to wear a shield of armor to get through her life. "You're asking for the world, you know."

His austere features seemed to soften, and he crooked a small smile. "I tend to overweening ambition, if you haven't already noticed."

In the fading afternoon light, he seemed taller and leaner than she remembered, the skin drawn tightly across his prominent cheekbones, the deeply set eyes and strong nose. It struck her, inappropriately and inconveniently, that he was a beautiful man.

"And if you persist in believing that I'm somehow the villain of the piece," he said with a glint of humor, sensing her disposition, "there's no need to concern yourself over my hurt feelings, if that's what's worrying you." He added a broad smile, changing the mood in the room in an instant.

Perhaps it was her weakened state, but it was as though the sun had just broken through the clouds. *Lord,* he was devastating when he wanted to be, more powerful than the most toxic poison to her system.

Her illness had done something to her head. Now was the time to keep a hold on her emotions and her suddenly wayward desires, at least when it came to this man, because she still had no idea who he was and where his connection with her began.

"More water, please," she asked, biding for time to sort out her reeling thoughts. But this time when she took the glass from him, she avoided his touch. She managed to take several sips before she continued, not quite resisting the uncharacteristic urge to confide in him. "Trust has not been common currency in my life. Other than my dear friend and mentor, Horace Webb, I've learned from experience, most of it bitter, that it's wiser to go through life as a skeptic. Although you make a good case, Ramsay, or at least the facts do."

Behind the dark gray of his eyes, something flickered. He sat down on the chair and crossed one long, muscled leg, encased in brown suede breeches, over the other. "We seem to be getting somewhere here, at long last," he said, bestowing another smile.

Her head swam, from lightheadedness brought on by her condition or by his undiluted dynamism, she couldn't tell. "Well, you must forgive me, but there are some areas where I have great difficulty . . ." she tried explaining, pulling the sheet up to her chin, uncomfortably aware that only a thin piece of linen and a nightgown separated her from the man by the bed. *Difficulties.* Quite the understatement, although she sensed that he knew to what she referred. Yet after what they had done together, her face warmed at the images, it shouldn't really matter.

She soldiered on. "Had you wanted me dead, for whatever obscure reason," she continued with what she hoped was a logical tone, "you would have let me drown and you would certainly have taken the chance to let the arsenic do its work."

"And?" he asked with a raised brow. His hair was disheveled, as though he had run his hands through it several times.

"And you admire my work. And you've given me, through the X Club and this journey, an escape from and recourse against Sissinghurst." She finished the statement on a huff of breath, not quite believing the narrative herself.

His eyes narrowed, his voice dropping into a softer but deeper register. "We have a truce then." From the beginning, the timbre of his voice, with its graveled undertones, had taken her prisoner.

The statement provoked a tentative smile from her. "I suppose we do." She returned her fingers, nervously plucking the sheet pulled up to her neck. She resisted the urge to move her hand the scant inches across the bed to touch him.

His returning smile was as deep and confidential as his touch might have been. Gone was the detachment, the disciplined dispassion of their previous association, and she wondered how she could have ever thought him cold.

Anything but cold.

He lounged gracefully, relaxed now, placing his hands behind his head. "And I have the perfect way to celebrate. Once we get to Cape Verde."

"Celebrate," she echoed.

"Your complete recovery and our détente."

His tone was playful, but his eyes, she would remember weeks later with piercing regret, were dangerously resolute.

Although he didn't visit the cabin over the next day, Helena was as nervous as a schoolgirl. Quickly regaining her strength on a sailor's rations, she spent her time reading, re-covering, and worrying.

Her presence had placed the entire ship in jeopardy. Un-forgivable. Her father had always told her she'd been born under a black cloud, trailing chaos and drama in her wake.

To ensure the safety of his men, Ramsay had jettisoned most of the supplies, keeping only basic biscuits and beef jerky, which he'd randomly sampled himself to ensure its harmless-ness. He was an unusual man, she was quickly learning.

Gathering up her cloak, she wondered for the tenth time who would try to kill her and why. She tied the toggles at her throat more tightly than necessary, her frustration growing as she wrestled with the specter of the Bishop of London and his Machiavellian machinations. He needed her alive, preferably certifiably insane and stowed away in Bedlam, at which point he would legally assume control of her fortune.

She was no good to him dead.

The ship tilted and turned into the wind, signaling that land was not far off. She wanted to catch a glimpse of Cape Verde on the horizon, her hunger to see terra firma almost as acute as her desire to see Nicholas Ramsay again.

She got her wish on deck.

With salt spray stinging her cheeks, she watched the faint traces of land slip over the horizon into her field of vision. Every hand seemed to be aloft to hasten the *Flying Cloud*'s race toward Santiago, every inch of canvas unfurled. She tried to stay out of the way, the shouted commands ringing in her ears like a foreign language. Looking up to the rigging above still made her dizzy, but her eyes locked on a dark-haired man, his breeches and shirt hugging his body in the high winds, scrambling over the bow rigging as he climbed the swinging ropes.

It was all she needed. Her breath stuck in her throat and she clung to a post mounted on the ship for fastening ropes. She recognized immediately the familiar athletic movements, the seamlessly coordinated muscle, sinew, and bone as Ramsay effortlessly ascended the rigging, his eyes squinting against the sun. If she had to, and she wanted to, she could draw the powerful arms and long, muscled legs blind, the broad shoulders that led to a narrow waist and hips that now straddled the rigging with unconscious grace. He was suspended in a canvas of empty sea and sky, an image that would be forever frozen in her mind's eye no matter what happened or how long she lived.

She didn't stop to analyze her stunning response to the man. While she wouldn't precisely trust him, she would simply take what he could give her with a ravenous appetite to make up for all the years of deprivation. Here was an opportunity for her to overcome her fears, to release the demons that for so long had kept her shackled better than any straitjacket ever could.

When they returned to England, reality would rear its ugly head soon enough, but she wouldn't think about that now. She didn't want to.

She knew the territory she was moving toward was dangerous, more perilous than the churning currents that swept Tierra del Fuego. And yet, these were the waters she would navigate to reclaim her life, and Nicholas Ramsay would simply serve as her conduit. Wasn't that what she'd tried to do back in London, randomly, desperately choosing a series of lovers, all of whom had left her cold and unmoved and unchanged?

Trying to read Ramsay's dark, opaque eyes the next day made her question her reason. She was mad to think this might work.

A warm wind blew over the promontory where they stood, his body shielding hers from the gales that raged like a hot embrace. Clad in only a light linen shirt and trousers, he seemed ever ready for the unexpected, invincible, and untouchable, as though welcoming the exotic and the dangerous. She turned away from him and toward the alien world unfolding before her eyes, a lush, verdant valley that rolled down to a swathe of impossibly white sand.

Yesterday morning they had anchored at Port Praya on the island of Santiago, where Ramsay had ridden ahead to the village of Ribeira Grande to expedite the reprovisioning of the ship. A Spanish doctor had boarded the *Flying Cloud,* examined her briefly, and pronounced her well. The plan was to set sail again within forty-eight hours, making the most of the prevailing winds. Feeling stronger, Helena had been desperate to spend some time on land, curious about what she had read in Darwin's writings about this series of unusual volcanic islands off the coast of Senegal. And even more desperate to spend time with her charcoal and sketchbook.

"This was a wonderful idea, thank you," she said over the sweet-smelling wind that perfumed the air. *This celebration of their détente.* "Your idea to come out here was simply brilliant." The sunshine, the air's softness, and the lushness of the surroundings were seeping into her veins. The warmth was unprecedented in her experience, the tropical heat relaxing her muscles and melting her bones. And her defenses.

He had come for her just before lunch with two horses and an invitation to spend the early afternoon just south of the small Spanish village of Fuentes. Packed in his saddlebags were her art supplies and what appeared to be a movable feast. Her appetite having returned with a vengeance, her mouth watered at the thought of both distractions.

He smiled down at her. She couldn't get used to his smile, *dazzling*, in contrast to his eyes, gray and forever watchful, giving away nothing. "I think this is the tonic you need," he said smoothly. "You've been through quite enough, and I'm pleased the doctor has determined that everything is in order."

Beckoning her to follow him, he began to make his way through a jagged pathway leading down to the strand. She watched him from under the brim of her bonnet, the broad shoulders and narrow hips, his easy, athletic pace, her fingers itching to trace the sharp, strong lines onto paper. Much as she wanted to capture the streaks of blue and pink angling up from the ocean and backlighting the fantastically jagged sky-line, she wanted to capture Nicholas Ramsay even more.

Dry gravel crunched under her boots as the pathway steep-ened. Picking her way carefully through the scrub, she saw a cove open in front of them, the bleached rocks behind the beach framing a stream spilling out of the hills.

"I've never seen anything like this," she said to his back.

He replied over his shoulder, "Nothing like England, is it?"

And she wondered again how much of the world he had already seen in his lifetime and why she still knew so little about him. "You've been here before."

"Once," he said enigmatically, "where I learned that, de-spite the indisputable beauty of these islands, this area has a brutal history."

In the cove, they were out of the wind and sheltered from the worst of the sun. He put down the saddlebag he was carrying, opened it, and began spreading a blanket on the white sand. "Tell me some of the history," she prompted, half wondering whether in the telling he would divulge something about himself.

"Take off your boots first—you'll love the feel of the sand between your toes."

Unaccountably, she blushed and turned her head away to smooth out a corner of the wool blanket. Bending over, she began unlacing her boots.

"Do you need any help?"

The last thing she needed right now were those hard hands on her legs. She made quick work of her laces before pulling off one boot and then the other. Her stockinged feet sank into the sand.

"You're right," she said more primly than she'd intended. "This is wonderful. But please continue. I'd like to know more about these islands."

Feeling suddenly awkward and ill at ease, she lowered herself onto the blanket, tucking her feet beneath her with her toes still buried in the warmth of the sand. She watched as he pulled off his boots and joined her on the blanket as unselfconscious about his actions as a wild animal.

"It's not a pretty story," he cautioned, stretching out his long legs and crossing them at the ankles. She couldn't help but notice that his feet were large and elegantly made.

"I'm not a stranger to unhappy endings," she said honestly, the sun hot against her face. She pulled her bonnet more securely over her chin, watching as he produced a bottle of wine from the saddlebags and two glasses.

"I promise this wine, at least, will deliver a happy ending," he countered, pouring them each a generous amount. "No arsenic. Here, I'll take the first sip."

Helena watched as he toasted her silently and took a healthy mouthful, aware of the man's contagious vitality. He was the most physical specimen she'd ever encountered, larger than life, exuding a strength that made every man she'd known before pale in comparison. She knew what he felt like under her fingertips, the tightly corded muscles and the powerful bone structure, the heat that emanated from his skin like a furnace. All of which contrasted, frustratingly, with a coolly contained vigilance as impermeable as an ancient citadel.

Willing herself to relax, she took a deep draught of the wine, listening to that low, persuasive voice.

"From the viewpoint of European history, the Guinea Coast is associated mainly with slavery," he said, leaning back on his elbows. "One of the alternative names for the region is the Slave Coast, but the nomenclature is entirely the result of the arrival of the Europeans in the fifteenth century.

"The Portuguese used slave labor to grow cotton and indigo in these previously uninhabited islands; then they traded these goods in the estuary of the Geba River for slaves captured in local African wars and raids. I'm sure it doesn't come as a surprise to you that these slaves are sold in Europe and, from the sixteenth century beyond, in the Americas."

Helena squinted into the sun. "I would assume that Britain's interest in the region has declined since the ending of the slave trade in 1807."

Ramsay nodded. "Leaving the Portuguese and the French to battle it out."

She had witnessed firsthand the tropical languidness of Fuentes that morning, the proud bearing of its people, the vibrant colors reflected off the brilliant ocean, and the small pink and coral houses of weathered wood, surrounded by small gardens, fenced pigs, and chickens running wild. Seductive scents, which she couldn't identify, had scented the balmy air.

She looked out onto the sparkling ocean, and unaccountably, the image of the *Scindian* rose in her mind, the squat and ugly boat replica she had spied at Conway House. The wine and the heat were going to her head. Grasping for a connection she couldn't quite make, she forged ahead, the awkward question balanced on her tongue.

"Please forgive me if I'm speaking out of turn," she faltered, "but it's a question I've wanted to ask you for a long time, having to do with a small boat replica, back in your library in London, on the mantel." She pulled her legs from the sand and tucked them protectively under her skirts. "Is there a story behind it? It seemed so out of keeping with the rest of the house, and I then assumed it might have some special meaning for you."

The late-afternoon sun pulsed over them. She couldn't see his features, blackened out by the sun. "You're very observant. The artist's eye, I suppose," he said neutrally. "Actually, it's a memento from another time."

She kept glancing at him, sensing that she was on the cusp of some discovery. "What type of ship is it?" The question ricocheted through her mind. "I'm hardly familiar with all things nautical, of course, so I was just wondering, not having seen anything like it before . . ." She trailed off.

Only the faint whistling of the wind and the murmuring stream broke the silence. She wondered if she'd gone too far.

"It was a barque built at Sunderland in 1844," he finally said. His profile was granite. "And it was employed as a convict transport."

The glaring tropical afternoon light seemed to fade, the sun sliding behind a lone cloud on the horizon. She swallowed hard, balancing her wineglass in the sand, acutely aware from the hair standing up on the nape of her neck that she was treading on unknown ground. "And did *you* have anything to do with the *Scindian*," she asked, unable to hold back.

He had yet to move, silhouetted by shadows, lying as still as a snake in the grass getting ready to strike. "And what if I did?"

Somehow, she had expected him to deny the association. As a matter of fact, she'd *wanted* him to deny an association with a convict ship. She could only imagine the wealth to be made from forced labor, a quasi-legal form of slavery that was still practiced by her own country. It would explain so much about him. Horace had warned her, and even Madame Congais, if she recalled, had alluded to this man's dangerous and unpleasant provenance.

"Of course, it's none of my concern," she said stiffly.

"No, it isn't."

Silence stretched between them. She had known him but for a short time and he'd killed at least one man, and possibly several men, for her. She had to be honest with herself. Morality was complex and her own conscience was hardly pristine. If she must recognize anything it was the fact that Ramsay was a complicated man who had clearly lived many lives, in the words of Mackenzie, making easy judgments inadvisable. He had, after all, involved himself with her—a madwoman—and pitted himself against Britain's most powerful brokers, without once asking her to justify her past or her actions.

"Actually, I didn't mean to intrude," she said as she tried again, pulling her knees up against her chest, tucking her skirts around her ankles. "It's just you know so much about me and I know so little about you. You can hardly fault me for asking."

He sat motionless, unnerved. *What have you done?* The voice was inside her mind before she could stop it. She could not bring herself to look directly at him. The silence lengthened until finally, he said, "The comparison is hardly fair. I don't know as much about you as you think."

He was right. He knew only the barest outline of her life, his passing references to her father and her family drawn in generalities. True, he had excavated a few inches beneath the surface, to the fears and repressed emotions that simmered beneath, but then she suspected he had a talent for uncovering unpleasant truths.

She glanced sideways at him and, unexpectedly, a shot of mutual vulnerability passed between them, as unsettling as an arctic blast on a summer's day. "It takes many years to get to know someone even if you care to," she said quietly. "And I don't know if it's even possible for people like us." Her voice didn't waver, her gaze was clear and steady, even if her heart was racing and she hoped there was no way he could know it.

"Interesting, your choice of words, *people like us*, as though we have anything much in common." His gaze was a steady, cool gray. He drained his wineglass and poured himself a second. "I'm wondering how productive this discussion is in all actuality. Perhaps we should be focusing on our shared goal, something we *do* have in common—that is, how we intend to go about finding the evidence that the X Club and you need to contain the Bishop of Sissinghurst."

He was smooth, as smooth as the carrera marble in the main atrium of the Victoria and Albert Museum, but the warmth and openness he directed at her were paper thin. Accepting his offer of another glass of wine, she decided she

needed something in her stomach to regain some equilib-
rium. As if sensing her mood, Ramsay sat up and dragged
the saddlebags toward him, rapidly revealing several covered
dishes.

"You need to eat." He was clearly at ease out-of-doors,
smoothly producing simple implements, coarse cotton napkins and a spicy Portuguese stew that she learned was made
of hominy, beans, and fish. A sweet and savory chicken dish
followed, which she devoured with unexpected enthusiasm.

Glancing up in between bites to survey the exotic scenery
spread before them, she attempted to get them back on an
even footing by changing the subject. "I recall reading that it
was on Santiago that Darwin made his first curious discovery
involving a horizontal white band of shells within a cliff face
along the shoreline of Porto Praya." It was a neutral enough
gambit compared with the tenor of their earlier conversation
and a welcome reprieve.

He nodded, wiping his hands on the napkin spread out on
his lap. "I believe you're referring to the fact that he noticed
that this layer happened to be forty-five feet *above* sea level."

"What else can one conclude except that at one time it lay
under the ocean, leading to the question of how it came to be
forty-five feet above sea level."

The expanse of water, seemingly limitless and fixed, glittered before them in the strong afternoon sun. "It certainly
does support a theory of a world slowly changing over great
periods of time," he said thoughtfully. "Of continents rising
and ocean floors sinking."

"Somehow that hypothesis doesn't strike me as so very
outlandish. I wonder at the resistance and intransigence,
given the inherent logic." She shook her head at the thought
of Sissinghurst and everything that he stood for. "I recall a
heated discussion between the bishop and my late husband"—
she paused—"about the queen's wish to confer a knighthood
on Mr. Darwin and Bishop Wilberforce intervening and convincing her to abandon the idea." Sissinghurst had said vocif-

erously that the ideas expressed in Darwin's work were dangerous to society, leaning natural science away from its respectable position as an investigator of God's creation.

Ramsay glanced at her sharply. "Science is the least of the worries generated by Darwin's investigations," he said. "Imagine, just last year, Mr. Huxley giving lectures to the poor working classes on the evolution of man from lowly apes. Such sermons are vastly appealing to people, the idea of man being a noble creature, not fixed in a certain social stratum, but with potential for progress. All of which places the clergy, the aristocrat, and the laborer on the same continuum. It's a political weapon intended to smash the spiritual basis of privilege."

"Dangerous, indeed," she conceded, wondering about his true views on the subject, this man who came out of nowhere with untold wealth and influence. She placed her plate and napkin aside, and scooped up a handful of warm sand, letting it flow through her parted fingers. "Things change, and so man is capable of change and transformation. Even these grains of sand, once having been part of a stone, a rock, or even a mountain face and over a millennium, are ground down to this fine, powdery substance. So why would we assume that other geographical formations, animals, or even humans, should be unchanging and immutable?"

"You're an intelligent woman, although I'm sure you already know that," he said. "But you also have an open mind willing to consider alternate perspectives." His compliment was decidedly unfamiliar, and it warmed her more than the blazing sun beating down on them. Intelligence was considered willfulness; her artistic ambitions, a form of madness. Never before in her life had her thoughts and ideas been weighed and considered free from condescension.

She took a deep breath. "Thank you," she responded simply.

"I was only stating the obvious." He sat up in one graceful motion. "Nothing remains the same in life, and you're a very wise woman to acknowledge the fact." Although he hadn't moved any closer to her physically, it seemed, somehow, that he was closing in on her.

"What are you doing?" she asked, watching him extract a silver case from the pocket of his shirt and extract two slender cigarettes and matches.

"Offering you an opportunity to smoke. Care to join me?"

His sudden change of mood struck like a bolt of lightning, and his low voice carried a command that she found difficult to resist. He put one cigarette in his mouth and lit it, cupping his hand against the brief flare of the match, then repeated the action with the second. Suddenly light-headed from the wine, food, and tropical warmth, she watched him lean toward her over the blanket.

He took one cigarette from his mouth and said, "Take it." She complied, but the touch of his hand on her face startled her, and the brush of his skin against hers was so light that she could almost believe she imagined it.

She watched as he drew deeply, signaled by the sudden bright ember of the tip. The scent of the blue-white stream was vaguely familiar. "Go ahead," she heard him say.

She took a mouthful, and the smoke stung her throat and stopped her breath. "This is opium, isn't it?"

Ramsay smiled. "No, it's hashish."

She didn't reply, knowing already where she was going and why. The fragrance was more aromatic than what she recalled from Madame Congais's; she drew the heat into her lungs and released it in a long, slow breath.

He smoothed the back of his fingers across her cheek. "Now take off your bonnet. . . . The sun is going down behind the cliffs," he added in the event that she needed extra inducement.

Helena loosened the bow beneath her chin and let the hat fall to the blanket, revealing her dark hair smoothly captured in a chignon. He looked at her for a long moment, his eyes hooded, unreadable.

They smoked in silence, the distance between them shrinking like a horizon at sea. She felt weightless, her anxieties falling away, replaced by a simmering yearning that she didn't want to fight. She watched him bring his cigarette to his lips, delighting in the action of his beautiful forearms and strong hands, the wide mouth.

"You're doing this deliberately, aren't you?" she asked into the long silence.

He didn't bother to pretend that he didn't understand her meaning. "Why not make things easier, and take the path of least resistance?" he replied, stretching out to face her directly.

Without his prompting, she leaned back, supporting herself on her elbows, watching the ocean turn a pearlescent blue with the setting sun. "You need help with my seduction," she said baldly, not believing it for a second.

He smiled slowly and then took another pull on his cigarette before crushing the remnant into the sand. "You won't do anything you don't want to do, Helena. We've already crossed that boundary. Remember?"

As though she could ever forget. The strange woman whose reflection glittered in the mirror. The shattering pleasure that was hers for the first time, unbound, unfettered, and uncoerced. Her blood rushed at the memory. She wanted to put it in words, to tell him about her past, her poisonous relationship with the duke, but the words wouldn't come. Instead, she took a final draw of the smoke into her lungs before abandoning the cigarette alongside his in the sand.

"You don't need to tell me." The voice was his, but the words could have come from her own mouth.

She swallowed hard, a lump in her throat.

"Don't think about that right now," he murmured roughly. "Think about this and how addictive it could be."

"What could?" she asked in halting syllables, slowed by the sensation of her tongue moving over her lips and teeth.

Then she lowered herself on her elbows to stretch out along-side him as though it were the most natural thing in the world.

They lay face-to-face on their sides.

"How addictive *this* could be." With his thumb, he dragged open the fullness of her lower lip and closed the distance between them. His mouth was firm and warm, as though he'd absorbed the sun's rays into his body. The barest ripple of her breath escaped and he drew her breath into his mouth. His hands moved down her back to her hips, pulling her tightly against his legs. She was aware of his hand kneading her backside through the layers of her skirt, of the warm plunge of his tongue and the smooth linen of his collar under her hand.

Whether she heard the roar of the sea or her own pulse in her ears, she didn't know. The pinks and blues of the ocean glistened behind her closed eyes as she sank into his slow, leisurely kiss. He trailed his tongue along her neck, under her chin, and then gave a tease of his tongue in the hollow of her throat. He nibbled her soft flesh, back up to her parted lips. She was helpless to do anything but fit her body tightly to his, aware that he was baring her flesh, pushing her bodice aside, kissing away the chemise that blocked his way.

The fabric parted and slid down over her breasts to her waist, sending a shiver through her. Her naked breasts yearned for his hands, his mouth to feast ravenously on her nipples. He lowered his head. The moist, heavy pull of his lips, the teasing teeth on a tender breast, first one and then the other, sent spirals of fire to her core.

She felt languorous, suspended between sleep and wake-fulness, but her skin had never been as alive. With every lick of his tongue across her flesh, she dissolved a little bit more. He ran his hands from the sides of her breasts down her body and with the tip of his tongue fed at the corner of her mouth.

She welcomed the heat of the heavy air on her waist, hips, and legs as, miraculously, the tiny concealed fastenings of her skirts and chemise eased under his ministrations to slide down around her ankles. Clad only in white stockings and naked to the sea and sky, for the first time she knew neither power nor shame but simply a desire to have this man inside her.

"I feel so different . . ." she whispered against the hot skin of his shoulder, the coarseness of his hair sharp against her lips.

He raised his head, his hands cupping the nape of her neck, eyes half closed. "That's how it should be. No hiding, no subterfuge, no manipulation. Just this." His words were hot against her mouth.

Weighed down by a languid desire that pooled in her abdomen, she watched as he stripped off his shirt, making quick work of the fastenings. He was lean, weathered, the corded muscles of his chest and abdomen a fresh assault on her senses. A formidable erection pushed through the fabric of his breeches. On her own volition, her hand trailed down to cup him, her palm spanning his hardness, the heavy fullness that was for her. At her touch, he inhaled fiercely, and she was about to say something else when he silenced her by kissing her eyes, then feeding fiercely at her lips.

The tempo changed. He bit into her nipples and then brushed away the fire with the back of his hands. She writhed between pain and pleasure, her hands barely encompassing his erection as he thrust it back and forth within her grip. The rasp of his breath pulsed in her ear; then he pulled away and began trailing his hot tongue between her breasts to play briefly with the indentation of her waist. She inhaled violently when, hands on her hips, he buried his face in the triangle of the soft, dark hair between her legs.

She stopped breathing, somehow outside herself, allowing him to arrange her, legs bent at the knee and spread wide apart so that her sex was exposed to the light of the late-afternoon sun.

Time stood still and she lay there, open and vulnerable. He rose to his feet and pulled off his breeches, and she had to raise her head to take in his long, muscled legs and the rampant erection that curved toward her. She stared into those intense gray eyes as he looked down at her, and all she wanted to do was reach out and touch him, to feel the weight of his sex in her hands and to take him inside her where her womb pulsed with knife-sharp need.

Then he was next to her again, spreading her legs, his hands on her mound, stroking the long cleft beneath. She felt like silk and velvet, warm and smooth in her liquid desire. He bent his dark head, opening, tasting, and after a lifetime of teasing, sliding over the pulsing center. With the heel of his palm low on her abdomen, he never stopped, the concentric circles of his tongue building in tempo with her racing blood, so fast and so hard, she knew that she was going to die.

Her hands bit hard into his shoulders and threaded through his hair aimlessly while she struggled to free herself from his lips. She couldn't stand it anymore, her blood rushing to the tight, throbbing center that threatened to explode. But he held her fast until she crested, clenching around his lips and tongue as she bucked against the hot flow of sensation that blotted out everything else.

She could hear her own panting, the rasp of his breathing. When she opened her eyes she saw him take his erection in his hand, massive and heavy, and use it to part her lips again with exquisite ease.

"I can't . . . I can't possibly," she gasped, turning her head aside against the onslaught to come.

"You can and you will," he said, pressing a soft kiss on her inner thigh, then licking his way to the inside of her smooth, satiny cleft.

He teased and he taunted then, using the heavy head of his erection to caress her opening with hard, seductive strokes. Penetrating no more than just the rim, and then out again, each time he opened her wider, making her ready, rubbing against her wet curls and tender flesh.

She moaned, desperate, her hands grasping his hips, whimpering, begging to receive the full thrust of his erection, to have it buried deep inside her. But he moved with an excruciating leisure, penetrating deeper but then withdrawing, his hands cupping, soothing the sides of her breasts. She felt the wave building again and she squeezed and rocked her pelvis. Only then did he quicken his pace and she called out to him in a strained and breathless voice, words that were strangled, incoherent, forever lost in the soft ocean breeze.

She opened her eyes, transfixed by the sight of him, his jaw rigid, the veins and tendons in his neck straining. Something flared in his gaze and he paused for a heartbeat before he slammed deep inside her with one relentless thrust. A violent shudder coursed through her body and she threw her head back, her knees opening wider as she pulled, gripped, and pulled him in farther. She was filled, impossibly stretched just as he surged upward and then withdrew, waiting that infinite second before thrusting again. Taut as a bowstring, blood pounding, she turned to those eyes, now concentrated with lust. With every thrust the pressure built deep inside her. His hands tightened on her buttocks as he lifted her lower body from the blanket, grinding against her, bearing down hard; then she felt the shudders begin, convulsing her body in a searing purge, an unending stream.

The smell, the feel, and the heat of him—there was nothing else. She bucked and she bit her lips against the scream that ripped from her throat. And at that moment he tensed and began to withdraw, but she clutched his hips, not wanting to let go. Not wanting to . . . She shattered into a thousand pieces.

"That's it," she heard him urge her on as he pushed fiercely into her wetness, drawing a ragged breath. He covered her mouth with his, eyes heavy lidded above her, his hips driving like a piston until suddenly, he shoved away from her.

The air was impossibly cool against the hot seed pouring in an unending stream onto her stomach. Her mind reeled, mesmerized by the rhythm of ragged breathing, his or hers, she couldn't tell, her eyes open to the purpling of the sky above her.

Afraid to turn her head toward him, she tried to get some control, to regulate the rise and fall of her chest. She wanted to say so much, but she didn't dare test the words aloud.

He seemed far away, although she could feel his hand heavy on her stomach. The atmosphere enveloping them was sultry despite the deepening sky overhead.

Her heart still racing so wildly, she was sure it would leap from her chest, she pulled the shambles of her clothes over her breasts. His hand circled languidly on the small of her stomach. "A little late for modesty, I should think." And then he sat up.

"Please don't look at me that way," she said, her voice small.

He shrugged his broad and very naked shoulders, perfectly at ease. "What way?" His opaque eyes darkened with what she now recognized as desire. The wind had died down and only the murmur of the stream and the occasional lapping wave competed with their presence.

She sat up, pulling her clothing with her, acutely aware that she wore only her stockings and nothing else.

"It makes you uncomfortable."

"As a matter of fact, it does."

"I suspect I know why," he said, his smile cool against his analytical words. "You equate male desire with tyranny, and for good reason, although I trust we've demonstrated that doesn't have to be the case."

In spite of or because of what they'd just done, she couldn't ever remember being so intensely aware of another human being. He was sublimely unself-conscious of his sprawling nudity, and she found it difficult not to drink in the sublime male beauty along with the brutal honesty of his assessment. Unaccountably disturbed, she let the froth of her chemise fall from her breasts. "Why are you bothering with me, Ramsay?" she asked, her voice husky. "I didn't ask for your help with all of this."

He put his hand against her neck, cradling her throat with his large land. "You're a physically beautiful woman, Helena, but there's much more to you than that, most of which your father, your husband, and other men in your life were afraid to acknowledge. But I'm not most men."

She could feel her pulse beating too fast underneath the heat of his hand, her nipples already tightening in desire. How could she begin to explain? Somehow she felt she owed him an explanation. She began tentatively, trying to keep her voice from wavering. "For me, relations with men have always been fraught with difficulty," she said, aware of his hand stroking her throat. Vulnerability was a luxury she could seldom afford. "I was either being used or I was using them."

He moved his face closer, his chest within teasing distance of her breasts, his mouth hovering just over hers. "I know, Helena, and I understand." The words were simple and it took everything to keep the tears from her eyes. His clever fingers brushed against her soft skin. "You can forget all of that. Leave it behind you. I meant what I told you: that true passion can be liberating in so many ways."

He moved away slightly, his gaze leading a scorching path down her breasts, waist, and the length of legs so close to his.

"Why are you doing this?" she whispered again. Why wasn't he just taking, demanding, coercing?

"Because it gives me pleasure to give you pleasure," he said. And while she couldn't entirely believe him, there was something there, a kernel of truth he kept hidden from her and from the world. His skin was turning a golden brown in the fading sunlight, the lines around his eyes and mouth more pronounced.

"But enough of all this seriousness, which obviously goes against the principles of pleasure we were just talking about." He gestured to the satchel abandoned at the foot of the blanket. "I have a suggestion to make. You wanted to come here to draw, so let's take the few hours left before we have to get back to the ship."

Before her bemused eyes, he produced one of her pads of paper and a box of charcoal, knowing that she couldn't resist the temptation of her one and only obsession: to create something out of nothing. He cleaned the remnants of their passion from her smooth abdomen, while she quickly pulled her chemise back over her head. Then, with a grateful smile, she took the materials from his hands and began to draw.

An hour passed in silence. Her charcoal scratched across the page, loose scrawls and small, controlled swirls. She abandoned one page after another, acutely aware of nothing but the sharpness and detail of her work as real to her as the ink-blue waves of the Atlantic crashing onto the deserted shore under the fading afternoon sun.

He sat quietly by her side, watching unobtrusively, the stillest man she'd ever known. His presence sent a permanent shock right through to her nerve endings, his splendid nudity driving the quickly diminishing piece of charcoal between her fingers.

Not knowing exactly how much time had passed, she looked up from her drawing, a slight breeze lifting the end of the paper held steadily on her lap. She flexed her fingers and fixed him with her gaze.

"Had enough? You're very patient sitting here with me like that."

He leaned back on his elbows and crossed his legs, a sculpture come to life. "Good of you to point that out. I just may have to demand some recompense for my time."

It was amazing that after what they'd done together, she

still couldn't discern whether he was serious or jesting. "What kind of recompense," she asked finally and carefully.

He cocked a dark brow. "It all depends. I'll give you a choice."

Closing the pad on her lap decisively, she tilted her chin toward him. "And what are my options, sir?"

He slanted a glance at her. "Show me what you've drawn. You know I've been an ardent admirer of your work from the first."

She didn't want him to see what she'd drawn. Not right now, and possibly not ever. "The alternative?" she asked, sliding the pad back into the satchel at her elbow.

His expression was serious, but his tone lightly mocking. "I won't pretend that I'm not offended."

"As if," she murmured, arranging the folds of her chemise carefully around her breasts.

His eyes followed the movement of her hands speculatively. "You're not going to ask what the other option happens to be?"

The air around them thickened and she felt a tingling pulse beat between her legs. "I'm sure you're going to tell me."

He smiled dangerously. "That stream looks particularly inviting." And before she could reply, he grabbed her hand and pulled her to her feet.

The water was deeper than it looked, sweeter and colder. She gasped for breath and laughed in spite of herself as he dragged her up to her waist, not letting go. He began washing her, cupping water in his hands and letting it run over her arms and shoulders. Rivulets of glistening droplets trickled over her breasts and teased her skin, the thin cambric of her chemise sticking to her body. She loved his hands, the long, strong fingers, the elegant sinews of her forearms. Hands that could give her such pleasure. The water soothed the pleasantly aching flesh between her thighs.

Suddenly, he paused, his cupped palm dripping water, midair. "Forget what I said earlier." His gray eyes were dark, and it struck her again how inconsistent the indentation in his firm chin was, an incongruity that scorned the austere cheekbones and assertive nose.

"Forget what, exactly?" she asked innocently, swaying closer toward him.

"You *are* a physically dazzling woman, and that's a difficult thing to forget."

She didn't respond but focused on the play of the water lapping gently around her thighs still clad in her now soaking stockings.

"And following the logic of that thought, shouldn't we get you out of those wet clothes?"

He was so quick that Helena hadn't the chance to say anything before he was deftly lifting one leg and rolling down her stocking, first one and then the other, wrenching them off her ankles. "That's much better," he said, his mouth lingering on the inside of her thigh before lowering her back into the water. "Except for the chemise, of course. And I'm pleased you didn't wear a corset." He trailed a long finger down her breastbone, his gaze scorching hotter than a tropical sun. Her curves were lasciviously outlined by the clinging fabric. "I think I like you this way for now."

He loomed over her, virile and massive, and she reacted with an increase in her pulse, reaching out to caress a muscular arm. "You're fairly dazzling yourself," she murmured. The artist in her couldn't resist running her hands along the ridges of his ribs, her sensitive fingertips registering the magnificent nuances of his honed body. "You know what I like to do when I go to the Victoria and Albert," she asked, sprinkling a little water onto his chest.

He stilled her hand in his, the ocean silhouetted behind him. "I can only guess it's something wicked, something truly mad."

She nodded slowly. "When no one is looking, I like to caress the sculptures, run my hands over that cool marble that's begging to be touched. Sculpture is three-dimensional and it's meant to be felt."

He placed his hands on her shoulders and pushed her closer toward the stream's edge where the water only came to their knees. "You're a very sensual woman, Helena, you just don't know it quite yet." He leaned over to caress her cheek. "Imagine I'm a sculpture then. Do your worst," he said, his voice dipping lower.

She responded with a faint smile, plunged her hands into the water and released it over his shoulders, across his chest, over his thighs, and between his legs until he gleamed like a magnificent bronze of her imagination. She was fascinated by the water cascading down his body, the way it turned his skin a darker gold. She turned him around slowly while still running her wet hands over him, transforming his strong back and hard buttocks into sleek marble.

He was as docile as a sleeping jungle cat, allowing her to spread his legs apart and slip her hand underneath him to hold and caress his heavy sex already rock hard under her ministrations. She was naked, bold, and she'd never felt more free, daring to fall to her knees in the shallow water to take him hungrily into her mouth.

She felt his groin tighten against her cheek and she looked up at him. His jaw was clenched. "You don't have to do this," he rasped with a steadying hand on her shoulder.

"I want to," she whispered, pressing her mouth on him with an urgency she'd never felt before. "I want nothing else right now."

A wave of dizziness washed over her as she tasted him in slow, luxurious swathes. Her hand tightened on his erection, barely closing her hand around its circumference, her tongue and mouth moving more tentatively at first and then more deeply. Ramsay was silent, his torso rigid, and only his hands moved, sweeping up her neck and into her hair, his long fingers moving sensually over her sensitized skin.

And on it went, the strange dizzy lust that she knew wasn't fueled by the hashish that had long ago been burned away by their passion. It was something else, a sensation that she didn't have to care, that she could slowly, deliberately feed her own pleasure as she took him wholly into her mouth.

And behind her closed eyes, the image of Nicholas Ramsay burned, the lines and strokes made by a piece of charcoal and by a sheaf of paper taking on a life of its own.

Chapter 16

Francine Congais, formerly known as Florence Cosgrove, fanned herself impatiently. The fires burned low in the grates of her salon on Regent Street, the atmosphere heavy and fetid. Her eyes narrowed as she made a quick scan of the main drawing room. A judge in a far corner, stooped, balding, but irrepressibly eager in the presence of one of the girls, craned his grizzled face toward her rosy bosom. To the right, on the red velvet settee, a young viscount, whose accounts were seriously overdrawn across the city, lounged decadently with his escort for the evening, a water pipe, and a suitably soporific expression.

All was well, the low hum of voices told her coming from the warren of rooms that was her townhouse. Then why did she feel as though she were hanging on by her last frayed nerve? She couldn't account for the growing knot in her stomach and, Lord only knew, her instincts were seldom wrong, sharpened by years of living on the thin gruel that gave her her wits.

Her eyes drifted back to the red velvet settee and the last night she'd seen Nicholas Ramsay in the company of that most unusual woman, Lady Helena Hartford. Half of London believed her to be mad, and there was Ramsay aligning himself with her no-doubt sumptuous hide and running off with her to the wilds of South America.

Francine didn't know the whole story, but she could guess. Her ears were sharper than her eyesight these days, and she'd pieced together a whole cloth out of snippets of lewd and whispered exchanges that passed for conversation at Madame Congais's.

Damn, she needed a drink. Gin preferably. Although generally it wasn't a good idea when she was working, and she was working, most of the time. Even the thought of Ramsay could do that to her, make her thirst for something she could never have.

They were similar, she often lied to herself. Both scrappers arising out of the quagmire that was England where only the fittest could survive the onslaught of cruelly delineated class distinctions. Had it not been for Ramsay those many years ago . . .

She saw herself as she was then, with two fatherless girls, stealing a gold fob watch. The face with its diamanté hands had sparkled with promise but delivered her to the gates of Newgate instead. Then Ramsay came along. She smiled to herself at the memory. How quickly money and influence applied to the right palms could change one's world around.

She never asked directly where his resources originated, but she did make certain assumptions, collecting pieces of the puzzle along the way. Her world was like that.

Instead of sending one of her servants to fetch her gin, she glided with her usual studied pace to the mahogany sideboard in the far corner of the salon. With its brass backrail and two central drawers, the piece of furniture was by no means the most opulent in her house. Her hands steady, she found the bottle she was looking for and poured herself a generous helping in a crystal-cut glass.

This should calm her nerves. The juniper berry vapors mingled with the perfumed air that permeated Madame Congais's, an integral component of the atmosphere she insisted on creating. It was this kind of attention to detail that made

her a successful businesswoman in the netherworld of pleasure that operated just beneath the law. And, of course, Ramsay's protection didn't hinder either.

She was taking another swallow of her gin when a discreet
tap at her elbow caught her attention. The majordomo bent
to whisper in her ear. When he finished, she smoothed her expression and the stiff bottle-green bombazine skirts of her
dress. "Please show him to my office," she said, relinquishing
her glass with a calmness she didn't remotely feel.

When she swept into the dark paneled room with its elaborate stained glass window, she was not surprised to see a
clergyman seated on the horsehair settee. A young man with
the face of an altar boy, he didn't bother to rise at her entrance. Her eyes narrowed speculatively, refusing to give in to
rising anxiety pushing at the stays of her too-tight corset.

"No reason to stand, Deacon Mosley," she murmured, allowing a tinge of sarcasm into her voice. She inserted herself
behind the golden oak twin pedestal writing desk and sat
down. "What is it that I can do for you? A particular diversion, perhaps?"

His pale blue eyes widened in feigned shock. "I am a man
of the cloth, Madame Congais." He adjusted his starched
clerical collar for her benefit, sitting almost as stiffly as the
horsehair stuffing of the settee.

She smiled tightly. "And since when has that made a difference, sir?"

He returned her smile showing small, even teeth, but she
wasn't disarmed by the feint at affability. "I shouldn't be putting
on haughty airs, *Miss Cosgrove*. For people of your sort it is always more helpful to be polite and accommodating."

Folding her hands on the desktop blotter, she noticed that
the stained-glass window, illuminated by gaslight, rendered
Mosley's otherwise pale complexion a lurid yellow. "I gave
up being polite and accommodating to people like you years
ago, Deacon Mosley."

"That's a pity."

"I shouldn't think so," she said, rising from behind the desk. "Now given that I don't like the tenor of this discussion already, and the fact that this is *my* house and property, I'm afraid I shall have to ask you to leave."

Deacon Mosley pretended to look offended, then shook his head as though admonishing a small child, not in the least dissuaded. "An unfortunate request on your part as you will see in a moment. My requirements are modest in that all I ask of you is for some small piece of information."

She remained standing. "I don't divulge the private concerns of my patrons, Deacon Mosley."

"More's the pity." His fine gold curls glowed in the gaslight, giving him the appearance of an evil cherub. "Because all I ask is for you to tell me a few things about your good friend and benefactor, Nicholas Ramsay, and about his unfortunate liaison with Lady Hartford."

Her mind spun back several months ago, to that moment in the kitchen where she had smoothed the progress of Helena Hartford's escape. By nature, she wasn't selfless, far from it, but there was something in the other woman's predicament that called out to her. Her reputation had already set most of London buzzing, particularly the wags who hated nothing more than a spirited and independent woman who refused to be brought to heel.

And who flaunted that independence by lending her name and fortune to the most unsavory prospects. So she dared to exhibit her art and join company with male artists, that hardly constituted madness. Further, if the woman wanted to comport herself as men did, seeking exotic diversions at Madame Congais's, all the more admirable. As far as she could tell, Lady Harcourt was as sane as a high-court judge.

"I have nothing to say about the woman in question, sir."

"You know of her reputation?"

"I know of *everyone's* reputation." She appraised him coolly. "What is your point? I shouldn't want to ask you to leave again. My majordomo can be remarkably persuasive in the event that I'm not."

Mosley made a small sound in his throat. He rose to his feet, standing taller than his fine bone structure would have suggested. "I'd always heard about the generous hospitality that could be found at Madame Congais's," he said with a moue of disappointment. "I must have misheard, *Miss Cosgrove*. Otherwise, I cannot account for this distinctly chilly conversation we're having when all I want"—his voice became steely—"is to discuss a few rather salient details regarding your relationship with Mr. Ramsay. My understanding is that you know him better than most."

"Nobody knows Ramsay," she said in a tight voice.

"I'm not so sure about that, particularly when there are certain inducements available to refresh one's memory." He sat back down on the settee and gestured for her to do the same. "So let's begin, shall we?"

One hour later, Mosley advanced across the vestibule of the Bishop of London's manse, his footsteps silent on the thick carpeting. He sniffed, inhaling a trail of incense, more evidence of Sissinghurst's High Church, Papist inclinations.

It had been a long and busy day but also a productive one, and he did not mind in the least to be kept waiting by the bishop. He'd never stopped to consider their uneven relationship, accepting it instead as an article of faith that was sent to test his spiritual fortitude. In the past, it was the mortification of the flesh that served as ritualistic practice, along with starvation, sleep denial, and scourging.

For Mosley, it was the Bishop of London.

He clasped his hands behind his back. Soon enough, Sissinghurst would come to appreciate his inimitable services, particularly when he learned of the progress he had made earlier in the evening—thanks to the good offices of Madame Congais. Miss Florence Cosgrove became affable enough when he'd lied to her that the *Flying Cloud* had been shipwrecked off the Falklands in a storm. No more Ramsay as protector, no more recourse from the law for poor Francine. If she was anything, Madame Congais was an astute business-woman who clung tenaciously to her livelihood.

Behind him, the door to the vestibule opened and, as expected, the heavy tread of the bishop followed.

"On time as usual, Mosley," he said distractedly. He had just finished having dinner with the archbishop, his labored breathing and straining girth testament to a lavish menu. A faint sheen of perspiration highlighted his beetling brow, and he clutched the ruby-encrusted crucifix around his neck reflexively. Quite possibly, dinner had not gone according to plan.

As always, he wore his purple cassock and Mosley had never seen his superior in secular clothes and suspected he never would.

Without preamble, the bishop made motion for the younger man to follow him into his study. The porcelain heater hummed in the background, casting the room and its furnishings in a deep, red light. Two wing chairs sat facing each other and Mosley made haste to pull one out for the bishop, who hefted his weight gratefully into the lavishly embroidered seat.

His question was peremptory. "What do you know about Australopithecus?" He folded his hands over his paunch, his tone accusatory.

Waiting for permission to sit, Mosley quickly drew from his storehouse of classical languages, always eager to demon-strate his erudition. His news would have to wait. "*Australis,* Latin for 'of the south,' of course. And from the Greek, *pithekos,* meaning 'ape.'" He gestured to the chair and waited for the bishop's nod before seating himself.

The bishop paused, staring straight ahead and past Mosley. At last he shook his head testily. "I wasn't testing your know-ledge of the classics," he said sarcastically, "as I'm already quite familiar with the etymology of the word in question, Deacon. As usual, you have missed my intention completely."

Grimacing, he looked down at the hands folded neatly on his girth. "What I want to hear from you is that you understand the implications of Australopithecus."

Mosley stared searchingly, his usually quick mind slowing like molasses in the presence of Sissinghurst. The term *ape*, of course, was one that was tentatively associated with Darwin's research. Mosley's fine lips thinned in frustration.

Sissinghurst nodded wearily, as if unsurprised. "Of course you don't understand. What was I thinking? *You* who have managed to hopelessly complicate the situation of Lady Hartford in ways I can't even begin to fathom. Of course I can't depend on you to appreciate the implications of a discovery that purports to prove the evolutionary origin of our own species."

At first, Mosley believed that he had misheard. "A discovery?"

"That's what I said. And we're not talking about a few useless bones."

It was apostasy, blasphemy, the worst sacrilege. And from the mouth of the bishop. To have the questions of origin and time that had plagued man's quest of knowledge *answered* and in a way that precluded any involvement from God?

"This is impossible," he stuttered, hands gripping the sides of his chair, "that there is proof that such a creature, such a being, has ever existed. It belies the fundamental belief that we were created in God's image." Marshalling his thoughts into a semblance of coherence, he tamped down on the panic that threatened his sanity by simply closing his mind and choosing, as a man of faith, to disavow what he was hearing.

The bishop snorted derisively, leaning forward in his chair. "Don't waste your religious protestations on me, Mosley, because I'm not in any mood to entertain them. Instead, I want you to *think*, rationally and coldly, about this. Whether God exists or not is a moot point," he ground out. "What's important is that we support the fiction of God and his role in creation in this best manner we can. Not because we're believers, but because—and are you listening closely here—because it serves our very worldly purposes."

Mosley stared and, if he was shocked, he didn't show it. Inured to what he was hearing, he dipped his head in a servile nod while Sissinghurst continued. "While you have failed to intercept the *Flying Cloud* and its passengers Lady Hartford and Mr. Ramsay, I have been busy discussing important matters with an individual whose loyalties to friends and colleagues are not as sound, shall we say, as his friends and colleagues would wish. What I have discovered is twofold."

The bishop paused, not looking very happy with himself or Mosley. "What I have discovered," he continued portentously, "is that Mr. Darwin has in his possession an unpublished manuscript titled *The Descent of Man,* and in this document he writes of his discovery in Tierra del Fuego of the remains of a primitive ape species that bear a striking resemblance to humans."

Mosley felt himself pale, the blood rushing from his head to his cold feet.

"And secondly, my good deacon," the bishop dragged out his next pronouncement for effect, "why do you think Mr. Ramsay and my fair aunt are traveling to Tierra del Fuego? Unless, of course, they're not because you've managed to have them poisoned or Mr. Ramsay has made good on his threat to do away with his lady love himself."

"Oh, dear God." The three words froze in Mosley's throat, despite the slowly simmering rage that chafed in his belly. He'd hoped Helena Hartford was still alive, that the poison had failed, because what he wanted most of all now was to see her trapped in a living death, beaten, diminished, and above all, begging for mercy, *his mercy,* in a prison far worse than even Bedlam. The feverish craving brought a flush of heat to his face. "Dear God," he repeated in a strange commingling of sexual and religious ecstasy.

"Never mind God," snapped the bishop impatiently. "Fortunately for you, I have received word that the *Flying Cloud* is still heading in the direction of South America, but whether my aunt is still alive and with us we have no way of knowing until the ship reaches the Falkland Islands, upon which our diocesan contact will apprise us accordingly."

Mosley thought it best to remain silent, focusing his intense hatred on the image of Helena Hartford chained and begging in some dank and benighted medieval cell.

"Are you still with me, Deacon?"

Mosley nodded mutely.

Producing a handkerchief from his pocket, the bishop mopped his brow delicately. "It only gets worse, I'm afraid."

"Is that possible?" Mosley croaked through lips dry with outrage.

With the flick of his handkerchief, Sissinghurst dismissed the question. "Upon the *Flying Cloud*'s return, the X Club has scheduled a very public debate between me and Mr. Huxley at the Royal Society. They will expect to have evidence, along with detailed drawings, of this Australopithecus, so generously provided by my aunt and Mr. Ramsay. Needless to say, we cannot allow this to happen for two very important reasons, the first of which is the Archbishop of Canterbury, with whom I had dinner this evening, who expects me to demolish, once and for all, any Darwinian claims regarding the origin of our species. The second concerns my aunt's fortune, which deserves to be in my hands."

The bishop heaved a deep breath. "Therefore, it is absolutely essential that we greet the *Flying Cloud* on its return and ensure that this time we have Lady Hartford in our custody."

"And the evidence?" Mosley managed to ask. He gripped the edges of his chair imagining Helena Hartford gagged and bound at his feet.

"Use your head, for once!" Sissinghurst fumed. "If Mr. Ramsay returns with her in tow, he will probably have developed a tendresse for my aunt and forgone his hopes of revenge. I know *you* do understand that my aunt exerts a certain *unhealthy* hold over men, witness my late uncle, the duke." He sighed despairingly. "Which means I have had to make certain arrangements, in the event that Ramsay does not prove accommodating." He tensed because Ramsay would not make it easy. "To ensure we get the evidence in exchange for his whore."

The porcelain heater hissed in the background. Through the haze of his suppressed rage, Mosley swam through the options at his disposal, courtesy of Florence Cosgrove's revelations. His recall of Nicholas Ramsay was a blur, based on a foggy but decisive encounter in an alleyway close to Conway House. In contrast, his rage, fueled by lust, was burnished to a bright flame for Helena Hartford.

"But if he still does intend to seek revenge," Mosley said slowly, aware that he was offering a valuable gem of information, "we may be able to offer our services, depending on his priorities, of course."

For the first time that evening, Sissinghurst's head snapped to attention. Mosley was aware that he had been preoccupied, absorbed in finding a way to control a man who was, it was all but universally acknowledged, uncontainable.

"Priorities?" His small eyes were almost lost in the ample flesh of his face. "What have you learned from Congais about Mr. Ramsay's interests in the X Club?" In contrast with his yielding corpulence, his instincts were sharper than ever.

Sensing that he was gaining a modicum of control in the proceedings, Mosley loosened his grip on the armchair and chose his words carefully. "His reasons have to do with revenge."

"I already know that." He gestured impatiently. "I want to know about his motives. The man is as rich as Croesus, why bother with all this science nonsense?"

"It has to do with Lady Hartford's late father."

"What about him?" Sissinghurst paused, raising a hand to his forehead as though searching for a memory. "Canny bastard, as I recall. Odd name. Made most of his money in factories, although you wouldn't know it to have heard him talk, what with his airs and affectations." He shuddered in recollection. "Robert Peacock Whitely, that's it." He rubbed his brow. "A man of the most middle-class sensibilities despite his fortune."

Mosley brought him back to the present with his next words. "At one point," he said distinctly, "Ramsay worked in one of his factories." And for the first time that evening and for the first time in a long time, he had the bishop's rapt attention.

The older man stiffened. "Do say." His small eyes narrowed speculatively. "Now we may have something here."

The younger man made the most of the moment, straightening his spine against the back of his chair. "Without going into too much tedious detail, when Ramsay was a boy of fourteen, Whitely had him shipped as convict labor to Australia. According to Congais, our man has never quite recovered from the indignity, despite the vast wealth he managed to accumulate."

Understanding along with a slow smile dawned on Sissinghurst's face. "Now *that* nugget of information has interesting possibilities." He pursed his lips thoughtfully. "A bitter man, our Nicholas Ramsay, the poor little urchin with nothing to recommend him except extended exile, courtesy of dear Lady Hartford's father. I do *so* love the irony."

He decided to throw Mosley a bone. "Well done, Deacon, although don't get too pleased with yourself as yet. We still have to see how you manage the information you have gleaned. Although I do have added ammunition should you require it when the time comes."

Fingering his ruby-encrusted crucifix, the bishop continued, "Of course, I now have an overwhelming suspicion that Ramsay won't simply do away with my aunt. That would be too easy and painless for her, after all."

"Had he wanted to, he could have had her disposed of without ever even dirtying his hands," concurred Mosley helpfully.

The bishop shot him a dark look. "But that's not at the heart of revenge, is it? The sins of the father, this time visited upon the daughter . . . the temptation would be too sweet for Mr. Ramsay."

"So, if we could somehow tap into that vein of vengefulness," Mosley proposed helpfully, his color rising in his excitement, "we could possibly secure both the harlot *and* this blasphemous evidence."

"Now you're beginning to think strategically, dear boy," Sissinghurst said.

And Mosley basked in the rare warmth of his approval.

Chapter 17

Ramsay leaned into the wind. The *Flying Cloud* was turning south toward the open sea. The gusts were fresh out of the northeast, enabling the vessel to coast down the channel under a full main. As night turned to day, he felt the unmistakable swell of the southern ocean, the mighty surf dashing against the headlands of Isla Hermite, throwing 100 feet or more of water and foam into the air.

He could read the signs. They were only twenty or so miles away from the pyramid that marked the southern end of the archipelago and the continent. The Horn was a symbol of that dangerous divide between the Pacific and Atlantic oceans, a graveyard for countless ships swept away by diabolical winds and awkward seas.

While he should feel fear, dread, or even exhilaration, he felt nothing. This destination, this jagged rock, was the culmination of a long journey, another graveyard of sorts where he could lay to rest his personal demons, wrapped in the form of Helena Hartford. There was no room for sentimentality, or whatever he chose to call that rock-hard erection that materialized whenever he thought of her. It had almost been too simple, hardly a challenge to ensnare her in a trap of her own choosing. While he hadn't liked the incursions on his territory—the attacks at the hands of Sissinghurst's men, the arsenic—cool logic dictated that they only made her more vulnerable. She'd been ready and primed for the dark, convulsive sensuality he could provide.

That she misinterpreted its meaning was entirely predictable and quite unfortunate—for her. She trusted him, possibly thought herself infatuated. As he'd intended.

And arrogance on his part had nothing to do with it. He'd dispensed with such useless and dangerous sensibilities long ago. That she'd fallen like ripe fruit into his hands was hardly surprising. Her story was common enough in their brutal age, a woman exploited sexually and financially, her individuality and talents smothered by male prerogative. The situation evoked a glimmer of sympathy for him, but not much.

Life was cruel, and Helena Hartford had fared better than most. That her father was a wealthy bastard of the first order, only one of hundreds in rapaciously greedy London, aroused nothing more than an old bitterness in him, best cauterized and then finally forgotten like fading burn marks. Emotions were dangerous, but once he finished with the daughter of the man who had separated a child from the only squalid, hopeless life he'd ever known, the slate would be clear.

He looked up at the tall masts that swayed with the churning currents. The skies were open, but he knew change was the only constant in the southernmost part of the known world. Storms arose with the rudeness of a lightning bolt, a gift or a curse of nature. There were too many stories about clippers pinned down on their starboard rails finding their final resting place by sailing straight and helplessly into the Horn's jagged ramparts.

Only the fittest survived. It was a naturalist's creed, but it didn't really need endorsement from the likes of Huxley and Darwin. Descending into the fetid hold of a convict ship, into its reeking bowels, provided plenty of evidence of the flesh giving up the spirit.

As for the weak . . . He allowed himself a grim smile. Like dogs circling each other, the weak were a component of nature. They succumbed to opiates, religion, useless emotion, and always, physical or material domination.

Helena Hartford would succumb. She already had.

She was mesmerized by their lust for each other. It was in every glance, every touch, in the eagerness of her exquisite mouth that promised ecstasy and delivered more. He refused to lie to himself. Already he felt himself hardening, the thought of her chafing his blood in a way that was unfamiliar, out of his control. And yet he knew it was simple fornication, spectacular in its own way, but a physical reaction no different from hunger or the need for sleep. They had fucked every way possible in the past several weeks, the method behind his particular madness, but he still wanted more.

His gut tightened. When the time came, he would and could leave her behind. Women's bodies were plentiful and he had the world at his disposal. The memory of Helena Hartford would wither and die, leaving him to deliver to the X Club the evidence it needed to secure what was most important to him. A single woman was nothing when compared with the hundreds of thousands of lives that would be forever changed, not only in the present but also in the future, by a scientific hypothesis made flesh.

The seas began to buck in earnest. Looking starboard, he saw Helena weaving toward him, hands clutching the rails, Mackenzie at her side. He'd wanted her to catch her first glimpse of the Horn with him. One more shared experience, he thought cynically.

Hair whipping in the wind, she glowed, her expression as open as a child's. "This is incredible! Thank you, Mac, for taking the time to bring me aboveboard."

"No problem at all, madam." The steward was smitten, it was written all over his hardscrabble face. Watching Mac, a man who'd survived the back-breaking labor in the copper and iron mines of Kapunda, Ramsay noted with dispassion, and not for the first time, Helena's staggering impact on men.

He took her arm to steady her. "To your left, around eleven o'clock." They had not sighted land since their brief stop for supplies in Cape Verde. But now, in the near distance, they saw the foaming, half-submerged rocks that lay just off the Horn, its power and remoteness highlighted by the surrounding cliffs.

It was a downwind sleigh ride, with rollers heaving astern and shooting the vessel forward. As each one passed, the bottom half of the great rock disappeared entirely and then came swimming back into view.

"What's our course?" For a woman who had never sailed before, her demeanor was steady and her curiosity insatiable.

The wind howled with intensity as he bent close to her ear, his hand secure around her waist. "If the weather cooperates, and I don't think it will, we can try to wait out the typical series of violent storms in this area and then enter the Beagle Channel as soon as we can. Otherwise, we'll anchor at Windhond Bay where we'll be relatively safe from the elements."

His words proved ominous and, as if on cue, the wind suddenly swung wildly to the southwest, the portent of a squall originating seemingly out of nowhere. "Get back down to the cabin," he said calmly. "Mac will take you and I'll join you when I can."

The next two hours were spent with his men and an eye on the telltale compass overhead. Deep thunder joined the roaring of the storm and the crash of the seas while they wrestled with taut ropes and lines while battening down the fore and main. Like an intransigent, intemperate god, the wind mocked them with driving rain and spray. Every time a tall sea struck the bow, its white head flooded the deck with solid water, obscuring the black reefs and cliffs that were perilously close by.

It was hard to determine how much time had passed when the *Flying Cloud* settled on the starboard tack, flanking across the seas with the steadily diminishing winds at an acceptable five knots. When they finally jutted into Windhond Bay, a familiar euphoria edged out exhaustion, a primal surge that had everything to do with having cheated death, the urge to seize life at its most basic level.

The cabin was dark, illuminated only by a small gas lamp that burned at Helena's side, her head bent over her sketchbook. He stripped off his oilskin and wiped the mixture of saltwater and rainwater from his face with a towel, until he stood reasonably dry before her in his breeches and shirt. Desire darkened the blue of her eyes. They had explored every variation of the sexual theme in the past weeks and, for some unexplained reason, he was reluctant to pursue, he exulted in the lack of trepidation in her gaze.

She put down her pencil and book, and rose from the table, clad only in a thin satin robe that teased more than it covered. He focused on her eyes and her mouth, so sensually alive, before his gaze wandered down over her body and its perfect flesh, the opening of her robe exposing a creamy expanse of her slender neck. He knew from experience that the skin beneath was smooth and silky and unblemished.

He drew her toward him, forcing a hand through the knot of hair at her nape, the coils loosening, as her hair tumbled down her back. She watched him, riveted by the simple action.

His hands went to unbutton the sleeve fastenings around her wrist, then turned her palm up and licked a small spot at its center with the tip of his tongue. And again, he tasted her skin from the palm of her other hand. She lowered her lashes and took a steadying breath that was already pulsing out of her control.

Stepping back behind her, he opened the sash tied around her waist and then slowly eased it off her shoulders to let it slip to the floor. He lowered his head to place a kiss on her naked shoulder, disciplining himself to take his time.

The ship heeled, but he didn't care, the listing delivering her into his hands. She groaned, a low, inchoate murmur that was as familiar to him now as his own voice. Her breasts tantalized, the already erect nipples with their pink nimbus, the weight and superb roundness that filled his hands. He slid his tongue down the side of her neck while skimming the cords of her pantalets from her hips to reveal the patch of black silk between her legs.

He burned hotter. The sight of her standing in her slippers, naked but for the provocative dark stockings held in place by long garters attached to a belt of matching lace, signaled sex.

He swung her off her feet in one swift move. Cradling her in his arms, he wrapped one of her legs over his hips, his fingers teasing the slick folds of her core and adeptly opening a floodgate of pleasure. She fumbled with the front of his breeches, releasing him with a small sound at the back of her throat. Her heartbeat raced against his chest and she bit the fullness of her lower lip to quell the rising tide of desire. Twisting her around to face him, he surged into her with one sudden, fierce thrust. She gasped and stiffened before he silenced her mouth with his.

With her long legs wrapped around him, he pushed her up against the nearest wall, her arms clinging to his neck. And then slowly and determinedly, he surged into her in rhythm with the rocking of the ship. Harder, slower, faster, his face buried in her breasts as he grazed and sucked her rigid nipples.

With every thrust, she gave a little more of herself to him, not with passive resistance or manipulative intent, but with an active responsiveness that stirred something in him he refused to recognize. She was magnificent in her naked longing, each whimper and moan the unmistakable sounds of a woman caught in a web of sensual thrall. He held her tightly, her body wrapped around him like a second skin. He was huge, hard, as he slowly moved in and out of her. Long, deep thrusts now. He slicked his thumb over her center, feeling her contract, sucking him into herself, then releasing him with a need all her own.

She came in a sweeping torment and he held back, wanting to give her the addictive pleasure, have her come again and again, until she drowned in her own carnality. In a paroxysm of pleasure, she grabbed his hair with both hands. She pulled his head down and kissed him with a wildness that was intended to undo them both, and it was only the rocking of the ship and the slap of her body against the cool, paneled wall that kept him on the shores of sanity.

He stopped thinking then, burying himself deep inside her for the last time. The climax hit him so hard, he almost cried out, but he continued holding her hips, fucking her slowly and calculatingly, until he felt her shudders a second time, her body rigid against him. He withdrew in the last second, losing everything on her smooth stomach and thighs, bracing her limp body against the wall until her legs stopped trembling.

He stepped away from her. Her eyes heavy-lidded, her breath rising and falling rapidly, and those long, shapely legs bent at the knee. He wanted her again with a fierceness that was mindless. He closed his eyes and cleared his senses of the heavy fog that was strangling him.

Because he knew this would be the last time.

When his vision cleared, she was shrugging into the abandoned robe with an unself-consciousness that was new to her. There was a freedom, an openness to her movement that, if she'd stopped to recognize it, was immoderately sensual.

"That was quite the greeting." She gave him a curious half-smile, tightening the sash around her waist. Her face was flushed, her hair a tangle over her shoulders.

"Let's just call it a welcome to Tierra del Fuego." He buttoned up his breeches, reluctant to say anything more.

"We've reached our destination, then." She bent over to slide on her slippers and then straightened to look up at him with clear eyes. "We now need to do what's necessary—for both of us."

Her words hit too close to the mark for his comfort. And it struck him, not for the first time, that it was unfortunate that she really was an innocent.

"But no matter what happens, Ramsay, I'll always remember this." She gestured vaguely and looked away from him, a faint pink suffusing her cheekbones. "You've given me a sense of myself that I've never had, even through my painting," she continued, examining his expression for something she wouldn't find. "And no worries, I shan't haunt your doorstep once we return to England. I understand the boundaries of our peculiar alliance." She paused, and there was courage behind her next words. "And regardless of what I intimated earlier in our relationship, it turns out that I have learned to trust you, despite the fact I know next to nothing . . . Clearly that's the way you prefer to keep things. . . ." She trailed off and then seemed to think better of it. "And thank you. Above all."

Her smile was tentative and her gaze so direct that had he been an honest man, she would have been his undoing. Perhaps he should have simply killed her a long time ago, or let the attacker on his ship or the arsenic do its work. Instead, he absorbed the words he'd been waiting to hear.

"Nothing to thank me for." He spoke the bitter truth.

"I won't accept that." A familiar hint of stubbornness threaded her tone. "And I'll help in any way I can to find this missing link that so concerns you and the X Club. I can capture its likeness and do anything else that assists in your efforts." She pushed her hair back from her face and into a loose knot. "I'll also concede that I do have some of my own interests at heart, as you well know, securing my independence against Sissinghurst."

She negotiated the now gently listing ship to sit down at the captain's table. The hurricane lamp sputtered before finally going out, allowing the early-morning light to pierce the cabin. "I won't ask—or take—anything more from you. Once we return home, I hope to move forward with my life, without Sissinghurst's threats and without your protection."

There was pride in her voice, and if he'd had a conscience, it might have affected him. He sat down across from her, keeping his expression blank. "You forget that my protection doesn't come without a price—your talent."

"I haven't forgotten. And I also haven't forgotten that you took a tremendous risk in your decision to associate yourself with me."

He wanted to laugh out loud at the solemnity of her tone. One wayward heiress that society happened to believe mad. And the Bishop of London, a mere obstacle in a much larger bid to undo centuries of oppression. "I wouldn't concern yourself unduly."

"But I do."

He dipped his head in acknowledgment. "Very well, then let's begin discussing what we can accomplish together now that we're here."

Her gaze was intense. "When will we go ashore?"

He looked out the porthole briefly before answering. "We'll land on the eastern side of the Beagle Channel, undoubtedly under the watchful eyes of native Fuegians on shore."

"Friendly natives, I trust."

He shrugged. "We can only hope because we'll need them."

"I can't wait to begin drawing them. With their permission, of course."

He looked up sharply. Her sensitivity unnerved him more than anything else about her. A woman raised in luxury and wealth, yet she still displayed an unerring sense of humanity. Would her father have been the same?

"We'll begin our search with the mission at Woolya Cove."

"I recall Darwin's account of a Reverend Richard Matthews and three anglicized Fuegians who settled down to run the mission," she said frowning. "Although I wonder at this attempt at Christianizing the natives. To what end?"

He crossed his arms over his chest. "Money and power, of course. It's what we colonizers do best. The British Empire, where the sun never sets, the discoverer of new lands and new people to exploit. When she's not exploiting her own."

Her eyes darkened. "I'd never thought of it that way."

She'd never had to. His resolve hardening, he disappeared into the small dressing room off the cabin. When he returned, he held a pair of trousers and a heavy linen shirt. "For you."

Her eyes widened as she pushed back her chair. "I suppose it makes sense," she paused, "rather than cumbersome skirts." She reached to take the fabric from him, scrunching it in her hands.

"I knew you were a practical woman at heart." To ensure her survival at the mission, he would have some of her more sensible clothing, her smocks and serviceable skirts, to be forwarded from the ship. Along with her art supplies. He couldn't deny her that.

"And to that end, let me wash quickly and get ready." She withdrew into the dressing room and he could hear water pouring, the slide of linen against flesh. It took every ounce of willpower to shut out the images of the damp material between her legs, the cloth kissing her skin. When she emerged, her skin was pink and flushed, and she wore a simple white chemise and sturdy stockings.

"Unless we get you dressed quickly, I don't know if we're ever going to arrive at the mission," he said, his voice thick. To counter an urgency he didn't want to feel, he pulled her toward him and held out the trousers. "Let's begin with one leg at a time."

With a small smile, Helena rested one hand on his shoulder and slid first one leg and then the other into the trousers. He tugged the fabric up and over her hips, his fingers deftly fastening the buttons. Gritting his teeth, he drew the linen shirt, over her exposed skin. "Your breasts are too beautiful," he muttered under his breath, mastering the ties beginning at her waist and marching up to her chin. His knuckles brushed soft skin.

Her eyes had closed and he sensed her own sharp anticipation. She cupped the back of his head, tangling her fingers in his hair. For a moment, he wanted to stay that way, to forestall the inevitable.

Helena moved first. "Had I only known," her voice was low, "how all this feels . . ."

To preserve his sanity, he stepped away from her just as she spun in front of him, displaying shapely buttocks and endless legs showcased in men's trousers.

"You're ready, then," he said, for once relieved that he wasn't touching her but wondering how he'd come up with the seemingly brilliant idea of dressing her in men's clothing. She was more blatantly female than ever. He turned away from her and moved toward the door, hauling the earlier discarded oilcloth over his shoulder. "We have no time to lose." The next few days couldn't be over quickly enough. "I'll explain what you need to know along the way."

The ride in the tender was swift. The water was choppy but the wind had yet to rise, and his men, six on each side of the small vessel, pulled with the required muster that the observing sailor at the helm fully expected. Helena sat composed, her gaze taking in the cliffs, glaciers, and deep blue waters that floated to the tops of the boat's gunnels. He recognized by her quiet intensity that she was already sketching the dramatic landscape in her mind's eye.

A bright sun hung in the sky as the boat proceeded down Ponsonby Sound to arrive at Woolya Cove. Disembarking, they saw three small huts, kitchen gardens, and the eager faces of several Fuegians who ran to greet them. Ramsay had already directed his first officer on the *Flying Cloud* to send one yawl and another whale boat filled with supplies for the mission, the textiles, medicines, books, and food that would see them through the next two or so years. An inner voice told him, if he cared to listen—and he didn't—that he'd discharged his duty.

With open curiosity, Helena nodded and gestured with the Fuegians. One lone woman in the group stood apart and surveyed her boldly, without saying a word. The men's limited English was compensated by their eagerness to engage the newcomers. Clustering around her, fingering the cloth of her cloak, they peered closely at her face.

Helena laughed, the sound echoing in the clearing. Although directing his men in unloading the tender, Ramsay was preternaturally aware of her. He moved to her side, saying a few words to the Fuegians in their language as their faces, daubed with white paint, observed him warily.

And just as Darwin had noted, they exhibited the most amazing ability to mimic gestures and words, often repeating whole English sentences verbatim. In their eyes was reflected their own amazement at these white people's abundant hair and pale skin.

"I find their bone structure most dramatic," said Helena, turning to Ramsay in an aside. "I shouldn't want to alarm them, but if there's time, I would like to make preliminary sketches."

The scent of her, which he should be accustomed to by now, was disorienting. He should be inured to her, not distracted. Dangerously distracted.

"We'll have discussions first with Reverend Hornby." He then motioned her to wait while he strode toward one of the huts in the near distance. Before he could enter, a short, thin man emerged with thinning hair and a sour expression.

"Hornby?"

"Mr. Ramsay, I presume." The reverend extended a bony hand. It was difficult to pinpoint his age, which could have been anywhere between thirty and sixty. Living in harsh conditions aged a man, Ramsay knew, from firsthand experience. "Please come in."

The small hut was choked in smoke, wreathing unproductively from the iron stove that sat in the corner. Furnished rudely with a few wooden chairs and a table that looked like it belonged in a village manse long ago, the room had one narrow window, next to which was suspended a simple crucifix. The effect was oppressive.

"I received your missive, sir," began Hornby, pulling out

two chairs. "We would be more than pleased to welcome Lady Hartford to our humble mission. Any pair of Christian hands is welcome in our work converting the heathens."

"You will not make mention to Lady Hartford of the arrangements I outlined," Ramsay instructed, declining the seat.

Hornby thinned his lips. "Of course not. We understand the difficulties presented by wayward women. Good charitable works, away from the temptation of the outside world, will help in shaping and, eventually with time, transforming her soul into a model of Christian womanhood."

"My first captain will ensure you have the supplies you need," he said without emotion. "And the recompense." Blood money, call it what it was. This man was a more insipid version of Sissinghurst. As for the surroundings, he surveyed the dirt floor and the worn furnishings, no worse than a convict ship or copper mines in Australia.

A sense of unease mingled with the smoke in the room. He hoped to hell he could get what he needed in record time and sail back to England.

"I shall make my introductions without mentioning any untoward detail," Hornby said crisply, his worn hands clasped in front of him. "I take it the young lady is waiting outside."

"Please send her in when you've concluded," Ramsay told him. "We have unfinished business."

Hornby shot him a curious look from watery, red-rimmed eyes before nodding and leaving the hut.

The smoke in the room was as heavy as his thoughts. He pulled open the one small window, letting in a weak breeze. The temperatures were comparatively moderate for early September, but he knew for nine months of the year Tierra del Fuego was under snow and ice. Survival was not assured.

A brief knock and he looked up to see Helena waving a hand in front of her face attempting to clear the air. She walked tentatively into the low-ceilinged room, her movements free under her swinging cloak. "These dwellings are primitive," she said, quickly assessing the immediate surroundings, the dirt floor, mismatched chairs, and table, her eyes lingering on the crucifix. "But at least outside the lay of the land is certainly compelling, like nothing I've seen before."

Compelling but not conducive to human survival. Leaning against the window sill, he asked, "Did you make your acquaintance with Hornby?" The man she'd be spending the next three years with.

She sat down at the table, her cloak falling open to reveal trouser-clad legs. "More of the same," she replied, not keeping the distaste from her voice. "What is it with these dreadful clerics? The Fuegians I've met, albeit I haven't met too many so far, hardly look in need of salvation." She crossed her legs. "And that poor woman—I wonder how she came to be part of the reverend's flock. I would absolutely expire if I were forced to take up with Hornby and his ilk." A shadow passed over her face. "Unfortunately, I speak from direct experience."

He refused to be drawn in. He actually welcomed the momentum that was hurtling them toward a dead end—and the faster the better. "Unfortunately, Hornby and this mission are all we have currently so we'll make use of the settlement as a base for the time being."

She nodded and he cursed her acquiescence.

The drone of Hornby's voice, clearly lecturing the Fuegians, drifted in from the open window, and it occurred to him that Bedlam could hardly be worse. He kept his expression neutral. "If we keep our focus and think strategically, we can be done with all this in short order."

Her chin rose at the urgency in his voice. "I think I may have discovered something as well, something that may help us, when I spoke with the Fuegians earlier."

"Spoke? I didn't realize you were conversant with their language."

"Unlike you, I don't know any words, but they have clearly picked up a smattering of English from Hornby. It's amazing what happens when one tries. Not to mention that simple gestures and a willingness to communicate help immensely." She folded her hands on the table as though ready to do business. "But never mind for now. I'm eager to learn about those details you promised me."

He wanted this to be over. Quickly. "Very well, here are the salient facts that I'll give you as concisely as I can." He pushed away from the window and Hornby's voice. "The X Club has seen an unpublished manuscript that Darwin has kept clandestinely for the past twenty years," he began without preamble. "It's entitled *The Descent of Man* and theorizes that mankind evolved from a sort of primitive ape species."

An astute woman, she didn't look surprised. "Why did he keep it hidden and unpublished for so long?" She frowned. "Or need I ask."

"He was probably anxious about the reception it would receive."

"I can commiserate," she said with an attempt at humor. She palmed the surface of the table absently. "Is this a theory or something grounded in reality?"

He walked to the opposite side of the room, conscious of the low ceiling only inches away from his head. "You're one step ahead of me." He couldn't keep the admiration from his voice. "The X Club has had direct discussions with Darwin, who has become somewhat of a recluse these past twenty years, and as it turns out, he has indicated that there exists physical evidence to support his theory. And not simply a few fossil bones to make the case but rather hundreds of hominid bone fossils that, if returned to England, will prove that these apes are the ancestors of the primates and humans that exist today."

"But why didn't he simply transport the evidence back with him when he was here with Captain Fitzroy on the *Beagle*?"

"If we had the answer to that question, we would also

know why he has kept the manuscript unpublished for as long as he has." He paused. "Fitzroy, by all reports, is also a deeply religious man and an unstable personality. One suspects that the two men had profound disagreements that have remained unresolved to this day."

She linked her hands and placed them over a crossed knee. "This is beginning to make more and more sense." She stared at a soot mark over the table by the lone window, keen intelligence lighting her eyes. "I know what I'm about to say next is a wild supposition, but unless you know where to begin searching for these remnants . . ."

The smoke in the room was beginning to clear. "I have copies of Fitzroy's logs and Darwin's diaries."

"But not the manuscript *The Descent of Man* itself."

He shook his head, leaning one hip against the table.

She sprang from her chair, her cloak whirling around her trousered legs along with dust from the floor. "The Fuegians were eager to take me somewhere. Particularly, the woman. They tugged at my hands, pulling me toward a hilltop in the distance."

Her eagerness was palpable, but then she had every motive to find the evidence that would give her the upper hand with Sissinghurst. "You're getting ahead of yourself. They may have simply been overwhelmed by your charms," he said dryly, for some reason keen to deflate her enthusiasm.

She remained standing across from him, looking like a young soldier ready to do battle. Her expression would have frozen a lesser man. "I don't expect condescension from you."

He'd done his job all too well. She'd actually expected better from him. "I was being perfectly honest."

Their eyes locked and he had the impression she was sizing him up for a portrait she was undertaking. "I am still uncertain about you, Ramsay," she said softly, consideringly. "Oftentimes I force myself to believe that we are simply two people who can help each other. Yet at moments like this, I'm convinced that you're like one of those icebergs floating in these waters, with only the smallest tip revealed to the air and sky. And I don't quite know what to do about it."

There was nothing she could do about it. And it was better she never knew what lurked beneath those cold waters. Until it was all over.

"Very well, we can do it your way," he conceded. "We'll see what we can get from the Fuegians and then somehow cross-reference it with Darwin's manuscript." He didn't have a hell of a lot to go on, and if his trust in her instincts bound her closer to him, all the better. He pushed away from the table eager to get some fresh air when her next words stopped him.

"What were you like as a child, Ramsay?" At first he thought he'd misheard. The question came from nowhere, knocking the air from his lungs like a well-aimed fist to his stomach. Her eyes had taken on a penetrating acuity, the same look she had when he'd seen her with a piece of charcoal in her hand. Her instincts were good, too damn good.

He decided to give her the partial truth. "I don't recall much detail, actually." Ironically, he couldn't even remember exactly what his father looked like. And he wouldn't have recognized his own mother if she'd collided with him in the streets. The deafening clamor of machines piercing a small boy's ears, the sweaty hold of a careening vessel, the stink of rotting flesh, and the sting of the beating sun on a bare back, day after day—that was what he remembered.

"What about your childhood?" His response was seemingly random, almost cavalier, but it was intended to redress the balance of power.

She leaned over the table to look directly at him and there was a faint irony in her smile. "You didn't really answer my question."

"Because there's not much to tell."

She cocked her head to one side. "I don't believe you, but that doesn't matter, does it?"

"And you haven't answered my question." He pinned her to the dirt floor.

She straightened, her eyes revealing everything. "You can guess, surely. There's not much *left* to tell."

The silence stretched between them until she was the one who turned away and exited the room.

Chapter 18

Tension knotted the muscles in Helena's neck. She'd never imagined that the southernmost tip of the world would look like this. As far as the eye could see there was low-lying scrub that was so brawny it barely moved in the strong winds. Squat, craggy hills loomed and led to higher mountains that were painted a uniform shade of brown. And despite the shelter of the bay, the mission at Ponsonby Bay was still enclosed by a vicious sea remarkable for its unreliable currents.

After a brief and terse dinner the night before with Hornby, who had informed them that the mission's two other members had succumbed to a mysterious fever last year, she and Ramsay spent several hours quickly reviewing the copy of Darwin's manuscript. Ramsay had already underscored passages in the work that could prove of value, but Helena still felt that something was missing, an important connection that the great naturalist had decided to leave out.

She was startled by the cogent argument underlying Darwin's hypothesis, the clarity with which he'd outlined the evidence of the descent of man from some lower form, including details on the manner of development, as well as a comparison of mental powers and principles of sexual selection.

The astonishment which I felt on first seeing a
party of Fuegians on a wild and broken shore will

*never be forgotten by me, for the reflection at once
rushed into my mind—such were our ancestors.*

Now on the second morning after their arrival in Tierra
del Fuego, it was that statement that echoed in her mind,
teasing her with the intimation of what Darwin *had not said.*

For whatever reasons, she felt anxious, a gnawing in her
stomach reminding her that all was not well. Buffeted by
winds coming from the east under a swell of low, dark clouds,
it looked more like dusk than the middle of the day.

Stretching her neck to rid herself of her nerves, she surveyed the humble collection of huts worn by the sea and
cold. Inhospitable and unforgiving, the landscape had with-
stood eons of time, harsh lines etched as geography while the
humble shelters were already showing wear in the way of
chipped paint and gaps in the thatched roofs. Helena knew
that the Fuegians were in the main cabin where she had spent
the night alone on a makeshift cot. The reluctant converts
were now participating in a Bible study class led by Reverend
Hornby, exposing a glaring incongruity that was impossible
to ignore.

She heard the crunch of gravel behind her and tensed at
Ramsay's approach. Turning to greet him with a false smile,
she pulled together the collar of her cloak protectively. She
felt raw inside, stripped of her usual defensive layers, leaving
her vulnerable to the inundation of unfamiliar emotions.

He took her elbow, the stubble of his beard somehow still
enhancing the clean planes of his face. "You slept well, I
trust. Your first night on terra firma in a long time."

And her first night without him in a long time. Although
she'd noticed that he never stayed with her in her cabin after
they'd finished making love, if that's what she could dare call
their sexual infatuation, and she'd assumed, possibly lied to
herself, that he was being taken away from her by the demands of the ship.

He squeezed her elbow and she turned like a sleepwalker

toward him. "I feel refreshed, thank you." His eyes were the same gray as the skies overhead. It's what frightened her most, that she couldn't reconcile those eyes with the man who had so carefully and determinedly broken through her defenses and offered her redemption.

"So how do we proceed from here?" she asked, drawing from a weariness deep inside. Their last and personal conversation had shaken her to the core, reminding her that while he demanded everything of her, he gave nothing of himself.

He scanned the horizon with its fractured mountains behind them. "We have several options," he said, scrubbing a hand over the stubble of his chin. "But one of them isn't exploring every inch of this territory until we find what we're looking for."

She looked up at him, clutching the collar of her cloak. "So what do you propose?"

"I keep coming back to something we read last night."

"Coincidentally, so do I." She was relieved to be back on firmer, more practical ground.

"You go first this time, but let's walk while we have our discussion as I suspect Hornby is suspicious enough of our intentions." He guided her over to a muddy bank several yards away from the circle of huts and where her boots immediately sank into two inches of thick mire.

At least she was wearing trousers, better insulation against the damp than voluminous skirts. "I keep coming back to what Darwin had to say at the conclusion of his manuscript," she began, collecting her thoughts. "How he managed to conflate the image of the Fuegians with our ancestors. There's a connection there that I don't think we're making." She paused, the cold of the mud seeping through the leather of her booted feet.

"You're making the assumption that the Fuegians know something that they're not telling. Or at least, they may have told Darwin but he didn't care to include it in his writings." Ramsay's attention was concentrated over her shoulder, keeping a focus on the huts behind them. Not for the first time, Helena wondered about his obvious distrust of Hornby, a man he'd presumably never met before in his life. "Possibly," she said mildly. "But that still doesn't help us with the physical evidence."

He nodded. "Which is why I keep coming back to something Darwin recorded in his diary about what he found near Whale-boat Sound."

Her silence pushed him to continue. "While searching for fossils along the shore, he came across an interesting find, the *complete* fossil of a very large animal that he could not readily identify. Later, it was determined that it was a giant ground sloth."

"Which only led to more uncertainties, presumably."

"Precisely. He played with all manner of questions. Why were there no living animals in South America that looked remotely like the creature he found? How long ago had this creature died? And given his presumption that land masses rose in tiny increments over eons of time, and based on where the fossil was situated, he concluded it must have died thousands of years ago."

A nasty drizzle began to fall and it was difficult to remember that the month was early September. Helena looked up into the darkening sky, shivering. They were frustratingly close; she could feel it. Or maybe it was simply wishful thinking because returning to London without the evidence to rein in Sissinghurst was unthinkable.

"You're cold." Ramsay pulled the cloak closer over her shoulders.

"It's not that," she murmured, afraid of the way she reacted to the warmth of his body next to hers.

"Then what is it?" The tone encouraged confidences. She didn't move away when he drew her closer to him, draping an arm over her shoulders. Strength left her body and she sagged against him.

"The thought of returning home, to London, to an asylum . . ." She couldn't complete the sentence. "We can't fail. For any number of reasons."

Instead of looking directly at him, she stared at the water that was beginning to bead on his oilcloth jacket, yet, coward that she was, she drew on the power of his body next to hers.

"We won't fail." His voice was soft and they were so close that he barely had to speak above a whisper.

She tried to breathe normally but graphic images crowded her thoughts. Patients stripped naked and chained in cells strewn with filthy straw. Or swinging from cages, on display to Londoners eager to spend a tuppeny for the opportunity to revel in someone else's misery. The wardens used whips.

It was grotesque—and the ultimate symbol for evil.

In a panic, she roused herself from his arms. It took her a moment to find her voice. "We have to look and I don't care where we begin, even if it takes clambering over every inch of this godforsaken scrub." She flung her arms wide. "But we can't stand here and do nothing."

He made no move to touch her and, perversely, she ached to feel the shift of his body next to hers again.

"I'm not suggesting we do nothing. And you're getting wet. Let's go inside." There was no impatience in his tone but only studied indifference and she felt a renewed jolt of fear.

Her feet were sinking into the mud, but she didn't care. "Going inside isn't going to help, and I don't even care if I catch my death from a cold," she said, knowing that she was beginning to sound incoherent. "We have got to find that missing link."

"We will."

"How do you know?" Her voice was close to breaking, but she hung on his next words that were predictably calm and unemotional.

"Because I always get what I want." It was becoming icy cold and she could see his breath misting the air between them. "And because this is important to me as well." He trained his opaque eyes on her. Terse and ambiguous, it occurred to her that this was the most he'd ever revealed to her about himself. And she thought again of the *Scindian* sitting on the mantel at Conway House. "You can get through anything, Helena, if you have the discipline."

Discipline. It was in his body's preternatural stillness. In his remoteness and reserve. In the way he made love to her.

"You think I allow my emotions free rein. You said that once and I haven't forgotten."

He smiled lightly, oblivious to the drizzle running down the side of his neck and into the opening of his coat. "Not the worst thing, as it turns out. Your instincts have proved remarkably accurate. That abbreviated conversation you had with the Fuegians upon your arrival—I think we should follow your lead and accept their offer."

She stared at him disbelieving. Her ideas had always been discounted, her art invalidated, and here was a man who was taking direction from her. She pulled herself from the muddy bank and turned toward the ring of huts on the hill, anticipation rising in her breast. "I knew it . . . I had the sense that the Fuegians wanted to show me something. Something important to them. Although why they seemed to want to trust me, I don't quite know."

He went to stand beside her. "I'm not surprised. Your open, unjudgmental manner must stand in stark contrast to the behaviors of most Europeans they've encountered. If you know any of your history, I'm sure you know we can be excruciatingly cruel to those we can crush under our boot."

She glanced at him warily. "That's the last thing I want to do. Achieve our own ends at the expense of theirs."

Ramsay shrugged, his shoulders straining the fabric of his overcoat. "They've already paid a high price, starting when the Spanish first settled on the islands bringing diseases such as measles and smallpox that the Fuegians had no immunity against. You can imagine how their population was devastated. As Darwin would say, I suppose, survival of the fittest."

"And you—what would you say?" She threw down the

gauntlet sensing that, as always, there was much he was leaving out.

He smiled. "I'd say let's really save these souls by interrupting the good reverend's bible study. For that alone, the Fuegians' gratitude should prove generous."

That evening in the shelter of a lean-to and the smoke of a damp fire, they sat in a circle with the Fuegians sharing a simple meal. Horace would be horrified by the deprivation of the surroundings. Helena bit back a small smile. She hadn't had the chance to think of her dear friend in days.

It had stopped raining late in the afternoon and the sky was a black bowl in which floated hundreds of constellations whose configurations Helena couldn't begin to identify. Her ears strained over the wind to hear the noise of insects, the call of a bird, or the cry from an animal, but the land was silent. The Fuegians spoke mostly among themselves, in a low, gutteral language, occasionally smiling and inserting a few English words or, emboldened by Ramsay's own attempts at communication, gesturing openly.

Over a wooden bowl, she picked carefully at roasted fish, barely tasting the stringy meat. She thought again about Horace and the short note she had penned him when they'd stopped in Cape Verde, wondering whether the missive would ever find its way to London.

Sitting cross-legged, comfortable in her men's trousers, she chewed with reluctance the bony fish meat while Ramsay relaxed across from her, his profile lit red by the firelight, strangely at ease in such exotic surroundings. He was one of the world's richest men and yet he sat on the dirt, his damp clothes hanging on his tall frame, attempting to understand and be understood. She decided that she would never know him.

Mercifully, Hornby had declined to join them for a meal that didn't take place around a table, his protestations making it clear that encouraging the natives to follow their natural habits would only discourage their assimilation into Christianity. Helena could still hear the high whine of his voice in her ears.

The lone Fuegian woman in the group sat silently at her left. An awkward exchange of names was all Helena had been able to summon. On a whim, she put aside her wooden plate and reached for her satchel. Mara's sharp eyes followed her every move, watching her as she extracted a block of paper and a piece of charcoal from the bag.

She began to sketch by the light of the fire. First a tree, then an outcropping of rock—the pencil scraped against the blank page. Although she hadn't moved from her position on a log, Mara's intense gaze was fixed on the images emerging from beneath Helena's fingers. After a few more moments of silence between them, Helena tore the page from the book and gave it to Mara.

"For you," she said simply.

Her dark hair gleaming by the light of the fire, she looked down at the pages on her lap, then back up at Helena, her black eyes inscrutable.

"May I?" asked Helena. Then she leaned forward and, while not actually touching the woman's face, traced the broad cheekbones with their slashes of white paint, with gentle gestures. Whether she understood exactly or not, Mara nodded.

The fire crackled and spit embers in the background while Helena's fingers flew across the page, first introducing wide strokes and then adding more detail and shading. Smaller, more refined charcoal lines captured the depth and contrasts of Mara's exotic features. Reverend Hornby had identified his group of converts as belonging to the Ona or Selk'nam tribe who lived almost exclusively in coastal areas and traveled by canoes around the islands of the archipelago.

Forgetting all about the time, Helena worked steadily while Mara sat patiently at her side. It was usually impossible for her to finish a portrait in one sitting, and she preferred to put it aside and then work on it at a later time. But this instance would be different, and before she could add the last stroke, she sensed Mara leaning infinitesimally closer

"Again—for you," repeated Helena, placing the sketch with the others on Mara's lap.

The older woman's eyes sparked with interest as she examined the portrait. "Again, for you," she echoed.

Helena smiled and wondered at the nomadic life Mara and her tribe had once lived. She'd learned from Ramsay that they had lacked permanent shelters, making their camps out of stakes, dry sticks, and leather. When they broke camp, they carried their things with them and traveled by canoe along the coast that provided fish, sea birds, seals, and even whales for sustenance. When Darwin had first arrived on the *Beagle,* the light and smoke of their fires in their canoes must have presented an impressive sight when seen from a ship or another island.

She heard the rustle of paper as Mara carefully gathered the sheets on her lap and rose from her sitting position across from the fire. It struck Helena again how much taller she was than the Fuegian when she felt the older woman lay a hand on her shoulder. Without saying a word, Helena sensed she too was meant to rise and follow Mara from the light of the camp to the edge of darkness where only the faint light of Reverend Hornby's lantern shone.

Her eyes quickly adjusted to the semidarkness, already familiar with the crunch of nettles and stiff brush under her feet. A few yards away, the shoreline beckoned, the currents gentled by nightfall and marked by the cadence of lapping waves. Several canoes were turned upside down on the shore like pieces of waiting crockery.

Helena stopped a few paces behind Mara, who seemed to be expecting her by the small wooden vessels. For a mad moment, it struck her that the Fuegian wanted her to get into the canoe and ride off into the night.

Shaking her head at her ridiculous thoughts, she made another attempt at conversation. "Handsome boats," she said, unable to rid herself of the notion that Mara was attempting to communicate something of significance.

"Handsome boats," the older woman echoed. Her mission-issue skirts fluttered in the light breeze.

Somewhere a fish jumped, the splash like sudden thunder in the still of the night. Helena took a step toward the shoreline. "Tomorrow we go in the canoe? You take me in the canoe?" She was feeling her way in the dark, but the direction seemed right.

Mara remained silent, her gnarled hand on the wooden bow.

Chapter 19

The sound was deafening.

Whirlpools of water, like hundreds of wild dervishes, swirled around her, pulling the front of her canoe in dizzying directions. Her palms sweating, Helena kept her upper hand on the paddle grips, pulling the blade through the water and making a shape as though she were stirring a huge kettle of soup. Behind her, Mara stroked steadily onward, nimbly negotiating outcrops of rocks and frothing vortexes that threatened to suck both of them into a wet grave.

When she'd left the mission hut quietly and alone just before sunrise, she knew that Mara would be waiting for her by the canoes with the same stoic expression that Helena had come to expect from her. Wearing her trousers and an oilskin she'd borrowed from a hook on the back of the door of the hut, she clutched her satchel filled with basic art supplies, a few coins, and a change of clothing. For food and shelter and transport, she would have to rely solely on Mara.

A spume of ice water stung her face, but she kept stroking, keeping time with the beating of her heart. The canoe swung sharply to the right, just before tipping dramatically to the left, and a shaft of cold water soaked her trousered legs.

Drowning was out of the question. She'd narrowly avoided that fate not long ago—although this time she wouldn't have Ramsay to save her.

A small brazier burned sluggishly behind her, its stingy warmth cold comfort. She switched the blade to her other hand and pulled it through the eddy, the resistance so powerful that she imagined the water was only a few degrees away from becoming ice.

Why hadn't she included Nicholas Ramsay in her plans?

It was a question she was reluctant to examine too closely. Her last wish was to frighten or alienate Mara, something Ramsay or Hornby might have accomplished with a fierce line of questioning. Besides, she couldn't even begin to articulate what exactly she was hoping to accomplish with the Fuegian.

It was time again to rely on herself. While Ramsay had given her much over the course of their voyage, he would be forever closed to her, a man so steeped in the darkness of his past, he would never allow himself to emerge in the light of day. It was that darkness that she didn't trust and the shadows that, for her own survival, she couldn't lose herself in.

But dear God, she was tempted.

The bow of the canoe sliced through a froth of rapids sending another splash of frigid water over the gunwale and into the canoe. She was now kneeling in a puddle, her cloak and trousers soaked from the thigh down. Either the cold had numbed her legs or a peculiar exhilaration had taken over her body because her belief in her own abilities and Mara's skills was unwavering. It was all she had.

She felt a stab in the region where her heart should be—and somehow she knew that she would never have Nicholas Ramsay. He gave nothing of himself. Except his body and that expert, controlled sensuality that had liberated her from a dark place of humiliation and oppression. But she knew, she suspected, deep inside, that a carnal connection would never be enough.

For what seemed like days, they paddled on and Helena stopped thinking, mesmerized by the heavy ache in her shoulders and arms. Her muscles had stopped screaming, the pain replaced by a stinging numbness. Yet she'd never felt so alive and so far away from her former life, which now seemed like a prison house that she would forever turn her back on. With every draw on the paddle, she was convinced that she was getting closer to the key.

The key that would guarantee her freedom.

When she finally looked up from the curls of water dripping off the end of her paddle, she could see that they were headed around the curve in the river. She had no idea where they were, having lost her bearings when they first left the sea behind and headed into an intercoastal river that snaked its way to the west. It was probably close to noon, but the heavy gray sky gave only a hint of the sunshine that lay beyond a bank of perpetual cloud.

Her neck cracked as she glanced over her shoulder to look at Mara who was stoically maneuvering the canoe into a gully that narrowed into what looked like a swamp. Helena pulled her paddle from the water, watching as the Fuegian carefully steered the vessel onto the muddy bank. With a lithe grace more familiar in a much younger woman, she exited the canoe to stand akimbo and knee-deep in the swamp's thick water.

At first she couldn't move. Every muscle protesting, Helena scrambled from the boat, peering around her to quickly take in the shapes and colors of the surrounding hills and brush. The water was like a cold, thick soup, choked with debris, and even more difficult to trudge through. The stink of decay assailed her nostrils.

But she felt the flush of anticipation. "That was an incredible feat, Mara, getting us here. Many thanks."

The older woman stared straight ahead, shouldering the pack on her back, her face impassive. "Incredible feat. Many thanks," she echoed. And not for the first time, Helena was desperate to learn a few words of her friend's native tongue.

She watched in admiration as the older woman doused the flames in the brazier of the boat, leaving one burning coal they could use to ignite the fire later.

Grabbing her satchel from the gunwhale of the canoe, she plodded behind her for a steep uphill climb that took them past several berms. She was wide awake and inexpressibly fatigued at the same time, invigorated and exhausted. Perhaps she was hallucinating, the terrain unfolding around her like a disorienting moonscape.

Keeping her eyes fixed on the steady trudge of Mara several yards ahead of her, she tried to keep focus, the weariness invading her bones warring with her spirit.

Where was Ramsay?

The silent question bounced off the surrounding hills that were becoming taller and narrower, blocking out more of the skies. Perhaps it was the fatigue, but she wanted him next to her, his pace matching hers, his arm around her waist, with a violence that scared her.

She wanted him more than she wanted her next breath.

Dropping the satchel at her feet, she stopped to take a shuddering mouthful of air.

When she looked up, she saw it.

Mara had stopped in front of what appeared to be a giant mound arising out of the ground. But if Helena squinted past her, she could make out the faint outlines of an entranceway, not exactly a door but an area where the dirt had been pushed away.

She ran the last few yards watching Mara shrug the pack from her shoulders and into her arms before disappearing into the small gap. Bending low, Helena followed eagerly, pleased for once that she had no fear of either darkness or confined spaces. The duke had locked her in her chambers many times without the benefit of tapers or a gas lamp and, out of sheer pride, she'd learned to repel and finally halt the waves of panic.

It would have been pitch-black had it not been for the

torch that the older woman removed from her pack, lit efficiently, and then held aloft.

The passageway slanted gradually downward, narrowing
the deeper they walked, almost overwhelming them with the
odor of graveyards and cemeteries, of damp, dank earth.

"Where are you taking me, Mara?" The whisper was
smothered by the dark—useless, aimless words—but she didn't
expect an answer.

The older woman pretended not to hear as she shuffled
carefully forward, the passageway curving slightly before ta-
pering to the width of a generously sized wardrobe. Her
shuffling became slower until she finally stopped.

Helena placed a hand on the wall, the moistness of the
earth seeping into her skin. It occurred to her that there had
to be a source of air in the cavern without which Mara's
torch would have gone out.

But right now she shone it to the side, down a strip of rock
floor that jutted suddenly along one wall. Astonishingly, three
steps, carved from solid rock, led to an extended mass of ash
that lay heaped in the center.

It looked like a freshly dug grave.

Holding the torch high, Mara made her way down the steps
and Helena quickly followed until they were both kneeling
on the ground. Aware that this was an extraordinary moment,
she waited for a sign from the older woman.

It never came.

A trickle of dirt skirted down the wall behind them. Then
another. Like pelting rain. She jerked her head upward toward the sound.

It was the first and last time she'd ever heard his approach
because Nicholas Ramsay usually moved with a preternatural stealth. He stood on high, a torch burning in his right
hand, surveying the strange scene below. The flickering light
elongated his body, making him appear taller and more alien
to her than ever before.

"You followed us." Blood rushed to her head with the im-

pact of a roaring ocean. She jumped up from her kneeling position and gripped the handle of her satchel, unaccountably
angry and oddly euphoric at the same time.

He had come for her. Ridiculous notion.

He had come for what Mara could reveal to them.

"Makes me wonder if I can trust you, Helena," he said in
his cool, unconcerned voice. He took the three stairs down to
the pit, his eyes fixed on the ash-covered mass. He nodded
briefly to Mara who had watched their exchange silently. "I
didn't think it was necessary for you to slip away from the
mission without apprising me of the situation first."

There was a proprietary edge to his tone. And she didn't
care for it. "I don't need your permission to do anything,
Ramsay." Never in her life would she answer to a man again.
"That was never part of our agreement."

"I'd wager you've never canoed before, not that a small
fact like that would hold you back, clearly. You could easily
have drowned."

"Mara is incredibly skilled and competent, and she ensured that both of us arrived safely."

"Fortunately for you."

She also didn't care for the cavalier dismissal. "I was tired
of waiting and doing nothing. And I discovered that Mara
and I"—she gestured to the woman beside her—"had a particular rapport that I couldn't risk by involving you. Surely
you understand that."

He shrugged as though the matter no longer concerned
him and turned his gaze to the older woman. "What are you
going to show Helena, Mara?" he asked gently.

"To show Helena, Mara?" she replied unhelpfully. Glancing at the torch in his hand with something close to suspicion, the Fuegian continued to kneel by the ash-covered
mound. She peered at Helena and then back at Ramsay.

He was a man who found it difficult to relinquish control,
but Helena could not spare a shred of sympathy. "I think she
wants you to leave," she said instinctively. In the gloom, his

eyes were dark and merciless, and it struck her she was seeing the real Nicholas Ramsay for the first time, a man who let nothing stand in his way. She shivered. "You know the way out," she said, keeping her voice strong before kneeling next to Mara on the dirt floor.

Conscious that he remained where he was, she deliberately tried to ignore him. Folding her hands on her bent knees, she addressed Mara directly. "What's under this ash? What did you want to share with me?"

The older woman simply nodded solemnly.

"We're not going to get anywhere unless you leave, Ramsay." She didn't try to modulate her impatience. "We're so close. I can feel it."

The scrape of his boots on the dirt floor told her that he was moving in closer, examining the mound over her shoulder. "This has nothing to do with *feeling* anything. Obviously, there are remains of some kind under that ash, ash being a superb preservative."

"You're remarkably well informed."

"I'm simply prepared."

"I refuse to do anything without Mara's permission."

"Then it's helpful that I don't have any of those reservations. I trust you haven't forgotten that your life and freedom hang in the balance."

That same mesmerizing, persuasive tone. Such an expert at deception, never revealing, *never, ever* open. "And what else is hanging in the balance?" Suddenly, she was weary. "Perhaps this is a good time to finally tell me."

She heard rather than saw his smile. "Still suspicious. Perhaps you're making things simpler for me, after all."

His words seemed out of context, but the muscles of her neck tightened like a cornered animal's. This was the man who could make her body explode with exquisite sensation. This was her *lover*, her first real lover, but she couldn't help but feel it was all an illusion of his deliberate making.

She trusted him. And then she didn't.

"You really are a ruthless man," she said with a coldness that matched his for once. "I'd forgotten how familiar I am with your type, someone who thinks nothing of others and lets nothing get in the way of what he wants."

"It's what the world demands."

"You needn't remind me. I'm all too aware of what the world demands," she continued, hoping her voice wouldn't break, "but I refuse to proceed without Mara's permission." She felt vulnerable kneeling, aware that she was inches away from the strong length of his legs behind her.

"Why don't you ask her, then," he said with that same peculiar lack of urgency that she knew hid an implacable will. "Simply ask Mara what she would like to do next."

Helena glanced at the woman beside her, convinced that she was somehow following the heated discussion. Her expression remained impassive, but in her eyes there was an intensity that was unnerving.

"And why would she respond to me when she's not responded to you?"

"Because," he said deliberately, "there is a belief in both the Selk'nam and Yamana tribes that women once ruled over men in ancient times." He added dryly, "A utopia, no doubt."

She frowned, looking over her shoulder and up at him. "Firstly, how do you know? And secondly, your sarcasm isn't contributing to this situation."

His gaze locked with hers. "Matriarchal cultures aren't unusual in prehistory, and furthermore, this theory supports the assumption that the Fuegians may be the descendants of Australian aborigines who colonized this area long ago. They share similar practices in religion, body painting, and rock art."

She looked away from him. Australia again. Ramsay's knowledge and experience were far-reaching and staggering in breadth. Mackenzie had been correct when he said that the man had lived many lives and that the realization was daunting.

"Very well," she conceded stiffly. "I will bow to your superior learning in this situation."

"And none too graciously, I notice."

The likelihood of successfully ignoring him was slim, but she tried.

"Mara," she began, "may I touch these ashes? May I remove them? Like this?" Tentatively, gently, she scooped a handful at the edge of the mound. The older woman moved her lips but emitted no sounds, perhaps mouthing a silent incantation or benediction under her breath.

Helena's hands hovered over the mass, unsure and unwilling to go farther. She'd forgotten about her aching muscles and the dank, close smell permeating the small enclosure. And she tried to forget about Ramsay, his body inches from her own.

Mute and fervent, she hoped and waited for a response.

When it came, it was the gentlest of gestures, a light touch on her arm. Then without a glance at Ramsay or Helena, Mara uncoiled her body and crouched at the edge of the mass of ashes, and began reverently and carefully to dig.

Helena waited a few moments before joining her. The ashes were cool to the touch, leaving an oily coating on her fingers and black crescents beneath her nails. With an elbow, she pushed a strand of hair from her forehead, suddenly afraid of what would be revealed when the digging stopped.

Ramsay stood back, watching the two women engaged in a strange ritual as they scooped handfuls of ash to the side. Helena would never be sure how much time had passed when she felt the first scrape of bone against her fingers.

It was a skeleton.

The pelvic bones appeared first. A female.

She was an artist and she had studied da Vinci's drawings of the human body with their precise layout of muscle and bone structures.

Then the legs emerged and, under Mara's hands, a cranium, curiously small. Helena did a quick survey of the body, approximately three-and-a-half feet tall. They had removed perhaps six inches of ash. She fell back on her haunches, a buzzing in her ears, whether from the lack of air in the cavern or shock, she would never know.

Ramsay's hands rested on her shoulders. "Are you all right?" The blood had drained from her face.

Mara had returned to her original kneeling position, her gaze rapt on the skeleton still reposing, half-buried, in ash.

"We all need some fresh air." Ramsay lifted Helena to her feet, while offering a free hand to Mara. She couldn't disagree. Wordlessly, they wound their way out of the cavern.

In spite of the overcast skies, the light of day stung Helena's eyes. A feverish energy pulsed around them, and her own heart was pounding like a trip hammer. Ramsay offered both women water from his flask, and first Mara and then Helena drank thirstily. They leaned against the packed earth of the cavern, lost in their own thoughts.

When Helena finally spoke, her first words were for Mara.

"Thank you. Thank you," she said simply, hoping the woman would somehow and someday know the enormity of the gratitude she was owed. Not for changing Helena's life, but for changing the world's.

Serene and untroubled, Mara wiped the soot from her hands on her coarse skirts. She looked up into the sky as though sensing an oncoming rain.

Helena glanced quickly at Ramsay who hung back, watching with detachment as though a performance was unfolding before him. Shrugging the satchel from her shoulders, with shaking hands she withdrew a piece of charcoal and paper. "May I draw? May I draw, Mara?" She gestured expansively and then pointed in the direction of the cavern.

The older woman's eyes were obsidian. "May I draw. May I draw, Mara." And then she continued her search of the sky.

"Thank you," Helena breathed, every muscle in her body suddenly collapsing.

"Are you certain you're up to doing this right now?" As

always, that voice tempted, channeling a semblance of concern to achieve his ends. "It's permissible to take a rest."

She turned to him, taking measure of the man as if for the first time. Even outside the confines of the cavern, he seemed taller, broader somehow. Chiseled from granite rather than the warmer bronze of her fevered and yearning imagination.

Foolish. That's what she was.

She grabbed her satchel and stuffed the paper and charcoal back into the bag. "I don't care to rest or to wait, Ramsay. Allow me two hours and I'll have a likeness that captures every nuance of this . . . this . . . I don't even know what to call her."

He looked deceptively at ease, as though everything were unfolding according to his plan. He was standing too close and she started to step back, away from him. "Ironic that Darwin's discovery is a female."

She looked into his unreadable eyes. "The irony isn't lost on me, I can assure you. I can imagine how disconcerting it will be for the Bishop of London and his acolytes to discover that evidence of *man*'s missing link is not only part ape and part human but also female." She thought again of the small cranium and the large jaw so reminiscent of primates coupled with the human shape of the pelvis and legs that could clearly support an upright body.

"It's extraordinary," she murmured. "I've never seen anything like it."

"Nor I."

In an uneasy truce, they left Mara sitting outside while they returned to the interior of the cavern.

For several hours and well beyond exhaustion, Helena attempted to capture the likeness of the form revealed from beneath the ashes. Holding the torch steadily above her, Ramsay watched her silently, but she felt he was calibrating her every motion. She blocked him out, concentrating instead on her memories of drawing classes, the droning voice of her instructors, and later Horace Webb's direction as they worked together in his studio, before she had one of her own. Often he would guide her hand or that patiently and objectively, point out that her proportions were off or that she had missed a crucial element.

But it had been a few years since she'd attempted an anatomical rendering. *Capture the skeleton from different viewpoints.* Not much help here. She only had a one-dimensional perspective as the frame lay on its back.

She began with the skull, finding the eye sockets, and then moved to the clavicle, dusting away more ash, to reveal it protruding just above the shoulder blades.

This was not the time for sweeping strokes of her charcoal pencil. The marks on the vellum were controlled and accurate, her eyes testing and measuring with every mark on the page to ensure the greatest accuracy.

She moved on to the top edge of the pelvic bone, the iliac crest, which revealed the placement of the legs and lower torso. The knees and the ankle bones both protruded enough for careful observation, and she sensed that capturing their fine distinctions would prove significant to the naturalists and scientists in London.

"So odd," she murmured to herself. "To my admittedly uneducated eye, the top half of our creature here appears primate and the lower half appears human."

Behind her, Ramsay waited. She flexed her fingers to relax the muscles and drew in a slow, deep breath.

"Water." He handed her his flask. As she took it from him without looking up, she noticed the fine tremor in her hands. She drank greedily, then absently set the container down beside her to finish her work.

Another hour passed before she unfurled from her sitting position and stepped away from the skeleton. She'd filled several pages of vellum, the frame of the long-dead creature rendered in as much detail as was humanly possible.

"Care to have a look?" She thrust the sheaf of paper at Ramsay.

He'd planted the torch in the ground over her shoulder to give her maximum light to do her work.

"I don't have to look. I know these drawings will be superb," he said evenly. It wasn't a simple compliment, it was the unvarnished truth and as close to honesty she would ever get from the man. She held her breath as he looked at her with those smoke-gray eyes that even in the gleam of the torchlight saw exactly who she was.

"Thank you," she said softly over the lump of unwanted emotion in her throat. "I'm pleased we're finished here."

Removing the sketches from her hands, he picked up her satchel from the floor and placed them carefully in the leather folio. "There's still more to be done, but your work is finished, Helena."

There was an uncomfortable finality in the statement. She froze. "What do you mean?"

"I'll explain, once we get back to the mission." He uprooted the torch from where he had planted it in the dirt floor, keeping his face expressionless. He stepped back against the wall, flattening his body so she could pass him in the narrow passage.

Reluctantly, she began to slide past, careful not to glide against him. In spite of her caution, a flush of lust, slow and inexorable, suffused her body. Even now, exhausted and emotional, she wanted him. She watched as her hand reached up to brush the hair from his forehead, then cupped his strong jaw in the curve of her palm.

His strong fingers closed on her wrist. "Don't," he said, his eyes dark. And it was as if he were closing a door on the both of them.

And she was afraid to ask why.

Chapter 20

"Lady Hartford, I cannot have you disappearing from the mission with one of the natives in such a spontaneous fashion." Reverend Hornby marched toward her, the ragged ends of his cassock snapping in the strong wind. His thin lips had disappeared in his face under the weight of his disapproval.

Helena marched straight past him, over the muddy bank and into the hut where she slammed the door decisively.

On all of them.

Most of all on Nicholas Ramsay.

Over his objections, she'd insisted on sharing the canoe with Mara on the return to the mission. This time they were going against the current, and every stroke of the paddle, under the vigilant eye of Ramsay, cost her last reserves of strength. Strangely and inexplicably deflated, she couldn't account for the unease that hung over her like a shroud, the dread intensifying once they'd returned to Woolya Cove.

She wrenched her oilcloth jacket from her shoulders and threw herself down on her cot, pulling the coarse blanket over her fatigued body. Blessed sleep is what she needed. But when she closed her eyes, visions crowded her consciousness, keeping sleep at bay. The skeleton with its gaping maw. Mosley and Sissinghurst, peering at her through a cage in Bedlam.

And her late husband, the duke, returning to haunt her, chasing her with a whip to the ends of the earth, to the lost and benighted place that was Reverend Hornby's mission.

But what she feared most of all was to dream of Nicholas Ramsay.

She cursed her imagination and her artist's eye. All she craved was sleep. Oblivion.

When she stirred, it was noon, an insipid stream of sun, high in the lone window of the room, nudging her awake. Wincing, she stretched her arms over her head and noticed that she was still fully clothed. Sticky and ragged, she pushed a tangle of hair from her face.

"You're probably sore."

She wasn't prepared for the specter of Nicholas Ramsay standing at the foot of her cot.

The sight of him was so sudden, so unexpected that she knew he must be a part of her nightmarish agony that by some means continued to trail her waking hours. Unease still saturated every aching muscle in her body, but despite the miasma of mistrust that colored their relations, she couldn't deny a tormenting flash of pleasure.

Ironically, more than her father, the duke, or Sissinghurst, she knew at this moment that Ramsay would be the death of her.

It was a nightmare colliding with the solidity of reality.

"I have a strange sense that muscle soreness is the least of my worries," she said with a grimace. She pushed back the coarse blanket and rose shakily to her feet, all too excruciatingly aware that this was not the way the conversation between them should unfold.

"I always said you had good instincts," he said. He seemed to take no pleasure from the words. They were simply a statement of fact. She wanted to look away from that direct gaze that was so daunting in its emptiness. It would never be her refuge, much as she wanted it, *craved it* to be.

"Indeed," she said, then moved to the table in the middle of the room to put some distance between them. He was dressed again in his oilcloths, looking rested and overwhelmingly physical, and she had the unshakable impression that he was ready to depart, to leave Woolya Cove.

And go where, exactly?

Something wasn't right, had never been right. "You're going back to the site, aren't you?" she blurted out, leaning her hip against a chair in an attempt to appear in control. A thousand irrelevant thoughts ran through her mind as she continued to stare at him. That she was wearing trousers and a wrinkled shirt streaked with soot. That her hair was not even tied back by pins or a ribbon. That her feet were bare, and that every inch of her body was alert and trembling and ready to betray her.

Anything for his touch.

"Already done."

Two simple words and she felt her control slipping away. Immediately she was swamped with guilt. "You *did not* disturb the site." She bit out the words. "Those remains are important to Mara and her people, and deserve to remain here. Mara trusts me to keep the site safe and I trusted you . . ." She caught herself on the edge of hysteria and an inhalation of breath, the words outrunning her thoughts. "Swear to me that you didn't remove anything."

"I can't," he answered.

That stopped her, but only for a moment. "Even Darwin saw sense enough . . . to leave things." She choked, knowing that it was useless.

Because I always get what I want.

"We . . . you have the sketches. The drawings. Surely that's enough," she tried desperately.

He walked toward her and braced his hands on the table, his gaze not leaving her face. He was clean shaven, but she detected a haggardness around his eyes and mouth, the lines drawn with a heavier hand. "You know that's not enough, Helena, even you can't be so naïve. The drawings aren't enough without solid evidence."

She took a frightened step back. "You mean that they will never believe the work of a madwoman. That's what you mean."

"If you must, yes, that's what I mean," he said, his neutral tones cutting her to her core.

"You can't do this one thing for me? For these people," she gestured futilely, thinking of the Fuegians.

"There's too much at stake."

She searched desperately for a way out. "If I'm willing to risk my freedom, to risk incarceration in Bedlam, for God's sake, then surely a man of your means and your power could see fit to use other resources, find another way, to convince . . ." It was no good. "If the drawings weren't enough, why did you bring me along in the first place," she asked in a burst of clarity.

"That's a complicated answer and the reason I'm here."

Dread built in her chest. "I see," she tried to say as calmly as she could, but suddenly she wanted to get away. Could not bear to hear what he had to say next.

He levered away from the table. Panic rising in her throat, he must have seen her glance at the door because he strode over and slid back the lock with a decisive finality. "Always running away. But running away this time won't help. There's nowhere to escape, just miles of ocean at subarctic temperatures."

She shook her head wildly. "I don't know what you're talking about. You're not talking reason." Sagging against the table, she pulled her hair back from her face with a shaking hand.

He smiled now and it was full of pity and what seemed like contempt.

For both of them.

"I've waited a long time for this and, strangely enough, I can't find the words to describe what this means to me, what I feel. Perhaps because I no longer feel anything at all."

She searched his face desperately. "I don't understand. Perhaps I'm truly and finally going mad!"

He looked at her with that same frightening smile. "Although it would make it easier for you, you're not mad, Helena. You never have been and you never will be. It's cold comfort, but at least you have that."

"I'm not listening." She pressed her hands over her ears and turned away from him.

He continued unabated, "Since our curious relationship began, you've been clever with your questions, always wanting to learn more, always probing. And now here I am, willing to disclose—"

"Stop it!" She dropped her hands and turned to him, her eyes wintry with despair. "How can you do this to me? You forced me to trust you. You saved my life more than once. Was it all for a purpose, something hidden, something ghastly? Did you ever feel anything at all for me?" She took a ragged breath, her voice breaking. "Even though you knew about my past, you used me, used sex for your own ends, as cold-bloodedly and ruthlessly as the cheapest whoremaster."

He didn't flinch. "And I thought I was the instrument of your salvation, as you informed me more than once." He barely raised his voice. "I recall you in the throes of delirium begging me not to stop, importuning me to go on. And the nights aboard the ship where *you took me*—"

She turned her head away.

"Look at me, Helena. Or is it too much temptation, now that you know what pleasure is. Are you afraid that your body will betray you, that you will succumb to the urge *to fuck* one last time?"

"Enough!"

But it wasn't enough. Helena felt a deep tear begin inside

her, a painful slash that was threatening to rip her apart. Because she knew with a sickening dread that there was more gathering like dark clouds on the horizon.

He came slowly around the table. "You think your own troubles outweigh the rest of the world's, don't you? Total self-absorption, like so many artists, ready and willing to sacrifice anything and everything for their art. That's your fatal flaw. Your blindness to the world's suffering. The poor rich heiress who had to earn her living on her back, in the services of her elderly, twisted husband, who found she couldn't live out her fantasies or her ambitions, or hang on to her wealth. Unfortunate, yes, but a tragedy it's not."

For a moment, she was unable to speak, unable to move. She stared at his hands, strong and elegant, relaxed by his side. Later she would always wonder at the sudden leap of intuition that permitted her to make the connection. It was immediately, stunningly clear.

"That's what this is all about." The words were ripped from her throat. *"Your past."*

He folded his arms over his chest, the mocking smile finally fading. "Understanding dawns, I see."

"This has everything to do with revenge. Against me."

"There you are again with that artistic sensibility of yours that prevents you from seeing past the end of your beautiful nose," he murmured softly, but his eyes narrowed. "And yet you were in the process of giving away a goodly sum of your legacy. To all types of charitable organizations. Guilt perhaps?"

A cold, clammy sweat coated her skin. Her mouth was dry with dread.

"I've asked you several times in the past—did you ever wonder where your fortune came from? The one you're so reluctant to give over to the bishop's control?" He shook his head mockingly. "I think not, probably because you sensed the stink of corruption and exploitation around your father, Mr. Peacock Whitely, and were reluctant to see beyond it. Beyond to the thousands of factory workers he misused and abused as slave labor. I say workers, but most of them were children. Small and limber enough to get caught in machines, sometimes losing a limb or a scalp, or succumbing to malnutrition.

"And when Mr. Peacock Whitely—was there ever a more ironic name?—heard about something he didn't like or decided that someone had outlived his or her purpose, he would simply ship them off, transform them into an even more valuable commodity by transporting them to places like Australia where they would live out the rest of their foreshortened lives in mine shafts, breathing in dust and decay until they simply lay down under their burdens and never got up again."

His voice was monotone, as though he were telling the story about someone else. "And I, like you, was just one person who, in the grand scheme of things, didn't really matter at all. Unfortunate, but hardly a tragedy," he said softly but with finality.

Horror dried the sweat from her body.

"And that's why I'm leaving you here, Helena. Closing a circle."

She looked across at him, hollow-eyed and disbelieving.

"The conditions are much more salubrious than a convict ship or a mine shaft in Australia, you'll agree," he continued calmly. "And you will be able to escape the clutches of Sissinghurst and his like, perhaps returning to London, in three years or so when the next vessel pulls into Woolya Cove. By that time, your wayward ways will have been forgotten, and perhaps if I and the X Club have our way, Sissinghurst will have been demoted to some parish outpost."

She raised her head finally. He looked the same but he was a monster.

Fighting against the tremors threatening to shut down her body, she clenched her fists until her nails drew blood. Physical pain—a reminder that she knew how to survive. She forced herself to breathe again, vowing that she would never allow this fiend to defeat her.

She straightened away from the table. "So you propose to leave me here. So I can experience a semblance of your own, damned-to-hell past. Or perhaps as a salve to your wounded pride." She took a step toward him, her every move defiant. "My father has been dead close to ten years. You would think that would have been enough for a normal man. Instead," she spat out the words, "you visit your pathetic vengeance on his daughter, all the while exploiting a native people who have already endured the dubious benefits of a relationship with all-conquering empires."

Ragged, sweaty, and exhausted, she didn't care, advancing toward him with venom spitting from every pore. "Hardly the actions of a real man intent on saving the detritus of society."

Energy flowed through her veins, every pulse beat thrumming with savage intensity. "And of course you're so innocent. You've never spilled blood. You've never exploited a single human being in your relentless pursuit of power and wealth. I've heard the stories. Human cargo, opiates, every manner of contraband."

She stopped a heartbeat away from him, her face upturned to his, their breaths mingling. She did not back down. "Every fortune comes with a price, Ramsay, as much as one would like to disown it."

"And you would know."

"I know the exact price, down to the last tuppence."

The rise and fall of his chest didn't change. He absorbed her words with studied disinterest. And she knew he had no intention of being around her a moment longer than he had to. Her first impression of him had been entirely correct, that long-ago night at Madame Congais's.

His face could have been minted on a Roman coin. Hard, cold, and resolute.

She stared at him, everything converging on that one moment. And then she reached out and slapped him, putting every ounce of remaining strength she had into her trembling arm.

She'd never hit anyone before in her entire life.

Her hand had left an imprint on his jaw. But he just smiled.

"As long as we understand each other," he said.

Chapter 21

Horace Webb crushed the letter in his fist. The rain beat steadily against the windows of his carriage house, a torrential staccato that underscored his mood.

She lives. Helena is still alive.

Smoothing out the crumpled letter on the heavily embossed leather desk blotter, he scanned the missive, the beautifully looped lettering as familiar to him as his own handwriting. Date-marked over two months ago at Cape Verde, it was irrefutable proof in Helena's own hand.

He swung around in the chair to watch the rain pouring in small rivers against the window. She was obviously enamored of Nicholas Ramsay, that much was clear. Unexpected and dangerous, it was a fact that he would have to deal with. After the duke had passed away and Helena had taken on a series of lovers with a desultory urgency that was as unusual as it was remarkable, she'd sworn to him, up and down, that she'd discovered she really didn't like or need a man in her life at all.

She'd clearly changed her mind.

Not that Nicholas Ramsay, from what he'd gleaned, would be easy to manage. Either for Helena or for Horace. Because if she returned to London under Ramsay's protection—

He would have to think carefully about this change in circumstances.

Ruthless as the devil himself, Ramsay was all but immortal, immune to public censure, above the law and infinitely disinterested in the approbation of society. Dear Lord, what had Helena done now, associating herself with such a man.

He dropped his head in his hands with a surge of anger. It had always been thus. Defying her father, shocking the academy with her work, baiting her husband, giving away huge portions of her wealth, enraging the Bishop of London, for God's sake. The litany was never ending.

And the latest was Ramsay.

All of it because she wanted to and she could, protected by an obscenely large inheritance that was both her making and her undoing.

A knock at the door of the study roused him from his fevered ruminations. Perdita's pert nose poked through the opening. "I don't want to disturb you, my darling, but there's a man at the door. . . . I directed him to your solicitor as you'd instructed me, but he refuses to leave."

Her voice was tremulous and he hated hearing the underlying quaver of misgiving in her words. Two weeks ago, he'd had to dismiss several of the servants, including the housekeeper who would have answered the door today, a sign that a woman of Perdita's background understood too well. It would be only a matter of time before she would find herself another protector.

The house he shared with his wife mercifully was in her family's name, along with a steady stipend that at least kept their children fed and clothed.

Webb swung around in his chair. "Perdita, I have told you several times not to answer the door," he said with barely concealed impatience. She was such a child, but he suspected the brain of a bookkeeper percolated under the lace cap she wore.

"I know, my dear." She bit her lower lip. "But since Mrs. Cranston was let go, I don't quite know how to go about managing the house." She twisted small, delicate fingers in a show of helplessness. "These economies are beyond my ken, my darling. I know you asked me to cut back on the lamp oil we're consuming, because of course I realize you need the lighting for your work, so in terms of quantities, I'm not quite sure. Because you see, there's probably a way to go about it that I'm not privy to. Never having to bother about such household details before." She rambled on, Horace beyond hearing the concerned chirping noises she was making.

He turned back to his desk, once again smoothing the crumpled letter on his leather blotter.

His debts. Even the last wager he'd made against Tyndall at the club in a fit of inebriated folly was just a drop in an ever-widening whirlpool that threatened to suck him to the very bottom of an ignominious fate.

When Whitely was still alive, he could have gone to him, asked him delicately for credit, as only a man of his aristocratic background could do. And although Whitely would narrow those shrewd eyes of his, he would finally acquiesce in exchange for a sponsorship to the Carlton Club or a timely and valuable introduction.

It was precisely how Whitely first met the Duke of Hartford. He had greased the wheels of that particular alliance.

"So what are we to do, dear Horace?" He wasn't about to turn and look at Perdita because he knew that her eyes would be innocently wide but not quite successful in hiding the threat beneath those fluttering eyelashes. She would be ensconced in Tyndall's townhouse before the fortnight was over.

And he would be in the poorhouse. The rain pelted on the windows and he shuddered, dropping his head back into his hands.

The odor was gut-wrenching, particularly for someone of the Bishop of London's delicate sensibilities. He held a handkerchief to his nose as he and Deacon Mosley were shown to a warren of rooms that were the madhouse-keeper's quarters.

The screams, punctuated by animal noises and the sounds of obscene bodily functions, faded to a faint roar.

The bishop was familiar with the history of Bethlem itself, once a monastic foundation dating from as early as 1247 and involved with the care of the lunatic since at least the early fifteenth century. Synonymous with chaos, danger, and disorder, the institution was considered one of the preeminent sights of London.

The little girl standing in the center of Dr. Munro's offices, with leather handcuffs binding her wrists, was anywhere from 8 to 12 years old. Sissinghurst found it difficult to pinpoint a precise age, but such were the effects of malnutrition.

Introduced as Missy by the affable doctor, she averted her gaze as they entered the room.

"Oh, my dear goodness," rambled Munro, quickly pulling out chairs for the bishop and Mosley. "I thought we had dispensed with this one here earlier today. I shall call the attendant immediately and have her returned to her cell," he said, ready to dart from the room to call one of the burly guards who patrolled the premises.

Sissinghurst held up a fleshy hand. "One moment, Doctor, if you would be so kind." He turned to the young girl, who remained motionless as a porcelain doll, with shrewd appraisal. "What precisely seems to be the dilemma? She appears to be sound and able-bodied. I have seen many her age in factories."

Mosley echoed the sentiment. "Sometimes nothing more than good honest work is what's needed to bring them back into the fold."

Munro hovered by the doorway, indecision marking his brow. He was the fourth of a family dynasty that had continuously presided over London's Bedlam since 1728. Their family had built on decades of contacts to create a remarkably extensive and extremely lucrative practice ministering to the mad. His father had even acquired madhouses of his own, obtained healthy retainers from his contacts with a range of establishments. After all, if undertakers and clerics could make death the occasion for profit, there was enough opportunity and fresh prospects to gain from the care of lunatics.

Disobedience, incoherence, melancholia, menace, uncontrolled rage, immoral behavior—the trade in lunacy was thriving. However, there was something in the bishop's targeted questions that was worth heeding.

Munro stepped back into the room, picking up a wooden pointer on his desk. He smiled at the bishop and Mosley. "So good of you to take an interest," he murmured, "in young Missy here."

The bishop's gaze was expectant, his hands resting calmly on his considerable girth. "Do proceed. I've yet to see demonstrated that she cannot be put to good and honest work," he huffed.

Munro's smile widened, his fingers tightening on the pointer. "I understand your momentary confusion, Your Grace. Missy here is a fair-haired, nice-looking girl. She even knows her letters enough to stand up and read from the New Testament if requested. Don't you, Missy?" He prodded her gently in the shoulder blades with the pointer. When she didn't respond, he continued, "However, in the factory where she worked, she began tearing her dress from her body, shrieking obscenities so unsuitable for a young girl her age, no matter what sewer her family emerged from." The doctor sighed. "As a result, she was brought to us, and unfortunately, we've had to put leather handcuffs on her wrists so tightly that they make her hands swell."

He demonstrated by tapping the small wrists with his pointer. Mosley and Sissinghurst watched closely.

"But you see, she pays no heed. It does not hurt her any. Why yesterday, she tied a canvas belt around her waist so tightly that it made my heart ache to look at it," he said, placing the pointer back down on his desk. "I'm certain it would have stopped her breath in a short time so the wardens saw fit to tie her to the back of the seat with the ends of it."

The little girl remained unresponsive.

"I see," said the bishop with equanimity. Mosley was staring, taking a peculiar interest in the proceedings, which was no surprise. The bishop sighed, letting a bit of his irritation show. It was a good thing that he'd decided to take charge of the Nicholas Ramsay matter. Mosley would have been entirely unprepared.

He turned his attention back to Munro. "Thank you for the comprehensive explications, Doctor. Please have the child removed and we can carry on with our business."

In short order, the girl was swept from the room as though she were no more than a piece of annoying debris. The bishop settled back in his chair, watching Munro slide behind his enormous desk, and aimed his first salvo at Mosley.

"Now as I understand it, Doctor, the deacon here has been in discussion with you about my charge, the unfortunate Lady Hartford."

"Indeed, we have," said Mosley.

The doctor rested his hands on the top of his desk and tried to look concerned. "He's apprised me of the widow's ill-fated condition, most likely caused by the effects of grief and, what we call today, a type of female hysteria most marked in women of unsuitably high intelligence who exhibit inappropriate interests that, in the interests of courtesy and respect, I shan't enumerate."

Sissinghurst smiled cynically but decided to play along with the charade. "Thank you, Doctor, for shielding us from the world's wickedness. Although I should like to clarify that, in my humble, unprofessional opinion, Lady Hartford suffers from a type of moral insanity." He smiled slyly at Mosley, who shifted uncomfortably in his chair. "The deacon here has also indicated that you have discussed some of the treatments available to my aunt. And I'm sure he has emphasized how crucial it is that she remains, physically at least, in robust health."

Mosley interjected, coughing lightly. "Indeed, the doctor

and I would only conscience the very latest, most modern protocols."

Munro nodded with confidence at the bookshelves, grimed with dust, lining the west wall of his office. "We now have a veritable arsenal of cures and remedies available."

"Such as?"

"We can begin with solitude and darkness," the doctor began, self-importance creeping into his voice. "If that does not prove effective, we can move on to mild corporal punishment, gagging, and of course, dousing."

Mosley added reasonably, "Munro explained that a prominent doctor in America found that enclosing a patient in a coffinlike box with holes and then lowering him or her into a tank, until bubbles of air ceased to rise, prepared the patient to be released, rubbed, and revived."

Munro nodded. "The concept behind the treatment rests on the premise that once a patient is nearly drowned and then brought back to life, he can make a fresh start, leaving his disease behind."

"I am most impressed," drawled the bishop.

Encouraged, the doctor continued, "Failing revivification, we can always try the tranquilizer chair. The patient is strapped into a gyration device suspended from the ceiling by chains. Then attendants swing and spin them for hours."

"Spinning reduces the force of blood flowing into the brain," concluded Mosley, "thereby relaxing the muscles and lowering the pulse, an effective means of taming their mad passions."

Sissinghurst made approving sounds under his breath. "How far we've come, gentlemen," he said, as though conferring a benediction. "I'm feeling very confident in leaving my aunt in your clearly capable hands. But I do believe you have omitted one possible treatment option, one that has proved quite salubrious in calming and sedating women, in particular, suffering from the type of moral contagion that my aunt is inclined to."

Munro pursed his lips, looking inquiringly at the bishop. "You are speaking of pharmacological interventions?"

"Precisely. Laudanum, or in the case of my aunt who may need stronger dosages, given her deteriorating condition, *opium* may be of help."

Munro once again picked up the wooden pointer on his desk, weighing the moral implications of the suggestion.

"Of course, extra expenses in this instance would not prove awkward in the least," added Sissinghurst helpfully.

Munro tapped the pointer before relinquishing it. "Of course," he amended with an ingratiating bonhomie, "we can certainly consider *every* option."

Mosley flushed a delicate pink. "I've already informed the doctor of my willingness to assist him in every possible way, and that I will be taking a *personal* interest in the ongoing care of Lady Hartford."

Sissinghurst gripped the arms of his chair, making to rise. Halfway out of the seat, he glanced sharply at the deacon and then back to Munro. "Of course, Deacon Mosley will make his time available to you, Doctor, but"—he paused deliberately—"only if he can execute his other duties in a timely fashion."

Mosley jerked from his chair. "This is one time I won't disappoint." The words were meant expressly for the bishop—who was not reassured.

"May we have a few moments alone, Doctor?" he requested, sitting back down in his chair.

Munro quickly assessed the situation, jumping out from behind his desk like a shopkeeper ready to fetch and display his most precious wares to his wealthy clients. "Of course, certainly. Take as long as you like. I should take this time to check in on our little Missy." He bustled out the door with brisk efficiency, closing it softly behind him.

The bishop heaved a heavy sigh expressly for Mosley's benefit, sparing a last look around the grimy offices. "I so do detest having to lend my presence to these types of proceedings. But given your performance up to this moment, I have justifiable concerns. I trust that you *are* prepared to meet the *Flying Cloud* when she pulls into port? And keep in mind that this increasing obsession with my aunt," he said with distaste thick on his tongue, "cannot interfere with your dealings with Nicholas Ramsay. He is not a man to be trifled with."

"Of course, Your Grace, I am well aware."

Sissinghurst continued unabated, "You do realize that the upcoming debate with members of the X Club, which the archbishop has expressly asked me to oversee, looms on the horizon." His lips curled in disgust. "I should think that it takes precedence over your indecorous fixation with my aunt."

Mosley started to speak, but he waved a hand dismissively, silencing him. "Fortunately, I have made it my business to obtain additional inducements to help with Mr. Ramsay should he prove intransigent. In which case you are to refer him to me."

Mosley's pale blue eyes widened in disbelief. "To you—personally?"

The bishop straightened from his chair, hard and regal, returning the look with one of his own. "I shouldn't look so surprised. He holds three quarters of the House of Lords and at least one half of Parliament in his hands. That's what great fortunes can do for one, if applied correctly."

Mosley opened his mouth as if to ask something, but Sissinghurst interrupted him. "Don't look so startled, and rest assured that I have simply used Ramsay's own modus operandi against him."

Anticipation surged through him. "He has covered his tracks well, but that doesn't dictate we can't create some of our own."

Chapter 22

The water in the basin was bloody, the face in the mirror dark and feral.

Ignoring the oozing cut on his cleanly shaven chin, Nicholas Ramsay tossed the razor to the side of the basin. He avoided mirrors these days.

Grabbing a linen towel, he looked away from the reflection, from the bastard that he had become, or more accurately, had always been.

The *Flying Cloud* had shuddered into the Port of London earlier that morning, but he was in no rush to leave the vessel. There were years when he'd been overwhelmed by the city's size and squalor, by its grandeur and its filth. Hundreds of ships entered the port each month bringing coal or grain, sugar and rum, tea and spices from the Indies, wine from the Mediterranean, furs, timber, and hemp from Russia, and tobacco and cotton from the Americas. It was the center of the universe, but Ramsay knew it as a place where the empire's palaces burned ever brighter against the darker shadows of its factories and slums.

The knock was discreet. Keeping his back to the door, Ramsay pulled a shirt from the small wardrobe and shrugged it on. Accustomed to cramped quarters, he could barely turn around in the cabin. "What is it, Mac?"

The Australian poked his head in the door. "The first officer reports that all the papers are in order and we can proceed with disembarkation." His eyes swept the cabin, taking in the narrow bed, the built-in cabinets, and little else that revealed the power and wealth of its occupant. "However, there is a gentleman that wishes to speak with you, sir. I suggested that he meet you at one of the warehouse offices at your convenience, but he insists on conferring with you at once, aboard the ship."

Ramsay buttoned the cuffs of his shirt and, without looking, grabbed a dark wool jacket from the wardrobe. "Tell him some other time, Mac."

"I could have him escorted from the *Flying Cloud,* sir, but I shouldn't want to create a disturbance." Mac leaned in the doorway, deliberately lingering. "It could be important, given that he maintains he has a message from the Bishop of London."

Ramsay lifted his head. "You don't say," he said coolly. "Tell him to fuck off." He smiled grimly. "Or on second thought I would prefer to do that personally in a public venue. Maybe I'll save it until we meet at the great debate, hosted by the archbishop and the X Club."

Mac coughed and cleared his throat, one foot in the hallway, the other in the narrow cabin. "I know that theoretically the bishop no longer serves as an immediate threat to Lady Hartford but, just to be sure . . ." He trailed off and Ramsay didn't register the contempt behind his old friend's words. Even hearing the name said aloud, *Lady Hartford,* caused him no more discomfort than the razor's nick on his jaw.

"You're still bleeding, sir. And it's getting on your shirt collar."

With a grunt, Ramsay grabbed the discarded towel hanging over the porcelain basin and applied it briefly to his jaw. "Don't give me that look, Mac. Lady Hartford is safer in Tierra del Fuego than she would be in London at present." The rationale sounded false even to his ears. "So whatever Sissinghurst or his acolytes have to say is immaterial." He discarded the towel. "And why is this any concern of yours, or need I ask?"

The Australian's expression was bleak. "You know, sir, I don't think it was entirely fair, how things ended."

"Truly."

"And I don't think you do either," he persisted. "You haven't set foot in the captain's stateroom since we left Tierra del Fuego. Keeping yourself here in this monk's closet when it's entirely unnecessary."

Ramsay sat down on the narrow bed to pull on his boots. "You're meddling like an old woman, Mac, and I see where this is going. As though I can't bear to set foot in the cabin that Helena Hartford had previously occupied."

Mac continued hanging in the doorway. "You said it. I didn't."

"Which means you're finished here at the moment." He stood and raked a hand through his hair, his voice cold. "It had to be done, and I don't care to discuss it further. I'll be up shortly and the bishop's representative had better be gone."

"Deacon Mosley."

Ramsay had a brief flash of that rainy night in June. Helena's face lit with panic, a chloroform-soaked cloth held tightly against her mouth and nose.

"I'm surprised he'd even want to meet with me again. The man must have a death wish."

Mac gave him a hard look from underneath heavy brows before exiting, leaving the door partially ajar.

Soon it would be over. All of it. Ramsay leaned over and opened the cupboard underneath the narrow bed extracting a leather folio with its damning sheets of vellum. His hands hesitated undoing the pigskin cords, before impatiently ripping them open and sliding out the drawings. He held them up in the late October sunlight, studying first one and then the next. The startling accuracy, the appallingly direct lines, the layered and nuanced strokes—her creation. And suddenly, after many weeks of a self-imposed emptiness, he felt her presence.

She was there. Standing next to him, her body pressed against his.

He was getting weak. And he didn't like it. He shoved the drawings back into the folio and threw them on the desk.

It was the last chapter. And then he could close the book on his life, finally lay to rest the personal grievances he could barely recall anymore. Helena hardly mattered, and he even less so. He couldn't remember what it was like to be a child, if he'd ever been one. Or the factory. Or that one glimpse of Robert Peacock Whitely.

In the years since, he'd circumnavigated the globe several times and claimed a fortune while losing his soul.

Ironic that. He'd told Helena she couldn't run away.

Yet he'd escaped from the children locked in factories for twenty hours a day who, when wounded and crippled, were turned out to die of their injuries. He'd run from the children who, late to work, or who fell asleep, were beaten with iron bars. From hands and arms regularly ripped to pieces. From little girls, their hair caught in the machinery, who were scalped from their foreheads to the back of their necks.

He looked out the small porthole that framed the body of another vessel two docks away, the shape of its hull wide and deep. Sometimes he wondered if his memories were even accurate any longer. He may have dreamed of human cargo, of the men and women tormented by unhealed wounds who could not all lie down at once without lying on each other. Or he may have invented the hatchway that was constantly patrolled by sentinels armed with hangers and blunderbusses. Imagined the stench, disease, and death.

The blazing heat of the pits. The time a ragged ten-year-old suffocated to death next to him in a narrow mining channel.

Useless memories. Hopeless sentiments. Worthless.

He scrubbed a hand down his face.

A belief in progress—for all—was what would finally matter. Greasing the wheels of politics, and he'd done his share with the wealth he'd accumulated, only went so far. Religion was the cornerstone of the social order, the House of Lords and Parliament mere props. He glanced at the folio on the bed and thought of the package, carefully parceled, below deck in the hold of the *Flying Cloud*.

That would make the difference. Finally, the embodiment of progress, to be used against a hide-bound society that believed it could rule over the poor with a whip and crucifix in one hand and a sherry in the other.

Because somehow it was supposedly preordained.

He was wasting time. He scooped up the leather portfolio and again it hit him with the force of a fist to his gut.

God damn, her scent even permeated the cabin. He needed fresh air, a drink, and a cheroot.

Impatiently, he turned around to rip open the top drawer of the small desk, filled with papers. He pawed through the contents until his hand closed over a silver cigarette case. He pulled it out, closed the drawer, and turned around.

To look directly into the eyes of Helena Hartford.

She was so close that, if she had a gun, it would already be over, a bullet lodged where his heart should have been.

But then again, it took a lot to kill him.

"Another stowaway," he said softly. "I never imagined that I'd have more than one to dispatch. Security aboard my ships must be getting careless."

She'd lost weight and there were circles under her eyes, as though she hadn't been sleeping well. "You look rather worn, Helena. Has Mac not been looking after you adequately?"

She was staring at him as though she couldn't believe her eyes. Up close, so he could see the fine texture of her skin and inhale her scent. She was dressed in a brown cloak, as though ready to make her departure.

A tiny, wild smile curved her full lips. She finally found her voice.

"I couldn't resist," she said in a low, throaty tone that almost penetrated his reserve but in the end couldn't crack the hard surface. "I could have simply walked off this ship and disappeared into London and then onto the Continent. But I simply couldn't resist."

"And I missed you too." And with a long arm, he pushed the door shut behind her, watching with satisfaction as a flare of alarm ignited in her eyes. They were alone, two bodies in a room that measured no larger than a vestibule.

But her smile only widened. "Still hiding, aren't you?"

"And you're still ruled by your emotions, aren't you?" he returned smoothly. "Otherwise you wouldn't be here. Confronting me like this is a dangerous proposition, far more dangerous than simply slipping off to the Continent as you'd intended. Because I could kill you"—his right hand snaked around her neck—"before you choke out the next epithet." A pulse beat, slowly and steadily, beneath the silk of her warm skin.

The blue of her eyes darkened to the color of the sea. "Or I could kill you."

"Then why didn't you rather than wasting this time with talk?"

"Because, unlike you," she said slowly and distinctly, "I don't believe vengeance is a good enough reason to have blood on my hands." She made no attempt to dislodge his grip around her neck. "You see, I just wanted to have the last word. To demonstrate to you that you could not relegate me to the outer regions of the earth to suit your twisted purposes." She grabbed his wrist with one hand, her own grip surprisingly strong. "That should be enough—*I got away.*"

He smiled through gritted teeth. "I wouldn't be so sure." He could smell her arousal and couldn't get away from his.

He slid his hand from her neck, under her heavy fall of hair, and drew her face up to his. She stiffened momentarily until his lips hovered over hers. "This is the reason you're here," he breathed into her mouth.

The softness of her lips went through him like a gunshot. Suddenly, he couldn't get enough, and deepening the kiss, he tasted and absorbed her soft moan. With one hand tangled in her hair, the other spanning the small of her back, he became a starving man.

He took her mouth again and again. Deeper this time and then more slowly, playing with her lips, until she shifted against him. The light in the cabin was dim and he couldn't get his fill of the texture of her tongue playing with his or rid himself of the acres of fabric between them.

He maneuvered her backward, untying the ribbons at her collar, her cloak billowing in a heap to the floor. Without breaking his kiss, he stroked his tongue into her mouth, slow and deep, shifting her toward the bed until both their knees touched the edge.

He stopped and stood back, saying nothing as he stripped off his jacket, tossing it onto the bed. She swayed on her feet, and he thought how fragile she'd felt beneath his hands.

"What are you doing?"

"Let's not talk. It never does us any good." He could tell that she wanted to back away, but there was nowhere to go. So she sat down on the bed and looked up at him, her eyes clouded.

"We're not doing this. I refuse," she said in a strangled voice. Her hair, dark, heavy silk, tumbled halfway down her back.

"Take off your clothes," he said calmly. "You know that's what you want. Surely I don't have to prove it to you." He shrugged out of his shirt. His hands reached out as he kneeled and began undoing the buttons that marched from her throat to her waist. His fingers caressed her warm skin through the silk, pushing it away impatiently, until only the thin cotton of her chemise and corset barred the way.

She was breathing heavily, her cheeks flushed. "This isn't fair," she said petulantly, already arching into his large hands settling on her hips. Bunching the wool of her skirts in his fists, he slowly drew the fabric, inch by inch, up her thighs. "There's no reason we should be doing this." Then she said his name in an urgent, restless whisper, clutching his arms in support.

"That's always been your problem, Helena," he said brutally. "Sex should have nothing to do with *reasons*. It's about nothing more than pure pleasure. It's about this."

She was wet. Drenched. His fingers had barely brushed her core when he felt the ripple of her orgasm begin, and he stopped her mouth before she could protest. He absorbed her moans and her shaking body, the trembling building. He refused to release her mouth, drinking in her incoherent cries that were sweeter than the purest vengeance.

Before the last spasm subsided, he thought she would push him away. Instead, she quickly unfastened his trousers, taking him, hard and hot, into her hands.

"I see you changed your mind," he said, dropping his fingers down the damp valley between her breasts to stroke the blue-veined skin beneath the thin cotton.

"As though you never had your *reasons*"—the words were choked and she looked broken—"to use this against me." He wanted her broken, and yet he allowed her hands to work his erection, the fingers greedy and female against his hard flesh.

He was ready to lie, but for the first time in his life, he couldn't. "Then stop now if this isn't what you want," he said without mercy for her or himself, pulling away with a self-control he never knew he had.

But it was too late. She pretended not to hear and, pushing him down on the bed, straddled him. It took only a moment and he was inside her, deep inside. She knelt over his hips, wrapping her legs around him, and began to move, and this time she refused to release his mouth.

"Bastard," she choked out against his lips. Taking a harsh, ragged breath, she traveled his torso with her eyes, the impact like a physical touch. She lifted her hips, poised above him before driving down again, sending violent ripples through his body. Breathing became impossible as he imagined her nipples hardening beneath her corset. He slid both his hands up her thighs and thrust upward inside her wet, ready heat with barely controlled ferocity.

She made a small sound at the back of her throat. And again she lifted herself on her knees, withdrawing from him, hovering just over his erection.

His hands clenched her buttocks, blood roaring through his veins. "Two can play this game," he said, rolling her over until she was beneath him. She crossed her ankles behind his back, hands clenching his biceps.

"I hate it," she hissed, helpless against the wanting, "when you do this to me."

He was huge, dark, and powerful between her thighs, playing with her as if they had all the time in the world. "When I do what—this?" He thrust between her legs, slowly and inexorably. And then pulled out, almost completely, dragging his erection deliberately over her slick folds. She bucked beneath him, clawing at his back, desperately trying to bring him back, but he decided to draw it out. Make it last. Make it harder. For her.

Anger, lust, the desire to punish—he didn't know anymore. All he knew was that he had her in his arms. He pinned her hips to the bed and pushed into her a fraction, pulling out again in a maddening, shallow rhythm that left her weak and breathless. Her moans came in small gasps, matching his own ruthlessly controlled arousal.

With each responsive cry, he gave her more, pushing in farther while she moaned in despair, clutching at his shoulders, at his arms. He skimmed a thumb over her clitoris and was rewarded by a clenching of her muscles, and only then did he allow himself to plunge to the hilt, feeling her hovering on the edge, where he wanted her, needed her to be, helpless against him.

Her eyes were the dark blue of the ocean and she was shaking. He stopped thinking then. He pulled her down to the edge of the bed and wrapped her legs around his hips, slamming deeper inside her, filling her, his body sweat slick. When her climax came he couldn't tell where it began and where it ended.

Her strangled cry of pleasure urged him higher. He wanted it never to stop. He wanted her with him forever. Like this.

He thrust into her, deliberately slowing his blood, holding her hips, reading her every action and reaction until the blood thundered in his ears and he lost it, pouring himself into her hot flesh, his mouth against hers.

It was impossible to say how much time had passed.

They lay silently on the narrow bed, breaths rasping in tandem. Then he felt her stir, sensing that she was moving away from him. It struck him then that they had never really slept together before, spent a night in bed, awakened with each other. He'd never wanted anything like that before. Letting his hand drift along her arm, he felt her immediate response, the heartbeat and the pulse that were as familiar to him as his own.

"Where are you going?"

She turned her head and looked at him with traces of tears on her face, her hair a tangle of silk. "Away from you. And off this ship."

And he wondered why she hadn't killed him. It would have been simple to do. A shot at close range would have hit its mark. Looking at her now, at her face shorn of bravado and rage, he wondered how he had been able to leave her behind on Tierra del Fuego. And for what? To reconcile a debt that was of his own making?

"Let's talk about this." The words were barely adequate and he couldn't believe he wanted her again. She moved away from him, sitting up on the side of the bed and looking more beautiful than ever, despite the concave shadows beneath her cheekbones.

Her voice, low and husky, was resigned. "You must be the one who's mad, Ramsay." Her slender back curved as she bent to pick up her blouse. She adjusted the lace of her chemise, her breasts trembling above her corset. "There is nothing to talk about once I walk from this ship. I spent the last six weeks in the captain's cabin thinking about my life and what I'm going to do about it. And the one conclusion I came to quickly is that it wouldn't include you."

He pulled himself up and sat beside her, surprised that he wanted to do nothing more than keep her with him, to never let her out of his sight again. She hurried to button up her blouse. "So it was Mara who helped you canoe to the *Flying Cloud* that day and Mac who took over once you were aboard," he said to fill the silence stretching between them.

"Very clever of you to guess." She pulled her hair into an impatient knot, jabbing a pin to hold it in place. "Although I wonder at your courage even mentioning her name in my presence. What you did to her and the Fuegians was unconscionable, no matter what your twisted motivation."

"There are some things in the world bigger than either of us."

She jerked around to face him directly, her breath warm on his face. "Spare me please, just this once. Because I know in my heart that all this is simply about your settling old scores, nothing more. And that's not good enough for me. Not now. And not ever."

She grabbed her cloak from the floor, but he seized her arm before she could make a move toward the door. She kicked the air, her foot making contact with the desk instead.

"I said you're not going anywhere."

Her eyes spat fire. "It's not too late for me to kill you."

Without letting go of her arm, he quickly buttoned his breeches. "Hear me out, Helena."

"You can't begin to know what you're asking," she seethed with undisguised hostility.

"For God's sake, would you listen for once in your life." His jaw ached from clenching his teeth. "Mosley is outside waiting for you. Can I say it any more directly?"

Suddenly, she stilled and stopped struggling to get her arm away from him. "Here? Now?" Her eyes widened, but in the next second she wrenched her cloak from his grasp. "And that's my problem and not yours."

There was nothing else he could do. She started to step back, away from him, when he lifted her up in his arms and deposited her on the bed, impersonally. He really wanted to shackle her to the desk. She stared at him in shock.

"Stay here until I get back," he said. "*I'll* take care of Mosley and the bishop."

And he locked the cabin door behind him.

Helena's hands shook with hatred. For Nicholas Ramsay. But more for herself.

She knew it had been over the moment she'd fastened her eyes on his broad back. And she knew she was finished the moment he touched her, her blood surging hot and fast. His open hand had slid from the ball of her shoulder to encircle the base of her throat, her breath catching. He had kept his fingertips pressed lightly to the pulse there, absorbing every erratic beat.

She jumped from the bed in a panic, nearly bumping her head on the low-beamed ceiling, desperately looking for her shoes even though there was nowhere to run. But she needed to get away. Now. She could still feel the pressure of his hands against her thighs, and she felt dizzy, disoriented, unwilling to relive the pleasure and the pain of his body hot against hers, his fingers between her legs as he looked down at her with those eyes that gathered only darkness into their depths.

From the first moment at Madame Congais's, his sheer physicality always had the power to unnerve her. But she'd learned that his pure, cold face was sculpted not from bronze or marble as she'd first believed, but from iron that nothing on earth could melt.

Both shoes lay discarded under the desk. She couldn't remember when they'd come off, but then there wasn't much she could focus on when her whole body was still thrumming with a liquid intensity that streamed from her head to the core of her being, when she could still feel him, the singular soreness, between her thighs.

Leaning against the desk for support, she jammed on first the one shoe and then the other. It was over. She was done with him. Done from the moment he'd turned away from her at the mission, leaving her at the ends of the earth and taking with him the remnants of a culture that had little enough to sustain it. She had cried silent tears, desperate and futile, unwilling to admit that the man who could make love to her with such tender intensity, who had taken her with such fierce possessiveness, had also given her redemption without relinquishing any part of himself.

Her eyes caught the leather folio on the desk, the edges of vellum spilling from its opening. She eyed the contents warily, unwilling to look in case the darkness of the cavern came hurtling back. She couldn't bear to relive the smell of the damp earth or the look in Mara's eyes. Mara, who had helped her escape back to the *Flying Cloud* so she could finally face her demons.

Picking her cloak off the floor, she pulled it around her shoulders, giving her a false courage she needed more than ever now. She had run from Sissinghurst the last time. The Continent would wait until she was finished destroying the man who symbolized everything and everyone who had sealed her in a metaphoric straitjacket since her life began. She shoved the leather portfolio beneath her cloak.

Experimentally, she rattled the latch on the door, first once and then repeatedly, the noise reverberating in the small cabin and in the narrow hallway outside. Mackenzie had helped her once and he would help her again.

A moment later, she was rewarded by the sounds of footsteps and the latch opening against her eager palm.

Chapter 23

The Bishop of London settled back in his chair, looked up, and offered his most engaging smile. "So good of you to take the time, Mr. Ramsay. I must say, I doubted that I'd ever have the pleasure."

Nicholas Ramsay yanked him up by his ecclesiastical collar and hauled him to the fine Persian carpet gracing the marble floor. He revealed a well-oiled revolver and aimed. "I want the papers necessary to release her now. And I won't ask again." He pulled back the hammer, the sound ominous in the room.

Leaning on his elbows, the bishop panted, a tuft of thinning hair askew. His round, fleshy face gave no sign of contrition. "Ah, I see that Deacon Mosley has finally delivered our Lady Hartford into the care she needs and deserves. Surely, Mr. Ramsay, in your long association with my aunt, you noticed her, shall we say, unreliable tendencies?"

His answer was the butt of the revolver jammed into the side of his head. "I'll count to five, Sissinghurst, after which Deacon Mosley will have a funeral service to plan." Ramsay's voice was as cold as the crypt that lay beneath the manse in the shadow of the great Cathedral of St. Paul. Only the ticking of the clock, the gift from the Duke of Hartford, calculated the seconds that were presumably left to the bishop.

"You will come to regret your actions, Mr. Ramsay," said

Sissinghurst conversationally despite the fact he was lying at Ramsay's feet, studying the pattern of a calla lily an inch from his nose. "Every indignity done to my person will be visited tenfold upon my aunt."

Without releasing his grip on the pistol, Ramsay hauled him to his feet and shoved him into a chair by the large stained-glass window. "I will bring you your stationery and you will to draw up the necessary papers to release Helena Hartford immediately."

The bishop nonchalantly dusted off his trousers. Except for an unnatural pallor, there was little sign of his discomposure. Without a glance at his desk and its ornate inkwell, he solemnly considered Ramsay. "Judging by your expression, I take it that Deacon Mosley managed to spirit my aunt out from under your nose and away from your ship. Or perhaps she went willingly," he added, spreading his empty, fleshy hands for emphasis. "Then again, we may never know and what does it truly matter."

Ramsay looked at him from cold eyes, more formidable in person than the reputation that had preceded him. And right now, noted Sissinghurst, he appeared ready to move heaven and hell to get what he wanted.

Well, he had arrived in hell, as he was about to discover.

"Please sit down, Mr. Ramsay. All this melodrama, as I pointed out before you so unceremoniously burst into my offices, is unnecessary and potentially dangerous to the well-being of my aunt. And I'm assuming by your intemperate behavior that you are somehow enamored of her." He made a clicking sound with his tongue, communicating his disbelief. "How unfortunate for you."

Ramsay ignored him, rummaging on his desk until he found and grabbed a sheet of paper. He tugged the pen from its inkwell. "I'm not here to discuss anything with you, Sissinghurst. Draw up the papers or I'll shoot you in your upper thigh where there's a large vein, which will ensure that you lose blood slowly enough to die an agonizing death."

"And you would risk a charge of murder?"

Ramsay shrugged. "I will say it was an accident and no one will question my version of events."

The bishop smiled widely, displaying his large white teeth. "I shouldn't be quite certain of that, Mr. Ramsay. Your word might not carry as much weight as it once did." He paused significantly, relaxing back into the chair that had been in the Hartford family for generations. "Particularly since certain circumstances have come to light."

Ramsay didn't even look up. He dropped the paper and pen onto the bishop's lap.

"Not even curious?" Sissinghurst asked. "I shouldn't be as concerned about these"—he gestured ineffectually at the stationery in his lap—"when there are other documents that pertain to you and, better still, are currently in the hands of the magistrates."

Ramsay merely cocked his pistol and aimed more carefully for his left thigh. The man had ice water flowing in his veins. "*Write,*" he said smoothly.

"I'm afraid I shan't," he returned calmly. "Which means, I suppose, that I will find myself bleeding on this lovely carpet very shortly while you, Mr. Ramsay, rush off intending to storm the barricades at Bethlem Royal Hospital—only to be intercepted by the magistrates who have orders to arrest you the moment you set foot in London. Which, by the looks of it, you already have."

Ramsay's eyes narrowed. "What are you talking about?"

"I see I finally have your attention. You may sit, if you like, it may make this difficult conversation more comfortable for you, sir."

"I prefer to stand." His voice was expressionless.

"Very well," said the bishop, willing to accommodate this rather rash display of discourtesy. But what could one expect from a guttersnipe? "Perhaps it's best that I begin with an acknowledgment of your background, Mr. Ramsay, which seems to have plagued you unrelentingly to this present day. But then rising as you have from the depths of poverty to your present circumstances is extraordinary by any estimation."

Framed in the light streaming through the stained glass, Ramsay said nothing.

"You are aware of the Slavery Abolition Act of 1833 and the Penal Servitude Act of 1853, I'm assuming, a man in your *trade*." The bishop made certain to emphasize the last word. He reached for the ruby crucifix around his neck reflexively.

"Your point, Sissinghurst. I'm running out of the little patience I had."

"My point, Mr. Ramsay, is that recent documents have been recovered that reveal from 1853 until this year you have been involved in a highly illegal exchange: transporting slave labor for use in mines—many of which you own, in Australia and South America."

Ramsay laughed, then gestured with his pistol. "The purest fiction, Sissinghurst, as you well know. My ships transport nothing more than materials and goods." He added, almost congenially, "I was expecting an old bastard like you to be difficult, but if this is your best gambit, then I overestimated you."

The bishop's small eyes were bright and alive. "I thought an intelligent man like you would understand the implications of what I'm suggesting. But obviously not," he sighed theatrically, his girth expanding and contracting. "People see what they believe to be true, and when they see a man appear out of nowhere with untold wealth and influence at his disposal, they are ready to believe anything. Even the worst."

Ramsay kept his voice low. "Highly creative but hardly credible." He seemed barely interested. "You've gone to great lengths to secure your aunt's fortune. It makes me wonder why a man like you would have such desperate need of resources." He glanced around the obvious comforts of the room, his glance lingering on the ruby-encrusted crucifix nestled in the crisp fold of the bishop's shirt.

Sissinghurst's mood suddenly darkened at the mention of

Helena Hartford. "She was always an interloper, my uncle's wife, a constant cross to bear and, worse still, she robbed me of the legacy that was legally mine."

Ramsay leaned casually against his desk, crossing his booted legs at the ankle. "The way I understand it, upon Helena's death you would receive the title but not the money."

The bishop looked incredulous. "Title! My uncle's estate is virtually bankrupt and his title, which is entailed to me, is as worthless as this piece of paper you're asking me to write on." He shoved what was on his lap to the floor.

"Which is the reason why you need to keep Helena alive, so as her legal guardian you have control over her wealth. But I have one question."

"Which I may or may not answer," the bishop responded somewhat crossly. His fingers closed spasmodically around the crucifix at his neck.

"To whom is her money entailed."

The bishop shook his head, his jowls shaking in wonderment. "All manner of ridiculous charities and a few hangers-on."

Ramsay absorbed the information quietly, his eyes giving nothing away. Sissinghurst, as a matter of fact, didn't care for the expression in them, cold, distant, like he didn't give a damn about much at all. "But while we're discussing legal matters," he continued in an attempt to gain control over the discussion, which had somehow slipped from his grasp, "I hope we can leave the subject of my aunt behind us and discuss opportunities available to us to reach a certain compromise."

"Is that another threat?" Ramsay asked lazily, caressing the snub end nose of his pistol.

And suddenly Sissinghurst tasted fear. He'd entirely underestimated Nicholas Ramsay, never dreaming that the man was as empty as a cathedral on a weekday, a man who appeared to have nothing to lose. His voice hardened. "I will relinquish the incriminating documents in exchange for"—he paused for good measure—"evidence of Australopithecus."

In turn, Ramsay looked bored. "At least get your strategy straightened away, Sissinghurst. I thought I heard you say that the incriminating documentation was already in the hands of the magistrates. So explain to me precisely what I would have to gain from this little exchange."

The bishop glared. Nicholas Ramsay was indecently tall and strong, and clearly not of aristocratic lineage. The observation lent him false courage. It was time to make his point. He rose from his chair, heedless of the pistol that tracked his progress. "Listen here, you upstart," he said, his lips peeled back in a grimace. "I am giving you a chance to walk away from the chaos that my aunt ever-so-predictably leaves in her wake. And if in your arrogance you refuse to see opportunity when it presents itself, then march out of here, leave me prostrate and bleeding or not, but you will find your life irrevocably and unrecognizably changed. I guarantee you that."

Ramsay shoved him back into his chair. "I didn't say you could move." He looked immeasurably unconcerned as though watching the antics of a particularly boring piece of theater. "I refuse to negotiate with you about Australopithecus, the clearly forged documents— that are or are not in the hands of the magistrates—or Lady Hartford. I've asked you twice and I won't ask you again to draw up the papers necessary for her release."

"You're making a mistake." But it occurred suddenly to the bishop that Nicholas Ramsay had killed for Helena Hartford before, and he would do it again before the day was out. His mind moved quickly, realizing that only the housekeeper and a scullery maid still working at the manse stood between him and the prospect of a premature death.

"Might I also remind you that every minute you spend here with me, Deacon Mosley and the mad-doctor have more time to practice their treatments with my aunt as their not-so-willing patient."

Ramsay watched him with mild annoyance. "I have a proposal for you, Sissinghurst. Instead of drawing up those papers I requested, you accompany me to Bedlam."

The bishop puffed up his chest in disbelief. "Why should I go with you anywhere when the minute you step outside these doors you will find yourself in shackles?"

"Because if I'm in shackles I promise you that you'll never get your hands on Australopithecus. Did you think I would leave evidence out in plain sight?"

The bishop clamped his mouth shut, then opened it reflexively. "I accompany you to Bedlam in exchange for what?" he whispered hoarsely, afraid to hear the answer.

"Your life. Or I put a bullet through your head right now."

Helena no longer knew what time it was. The window was blacked out with heavy velvet fabric, but the sputtering of oil lamps lit the small room, casting two large shadows on the wall. The first belonged to a man she had quickly come to know as Dr. Munro; the second belonged to Deacon Mosley.

Her stomach clenched in fear.

"Now you see, my dear Mosley, this chair, where we have Lady Hartford ensconced, offers the complete constraint of a patient's every move." Dr. Munro tapped his pointer to demonstrate. "Note that this board is attached to the back of the chair, which is devised to rise and fall according to the height of the patient. To the end of the board is attached a wooden box lined with stuffed linen in which the patient's head is held immobile so it cannot move backward or forward, nor incline to either side."

Munro rapped the board to test his hypothesis. "Am I not correct, Lady Hartford," he asked rhetorically.

It was like being buried alive, nailed into a coffin sitting up. Helena wanted nothing more than to give in to the urge to scream, but she didn't, struggling to maintain her sanity, the only way she was going to survive.

It was too late to curse herself for believing that she could leave the *Flying Cloud* without falling into Mosley's hands. She had persuaded Mackenzie that she had only wanted to return to the captain's quarters to await Ramsay's return. And instead, she'd slipped down the gangplank to find herself bundled into a carriage and into Bedlam and this horrible little room.

"Now come closer and examine these chest and stomach bands, Deacon." Although she couldn't turn her head to see him, she sensed Mosley's approach by the hot gaze that lingered on her body. "These bands," continued Munro, "are made of flat pieces of strong leather that confine and limit the body's movement in the chair. Similarly, we have leather bands that confine the arms and hands of the patient to the arms of the chair."

Not for one moment did she hope that Ramsay would come and save her. She could afford no such illusions. He had what he wanted, the evidence the X Club required and the weapon he needed to assuage his guilt, his past, or whatever it was that could possibly fill the hollowness that marked his existence.

As though she could afford to care.

Munro's voice droned in time with the sibilant hiss that was Mosley's accelerated breathing. "Now you see these pieces of wood that protrude slightly from the chair and to which the patient's feet are confined, these are devised to prevent their moving in any direction. And this stool—" The doctor thumped the pan half filled with water under the chair with his foot. "It is attached so it may be drawn out from behind the chair and emptied and replaced without removing or disturbing the patient."

The reality of the degradation to come was almost too much to bear. A scream welled up in her throat. She bit down on her lip hard, so hard that she could taste the blood. This was what her life had narrowed to, this moment in time where the ties that once bound her spirit now bound her body and soul. She struggled to shut the two men out, to think about her work, the feel of a paintbrush in her hands, to follow patterns and shapes in her mind's eye.

And she thought of Horace and whether he would have a chance to visit her in this horrible, horrible place. And perhaps after a while, after all the torment and the terror, she wouldn't be able to recognize him at all.

Mosley's boyish voice interrupted her nightmarish thoughts. "Thank you for your thorough and comprehensive explanation, Dr. Munro. Now that I am familiar with the workings of these restraints, you may leave us so as I may have some time to minister to Lady Hartford's soul, which has been, as you know, placed in my charge by the Bishop of London himself. She is in dire need of Christian guidance."

Reality ceased to exist. She couldn't see him, she couldn't lash out at him. Only her mind continued to work, a cruel irony that would have her witness this evil little man's every unbearable perversion.

The door closed, followed by the grinding of a key in the lock. And she knew without even having to look, as though she could, that the covered window was most likely fixed with bars.

"At long, long last, Helena." The words were breathed in her ear, a vicious whisper of sound inside the horrific box that held her head immobilized. She strained away from him, trussed and bound in a dark space, and tried to swallow her panic. She couldn't see his face and she wondered whether that would make it better or even worse.

"I'm sure we will get along just splendidly, helped all the more by the mad-doctor's guidance," Mosley continued conspiratorially. "He has given me many tracts to study, particularly concerning female disorders such as nymphomania, moral insanity, hysteria, and neurasthenia. Did you know, for example, that Dr. Charcot has publicly demonstrated that most mental disease in women results from abnormalities or excitation of the female external genitalia? These clinical tutorials of his, by the way, are very well attended by scores of men."

Helena had never fainted in her life. Now she prayed as she had never prayed before to a God she didn't even believe in, with a pitiable combination of desperation and hopelessness.

"It is a well-studied area of medical practice, you will be pleased to discover, given that this abnormality can lead to a series of disasters progressing through insomnia, exhaustion, epilepsy, convulsions, melancholia, paralysis to eventual coma and death. Now we wouldn't want that—the bishop would be most disappointed."

Helena tried not to react, reasoning, with the scant sanity that she had left, that total passivity could prove her best and only defense. She'd just closed her eyes when she heard the scrape of the key in the door.

"Good, Deacon Mosley," boomed the bishop, his plummy voice exuding triumph. Heavy footsteps indicated that his corpulent form was shambling into the room. "I see you have things well in hand with my aunt. How are you feeling, my dear?" he asked, clearly amused. "Not that I think you can feel much of anything, what with those bands cutting off your circulation. But never mind that, I'm sure Mosley will take matters into his own hands soon enough."

Mercifully, she could feel the deacon move away from her. "I see you have a brought a guest, Your Grace, although who would have guessed it that Nicholas Ramsay would allow himself to be shackled ever again in his life."

Helena's eyes flashed open, staring straight ahead through the darkness to the square that framed the brightly lit room.

"Well, he *insisted* on accompanying me to visit my dear aunt," the bishop responded in the same smiling tone. "But when we arrived I made sure that these three robust attendants had him suitably subdued." He seemed to turn toward Ramsay. "I didn't like your manner from the first, sir. Such

effrontery from the lower orders! You should have simply ac-
quiesced to the exchange I was offering. The evidence in return for those incriminating documents that will have you
languishing in prison for years."

"I should have shot you or slit your throat when I had a
chance."

Helena stiffened. That voice sent a chill down her spine.

Then a series of blows, the sickening sound of bone meeting flesh. Her stomach roiled, rising to her throat. She couldn't
move, even turn her head an inch.

Silence, punctuated by heavy breathing.

"Ordinarily, I don't like to resort to violence, but, sir, you
do seem to make it difficult for yourself."

Despite the blows, Ramsay's voice remained unchanged.
"Fuck you," he said.

An inhalation of breath and then Mosley's clipped words.
"I think you just may live long enough to regret the sentiment."

The bishop heaved an audible sigh. "I told him earlier
today that every indignity visited upon me would be amply
rewarded. And so I believe it's time to put my warning to the
test. And we shall see how long Mr. Ramsay lasts and how
quickly he divulges the whereabouts of the evidence that the
X Club is so keen to have."

There was a shuffle of feet and then Mosley's voice. "I
managed to confiscate this from Lady Hartford's person."

Helena ran the images through her mind—Mosley's small,
delicate hands giving over the leather portfolio with its sheets
filled with drawings. The result of her rashness. She screwed
her eyes shut. Why had she taken the sketches from Ramsay's
cabin rather than leaving them there, in a place where they
would still be safe?

Her lungs burned and she deserved the pain, the bands
around her chest and stomach cutting off her circulation, invading her body with a deadness that she hoped would come
to her aid when she needed it most.

"Well done, well done, Deacon," murmured the bishop, and she could hear his footsteps coming near. He peered at her through the front of the box that held her head in a vise-like grip. His eyes shone small and reptilian. "My, my, we're certainly not looking well, dear Helena," he said softly, as though he wanted no one else to hear. "Although I don't think the good deacon will mind at all, what with his peculiar interest in your person. But then again, he's fulfilled his duties admirably, so I shouldn't wish to deny him—and Ramsay here—his just rewards." He patted her hand. "Now I wonder if these two gentlemen would mind an audience?"

Helena stared straight ahead, trying not to cringe away, sending a beam of hatred toward the man who would deliver her to a living death.

The bishop shuffled away. "I do believe that a demonstration *à la Charcot* is just what Mr. Ramsay may need to persuade him to divulge the whereabouts of that elusive Australopithecus. What do you say, Deacon? And are you quite comfortable, Mr. Ramsay, what with your three sturdy attendants watching your every move?"

Helena closed her eyes, bracing herself. She was losing her mind, finally. She didn't know why Ramsay was in the room with her, shackled and imprisoned. But she did recognize, with a desperate inevitability, that he would never give up the evidence that meant so much to him.

Mosley coughed discreetly, announcing his presence. "I don't believe Helena will mind an audience given that I already apprised her of the fact that the doctors Charcot and our very own Isaac Baker Brown are in the practice of conducting seminars attended by scores of men." He rubbed his hands together. "Now, where shall I begin?"

There was a scuffle and a dragging of chains. Helena shut out the image of the men gathering around her. She sensed Mosley's approach.

"Of course, we do know something of the causation of hysterical attacks in women," he began in his strange, high voice. "Much like Helena Hartford's case, with her inappropriate and unwomanly obsession with art and her unfortunate addiction to promiscuity—witness Mr. Ramsay's presence with us today. This is a disease that requires a radical cure, the literature tells us, without which any religious counsel will fall on hard ground."

He had yet to touch her and what was left of her spirit rallied. She tried to close herself off from the words that invoked hideous, vicious images.

"Initially, we understand that treatment involved applying leaches to a woman's private areas, and excuse me for the crudity, Your Grace, but in the interests of science, it must be said, the female genitalia is always suspect. Neither corporal punishment such as whipping or restraints helps, according to the literature, and only electrocautery, or more effectively, applying a red-hot iron heated in coals, *repeatedly,* can address the problem adequately."

"Shall we call Dr. Munro to demonstrate?" asked the bishop helpfully.

"I don't think that will be necessary, Your Grace. I shall simply ask one of the attendants here to fetch the required implements and we shall be on our way. But first, I believe we should examine the area in question."

Helena hoped she would die. She stopped breathing, willing herself to cease living, hearing in the periphery the scrape of the key in the lock.

"Are you still with us, Mr. Ramsay. You are unusually silent," the bishop inquired.

"I shouldn't want to interfere with your sport, gentlemen," Ramsay said in that cool, disinterested tone that was empty of emotion. "Although if you knew me better, you would recognize that it will take much more than watching a woman undergo mild discomfort for me to give up something as significant as Australopithecus." There was a hint of mockery in his voice. "Do your worst."

The bile in her throat. She was going to wretch, choke to death. And she welcomed it. She heard the men laugh and then felt Mosley's hands groping under the chair with its obscene opening. The fabric of her skirts tore and she felt the cold air on her bottom.

Please, please, she could not bear his touch.

"In females, Dr. Kellogg has found that the application of pure carbolic acid as an excellent means of allaying the abnormal excitement and preventing the recurrence of dangerous thoughts," said Mosley, "particularly in those whose will-power has become so weakened that the patient is unable to exercise self-control."

Helena jerked and went still. There was a flash of silence and she wondered whether she'd finally fainted. At first she thought she was hallucinating, but something hit the floor, solid and heavy enough to vibrate her chair. Then something metallic ground against the cold, hard concrete of the walls. Grunts, a wild shout, followed by the all too hideously familiar crunch of flesh and bone filled the room.

Whether the chaos lasted one minute or an hour, she would never know. Suddenly the wooden box around her head lifted, the light burning her eyes. Nicholas Ramsay was standing over her, his face hard and his gray eyes reflecting back to her a familiar void. Heavy chains encircled his wrists and one of his ankles. Jerking a small knife from his boot, he hacked through the leather belts restraining her waist, chest, arms, and hands.

Sheer force of will allowed her to stand. She shut out the pain that shot through every limb of her body now pulsing with blood. Frozen, she took in the bodies of four men in various states of lifelessness scattered across the small room. Her atelier and that June morning that seemed like a lifetime ago flashed before her eyes.

And this time she watched Ramsay tow the bishop's heavy bulk over to the hideous contraption she'd just vacated.

Moving with a sleek efficiency that scared her, he tied the heavy man in place, draping the limp body of Mosley across his lap.

They hadn't exchanged a word. Ramsay grabbed the leather portfolio with her drawings and then her arm, his fingers gripping tightly as he dragged her toward the door that was partially ajar and awaiting the return of the attendant with the *required implements*. She began to shake.

"How will we get out?" She choked back her fear. "There are at least three locked gates with attendants. . . ."

Before he could answer, he shoved her against the wall behind the door, covering her body with his until an attendant set his first foot over the threshold. In a move that was lightning fast, Ramsay had broken his neck, forever transforming the man's expression of stunned surprise into a frozen grimace as he slipped to the floor.

"I have keys," he said curtly, ignoring the fact that she was rooted to the spot, her hands hugging her body in shock. She wanted to call his name, in horror or in need, she couldn't tell. Instead, she bit her lips before anything more than a ragged intake of breath could emerge.

He regarded her with hard eyes. "When I first came through the doors with Sissinghurst, I ensured the struggle with the attendants resulted in my securing a set of keys without their knowledge."

She shook her head with sick dread, not trusting her voice. Watching as he unlocked and then kicked himself free of his shackles, she stumbled after him, down the narrow, unlit corridor that smelled of human excrement and misery. They were in one of the back wings of the hospital where all manner of treatments occurred and she thought she heard faint screams penetrating the walls.

The first gate was unattended and Ramsay swiftly fit a key in the lock. She held her breath as they ran down the corridor, her legs entangled in her torn skirts. He seemed to know where to go and where to turn and she followed him blindly, refusing to think about the little room. She would survive at least this night.

Suddenly, they stopped and he shoved her up against the wall, followed with a quick admonishment to wait. And she did, numb and obedient and unwilling to witness one more act of violence. When he returned, he shook her from her nightmare, dragging her past two more miraculously opened gates. Cowardly and ashamed, she refused to look right or left, desperate with guilt to avoid seeing evidence of his actions on her behalf.

The cold, late October air chilled her lungs, a reminder that she lived. She could not stomach looking up at the night sky against which the magnificent, palladium splendor of Bethlem Royal Hospital was spread.

Her body felt heavy as she was pushed into the seat of a phaeton with extravagantly large wheels and a minimal body that made it fast and dangerous. The street was deserted, and she had no idea how Ramsay had managed to find a conveyance or, if indeed, they were in the process of stealing one.

The two horses jolted into an immediate trot, and she glanced briefly at Ramsay's profile, calm and controlled, holding the reins in one hand. They drove fast along the dark, moonlit roads, and he took each corner with the speed and skill of an expert equestrian. She wondered again at how little she knew this man of many lives who had appeared to her at midnight and out of nowhere so many months ago.

"Where are we going?" she asked finally, shivering in her thin dress.

"There are a few things I need to do," he said, not sparing her a glance. But with his free hand he tugged a lap rug, which was bunched on the seat between them, around her waist.

She was tired and so confused, barely able to hold herself upright while trying to pull together facets of a personality that refused to fit. He had saved her life over and over again, and yet she couldn't shake the sense that he felt nothing at all for her.

"I want to go to my friend Horace Webb." She hoped her voice was strong. That's what she needed right now, to see Horace's dear, familiar face and his warm brown eyes brimming with concern. "His carriage house isn't far from here and I know that he will take me in for the time being. He's a good friend," she said simply.

It was cold and damp but at least it wasn't raining, the clatter of the horse hooves moving crisply across the cobblestoned streets. It was as though he were pleased to be rid of her. "You may be safer with him than with me for the time being," he agreed shortly.

"Turn left here." She wondered if she'd ever see him again.

Ramsay deftly maneuvered the carriage around the bend and into a narrow mews, following her directions. She shouldn't ask, but she couldn't help herself. "Where are you going to go?" she said in a faint voice, shuddering at the thought of Sissinghurst and Mosley, wondering when, like ghouls that refused to remain dead, they would rise again.

He eased the phaeton to a stop in the shadows, across from Horace's carriage house. "I'm going to ensure that Sissinghurst and any and all of his acolytes are released from Bedlam tomorrow morning."

She clutched at the rug covering her lap. "What?" Her disbelief rang in the silence of the night.

"Tomorrow morning will see them transferred to an asylum in Ireland where they will be held permanently," he said coldly, and she was relieved that she couldn't see his face in the darkness. "There's something Sissinghurst is hiding and I intend to find out what it is even if it means rousing my solicitors from their beds to begin the hunt. And once I do, I'm certain the Archbishop of Canterbury will prefer to bury any embarrassing revelations along with Sissinghurst and Mosley deep in wilds of Ireland."

The mews was deserted, but she could see a welcoming light still burning in the window of Horace's carriage house. She was tired, bone weary, and close to falling off the edge of exhaustion, otherwise she would never have asked. "Will I see you again?" she blurted out, quickly flinching away from the question. She couldn't bring herself to move, much as she wanted to, or to surrender to a primal need to reach up and pull him toward her.

The silence was suffocating. His gray eyes were unreadable in the dimness and half-closed as he leaned in, filling her senses with his heat and the scent that was uniquely his. For a mad moment, she thought he was going to press that wide mouth against hers. But he didn't.

Instead, just the warmth of his breath brushed her face. "There's too much to forgive to make much of anything possible."

Helena shook her head, more afraid now of the memories than anything else, even though it was all they had left between them. "Then why are you doing all this? Risking your life for me, jeopardizing the Australopithecus evidence when you could have simply walked away from it all?"

"I don't know," he responded with mild surprise. The words were cruel, harsh, made more so by their emptiness. And at that desperate moment, she knew she loved him, truly and irrevocably, despite the pain hidden so deep inside both of them.

She touched his wrist then, lightly, not to convince him to stay with her, because that was impossible, but simply to touch him for what was probably the last time. They remained like that, motionless, for an endless moment. Until she knew it was time to go.

"Thank you," she said, knowing that the hopelessly banal words were hardly enough and that filling them with pure, unadulterated emotion was all she could do. "For every-thing."

And she turned away from him and from the tears frozen in her chest, scrambling from the phaeton without a backward glance. He waited, until she'd finished knocking and the door of the carriage house opened, before driving away.

Something was wrong. Ramsay felt it. And it made no sense.

He tightened his hands on the reins and his emotions. Cold rage claimed every inch of his body, hovering in the air around him like a shroud. He had few regrets, but the one he would live with forever was not snapping Sissinghurst's and Mosley's necks.

Killing would have been satisfying but too simple. Giving in to raw instinct was never a good idea, particularly when a far more horrific fate could be arranged. The bishop was hiding something—and when it came to light it would be ugly indeed.

Urging the horses into a faster canter, he ignored the emptiness clawing without mercy at the pit of his stomach. He couldn't remember the last time he'd felt so powerless, almost helpless in the face of a reality he couldn't, for once, control. He thought that had ended over two decades ago when he'd crawled out of the *Scindian*'s hold and into the unforgiving sun of the Australian badlands. And he believed he'd ultimately laid it to rest when he'd left Helena Hartford behind at Woolya Cove.

Except that he hadn't left her behind at all. She would never leave him. Beautiful, talented, and disturbingly complex, she refused to be abandoned, and that reality would serve as his own personal, exquisitely painful destiny. He would be haunted for the rest of his life by a woman he could not live without.

He hauled the horses to a halt, watching the steam rising from the animals' haunches in the cold night air. And suddenly he knew why he'd killed for her, why his hands had shaken when she was ill, why he couldn't last a minute in her presence without a fierce desire to make love to her, and why he hadn't been able to leave Tierra del Fuego with—

The silence was deafening. He wondered why it had taken him so long. The cold rage was not dissipating but intensifying as the pieces of the puzzle shifted into place. Brutal honesty was all that was required.

He wanted his pistol, smooth and cold in his hand.

He swung the phaeton around so quickly that it nearly slid halfway across the street, the highly strung horses neighing in shock before breaking into a gallop. He'd relinquished his gun in the scuffle he'd engineered at Bedlam, allowing him to relieve the attendant of his keys.

So he would have to find another way to stop Horace Webb from killing Helena.

And for the first time in many years, he thought he might lose. He should never have let her go, allowed her out of his sight, out of his arms.

And he never would again.

The phaeton careened to a halt in front of the carriage house. He leapt from the seat and quickly assessed the front door and the one window where the small lamp still burned innocently behind the chintz curtains. Realizing the element of surprise was his only weapon, he pushed back the shutters and smashed through the mullioned paned window before catapulting his body through the low opening.

Horace Webb looked up in mild surprise, a harmless middle-aged man with a receding hairline and warm brown eyes. Helena lay on a low divan by the fire, asleep.

The syringe in Webb's hand never wavered. "You are Nicholas Ramsay, no doubt," he said in a pleasant voice. "Helena had mentioned you," he continued vaguely, seemingly unconcerned about the broken glass lying in shards at his feet. "Unfortunate, these circumstances."

"Is she dead?"

"Soon, I think," he answered, the syringe poised intimately against Helena's bare arm. The rolled-up sleeve revealed her soft skin, white and vulnerable. "I think the first dose of opium I gave her in her tea should have been enough. But just to make sure, I was going to follow up with an injection. I would not want her to suffer, you understand."

Ramsay advanced carefully into the room, his glance taking in a cheerful fire in the hearth, two cups, both empty, on the side table and then back to Helena who lay on her side. He looked desperately for the rise and fall of her chest.

"I shouldn't come much closer, Mr. Ramsay," Webb warned amiably, "as it won't make much difference. You wouldn't have the time to intervene given that I'm simply a pinprick away and"—he continued reaching into his evening's coat's side pocket to reveal a small pistol—"I also now have a reason to use this. A shame."

Ramsay held out both hands, palms up. "I'm unarmed, Mr. Webb, as you can see."

He nodded formally. "You seem an honorable man. And a courageous one. I can understand why Helena has fallen in love with you."

Ramsay hoped the shock didn't show in his face. He tried to keep his voice even. "You wouldn't want to take that away from her, would you, Mr. Webb, now that she has found someone to love who returns that love?"

The fire spat and shot a stray ember into the room, but Webb remained unperturbed. He seemed bewildered, his brown eyes shadowed with something approaching grief. "That's the strange thing, you see, I do wish her the best, always have done, and yet," the features of his thin face tightened, "she has so much. So much talent, so much wealth, and so much potential. And now she even has you. While I find myself languishing . . ." He smiled with self-deprecation. "Even my mistress Perdita has left me. So I have no choice and nothing left to lose."

Ramsay kept a close eye on the pistol and the syringe, neither good news for Helena. "You're the one who had the men ransack her atelier and who planted the assassin on my ship," he said matter-of-factly, the cold breeze from the broken window fluttering the curtains behind him. "And you are named the beneficiary in her will, I assume."

"Both assumptions correct, Mr. Ramsay. I'm also the man who first introduced Helena's father to the Duke of Hartford," he continued almost proudly, the moment seeming to rally his spirits. "It was a liaison I encouraged. I believed sincerely that the marriage was advantageous for Helena had she ever allowed herself to admit it."

Ramsay didn't know whether he was imagining it, or whether he willed it with a single-minded ferocity, but he thought he saw Helena's eyelashes stir. A damp spot, just beneath her head, made him wonder whether she had consumed the last drop of her tea. He drew Webb's attention away from the figure on the divan.

"You're envious of her abilities, aren't you? And you believed that the duke would be able to suppress her talent."

Webb drew back the hammer of the pistol, a small smile on his face. "You're a very astute man, Mr. Ramsay. It's unfortunate both you and Helena will have to die in a suicide pact or crime of passion, or whatever the authorities will choose to call it. Given her history of mental instability and all." His eyes projected a deep sadness. "This last dose of opium will ensure that my dear friend never wakes up."

Horace Webb never saw the sharp elbow coming. Uncoiling from the divan like a spring, Helena knocked the syringe from his hand and followed it with two flailing fists to his chest and stomach.

Doubling up in pain, he shot wildly at the ceiling, the bullet ricocheting off the wall harmlessly. In an instant, Ramsay had hauled him up against his chest with a chokehold around his neck. "Drop the gun, *now.*"

The moment had become unreal and a strange glance passed

between Helena and Webb before her old friend slowly raised the pistol to his temple and, like a carefully choreographed ballet, released the hammer.

One month later

"Hold still," Helena said with laughter in her voice. "You are a most impatient man!"

"Impatiently waiting for you to join me, my friend, my lover, and my wife," responded Ramsay, walking, resplendently and unapologetically nude, toward the pillow-strewn bed in her atelier. A rare and beneficent ray of late-November sunshine cast the cavernous room in a warm glow.

He was the most beautiful man she knew. Would ever know. And he was hers. He watched her with those gray eyes, once dark and unfathomable, and now lit with a combination of amusement and passion.

"Stop tempting me, Nicholas. And by the way, you're the worst model I've ever encountered. I just need a few more minutes to finish this." She narrowed her eyes at the canvas on the easel, playing with the palette knife in her hands.

"You are wonderful and the paintings will be wonderful," he said, sitting up, his broad shoulders incongruous against the white lace-trimmed pillows. "London will never see anything of this caliber for years to come." His confidence in her abilities was unassailable, and he had cleared the first floor of Conway House for an exhibit that would be opening in the first week of the new year. "Only I wish to purchase the portrait you're working on at the moment." He waggled his dark eyebrows at her roguishly. "I think I'd like to keep some things private."

She put down the palette knife and feigned a look of surprise. "The last thing I would have accused you of is modesty, but then one always learns new things about one's husband I suppose." She walked to the side of the bed, the satin of her dressing gown moving sensually against her skin. "But I hadn't intended to put it in the exhibit in any case. Your portrait is mine alone to enjoy."

His warm hand pulled her down beside him, his skin burning through the thin fabric of her night rail. "Relieved to hear it," he growled into her ear. Already she trembled at the need coursing through her body in a rush of heat. They had spent days in bed, hundreds of hours talking, and still she felt the fierce intensity of the bond that would never break and would leave her shaken, exhilarated, and forever changed.

"You're everything to me, I hope you know," she turned toward him, bringing his palm to her lips.

He smiled at her, a slow and sweet smile that he shared only with her. "And I couldn't live without you. Which I learned the most painful way possible. I almost lost what matters most."

Helena still found it difficult to think about Horace Webb, her dear friend twisted by envy and hate. She wanted the horror of that night to stay locked away and buried forever.

She shook her head. "There are greater issues in this world. You were right months ago when you told me that my life wasn't of particular significance. And you were right to bring the evidence of Australopithecus to the X Club. It will make a world of lasting difference." Even more than the resources they were providing to fund schools, workers' unions, public libraries, and mechanics' institutes. Better still, Mosley and Sissinghurst had been locked away in an asylum after Ramsay's solicitors discovered that the bishop had been selling children from poorhouses into servitude to factory owners.

"But"—she punched him playfully in the chest—"you could have let me know sooner."

He captured her hand in his hard one. "I may not be an artist, but I do know how a plaster cast is made." The original remains rested in Tierra del Fuego with Mara and the Fuegians. He pressed a soft kiss to the sensitive skin on the side of her neck.

"I was wrong to doubt you."

"You can spend the rest of your life making it up to me," he said, pulling the satin down around her shoulders, his fingers cool against her heated flesh. She was already lost, sinking down into a sensual lassitude as his lips played relentlessly with her mouth. His image burned against her closed eyes, the sharp planes and angles of his face, the overwhelming masculinity marked by lines of hard-won experience. Suddenly, she pulled back in a rush of tension.

Ever attuned to the most minute response of her body, he raised his head. "What's wrong?"

She didn't answer but leaned over the side of the bed to grab a slender leather portfolio. Withdrawing a sheet of paper, she handed him the drawing. "Cape Verde Island. The first time we made love."

They both looked down at the sketch of his face, the one she'd sworn to keep from him forever.

He took it from her hands. And his touch was all she needed.

If you liked this book, you've got to try
WANTON,
the newest from Noelle Mack,
out this month from Brava . . .

London, 1816. The Pack of St. James meets in secret in their elegant lair. An unknown assailant has begun to prey upon the women they love—and a poisoned communication threatens worse things to come. Marko Taruskin begins to investigate and finds the trail leads to a scandalous beauty known as Severin. Well aware of how a clever woman can hide more than she reveals, Marko must employ all of his powers of sensual persuasion . . .

The last chord died away and Marko heard the almost noiseless click of a piano lid closing. The woman who had been playing so beautifully sighed as she put the sheets of music in order before she rose, pushing back the padded bench with a faint scrape. He heard the faint miaou of Severin's cat, following her mistress about the adjoining chamber. Silk skirts rustled over polished floors. Then Severin swept through the double doors that led to her bedroom and stopped, her lips parting with surprise.

"What are you doing here?"

"Waiting for you."

Severin glided past the bed upon which he lay to her mirror-topped dresser. "I do not remember inviting you." She began to take down her hair, looking at his reflection in the silvery glass, her back to him.

"No, you didn't."

"Then how did you get in?"

Marko shrugged. He was quite at his ease stretched out upon her featherbed, luxuriously so, in fact. He rolled to his side, bracing himself with one arm and letting the other rest upon his hip. "Through the front door."

"Hmm. Unusual for you."

"What do you mean?"

Severin gave an unladylike snort. "You're a great one for trellises and balconies. Ever the romantic hero."

Her gleaming hair ripped over her bare shoulders. He longed to bury his face in its fragrant softness, lift it away from her neck, kiss her madly—but he stayed where he was.

"It is raining."

"Oh? I did not notice," Severin said, turning to face him. She put her hands on her hips and looked him over.

Marko could almost feel her gaze. He was nearly as aroused as if she had actually touched him. Since he was fully dressed, from his fitted half-coat to the breeches tucked into his high black boots, the sensation was not entirely comfortable. He drew up one leg and bent his knee to conceal his reaction to her cool study of his body.

"Boots in the bed?" she murmured. "How uncivilized of you."

"I could not very well strip, Severin. You might have screamed."

She permitted herself a small smile. "I don't think so. I've seen you naked before."

He remembered that night with chagrin. "Yes, but—nothing happened."

Her amber eyes glowed with amusement. "You wanted something to happen. But I was not ready."

"Are you ready now?"

The question was bold, but she was bolder.

"Yes," she said. And she came to him . . .

And here's a peek at Donna Kauffman's latest,
THE BLACK SHEEP AND
THE ENGLISH ROSE,
in stores now from Brava . . .

She laughed. "Oh, great. I'm supposed to sign on to help you recover a priceless artifact, in the hopes that when we retrieve it, you'll just let me have it out of the kindness of your heart? Why would I sign on for that deal?"

He turned more fully and stepped into her personal space. She should have backed up. She should have made it clear he wouldn't be taking any liberties with her, regardless of Prague. Or Bogotá. Or what they'd just done on her bed. Hell, she should have never involved herself with him in the first place. But it was far too late for that regret now.

"Because I found you tied to your own hotel bed and I let you go. Because you need me." He toyed with the end of a tendril of her hair. "Just as much, I'm afraid, as I need you."

"What are you afraid of?" she asked, hating the breathy catch in her voice, but incapable of stifling it.

"Oh, any number of things. More bad clams, for one."

"Touché," she said, refusing to apologize again. "So why are you willing to risk that? Or any number of other exit strategies I might come up with this time around? You're quite good at your job, however you choose to label it these days. Why is it you really want my help? And don't tell me it's because you need me to get close to our quarry. You could just as easily pay someone to do that. Someone who he isn't already on the alert about and whose charms he's not immune to."

"Maybe I want to keep my enemies close. At least those that I can."

"Ah. Now we're getting somewhere. You think that by working together, you can reduce the chance that I'll come out with the win this time. I can't believe you just handed that over to me and still expect me to agree to this arrangement."

"I said maybe. I also said there were myriad reasons why I think this is the best plan of action. For both of us. I never said it was great or foolproof. Just the best option we happen to have at this time."

"Why should I trust you? Why should I trust that you'll keep to this no-secret-maneuvers, no-hidden-agenda deal? More to the point, why would you think I would? No matter what I stand here and promise you?"

"Have you ever lied to me?"

She started to laugh, incredulous, given their history, then stopped, paused, and thought about the question. She looked at him, almost as surprised by the actual answer as she'd been by the question itself. "No. No, I don't suppose, when it comes down to it, that I have." Not outright, anyway. But then, they'd been careful not to pose too many questions of each other, either.

"Exactly."

"But—"

"Yes, I know we've played to win, and we've done whatever was necessary to come out on top. No pun intended," he added, the flash of humor crinkling the corners of his eyes despite the dead seriousness of his tone. "But we've never pretended otherwise. And we've never pretended to be anything other than what we are."

"Honor among thieves, you mean."

"In a manner of speaking, yes."

"I still don't think this is wise. Our agendas—and we have them, no matter that you'd like to spin that differently—are at cross purposes."

"We'll sort out who gets what after we succeed in—"

"Who gets what?" she broke in. "There is only one thing we both want."

"That's where you're wrong."

She opened her mouth, then closed it again. "Wrong, how? Are you saying there are two priceless artifacts in the offing here? Or that you can somehow divide the one without destroying its value?"

He moved closer still, and her breath caught in her throat. He traced his fingertips down the side of her cheek, then cupped her face with both hands, tilting her head back as he kept his gaze directly on hers. "I'm saying there are other things I want. Things that have nothing to do with gemstones, rare or otherwise."

She couldn't breathe, couldn't so much as swallow. She definitely couldn't look away. He was mesmerizing at all times, but none more so than right that very second. She wanted to ask him what he meant, and blamed her sudden lack of oxygen for her inability to do so. When, in fact, it was absolute cowardice that prevented her from speaking. She didn't want him to put into words what he desired.

Because then she might be forced to reconcile herself to the fact that she could want other things, too.

"Do we have a deal?" he asked, his gaze dropping briefly to her mouth as he tipped her face closer to his.

Every shred of common sense, every flicker of rational thought she possessed, screamed at her to turn him down flat. To walk away, run if necessary, and never look back. But she did neither of those things and was already damning herself even as she nodded. Barely more than a dip of her chin.

But that was all it took. Her deal with the devil had been made.

"Good. Then let's seal it, shall we?"

She didn't have to respond this time. His mouth was already on hers.

There's nothing more irresistible than
EVERLASTING BAD BOYS.
Keep an eye out for the anthology
from Shelly Laurenston, Cynthia Eden, and Noelle Mack,
coming next month from Brava.
Turn the page for a preview of Shelly's story,
"Can't Get Enough."

Ailean didn't know what woke him up first. The two suns shining in his eyes—or the paw repeatedly slapping at his head.

Yawning, he glared at the little monster trying to claw him to death. "Oh, now you're feeling fine, aren't you?"

He yipped in answer and that's when Shalin murmured in her sleep.

That's also when Ailean realized Shalin was asleep on his chest.

Slightly terrified, Ailean desperately tried to remember if they'd done anything the night before. He didn't think so and, when he looked down at her, she still wore the red gown from yesterday, and the fur covering he'd brought with him still lay between them.

He let out a breath, but still didn't know what had come over him. He may not have touched her, but all the things they'd discussed . . .

Ailean never talked about his father with anyone but his brothers, and those two never mentioned the old dragon unless necessary. Ailean definitely never discussed his mother and what happened that awful day. His own kin knew never to mention it. Nearly a century ago, one cousin drunkenly brought it up after a family hunting party and lost both his horns when Ailean snapped them off.

But Ailean had told Shalin pretty much everything. God . . . why?

The puppy yipped again and Shalin's head snapped up from his chest. "Wha—where?"

"You're safe, Shalin," he told her, seeing the confusion and panic on her face. When she looked at him, her panic seemed to pass and she smiled at him with real warmth.

"Good morn, Ailean."

"Good morn to you."

She turned a bit to look at the puppy, but seemed more than comfortable cuddled up on his chest. "And look at you, Lord Terrify Me."

The dog yipped again and Ailean said, "You best let him out, Shalin. Or there'll be more mess to clean up."

"Let him out?"

"Just open the door. He'll find the rest of the dogs."

"All right."

He thought she'd roll away from him, but instead, she moved across him to get to the edge of the bed. Ailean gritted his teeth and willed his body not to react. It had to be one of the hardest things he'd ever done, and he'd gotten in a fight once with a giant octopus.

"Will he come back?"

"I'm sure. He's bonded to you, Shalin." And he knew how the little bastard felt. Ailean knew if he left this moment, he'd probably come back too.

"Come on then, you little terror." Shalin picked the dog up and walked to the door. Ailean heard it open and then Shalin's strangled "Uh . . ."

"What's wrong?" He rolled to his side, raising himself up on one elbow, and looked toward the door. "Shit," he barely had chance to mutter before Bideven pushed past Shalin and stalked in, Arranz and the twins right behind him.

"You dirty bastard. Couldn't keep your hands off her, could ya?"

Ailean slid off the bed and stood in front of his kin, the only thing holding up that fur covering his hand.

"I'm not quite sure what it has to do with you, brother."

Bideven moved toward him but Shalin calmly stepped between them. "He never touched me."

Arranz sighed. "Shalin love, could you move? You're in the way of some lovely violence."

Giving no more than an annoyed sniff, she didn't respond to Arranz and instead said again, "He never touched me, Bideven."

"Then why was he here?"

"I needed help with my puppy."

Arranz and the twins started laughing and didn't seem inclined to stop while Bideven's accusing gaze shot daggers at Ailean.

"You bastard!"

Shalin rested her hand against Bideven's chest. "Stop this now."

"Shalin, you're an innocent about this sort of thing—"

Ailean didn't realize he'd snorted out loud until they all looked at him.

He glanced at Shalin and shrugged. "Sorry."

"—and his intent," Bideven finished. "We're just trying to protect you."

Shalin folded her arms over her chest. "Do you think so little of your own brother?"

The confusion on their faces would be something Ailean remembered for ages.

"What?"

"Do you think so little of him? That he'd take advantage of me. Force me,"

"I never said—"

"Is that truly what you expect of your own kin? I thought the Cadwaladr Clan loyal to each other."

"We are."

"I haven't seen it. Not when you barge in here and accuse your own brother of being all manner of lizard."

"I never meant to—"

"Then you should apologize."

"Apologize?"

"Yes."

"You can't be—"

Shalin's foot began to tap and Bideven growled. "Fine. I apologize."

Patting his shoulder, Shalin ushered Bideven and the rest out. "Now don't you feel better?"

"Not really," Bideven shot back, but Shalin already closed the door in his face.

Ailean stared at Shalin. "That was . . . *brilliant!*"

Shalin held her finger to her lips while she bent over silently laughing. "He'll hear."

"Good!" Ailean watched her walk across the room. "How did you do that?"

She shrugged before falling back on the bed, her grin wide and happy. "Years of court life, my dear dragon."